Praise for Chloe Neill's
CHICAGOLAND VAMPIRES NOVELS

"I was drawn in . . . from page one and kept reading far into the night."
—Julie Kenner, *New York Times* bestselling
author of the Devil May Care novels

"Neill creates a strong-minded, sharp-witted heroine who will appeal to fans of Charlaine Harris's Sookie Stackhouse series and Laurell K. Hamilton's Anita Blake." —*Library Journal*

"It's witty, it's adventurous, there's political intrigue, murder, magic, and so much more." —*USA Today*

"The pages turn fast enough to satisfy vampire and romance fans alike." —*Booklist*

"Despite all that has [been] and continues to be thrown at her, Merit's courage, guts, and loyalty make her one amazing heroine. Terrific!"
—*RT Book Reviews*

"Action, supernatural politicking, the big evil baddie with a plan, and, of course, plenty of sarcastic Merit one-liners. . . . Chicagoland Vampires is one of my favorite series." —All Things Urban Fantasy

"Neill's Chicago is an edgier, urban Bon Temps."
—Heroes and Heartbreakers

"All I can say is *wow*." —Bitten by Books

"An absolute treat not to be missed." —A Book Obsession

"Delivers enough action, plot twists, and fights to satisfy the most jaded urban fantasy reader." —Monsters and Critics

A CHICAGOLAND VAMPIRES NOVEL

BLADE BOUND

CHLOE NEILL

BERKLEY
NEW YORK

BERKLEY
An imprint of Penguin Random House LLC
375 Hudson Street, New York, New York 10014

Copyright © 2017 by Chloe Neill
Penguin Random House supports copyright. Copyright fuels creativity, encourages
diverse voices, promotes free speech, and creates a vibrant culture. Thank you for
buying an authorized edition of this book and for complying with copyright laws by not
reproducing, scanning, or distributing any part of it in any form without permission.
You are supporting writers and allowing Penguin Random House to continue to
publish books for every reader.

BERKLEY is a registered trademark and the B colophon is a trademark of
Penguin Random House LLC.

Library of Congress Cataloging-in-Publication Data

Names: Neill, Chloe, author.
Title: Blade bound: a Chicagoland vampires novel/Chloe Neill.
Description: First edition. | New York: Berkley, 2017. | Series: Chicagoland
vampires; 13
Identifiers: LCCN 2016046106 (print) | LCCN 2016054796 (ebook) | ISBN
9780451472342 (paperback) | ISBN 9780698180734 (ebook)
Subjects: LCSH: Merit (Fictitious character: Neill)—Fiction. | Vampires—Fiction.
| Magic—Fiction. | Chicago (Ill.)—Fiction. | BISAC: FICTION/Romance/
Paranormal. | FICTION/Fantasy/Paranormal. | FICTION/Fantasy/Urban Life. |
GSAFD: Fantasy fiction. | Occult fiction.
Classification: LCC PS3614.E4432 B63 2017 (print) | LCC PS3614.E4432 (ebook) |
DDC 813/.6—dc23
LC record available at https://lccn.loc.gov/2016046106

First Edition: April 2017

Printed in the United States of America
1   3   5   7   9   10   8   6   4   2

Cover illustration by Tony Mauro

ACKNOWLEDGMENTS

I had no idea, eleven years ago, that I'd written a novel that would be published, much less that *Some Girls Bite* would be the first in a thirteen-book series. I hadn't been one to hope fiercely back then, but I'm grateful and awed by it now.

Writing a book is both a team effort and a solitary one—and both in fits and starts. I am so grateful to everyone who has contributed to this process, especially my editor, Jessica Wade, who pulled Merit from a slush pile all those years ago, and my agent, Lucienne Diver, who took a chance on an unknown. My assistant, Krista, keeps the machine working, and my boys, Jeremy, Baxter, and Scout, provide support and comic relief. My family and friends, including my mother and Jeremy's, distribute copies of *Some Girls Bite* across the country, hoping to snare readers into continuing the series. And my friends and work colleagues have been remarkably supportive, from assistance with scenes to helping me balance, as best I could, the two strange worlds in which I live. Thank you all for your support and love.

Readers, you've stuck with me and Merit—with food and sarcasm, bad puns and eyebrow arching—through thirteen novels. Words are insufficient to express how grateful I am that you offer your time to us. I hope that you've found joy and sanctuary in reading these books just as I have in writing them.

Most of all, I suppose thanks are due to Merit. She is me and not-me, a friend, and, as my creation, a kind of child. She was origically Kate, once in a band, and eventually dropped into a world that would have confounded the bravest of humans. Sorry about that, Mer, and good luck to you and your beloved.

I can't wait to see what's next.

"Tis now the very witching time of night . . ."

—William Shakespeare, *Hamlet*

BLADE
BOUND

CHAPTER ONE

◆—✠—◆

FIVE BY FIVE

Late August
Chicago, Illinois

It was midnight in Chicago, and all was well.

I stood in front of Cadogan House, a stately and luxurious three-story stone house on a rolling bit of lawn in Chicago's Hyde Park. It was surrounded by an imposing fence meant to keep our enemies at bay, guarded by men and women who risked their lives to keep the House safe from attack.

Tonight, as summer gave way to fall and a cool breeze spilled across the quiet dark, there was peace.

Katana at my side, and having finished my patrol of the expansive grounds, I nodded at the guard at the gate and jogged up the stairs to the glowing portico. One final look, one last glance, to ensure quiet in the realm, and then I opened the door . . . and walked back into chaos.

Cadogan House's pretty foyer—hardwood floors, pedestal table bearing richly scented flowers, gleaming chandelier—was crowded with people and noise. A vampire manned the front desk, and three others—supplicants seeking time with Ethan Sullivan, Master of the House—waited on a bench along one side. Vampires carried boxes toward the basement stairs for the waiting truck, watched with an eagle eye by Helen, the House's den mother.

There was a flurry of movement and activity because the Master of Cadogan House was getting married tomorrow.

To me.

A vampire with dark skin and a shaved head rounded the corner into the foyer. This was Malik, Ethan's second-in-command. He wore a slim-cut dark suit—the official Cadogan House uniform—his skin contrasting vividly with the crisp white shirt and pale green of his eyes. He tracked the room, found me, and walked my way.

"Busy night," he said.

"It is."

"Is there a crowd outside the House?"

I shook my head. "No, but Luc said they're already filling the sidewalks outside the library. The CPD had to pull in extra staff to monitor."

Ethan and I would be married at Harold Washington Library, the city's main branch in downtown Chicago. The city's humans were lining up to watch.

Malik grinned. "'The wedding of the decade,' I believe the *Tribune* said."

"I just want a wedding without supernatural drama," I said. Chicago, and Cadogan House in particular, seemed to attract it.

"Luc has that in hand," Malik said of the captain of Cadogan's guard corps. "And the rest of us are doing what we can."

I couldn't argue with that. The entire House had rallied around us, thrilled to help celebrate the marriage of their beloved Master, the man who'd given them immortality. Cadogan's vampires had ironed linens, polished silver, slid invitations into envelopes lined with crimson silk.

"The effort is very much appreciated," I said. Their help gave

Ethan more time to lead the House, and me more time to ensure its safety.

A hush fell over the room, all talk and activity coming to a stop as Cadogan House's Master stepped into the room. Every eye in the place turned to him, including mine.

That we'd known each other for more than a year didn't make the sight of him any less thrilling. To the contrary—that he was mine, and I was most assuredly his, made the impact even more forceful.

He was tall and lean, with the body of a man who'd once been a soldier. Even now, as a leader of vampires, he'd kept the same chiseled physique. His hair was golden blond and shoulder length, his eyes the green of new emeralds. His jaw was square, his nose straight, his lips usually either quirked in a wicked grin or pulled into a serious line—the expression of a Master with weight on his shoulders.

He also wore the Cadogan uniform—a trim black suit that fitted him like the expensive, bespoke garment it probably was. He wore a white button-down beneath, the top button unclasped to show the gleaming silver teardrop of the Cadogan medal that hung at his throat. It was a mark of solidarity, of unity, among the vampires of Cadogan House. And he wore it as well as he did everything else.

Beside him was a small woman with tan skin and dark hair. She was a vampire, at least based on the invisible buzz of magic around her. And given the tightness around her eyes, she was a vampire with worries.

"We'll be in touch," Ethan promised, and she knotted her fingers together, inclined her head toward him.

"Thank you so much."

"You're very welcome," he said, and we watched as she headed toward the door.

But when I looked back at Ethan, his gaze was fixed on me.

Sentinel, he said through our telepathic connection, taking in the leather and steel of my ensemble. *I like the look of you.*

Good, I said. *Because you're marrying me tomorrow.*

His smile was just a little bit wicked. *So I am.*

Malik and I walked toward him.

"Mrs. Bly?" Malik asked.

"She has a human nephew she'd like to consider joining the House. His parents are less than enthused, and she'd like us to talk to them."

Malik smiled. "She wants us to sell them on the House."

"Like we're working on commission," Ethan said with an answering smile, and glanced at me. "You'll be leaving soon?"

Tonight was my bachelorette party, organized by Lindsey, a friend in the House and a guard, and Mallory, my oldest friend and maid of honor. Malik and Luc, Lindsey's boyfriend, were in charge of Ethan's bachelor party. I wasn't sure what any of them had planned, and I wasn't entirely sure I wanted to know.

"In an hour."

"Let's go to my office," Ethan said, nodding at Malik, and put a hand on my back, steering me through vampires and boxes and down the hallway.

"From head of security to wedding mule," said a vampire with a mop of wavy curls, his arms roped with the effort of carrying an enormous box down the hall.

"I'm pretty sure mules complain less, Luc," said the pale vampire with a swinging blond ponytail who followed him with a much lighter load—a bundle of long, spiraling branches.

"Sticks," Luc said, setting his box carefully on the floor and offering us a crooked grin, his face framed by tousled blond hair. "Why do you need sticks for a wedding?"

"They aren't sticks," Lindsey said. "They're willow branches, and they're for ambience."

Luc shook his head ruefully, glanced at Ethan. "Your orders, Sire?"

Ethan smiled. "Wedding decorations are outside my wheel-house, and Merit's, I suspect."

No argument there. I was technically the House's social chair, but I fell less into the Soiree Planner category than the Crash a Party with a Sword category. I'd left most of the planning to my mother and Helen, the House's den mother, both of whom were skilled at planning soirees. And when a Master vampire married a real estate mogul's daughter, a soiree was unavoidable. I told them "simple and elegant" and "white peonies," and let them have the run of things. Which meant they'd asked me at least twenty-five questions a night for the past four months.

"Hashtag wedding," Luc said with a smile.

Lindsey shook her head, mouth tight. "You're still not using that right."

"Hashtag oppression," Luc said. Not for lack of trying, Luc never quite got the references right. Probably not entirely unex-pected for a century-old vampire.

"I'm sure Helen appreciates your efforts tonight," Ethan said. "And I'm sure we will tomorrow."

I glanced at Luc. "You'll keep him out of trouble tonight?"

"Scout's honor," Luc said, his expression perfectly bland. Since vampires were experts at bluffing, I couldn't tell whether that was really the truth or a cover for a night of carousing and mischief making.

"If the CPD calls me," I said, looking at Luc and Ethan in turn, "there will be hell to pay."

"Ditto," Lindsey said, flicking Luc's arm.

Ethan slid his hands into his pockets, lifted his chin in amuse-ment. "Since Catcher will be with us, the odds of an arrest are slim."

I narrowed my gaze. "Because he works for the Ombudsman's office, or because he could magic over any trouble?"

"Both."

As long as it worked.

"And what do you have planned for your soiree?" Ethan asked. "I'm guessing it won't involve tea sipping and heavy reading."

I pretended to adjust invisible glasses. "Well, we will be reading the *Encyclopaedia Britannica* aloud and watching Neil deGrasse Tyson videos on the YouTubes. We might also make time for macramé."

"I'm sure," Ethan said. "And as long as you're back by dawn . . ."

"I will be."

When his gaze settled on my lips, Lindsey cleared her throat, adjusted her willow branches to check her watch. "We're leaving in exactly one hour," she said, then pointed at me. "Prepare to get your groove on."

Luc narrowed his gaze at her. "You said there wouldn't be strippers."

"There won't be. A bachelorette can get her groove on without strippers. And, dare I say, she is entitled to do so the night before she signs up for an eternity of . . ." She glanced cautiously at Ethan. "Of what I'm sure will be faithful and obedient service."

Ethan made a sound of doubt. "Faithful, yes. Obedient?" He gave me a considering glance. "Rarely."

"I'm obedient when it counts."

"And that is our cue to no longer be in this room," Luc said. "Come on, Blondie."

"An hour," Lindsey repeated, stealing another look at me. They walked on, and Ethan and I continued to his office.

When we were alone, I slipped into his arms, savoring the steady sound of his heartbeat, the crisp smell of his cologne, the warmth of his body.

"There haven't been many moments like this lately," he said, strong arms around me, head atop mine. "Not with wedding plans and supplicants and Nicole."

Nicole Heart was head of Atlanta's Heart House and the founder of the Assembly of American Masters, the new organization of the Masters of the country's twelve vampire Houses. Chicago had been through a lot supernaturally recently, mainly because a sorceress named Sorcha Reed, Chicago's high-society version of Maleficent, had ripped through downtown Chicago. We'd taken her down—and prevented her from creating an army of supernaturals—and the mayor had been pretty happy with us. She'd escaped the CPD, but four months later, there'd been no sign of her, and the mayor had stayed happy with us. Nicole wanted to capitalize on those good feelings, which meant lots of phone calls and interviews for Ethan.

"I was just thinking the same thing," I said. "I'll be glad when tomorrow is done."

He arched a single golden eyebrow, his signature move. "You're already ready for our wedding to be over?"

"More that I'm ready for our lives to begin, and to be done with wedding planning. And," I admitted, "to see what Mallory and Lindsey have in store."

"You'll be good tonight." As if sealing the obligation, Ethan lifted my chin with a finger, then lowered his lips to mine. The kiss was soft, teasing. A hint of things to come. A promise and a dare.

"As good-bye kisses go," I said when I could form words again, "that wasn't bad."

"I'm saving some of my energy for tomorrow, of course." His eyes went flat. "You know they want us to sleep separately."

Vampires weren't usually superstitious, but they did like their rules. One of those, we'd been advised, was the bride and groom sleeping in different rooms so they wouldn't see each other, even inadvertently, on their wedding night.

"I saw Helen's memo." Another reason she wasn't on my favorites list. "She wants to put me in my old room."

Ethan smiled. "That hardly seems fair, since I'll have our suite to myself."

"You're the Master," I said in Helen's clipped tone.

"That is a disturbingly good impression."

"I know. I've heard it a lot the last few weeks." The clock on the opposite wall began to peal its midnight chimes. "I should get dressed. Lindsey has specified our outfits."

His gaze narrowed. "Has she?"

I patted his chest. "She has, and mine will be completely bachelorette-party appropriate."

"That's what concerns me. You'll be careful?"

"I will, but there's nothing to be afraid of. Not now."

The union of sorcerers, finally realizing that Sorcha's destruction had been partly their fault, had set wards around the city. We couldn't stop her from walking into the city—that was the CPD's job—but if she attempted to use magic within that barrier, we'd know it.

And for four months, there'd been nothing from Sorcha. And other than a run-in with some unethical ghost hunters and a murderous ghost a couple of months ago, Chicago had settled into a beautiful and golden summer.

It was weird. And wonderful.

"You'll be good," Ethan said, nipping at my ear. "Or I'll be bad."

I'm pretty sure that was a win-win.

CHAPTER TWO

THE GOOD WORD

"Well," I said, staring at the white stretch limo that sat at the curb, "at least you didn't get the one with the hot tub."

"Only 'cause it was booked," Lindsey said. She'd worked soft waves into her hair and squeezed into a short black bandage dress that looked absolutely phenomenal. She glanced at me, gestured with a finger in the air. "This was a good call."

We all wore black dresses—that was the rule Lindsey had set for us—and I'd been decked out in a knee-length number with a square neck and cap sleeves. The fabric was snug and stretchy and left very little to the imagination. Thank God for my forgiving vampire metabolism, since dealing with Helen and my mother, who'd become a united front, had me raiding the kitchen's chocolate stash a lot more than usual.

We were sharing the limo with Margot, the House chef. Margot had dark hair and plenty of curves, and she'd opted for a fit-and-flare dress.

"I'm sorry! I'm sorry!" There was clipping down the sidewalk as a petite woman with blue hair ran toward us. "I'm late!"

Mallory's LBD was knee-length, sleeveless, and flowy, which

she had the petite frame to pull off. She'd styled her ombre blue hair so it curled across her shoulders, and wore enormous silver earrings in the shape of flowers.

She reached out and squeezed me, smelling faintly like lavender and herbs. Probably something she'd concocted in her craft-slash-magic room. "Happy Darth Sullivan Eve!"

I couldn't help but snort. "Is that the official title?"

"It is," Mallory assured me, and pulled a satin sash out of her tiny clutch purse. It read FUTURE MRS. DARTH SULLIVAN in glittery letters.

I'd been prepared to say no to any "Future Mrs." or "Bride-to-Be" sashes, but I decided I couldn't pass up glitter and snark together, so I let her pull it over my head.

"Oh, that turned out nicely," Lindsey said, hands on her hips as she surveyed it, then smiled at Mallory. "Is your house just covered in glitter now?"

Mallory stepped back, adjusted my sash carefully. "It's every-freaking-where. It's probably the perfect vector for worldwide contagion, should any bad guys figure that out."

The tall, lean, liveried driver walked around the car, raised two fingers to his strawberry blond hair. "Ladies, I'll be your chauffeur for the evening."

"Hi, Brody," said those of us from Cadogan House to the guard who'd also become our occasional transporter. He had solid moves behind the steering wheel.

Lindsey's gaze narrowed. "You weren't on the list as driver. Are you playing hall monitor?"

Brody held out his hands, and his expression looked innocent enough. "I'm just here to drive. I'm not a nark."

Lindsey stepped up to him, gave him her fiercest look. Which was actually pretty fierce. "If one word of what happens tonight gets back to anyone, I will know that word came from you."

"And that would be bad."

Lindsey's eyes gleamed silver. "It would be the most possible badness. Did I mention Merit and I have been practicing with the throwing knives?"

Brody swallowed visibly. "Are you good at it?"

She smiled, showing fang. "Very."

Brody wasn't the newbie he'd been before, and he didn't look as fazed by Lindsey's hazing as he once would have. But she still outranked him, so he nodded.

"You're the boss."

"Damn right," she said with a cheeky grin, and gestured to the door. "Ladies, if you please, we can get this show on the road."

Since she was the boss, I maneuvered carefully on ice-pick heels from curb to car and climbed into the limo.

Margot slid into the seat next to me. "Thanks for the invite. It's nice to get out of the kitchen."

"How's that going?" Margot refused to allow us to hire a caterer for the wedding, much to my mother's chagrin. Since my mother's pick would have resulted in shrimp foam at our wedding, I was fully behind Team Margot.

"It's going," she said. "Total Bridezilla situation. 'I don't want shrimp foam. Don't give me shrimp foam.'"

"Can you blame me?"

"I really can't. And that's why the mini Italian beef sliders will be a huge hit." She gave me a good looking-over. "How are you feeling? Are you nervous?"

I watched Lindsey through the window as she and Mallory talked very seriously about something. I couldn't hear what they were saying, but Mallory checked her watch. Maybe the entertainment was running late.

"About what Lindsey and Mallory have in store for tonight?" I asked, trying to read their lips. Turns out, I did not have that skill. I did recognize excitement on Lindsey's face and worry on Mallory's, but she hadn't said anything to me about something bothering her. And now that I was looking, there were dark circles beneath her eyes. I'd have to ask her about that later; I hoped the wedding wasn't the reason for it.

"About the wedding," Margot said with a laugh.

I smiled, glanced back at her. "The marriage, no. The wedding, a little," I admitted.

She winked, patted my knee.

"Where are we going?" I asked when Lindsey and Mallory settled along the back wall and Mallory began passing out champagne flutes.

"To celebrate your last night of freedom!" Mallory said. "Now, stop asking questions and relax. Everything is in our hands."

"That's exactly what I'm afraid of."

I'd spent the last month—when not patrolling the House or attending fittings—trying to figure out what Mallory and Lindsey were planning. I'd checked off all the stereotypical ideas—strippers, barhopping, rounds of half-drunk karaoke. None of those were me, and I didn't think they were particularly us. But that left me stymied. Lindsey was plenty full of flirty bravado, Mallory of wicked creativity, and I was stuck in the middle between them, hoping my evening wouldn't involve squealing, feather boas, and body shots.

The alcoholic kind, anyway. I wouldn't say no to a good, sweaty round of sparring.

Brody drove north, the lake a shadow to our right, away from Hyde Park and toward downtown Chicago. It figured that we'd head toward the city's center, which offered pretty much any activity a girl could want—from boat rides to museum tours to really good blues. So it didn't give me a single clue.

When Brody pulled the limo in front of a small slip of a building, I had to reassess. It was modern in design, with a tall, narrow window and offset door in flaming red. There were no signs, no names on the door, not even an address number.

Intriguing. "What is this place?" I asked.

"My half of the party," Mallory said as we climbed out of the limo one by one—and then tugged our dresses back into place. "A little something for you and for me."

She walked to the door, pressed a small buzzer.

After a moment, a thin woman with dark skin smiled out at us. "Merit party?" she asked with a smile.

"Merit party," Mallory agreed.

"Welcome to Experience," the woman said, and held the door open so we could walk inside.

The door opened into a long, narrow room with gleaming wood floors and a long, dark table in the middle. The walls glowed pale amber behind crisscrossing pieces of the same wood, like they burned from the inside. Rectangular sconces hung above us at varying heights. Jazz played warmly in the background.

There were women already in the room with champagne flutes in hand—including my sister, Charlotte.

"Hey, baby sister!" Charlotte said, walking forward and embracing me. Like me, she had my father's dark hair and pale blue eyes. She wore a sleeveless black dress with a flared skirt and patent flats with bows on the toes. She smelled like lilacs, the same perfume she'd worn since she was a teenager.

"Hey, Char," I said, squeezing her back. "How's my favorite niece?"

"Being quite the two-and-a-half-year-old, Olivia believes she is a debutante and is very disappointed she can't go to her aunt Merit's party tonight. But she is very excited about being a flower girl. And she's been practicing."

"Oh my God, I bet that's adorable."

Charlotte put a hand on her heart. "Granted, she's my kid, but yes. It is quite possibly the most adorable thing I've ever seen."

"I'm sure she'll toss those petals with aplomb."

Charlotte nodded. "If she remembers to toss them, yes. So far, it's been more of a petal-free sashay."

Sounded entertaining either way.

The woman who'd opened the door, who wore a dark, fluid tunic over dark leggings, walked to the table and pulled out the center chair. I glanced back at Mallory, who nodded.

"Go for it, sister," she said and, when I was seated, took the chair next to mine.

"We're having dinner?" I asked her. I'd actually grabbed a bite before leaving the House, to lay the foundation for what I assumed would be ample champagne.

"Not exactly," Mallory said, and gestured toward the doorway that led to the back of the building. The moment we were all seated, a bevy of waiters in black button-downs and jeans walked through, domed trays in hand. With the perfect timing of practiced dancers, they each walked to a spot at the table and simultaneously placed the trays in front of us, leaving the domes in place.

"The first course," the hostess said, hands clasped in front of her, and the waiters whisked away the domes, revealing gleaming white plates dotted with a rainbow of fruit around a pretty cube of chocolate cake, a small dish of what looked like chocolate mousse, and some kind of lacey and delicate cookie.

I glanced at Mallory as the women around the table oohed and aahed. "You got me chocolate." My heart lifted, sang. I should have trusted that these two would do it right.

"It's a chocolate-tasting table!" Mallory said, hands clasped together at her chest like a kid with a burning secret. "Five full courses!"

I wiped away an imaginary tear. "I love you guys."

"Damn right you do." Mallory lifted her glass. "To my immortal sister from another mister, and the future wife of the hottest damn vampire in the United States."

"To Merit!" Lindsey said, and everyone raised a glass. "Now, for God's sake," she said, "let the girl eat!"

I had to give the chefs credit—and sent my compliments back. I'd had my own chocolate stash once upon a time, but I still hadn't realized how diverse chocolate could be in the hands of a talented person. There was chocolate soup, chocolate foam, drinking chocolate, smoked chocolate. Chocolate with pistachio cream, chocolate with Scotch bonnet peppers, chocolate with bacon (a personal favorite), raspberries injected with chocolate, and a dozen more.

Somewhere near the bottom of the fifth inning, I decided even my immortal body couldn't hold any more. I spent a few minutes chatting with the guests and watching Mallory. The worry I'd seen earlier hadn't dissipated. Either they hadn't managed to work out the kinks in tonight's plan, or something else was bothering her.

I didn't like thinking about what might be worrying my oldest friend and talented sorceress—and the woman who'd outmagicked Sorcha Reed. But I also knew that she probably wanted the break and release of a party as much as the rest of us. So I decided I'd bide my time—and interrogate her later.

The hostess returned with a large silver tray of mints, fruit, and cheese.

"Please, sir," I said, hand over my stomach, "I do not want some more."

"With you," Mallory said, waving off the tray when it was offered to her. "That mousse-cake square did me in."

"It wasn't the half dozen before it?" Margot asked dryly, chocolate hangover clear on her face.

"I didn't eat six mousse-cake squares."

"I think you had eight," Lindsey said, licking chocolate off her thumb.

Mallory looked a little horrified, and a little nauseous.

"It's all good," I said, patting Mallory's hand. "Special occasion."

"Says you. I can actually gain weight, vampire girl. Still, though . . ." This time, when she looked at the empty plates in front of most of the women at the table, there was pride in her eyes. "We did damn good work here tonight."

"To us," Margot said, and lifted her glass. "And to Merit, and Darth Sullivan."

"Hear, hear!" Mallory said. And then she burped. Which seemed appropriate.

Still a little chocolate drunk, we were whisked back into the limo and shuttled to our next stop, which I hoped was a place for quiet contemplation of my bellyful of seventy-five-percent bittersweet.

"My turn!" Lindsey said. "And be warned—I am hopped up on sugar and chocolate."

"Oh good," I said. "Because you're usually so quiet and reserved."

That got the chuckle it deserved.

"What's next?" I asked.

"We're going to do the party a little more Cadogan style," she said.

By Cadogan style, she'd meant at Temple Bar, Cadogan's official watering hole. It was located in Wrigleyville, a neighborhood north of the Gold Coast and also home, as the name hinted, to Wrigley Field.

We pulled up in front, Sean holding open the door and his brother and fellow Irishman, Colin, ringing the brass bell behind the bar.

"Merit is on the premises!" he yelled out, to the applause of a crowd of vampires. There were plenty in the packed bar I didn't recognize, but all of them were women.

Our table was near the front of a make-do stage at one end of the long, narrow bar. Maybe I was getting a stripper tonight, although I couldn't imagine wanting to see anyone naked as much as I did Ethan. His long, lean form was pretty much a continuous delight.

The vampires dispersed among the crowd to chat with the others in the room. Lindsey grabbed drinks from the bar, gin and tonics all around, while Mallory sat beside me, checking her phone with a worried expression. Even when Lindsey brought an armful of sparkling gin and tonics for us, she didn't seem to perk up.

"I'll be right back," Lindsey said, kissing the top of my head. "Just need to check on something." She disappeared into the back of the bar.

"Everything okay?" I asked Mallory when we were alone.

"Why wouldn't it be?"

"Well, for starters, you're in a bar full of vampires, which a year ago you'd have been crazily happy about. You're practically famous after Towerline, and every Comic-Con in the country wants you as a guest sorceress, which is apparently a thing now. But you don't look very happy about it."

She put a hand over mine. "I am happy."

"For me," I said. "And I appreciate that. But there's more to it. What's going on?"

Mallory shook her head as if to clear it. "Nothing. This is your bachelorette party, and we are not going to worry about me."

I used the same look I'd given Helen, stared at her with narrowed eyes. "Mallory Delancey Carmichael Bell."

"Nothing, Merit."

"Mallory."

She tipped back her head, let out a frustrated sound. "It's just—I feel weird."

"Weird? What's wrong? Are you sick? Are you sleeping? You look tired."

"I'm not sick, and I'm not pregnant, since that seems to be the other frequently asked question." She shook her head. "I have . . . a malaise?"

I frowned. "About the wedding?"

"Oh Lord, no. You and Ethan were made for each other, even if he did have to wait four centuries to find you. Which, if you ask me, is probably good for him." She winked. "Makes him more grateful."

"Then what kind of bad feeling?"

She shrugged. "I don't know. It's just this vague magical feeling. A kind of unease, I guess?"

"From what? From where?"

"I have no idea. There's nothing specific in it. Not even a speck of what I could call a thing, or a threat, or a looming damn cloud." Her words picked up speed with the rise of her frustration. "Just unease. Catcher's being supportive, but I know he doesn't feel it. And that makes me feel like I'm being paranoid."

"So, let's assume you aren't being paranoid. What could be bothering you? Not You Know Who." That was as much as I wanted to mention the woman who'd tried to control us.

"No," she said. "It's been four months, there's been no sign of her, and the city's warded even if she did come back. Other than that, I don't know."

Mallory looked at me, and the concern in her eyes was even deeper than I'd thought. Whatever this was, she wasn't done with it.

"What if I can't do happy, Merit? I mean, I'm married, and you're getting married, and with the exception of the world's most idiotic ghost hunters, no supernatural drama. No River nymph infighting. We haven't been thrown to the wolves by the mayor or anyone else looking to use us for political fodder. I should be freaking thrilled. Instead . . ." She sighed, shrugged.

I took her hand, squeezed it. "Mal, you are the happiest person I know. The brightest person—except when you were evil."

"Except for that."

"And even then, you crawled out of it. So if you tell me something's off, I believe you. Have you talked to the Order about it? I thought you guys were on better terms."

"They already think I'm crazy."

"Well, what about Gabriel? Maybe the Pack's felt something similar." Although I hoped Chicago's resident shifter alpha would have come to us if he'd believed something was wrong.

"I don't even know what I could tell him. 'Gabe, I know you're busy being hot and wolfy and all, but all this peace and prosperity is making me antsy'?"

"Then I'm officially out of ideas."

"So you think I'm crazy, too?" She must have heard the rising panic in her voice, as she held up a hand. "Sorry. I'm sorry. This is just wearing on me."

I put an arm around her, squeezed. "We're going to be fine, Mallory. Everything is going to be fine. I'm going to get married, and Ethan and I are going to have a wonderful week in Paris."

"You're right. I know you're right." She shook out her hands, her shoulders, obviously trying to loosen up. "What's going to happen is going to happen, and there's no point in worrying about it now. Let's just have fun."

"Let's just have fun," I agreed, and clinked my glass against hers.

Because, paranoid or not, the other shoe was bound to drop. It always did.

"All right, ladies!" Lindsey said, standing on a chair in her bare feet, ringing her glass with a spoon. When the crowd quieted, she glanced around the room. "We've reached the, ahem, climax of tonight's Bachelorettetravaganza!"

"How many names does this thing have?" I whispered to Mallory.

"I think seven? We threw out 'Merit Does Chicago' and 'Sullivan Two: The Resullivaning.'"

"Good call."

"Colin," Lindsey said, gesturing to the bartender. "If you would?"

The overhead lights dimmed, but the spot on the small stage in front of us brightened on a single black chair that sat in front of a microphone. Music began to play, a jazz song with a playful, flirty rhythm.

As Lindsey sat down to join us, a man walked out of the back room, onto the stage.

Tan skin, dark hair, dark beard, his hair in a very well-executed knot at the top of his head. His eyes were green, his lashes as thick and dark as his beard, his mouth a long line that turned up at one corner. He wore jeans, boots, and nothing else. The terrain of his body was all smooth skin and hard, curving muscle, his left arm marked by a complicated monochrome tattoo.

The room went absolutely silent.

"Well," Margot said quietly. "He is . . . rather attractive."

"Attractive," Lindsey said, tilting her head as she stared at his biceps. "And well-defined."

"A dictionary couldn't do it better," Mallory said, eyes glassy as she stared at the man.

I glanced at Lindsey. "I can't believe you hired a dancer. Ethan is going to kill you. Or me. Or both of us."

"Oh, honey," Lindsey said. "He isn't here to dance."

Regardless, with the grace of a dancer, the man spun the chair around backward, took a seat, and pulled a thin, worn paperback from his back pocket. He looked up at me, smiled. "Your party?"

I nodded, suddenly nervous.

"Cool. Lord Byron work for you?"

I actually felt my face warm. "Sure?"

Beside me, Lindsey snickered, the sound full of satisfaction.

He nodded, thumbed through some pages. "Ladies," he said, meeting our gazes. And then, looking down at the page, he began to recite.

"She walks in beauty, like the night / Of cloudless climes and starry skies; And all that's best of dark and bright / Meet in her aspect and her eyes."

Every single woman in the room sighed.

I wasn't sure whether he was a grad student, poet, actor, stripper, or brilliant combination of all those things. But the man knew Lord Byron, and he knew words. He knew the rise and fall of sentences, the way to pause, the moment to look up, catch our gazes, smile. He knew emphasis and speed, pacing and clarity. He was a prince of poetry, and he had us mesmerized.

Champagne was uncorked and dunked into gleaming silver

chalices of ice, then poured into tall, thin glasses while we listened, legs crossed and perched forward in our chairs.

"Is it better if we're objectifying his body *and* his brain?" Margot asked, lifting the thin straw in her gin and tonic for a sip.

"I don't much care," Mallory said. "He gives good word."

I couldn't have put it better myself.

CHAPTER THREE

◂━━❧❦❧━━▸

FIVE SECONDS OF
(SUPERNATURAL) SUMMER

We left Temple Bar about two hours before dawn, dropped Mallory off in Wicker Park, then headed back to the House.

We separated on the first floor. The foyer was quiet and empty, the desk closed down for the evening, the supplicants home again, their issues addressed, or to be back in line to see Ethan another night. There was only so much one vampire could do.

There wasn't a single box or candlestick or willow branch in sight, which meant everything had probably made it onto the truck and over to the library. Or Helen had gotten sick of all of it and hosted a bonfire in the backyard. That seemed unlikely, so I'd just assume the wedding would go forward as planned.

"The wedding would go forward as planned," I whispered with a smile.

There'd been more showers, brunches, and cake tastings than I'd have thought possible—and still more than I thought was reasonable. Ethan had enjoyed the process, the preparations for our life together, so I'd humored him, and now the bachelorette party had been the last of them. The last hurdle before the wedding, before we took vows of fidelity—for an eternity. Nothing stood between us now but the rise and fall of the sun, and even Sorcha Reed couldn't change that.

That was when the nerves set in. Not fear, but anticipation. Excitement. Tendrils of desire, possibly stoked by a little too much time with Lord Byron.

The hallway was dark—Malik's and Helen's offices were dark, as was the cafeteria at the end of the hall. Ethan's light was still on. I doubted he was back yet; it seemed more likely they'd enjoy whiskey and cigars until the last possible moment. Probably the cleaning crew had forgotten to turn the light off, or maybe Helen had forgotten some last-minute bauble for the wedding.

I could leave him a note. A message to say good night, that I'd be thinking of him during our vampire-imposed exile, and that I'd see him tomorrow at the library, books optional.

That I thought that was funny probably said more about the gin I'd enjoyed at Temple Bar than about my comedic skills.

I walked into the office, headed for his desk . . . and didn't realize I wasn't alone until I caught the flicker of movement across the room.

He stood in the conversation area, a man in jeans and a long-sleeved shirt, the fabric mottled with dirt and ratty on the edges. His pale skin was smudged with grime, his dark hair tufted from what looked like constant pulling by the hands that now scratched nervously at the legs of his jeans. The House was still saturated by the scent of wedding flowers, but I caught the odor of unwashed male beneath it.

He was a vampire. Older than most I'd seen, but the faint, effervescent magic proved his supernaturalness. His magic did have a different sense about it—a chemical smell, like uncapped markers. I also didn't recognize him. If he was Housed, he hadn't been in a House recently. Not given the look of him.

"Hi," I said. "Can I help you?"

He looked up at me, dark circles beneath eyes nearly slitted with exhaustion. "You're here to help?"

"Sure. Are you here to see Ethan?" Supplicant seemed the best guess. How else would he have gotten past already bulked-up security? Maybe he'd been in the House to talk to someone, had slipped away undetected.

His shoulder twitched, nearly lifting enough to meet his chin. "Help. There's so much talking." He tapped his palm against his forehead. "Talking. I can't stop it."

"I'm sorry?"

I wished Ethan or Malik were here. They'd know better than I how to handle a supplicant who seemed imbalanced, or at least confused.

"It's talking. The voice. It's screaming—the same things over and over and over again. *Hello. Hello. Hello. I am here. I am here. I am here.*"

I was leaning toward imbalanced. And we didn't need imbalanced running around the House.

Ethan, I silently said. *If you're in the building, get Luc and some guards and come to your office.* I didn't know if he was close enough to hear me, doubted that he was.

"Let me just call someone to help you," I said, and reached for my phone, belatedly realizing I'd left my small clutch—and my phone—in the limo. I'd have to use the one on Ethan's desk.

His gaze narrowed on me, his eyes silvering—the mark of heightened vampire emotion. "Why is it screaming? Do you hear it? Why don't you hear it?"

I didn't especially want to turn my back on this clearly troubled man, but I didn't really have a better option. The first floor of the House had been mostly dark, and until I could get to a phone, or otherwise signal someone, I had to handle this on my own.

"Don't have my phone," I said easily, trying to keep the mood light. "Let me get the one on the desk."

"No!" His voice was loud, the word a bark of sound—and alarm. "No more screaming!"

His fangs were long, white, needle sharp. He launched toward me so quickly I had only a moment to turn, to brace myself against his impact. I managed to dodge most of the force, but he tripped me up, sent us both slamming to the ground. My head bounced against the floor, making my vision waver and putting stars at the edges of the room.

"It's your fault!" he said, and reared back to punch me. I raised an arm, blocked the punch, grabbed his forearm, and twisted, trying to unbalance him. But he was enormous, and he seemed to believe I was one of the mental demons he was fighting. He raised both arms, slapped at his forehead, and then tried to slap at me. I blocked his shots, but a couple put bone against bone, which sent pain singing through my arm.

"If anyone's in the hallway," I yelled out, "I could use your help right now!"

"Stop it!" he cried, missing the irony. "Stop doing this to me! I just want it to stop!" His eyes were red and brimming with tears, and he lifted his arms, beat the sides of his fists against his head. "Stopstopstopstop!"

The dress hiking up around my thighs, I managed to get a leg between his and scissored to twist him off. The vampire grabbed my sash, ripped it away as I reversed our positions, and he hit the ground with a thud.

I scrambled to my feet, shoving the dress back down and kicking away the stiletto heels. They'd make a decent weapon if I needed it, especially since my dagger was with the phone in my bag. And since no one had responded to my yelling, I'd have to hold my own until someone, in these predawn hours, happened to walk through the first floor.

The man climbed to his feet again, those fists beating against his ears. "Stop screaming! Stop talking! I don't want to hear it anymore! I don't want to hear it!" He looked up at me, fury and fear matching beat for beat in his expression. "Make it stop!"

I took my chance, dodged back to the desk and the phone. I managed to grab the receiver before he followed me, snatched up the letter opener from Ethan's desk—a long, silver, double-sided blade. I raised an arm, expecting him to stab forward. Instead, he stumbled back, put the dagger's gleaming point at his temple. There weren't many ways to kill a vampire, but I had to guess stabbing himself in the head would do the job.

"I'll silence it," he said, silvered eyes frantic. "I will end it."

I was no longer the victim—he played that role now, too. I put the phone down, held out my hand.

"Let me have the dagger. There's no need for it. I can help you with the screaming."

I jumped forward, wrapped my hands around his wrist, worked to force it down and away.

"No more screaming!" He kicked out, trying to push me loose, but I dodged the sloppy shot. He screamed, began pushing me backward until we hit the shelves on the opposite wall. Something crashed to the floor beside me. But my focus was on the blade in the vampire's hand, and my own fingers, which were white-knuckled around his.

"Just put down the blade," I said, ducking as he swung out with his free hand. He made contact with something on the shelves, which hit the floor with another crash. If they hadn't heard me yelling, maybe someone would hear the trashing of Ethan's office.

He pushed me hard against the shelves again, then pushed

me back toward the windows, trying to scrape me off like a barnacle. My hands were getting sweaty, and his eyes looked more desperate.

He pulled away, freeing his arm and sending me backward. I stayed on my feet but hit the shelves again. Eyes on him, I scrambled fingers against rows of books, searching for something I could use as a weapon. Delicate things hit the floor, upended by my questing fingers, until I touched something cold and hard. I grabbed it. He lurched forward. Weapon in hand, I swung and nailed him in the temple.

He staggered forward, hit the back of the couch, bounced backward again, and nailed me. We hit the ground together, his weight across my middle.

"Merit!"

I heard my name, and then the man was lifted off my chest. Brody had grabbed the man under his shoulders, laid him on the office floor.

Brody hadn't been a guard very long, and his eyes widened as he looked at me, dress ripped, hair around my face, and a bloody marble obelisk in my hand.

"I saw the light on," he said, offering a hand to help me climb to my feet. "I didn't think Ethan was back yet, so I was going to check it out. What happened in here?"

I edged around the man on the floor, his chest rising and falling, which was good enough for me. He was still breathing, but he'd have one hell of a headache when he woke up. And he hadn't killed himself, which was something. Beneath him was the crumpled ribbon of satin and glitter that had been my bachelorette sash.

I put the paperweight on the bookshelf, pushed my hair from my face. "I'm not entirely sure. I walked in, and he was here, and he went ballistic."

"He attacked you?"

"Yeah." I looked down at the man, at his unfamiliar face and grubby clothes, the chewed fingernails and cuticles. Even on a longer look, no one I recognized. "He look familiar to you?"

"No. Should he?"

"No," I said, but that was really a guess. I didn't know if he should be familiar, if he was someone we should have been aware of, or if this was as strange and random as it seemed.

I gestured to the phone on Ethan's desk.

"Call the Ops Room and lock down the House. Then call my grandfather," I said, chest still heaving. "Tell him we've got a vampire, maybe sick, maybe mentally ill. Definitely unconscious. Tell him to contact the CPD or an ambulance or both, and get over here. And find Ethan."

He didn't hesitate. "On it," he said, and double-timed it to Ethan's desk, picked up the phone.

One night before our wedding, and we had a hell of a mess on our hands.

Brody called my grandfather and Luc, so everyone headed back to Cadogan House. He stayed with me and the vampire in Ethan's office. We asked the human guards to do an extra sweep of the grounds, and Juliet and Kelley, also guards, started a top-to-bottom search of the House.

Ethan practically ran into the room, Malik behind him, the scent of cigar smoke trailing them. "Sentinel," Ethan said, scanning the room, then focusing his gaze on me. "What the hell happened?"

"He was in your office. I turned around, and he was standing there, talking about hearing someone screaming. He kept hitting his head, staring at things that weren't there."

"Paranoid?" Ethan asked. "Schizophrenic?"

"I don't know. Strong, and irritated, and I think afraid."

"Irritated?" Malik asked.

I frowned. "Like the voice was an itch, something he couldn't get rid of. He was afraid."

"He attacked you," Ethan said.

"He attacked *at* me. I don't know if he was aware of who I was. And then he tried to kill himself—stab himself with a letter opener." I pointed to where it still lay on the floor. "I knocked him out with your paperweight."

"I'm glad it was handy." He narrowed his gaze. "What were you doing in here?"

"The light was on. Given Helen's memo, I was going to leave you a note, say good night." I glanced down at the vampire. "I didn't quite get that far."

Luc ran into the room, eyes darting from the vampire to Ethan to me. "What happened?"

"That was my question as well." Ethan's eyes were hard. "An unfamiliar vampire gained entry to the House and attacked my Sentinel. And I will damn well know how that happened."

We waited for my grandfather, Catcher, and Jeff Christopher, my grandfather's computer ace, to arrive with a pair of CPD uniforms and a medical squad. The medical squad restrained the vampire, lifted him onto a stretcher, and removed him from the House.

I felt some of the tension finally leave my shoulders when he was gone, the House clear of him and his delusions. My grandfather, in his grandfatherly slacks and short-sleeved button-down, patted my back. "You all right?"

"I'm fine," I said, taking another drink from the bottle of Blood4You Ethan had pulled from the small fridge built into his bookshelves. It was the vampire version of comfort food. "Got my adrenaline going, but mostly because he took me by surprise."

"His name is Winston Stiles," Catcher said. He was taller than my grandfather—not to mention younger and bulkier—with a shaved head, pale green eyes, and a muscular body. He wore jeans and a well-worn T-shirt with MAGIC IS AS MAGIC DOES across the front. "Wallet was in his pocket."

"Where will you take him?" Ethan asked.

"The ceramics factory," my grandfather said. The former industrial site near the lake had been turned into a holding facility for supernaturals that normal jails weren't strong enough to contain. "He'll stay there, at least until he's evaluated."

"We'll talk to him," Catcher said.

Jeff, his tall, thin frame belying the white tiger that lived within, pushed his light brown hair behind his ears. He wore khakis, Converse, and a white button-down with the sleeves rolled up. It was his favorite look, and there was something comforting in the familiarity of it. "And check out his background," Jeff said.

"If you don't mind," my grandfather said, gesturing to the chairs, "it's late, and I'm going to sit. Would you join me?"

"Happy to," I said, but I knew it wasn't really "late" for my grandfather. He worked with supernaturals, so he worked long, late hours. He just wanted me to sit, to relax. Since I didn't disagree that I needed a moment, I took the chair across from him, and the finger of amber liquid Ethan extended in a short crystal glass.

I glanced up at him, brows lifted.

"Good Irish whiskey," he said. "It'll take the edge off."

I wasn't sure I needed to take that much edge off, but I could see the worry in his eyes, so I indulged him, too, and downed it in a throat-searing gulp.

"Take me through it," my grandfather said, and I walked them through the event from beginning to end.

"He kept talking about hearing a screaming voice, that he didn't want to hear it anymore. He seemed confused, afraid, and angry."

"At me?" Ethan asked. "At Cadogan?"

That was logical, since the vampire had been in Ethan's office. "He didn't mention you. I thought he was a supplicant, but not one that I saw tonight. And he didn't say anything else specific." I closed my eyes, tried to replay what he'd done, what he'd said.

"I'm not sure if he was capable of being that specific. You saw him—it looks like he's been living on the streets for a while. Hard to say if that's because of his demons, or if being on the streets created the demons. But it was all about the voice he was hearing—he wanted me to stop it, and when I told him I couldn't, that I needed to get help, he grabbed the letter opener. And that had been closer than I'd wanted it to be."

"How did he get in here?" Ethan's voice was low, and his dangerous gaze settled on Luc. Luc's expression wasn't any friendlier.

"I don't know. And I'm going to find out." He looked at me. "I'm sorry, Merit."

I shook my head. I wasn't angry he'd gotten in; I'd handled myself. But if he'd found a vampire who hadn't been able to protect himself? That would have been bad.

"I'm going to look at the security tapes right now," Luc said.

"If he came in as a supplicant," Ethan said, "he'd have had to sign the log. But I don't recognize him. Did you?"

My grandfather shook his head, looked at Catcher and Jeff, who did the same. "He hasn't been to the office."

"Did he give you any details about the person or thing he was hearing?" my grandfather asked me. "Vampire? Human? Male or female?"

I shook my head. "Just that it kept saying hello, that it was screaming and wouldn't stop. I can imagine how that would make someone feel crazy."

"Sounds like he needs some help," my grandfather said, rising. "We'll go, help get him processed." He pressed a light kiss to my cheek. "Make sure you get some rest. You've got a big night tomorrow."

"That's what they tell me," I said, offering a smile I hoped would lift the shadows from Ethan's face.

"We'll be in touch if we find out anything," Jeff said. "And we'll let you know."

Catcher didn't say good-bye, but squeezed my arm as he passed. Coming from him, that might as well have been a bear hug.

They'd been gone only a minute when Luc knocked at the threshold, his agitated magic clear even across the room. "The House is clean," Luc said. "We've started pulling the tapes, and we'll review them and present a report to you tomorrow. It would be sooner, but dawn's on the way."

"No objection," Ethan said.

Luc waited for a moment, opened his mouth to say something else, but then turned and disappeared again, irritation in every step.

"Are you and Luc going to be okay?" I asked, when we were alone in the office again.

"I'm irritated because I'm the boss," Ethan said. "It's my job to be irritated. And he's irritated because he doesn't like screwing up. That's why he's good at his job. Or one of the reasons. Did you know he can wrestle a steer?"

"I did not. Good to know." I looked back at the remains of the bookshelves, the glass and books and mementos scattered on the floor. "This night took an ugly turn."

Ethan put his hands on my cheeks, drawing my attention back to him. "You're okay?"

"I'm fine. It was just . . ." I took a deep breath, blew it out again. "A lot to come home to. I'd expected a very lighthearted night, and got it, for the most part. Kind of a weird ending to my singledom."

Ethan brushed a lock of hair behind my ear. "You single-handedly dispatched an intruder without a weapon in a very lovely party dress. I'd say that's an appropriate ending."

"Better. But still unsettling."

I had sudden sympathy for Mallory's feeling of existential dread, for the interminable sense that life was never going to be easy, that we'd never really be safe.

Cold feet, I told myself. It was the night before my wedding, and I was understandably anxious, and this weird incident wasn't helping. But I didn't have time for it right now, so I pushed the thoughts away.

"I doubt this was personal," he said. "Not an attack against you or me, but an individual who needs help—and now can get it."

I nodded. "You're right. Not a harbinger. Just a lonely soul."

"And we'll do what we can to set him to rights."

The clock chimed five, each peal ominous in the silence of the room. Dawn was approaching.

"I should get to my room," I said. "Try to get some sleep."

"Oh, you won't be leaving my side tonight, Sentinel."

I felt instantly relieved. But considered the repercussions. "But tradition—the whole thing about not seeing each other?"

"I am Master of this House," Ethan said, and, as if intent on proving it, pulled me against him, melding his mouth to mine. His kisses could be sweet or tender, teasing or incendiary. This one was possessive and promising—that he was here and I was safe.

"Let's go upstairs," I said when the kiss was done, burying my face in his shirt, in the scent and feel of him. "Let's leave this night behind and get started on tomorrow."

"I've no objection to that, either, Sentinel. None at all."

Our apartments on the top floor of Cadogan House were dark and cool, a few golden lamps burning away the darkness. There was no bedtime basket from Margot tonight—she'd been out of the House and probably thought I was sleeping in the small dorm room that had been my first home in the House.

I followed Ethan to the enormous closet, where my dress and his tux hung from valet bars in matching black bags, waiting for the sun to rise and fall again.

"Are you ready?"

I glanced at Ethan. He smiled at me while working his nightly ritual, taking off watch, removing keys and wallet.

"I think everything's ready for the ceremony and the reception, if that's what you mean."

"You know it isn't."

"I guess you'll have to see if I show up."

He cocked an eyebrow at me while unfastening his cuff links. "I am confident that's a joke, since you know I would hunt you to the ends of the earth if you failed to show up."

"I'm pretty sure I can outrun you."

His smile went sly. "Let's test that theory," he said, and launched toward me.

After he'd hauled me into the bathroom over his shoulder, we brushed our fangs like good little vampires. When we climbed into the bed, the blankets fluffy and cool, the automatic shutters *shush*ed softly over the windows, locking into place to protect us from the murderous sun.

I curled against the side of his body, his arms enclosing me.

"Much preferable to sleeping alone," he said. "Even if it comes with a little bad luck."

I wasn't sure how much "a little" would change the already sizable pile of it.

"And how was your bachelorette party, at least before the darker turn?"

"Good. There was poetry and chocolate. Mallory and Lindsey did a very good job of planning."

"And no strippers?"

"And no strippers." I glanced at him. "And you?"

"No strippers," he said. "Although the liquor was ample and the cigars were very definitely Cuban."

"What is it with bachelor parties and cigars? I mean, that's a pretty phallic symbol for a pre-wedding celebration."

"It's a bachelor party," he said with a wink. "We aren't celebrating the wedding. We're celebrating the bachelor."

"You hardly need celebrating. I think your ego's big enough."

I'd barely gotten the words out of my mouth when he pounced, covering my body with his and pressing me back into the bed. Pitched forward on his elbows, he brushed the hair from my face.

"You had something to say about my ego, Sentinel?"

I smiled at him, pushed a lock of hair behind one ear. "You're doing just fine, I think."

Eyes closing, he lowered his mouth to mine, teased with kisses that were soft and sweet, hints of things to come. "You are mine, Sentinel. Bachelor party or not, that is an undeniable truth."

"I think I was always yours," I said, and his eyes darkened. "There's something inside"—I put a hand over my heart, then his—"that was always waiting for you. I just had to get ready for it."

He grinned. "You had to ripen."

"I don't like the sound of that. And even if that's true, I'm not sure what it says about you." I patted his cheek. "But four hundred years isn't *that* long."

He nipped playfully at my neck. "It's nothing in vampire years."

"Which are like dog years, but longer?"

He made a haughty sound, nibbled harder.

"I forgot," I said. "There's actually something I wanted to talk to you about."

"Mmm-hmm." One of his hands cupped my breast, sending shivers of anticipation along my skin.

"But you're making it difficult to concentrate."

"That's the general idea," he said, and applied those nips to my jaw.

"This is a serious talk, though. For real."

He looked up at me, a lock of blond hair over his eye, so he looked very much like a pirate interrupted during a very interesting journey. Eyes narrowed, he sat up and looked at me consideringly.

I pushed up to sit beside him, legs folded beneath me. "It's about our names."

"Our names," he repeated, expression blank.

"Only Master vampires use last names, which is a rule I'm technically breaking, since Merit is my last name. I guess, technically, I could play the 'Caroline Merit Sullivan' game, but that's too much. There's too much baggage, and it just—I don't know."

He lifted his eyebrows.

I held up my hands. "I'm not saying this very well. The point is, after we're married, I'd like to stay 'Merit.' I want to keep that name."

He smiled. "Ah. I see."

"I've been putting this off. I didn't want to hurt you."

He smiled at me. "You were born Caroline, and you made yourself Merit. I demand your love and your faithfulness." He smiled slyly. "Your identity is yours to keep."

That was it, exactly. The thing I hadn't been able to put into words. I shouldn't have doubted that he'd understand what it was to feel like you'd made your own identity. He'd done the same when escaping from Balthasar, the vampire who'd made him.

"Come here," he said, pulling me against him as he lay down again.

I put a hand on his chest, felt his heart pounding beneath my hand. "You were born a soldier, turned into a monster, or so you feared. And you made yourself a Master. You made your identity."

"That was more of an 'it takes a village' effort, but to your point, yes." He lifted my fingers to his mouth, pressed lips to soft skin. "Others wanted us to play certain roles. To be certain people. But we made ourselves. So keep your name, Merit of Cadogan House. I have your heart."

He certainly did.

"Besides, I wasn't born 'Sullivan.' And I don't believe I've told you that story yet."

Before being outed, vampires had changed names every few decades to avoid detection. "You haven't," I said, a little guilty I hadn't thought to ask him before.

"Television anchor in the seventies," he said with a grin. "Name was Sullivan Steele."

"No."

"Absolute truth. He wasn't nearly as suave as the name suggested—I believe there was a double-knit suit in there, but I liked Sullivan."

"And Ethan?"

"That was Aaliyah's idea." Aaliyah was Malik's wife, a writer who tended to keep to herself. "Found it in a book of baby names, which is what we used back then for ideas."

"In the days before the Internet tubes."

"I don't think they're tubes, but yes. When the library was truly necessary."

I narrowed my gaze at him. "I hope you don't mean to suggest it's not necessary now. Because it is."

He wrapped his arms around me. "Easy, Sentinel. There are plenty of vampires who use the library, including us. The Librarian would certainly lead the charge for my assassination or dismissal in any event."

"Good," I said. I kissed him lightly. "Because that would endanger our relationship."

He nodded. "Besides, what would I do with the space? Although a conservatory would be nice . . ." He smiled again, but there was still a troubled tightness around his eyes.

"You're trying to calm me down," I realized. "By lightening the mood."

"Since we met," he said, putting his chin atop my head, "I've been telling you to be still."

"So you have," I said, and let myself be drawn in by the warmth and scent of him, by the comfort of his nearness, of having him as a lodestar. "I love you, Ethan Sullivan."

"And I love you, Merit of the Single Name."

And that was good enough for me.

CHAPTER FOUR

COLD FEET

We'd ignored the tradition of sleeping in separate rooms, but Ethan was still gone when I woke. Margot had left a breakfast tray of muffins, fat red strawberries, and a pot of Earl Grey that fragranced the air with citrusy bergamot.

"Let the wedding-night pampering begin," I said, and poured myself a cup, settled into a chair in the sitting room for a few minutes of peace and quiet before the chaos began.

Ethan had left a business card on the tray. His name was printed on the front, and on the back, in watercolor blue ink, was a heart and a note in his slanting script: "*See you soon, my beautiful bride.*"

And because it was Ethan, a postscript followed: "*Security briefing at D+1,*" or one hour after dawn.

This might have been my wedding night, but we still lived in Cadogan House.

After the security briefing, I'd be whisked off to the Portman Grand, where I'd be dressed and primped up, then off to the library for the ceremony and reception.

The implications of my having left the details to my mother and Helen suddenly hit me—they'd be in charge of my wedding day, and how and where I spent my time. Nice that I wouldn't need to worry about it, but not as nice as having relaxed friendlies in charge of the events.

I'd wear comfortable clothes to the primping session, I decided. Jeans, an old T-shirt, and a favorite pair of Pumas. My Cadogan medal, as always. And my hair unwashed, as the stylist had instructed me to do.

The House was somehow even more chaotic than it had been the night before. There were more human guards and a last rush of preparations for the wedding.

The door opened, and the captain of Grey House's guards walked in. Jonah was tall and handsome, with blue eyes, a perfect jaw, and auburn hair that just reached his shoulders. He was also technically my partner in the Red Guards, a secret organization created to monitor Masters and stand up for the rights of vampires. Jonah and I were fine, but the RG and I were still fighting because it preferred to ignore challenges instead of face them.

He looked up at me, smiled. Jonah had a crush I couldn't reciprocate, which probably put that slightly guilty look on his face.

"Hey," he said.

"Hey."

He ran a hand through his hair, and there was something wonderfully bashful in the gesture. "I didn't expect to see you. Before, I mean."

"It's only Ethan I'm not supposed to see tonight," I said with a smile, "but we're going to ignore that rule. Why are you here?"

"Security," he said. "After last night, Luc asked if I'd mind keeping an eye on the House, at least until you and Ethan are off premises. Sounds like you had quite an eventful evening."

"'Eventful' barely cuts it. We've got a senior staff meeting, and then he should be downstairs." Although, I thought, glancing toward the kitchen, I could probably find something for Jonah to do in the meantime. Something that would kill two birds with one stone. Or at least give them a little love tap . . .

"Could you do me a favor first?" I asked.

"Sure. What's up?"

I gestured toward the kitchen. "Could you go check with Margot—the House chef? See if she needs a hand with anything? She's catering the wedding."

Jonah looked a little suspicious at the request, but seemed willing to indulge me, probably because it was my wedding day. Which was fine by me. Whatever worked.

"Okay, sure."

I gestured to the hallway, walked him as far as Ethan's office, then made sure he walked into the kitchen.

Fate, I hoped, would do the rest.

The mood in Ethan's office was grim. Not exactly the feel one wanted on one's wedding night, but business was business, and vampires were vampires. Drama was inevitable.

Ethan sat behind his desk, Luc and Malik on the other side of the room futzing with the electronics.

"Good evening," I said, when Ethan glanced up at me.

"Sentinel. Happy wedding night."

"And to you. How are you feeling?"

Ethan sat back in his chair, arms crossed, fairly glowing with power and confidence. And he didn't seem overly worried—a good sign. "As well as a man might, when he's set to marry a beautiful and brave woman."

Not a bad sentiment to start the day.

"Your grandfather called. Winston Stiles is at the supernatural holding facility. He came to during the day still delusional and violent, so they sedated him. He remains sedated."

Ethan might have called it a holding facility, but in reality it was a prison where the city's supernatural convicts were held. Those men and women included a vampire named Logan Hill, the man who'd attacked me and left me for dead, the reason Ethan made me a vampire. The man whose identity I'd learned only a few scant months ago, when he'd been helping Sorcha.

The man I'd let live.

"Was he able to tell them anything about the source of the delusions?" I asked.

"No," Ethan said. "When he surfaced, he talked about the voice again, begged them to stop it. And then he broke through one of his restraints and got his hands on a guard. He was sedated after that, at least until they can figure out what to do."

"Does he need medicating?" I asked.

Ethan shook his head. "There's no history of mental illness in his medical records. He was a night watchman at a bank in Skokie, at least until he was laid off. There's a physician at the prison, but at the moment, this appears to be a mental breakdown of some sort."

"Caused by something he wanted to talk to you about?"

"Perhaps," Ethan said. "Catcher and Jeff started the investigatory workup during the day." He smiled a little. "They didn't want you running around tonight before the wedding. Had some concern you'd show up late, filthy, or injured."

"And what are we going to do?"

"We're going to get married," Ethan said. "And then we're going to Paris, just as we planned. We're going to let the Ombudsman's office deal with supernatural issues, as is their responsibility. And we aren't going to stress over it."

I narrowed my gaze at him. "How long have you been preparing that speech?"

His smile was sly. "Since I talked to your grandfather." He rose, walked around the desk, and put his hands on my face. "We are allowed to live, Merit. We are allowed to leave problems to those best able to solve them."

I nodded, tried to accept that. It was hard not to when looking up into those deeply green eyes. And I did have other things to worry about today. But it was hard. Hard not to think about the state of the world. Even if we were promising "for better or worse," that didn't mean I wanted "for worse" to become apocalyptically bad.

"We'll protect the House," Ethan said. "We'll watch the video, discover how he avoided our security, and let your grandfather handle the rest of it."

"You're right," I said. "You're right. It's our wedding night, and we can't solve every problem for everyone." Winston would have to find his own way. Maybe my grandfather's office could help with that.

"We're ready," Luc said after a moment, looking up and around the room. Ethan and I walked to the sitting area, where leather chairs and couches surrounded a low table.

"We've pieced the vampire's movements together from the various cameras," Luc said, his face void of expression, clearly still upset about the security lapse. I could understand the feeling. "This is from four nights ago."

He pressed a button and the video began, the screen filling with the shot of the House foyer. The camera was positioned in the middle of the space, angled down to catch the closed front door, bench of supplicants to the left, and desk to the right.

The front door opened, and our vampire walked in, the dark of night behind him. He moved to the front desk, signed in, took a seat on the bench beside four other vampires.

"He was a supplicant," I said.

Luc nodded. "He signed in as Winston. Didn't identify any last name or House, just 'UNAFF,' which I take to mean unaffiliated."

The clock on the screen ticked along, half an hour, forty-five minutes, then a full hour, and still Winston waited. But if he was agitated—or experiencing the delusions—he didn't show it. He looked bored and perturbed by the wait, but an hour on an uncomfortable bench would do that. And then I saw it.

"Zoom in on him," I said. "On his right hand, if you can manage it."

"Zooming," Luc said, and the image grew closer. It was more pixelated, but the movement was clear.

"He's hitting his leg with his fist," I said, and drew my fingers together, demonstrated. "Not a tap, or a nervous habit. It's irregular. And he's putting some force behind it."

"You're thinking it's a tic?" Ethan asked.

"This guy looks clean-shaven, reasonably put together, average appearance. And we know what he became. I'm wondering how much of it was in there before."

He crossed his arms, then raised his right hand to his temple, knocked the side of his fist against his head. Just once, but once was enough.

Time passed, and the other four vampires left and were replaced, which presumably put Winston next in line for Ethan's office. But then he looked at his wrist, and probably his watch, rose from the bench, and walked out the door.

"He didn't sign out," Malik said.

"No," Luc agreed. "And he didn't linger." The video shifted to the House's front lawn. The vampire walked down the sidewalk, disappeared through the gate. The video shifted again, and he continued down the street, disappeared into darkness.

"No further sight of him at the House this night," Luc said, then glanced at Ethan. "Does he look familiar?"

"No. Not at all."

Luc nodded. "But this is from two days ago." The video shifted to the next segment, and the foyer appeared on the screen again.

The vampire walked in again. This time, he looked the way I'd seen him last night. Disheveled—in the same clothes he'd worn before, but in worse condition—his movements more erratic. His lips moved as if in silent conversation.

A different Novitiate was at the desk, so she wouldn't have recognized him from the previous visit.

The vampire moved to the bench, took a seat. And the waiting began again.

He stayed seated but rubbed his temples vigorously, one foot tapping a quick and agitated tattoo. The vampire at the desk occasionally looked up but didn't ask the man to leave or otherwise interact with him.

"We take all comers," Ethan quietly said, gaze intent on the screen. "She wouldn't have turned him away unless he was violent. As it was, he just seemed . . . nervous?"

"Afraid," I agreed. "Or perhaps like he's in pain, not that he's planning to hurt anyone." And he probably never had been. I was in the wrong place at the wrong time, if his intent was to make the screaming stop.

"Still," Malik said. "They could use more training at the front desk. I'll make plans."

Once again, time passed, and vampires who'd arrived before him left to talk to Ethan, then returned to the foyer and left the House.

Forty-seven minutes had passed when two vampires moved

through the foyer and to the front door with boxes. Since Helen was leading them, it was probably more gear for the party.

The second vampire carried box atop box, and one of them tumbled over, spilling its contents across the floor. The vampire at the desk, and two of the other supplicants, began gathering up the supplies. And as they did, Winston walked past the desk and stairs and into the main hallway. The view shifted, followed. He stopped in the middle of the hallway—empty, fortunately for him—and seemed to fight back the voice he'd started hearing.

"Storage closet," Ethan said, and Luc nodded.

"He stayed there through the day. No one came in or out, and there's no camera in the closet. Nothing disturbed, except a few linens on the floor."

"He bedded down," Ethan said.

"Yeah. Stayed there until four a.m." The view returned to the hallway. The vampire walked to the dark cafeteria, and from those cameras, we watched as he drank bottles of blood right out of the case, then shoved the empties back inside. Then he walked into Ethan's dark office, and the view shifted to a camera mounted somewhere behind Ethan's desk.

A new horror occurred to me. *I didn't realize there were cameras in here*, I silently said, my face heating as I frantically tried to recall what unspeakable acts Ethan and I had performed in that room. And I'd think twice before kissing him in there again.

I'm the only one who has access to it, Ethan said, squeezing my hand. *Your secrets are safe with me.*

The vampire and I wrestled around the room; then I grabbed the paperweight and brained him with it. He hit the floor, and that was that.

Silence fell over the room.

"So let's summarize," I said. "He wanted an audience with

Ethan. Four nights ago, he makes his first attempt. He seems relatively stable, if impatient. Two nights ago, he comes back. He's more agitated, and his illness—if that's what this is—has progressed. He's impatient again, but this time manages to get into the House proper because of our all-comers policy and a coincidental distraction. He spends most of that time alone, until he looks for Ethan again, and doesn't find him. I find him, and he's almost completely succumbed to his demons."

"He escalated," Malik said. "Or worsened."

"From relatively normal to incapacitated in five days?" Luc asked, crossing his arms. "That seems impossible."

"Not if he was off his meds," I said. "Incapacitated could be his usual state, and we watched him wean himself off."

"Intentionally or otherwise," Ethan agreed, and looked at me. "It's also possible he isn't suffering from an illness, but magic. He's in custody now, and there's no reason to believe this was anything other than an isolated incident; Catcher confirmed that. But there is a bigger lesson—this might have been avoided if I'd made time to see him. Two separate nights of waiting, and I didn't let him in. I didn't talk to him."

"He didn't wait to be let in," Malik pointed out. "He didn't wait for longer than an hour either time, which is faster than he'd have gotten into an emergency room. And he didn't call the House or the Ombudsman," Malik added before Ethan could argue. "If there was an emergency, he could have reached us that way. It wasn't an emergency, and evidently not worth more than an hour of his time."

I bit back a smile. Malik was normally the strong and silent type, which made his strong defense of Ethan that much more enjoyable. And the tension around Ethan's eyes seemed to soften, just a little.

"I'll work with Malik," Luc said. "We'll talk about new procedures for supplicants." He lifted his gaze to mine, and it was heavy with guilt.

It took me a moment to understand. He was afraid the vampire might have seriously hurt me—or taken me out altogether—the night before the wedding. That he'd have taken out the bride of his Master, the man to whom he'd pledged an oath. The wedding was doing a number on all of us.

"You're not thinking," I said, and fire lit in Luc's eyes at my harsh tone. Good. He could use the fire.

"Excuse me?" he asked, not used to my questioning him—at least not when he was in guard-captain mode.

"I'm stronger than him, and better trained. He'd been on the street for who knows how long, and having some sort of psychotic breakdown to boot. My handling it was inevitable. And more importantly, I was in the best position to handle it. Better me than Helen or Margot or anyone else who isn't trained for combat."

Luc's jaw worked as he mulled over my thoughts.

Ethan reached out, squeezed my hand. "You did train her well," he pointed out.

"Damn right I did. Don't entirely like having it thrown back in my face, especially when I fuck up."

"And none of that, either," I said. "This wasn't your fault."

He looked up at me. "It was," he said. "House security is my responsibility."

"Yours *and mine*," I corrected. "I stand Sentinel. It's my job, at least in part, to protect the House. We both had that responsibility, so if there's any blame to pass, it's mine, too." I looked at Ethan, hated the uncomfortable clutch in my belly, the fact that I'd only just now taken responsibility for the breach. It shouldn't have taken me that long to acknowledge my contribution, or apologize for it. "I'm sorry for that."

Fire blazed in Ethan's eyes, and I hoped it was pride, not anger.

"She's right," Ethan said, looking at both of us. "We've identified a gap in our security—one we hadn't known existed. We know now, and we'll adjust our processes. We'll correct and move forward. That's what we do. That's what we always do. And speaking of moving forward," he said, glancing at me, "now that we've all donned our particular hair shirts, we should probably prepare for the evening."

"I think that's our cue to go," Malik said with a smile, rising and patting Luc's shoulder as he passed, a sign of solidarity.

"Sentinel."

I looked back at Luc.

"I just want you to know—your taking responsibility tonight shows . . . that I trained you really well."

I mostly bit back a smile. "That's what you're going with?"

He smiled. "Yeah. I think, tonight, we probably need it."

They disappeared, and I'd only managed to move a step closer to Ethan when another figure stepped into the doorway.

The man had tan skin, dark hair, and dreamily wide brown eyes. He wore jeans and a cotton tunic of deep saffron on his tall and lean frame, and a cheeky grin on his face. "Isn't it bad luck for the bride and groom to see each other before the wedding?"

The smile traveled through the crisp accent that edged his warm voice.

He and Ethan walked toward each other, met in the middle, and shared a manly, back-slapping hug. "It's good to see you, Amit."

Amit put a hand on Ethan's shoulder, squeezed it. "And you as well, my friend."

The most powerful vampire in the world—and Ethan's best man—glanced at me and held out his hands, a silver ring glinting on his right thumb. I walked to him, offered my hands. He raised them to his lips, pressed kisses as a frisson of magic passed between us.

"Amit. It's so good to see you!"

He grinned. "Have you changed your mind about marrying this reprobate yet?"

"I have not," I said, glancing at Ethan. "And I don't think I will."

Amit nodded gravely. "You're a brave woman."

"She is," Ethan agreed, eyes gleaming with pleasure. "That's why I named her Sentinel." He glanced back at Amit. "Did you just get in? Can we get you settled?"

Amit held up his hands. "I'm fine. Helen has seen to my luggage and accommodations. And speaking of which, what's happened?"

Ethan and I exchanged a glance.

"I'm Very Strong Psych," Amit said, a reference to the vampire ranking system. "There is an unusual energy in the House, and not just because of the wedding."

"Merit was attacked here last night."

"I wasn't attacked," I said, putting a supportive hand on Ethan's arm. "An unbalanced supplicant holed up in a closet, made his way in here. I was the unlucky vampire who found him, and he wasn't happy about it."

Amit's eyes widened with alarm, and he glanced at Ethan.

"Isolated incident," Ethan said, repeating the party line. "The Ombudsman's office is investigating, and the individual was apprehended after Merit beaned him with my Greenwich Presidium service award."

Amit nodded approvingly. "That's the way to do it."

"I'd have preferred not to bean him with an award or otherwise. But a Sentinel's gotta Sentinel."

"Put that on a T-shirt," Ethan said.

There was a polite throat-clearing in the doorway. We looked back, found Lindsey in jeans and a pink BRIDE'S CREW T-shirt, my dress bag in hand.

"Sire, Sentinel." She smiled at Amit, nodded, held the bag a little higher. "It's time to go."

The pre-wedding nerves hadn't sparked yet, but seeing her standing there with the dress she hadn't yet seen made everything suddenly real. We'd reached the point where there was no more time to guard the House, investigate threats, plan for security.

I was getting married today.

I was getting *married* today.

I was getting married *today*.

"Merit," Amit said, laughter in his voice. "You've gone a bit pale."

I swallowed hard, looked back at him and then Ethan. "I feel like I'm about to give my ninth-grade history speech."

Ethan smiled. "You made it through ninth grade, or so I assume, since you've got a master's degree and a half. I feel like U of C, among the others, would be particular about that kind of thing."

I blew out a breath through pursed lips. "Everything will be fine." But I grabbed his lapels, pitched forward. "What if my mother got doves? What if the DJ only plays the chicken dance? What if Amit messes up the toast?"

"I have no plan to mess up the toast," Amit said crisply. "I will bring the crowd to the cusp of tears, then amuse them with stories of your groom's wilder days."

Actually, that did sound entertaining.

Ethan kissed my forehead. "Steady on, brave Sentinel. You deferred the wedding planning, and now you must face the music—

and possibly the doves." But he looked down at me, skimmed a finger over the House necklace at my throat.

Regardless of the rest of it, he said silently, *there will be you and me. That will be enough, and that will be perfect. This night, and all of its dark beauty, is ours.*

Who needed Lord Byron anyway?

· ·——— ✦ ———· ·

CHAPTER FIVE

WHEN DOVES CRY

They stood in the foyer like a posse come to collect their due.

And that "due" was me.

Helen and my mother, Meredith Merit, looked like business partners. Both wore trim suits and pearls, their hair perfectly coiffed, makeup precisely elegant. There was something very *Stepford Wives* about it. Or the Oak Park and Hyde Park versions, anyway.

Mallory stood with them in jeans and another BRIDE'S CREW shirt. She stood beside a pile of suitcases and what looked like black tackle boxes.

They turned together, glanced at me with the same assessing gaze.

"Merit," my mother said, walking forward and pressing her hands to my cheeks. Her palms were soft and cold, and she smelled like powdery perfume. "How are you feeling, darling? Are you nervous? Excited?"

My mother and I weren't especially close. As my father focused on business, my mother focused on socializing—leading charitable guilds, hosting socials, arranging donations that got "Merit

Properties" on buildings or plaques or benches. Things that Charlotte dealt with better than I did. But given that she'd coordinated my wedding, this wasn't the time to be ungrateful.

"Both, I guess." As she turned to slip an arm around my waist, I glanced at Helen. "Before things get too chaotic, I wanted to say thank you for everything that you've done to get this wedding off the ground. Without you, we'd probably be eloping at a Waffle House."

"Perish the thought," my mother said with a smile. "It has been a great pleasure working with Helen." She reached out and squeezed Helen's hand like they were old friends, which disturbed me more than it should have. Helen already wasn't a fan of mine; I didn't think her having my mother's ear would improve the tension.

"The wedding will be beautiful," Helen said. "As befits a Master of Cadogan House."

Not as befit a Sentinel, or two vampires in love, but as befit the Master.

I would be the bigger vampire. "Of course," I said simply, and saw the surprise in her eyes that I'd agreed instead of arguing. Or maybe because I hadn't let her see that the arrow had found its home.

My mother glanced around at the group. "I think we're all here. Let's get started!"

She opened the door, and the group began to funnel into the night.

Mallory slipped an arm through mine. "That was well done, Merit. Saying thank you."

"If it's all doves and chicken dances, I'm retracting it."

"I'm not sure what that means, but I've noted it for the record."

That would have to do.

*   *   *

Another night, another limo. But while last night's mood was light and a little sassy, tonight's was much more serious. Led by Helen and my mother, we were serious people heading off for serious events. Prestigious events. Socially important events.

But I kept smiling as I watched the dark city pass as we drove toward the Loop.

I was getting married today. And I was feeling pretty damned good about it.

Mallory, who sat beside me, chuckled. "If you keep smiling, you're going to wear out your cheek muscles before things even get started. You're going to be asked to smile a lot in the next few hours." She cast a considering glance at my mother and Helen, whispered, "How many people at this shindig?"

"Four hundred," I whispered back.

"And you're going to have to say hello to each and every one of them."

I hadn't thought about that—not in so many words. But it couldn't be helped. It was my wedding night, and I'd make the best of it.

"I like those T-shirts," I said, plucking her hem.

"Lindsey's idea," she said. "She didn't want the mood to be too starchy." Another glance at my mother and Helen. "All things considered."

"All things considered," I agreed, and gestured to the chilling bucket of champagne. "Let's get this party started."

We pulled up in front of the Portman Grand, the grandest of grande dame hotels. We'd get dressed in a suite Helen had reserved for the wedding party—or the female half of it, anyway.

We'd party until dawn, and Ethan and I would also spend the

day here before tomorrow's overnight to Paris, where we'd enjoy the gardens at Versailles (by night, of course), excellent champagne, and each other.

A woman with blond hair in a low ponytail and a dark pantsuit stood in the gilded lobby, clipboard in hand. She strode forward on needle-sharp heels, hand extended. "Merit," she said with a smile, shaking my hand with brisk efficiency. "Welcome to the Portman Grand. Thank you for allowing us to have a part in your wonderful evening."

"You're welcome."

"If you'll come this way," she said, gesturing to a bank of elevators, "we'll get you to your suite. Your limo will remain in front of the building, under guard, until it's time to proceed to the site."

The "under guard" took me a moment to process, but I nodded and followed her into the elevator, one of the glass-walled variety that looked out on the city. The brass doors closed, and the car dipped slightly as everyone piled on, and then it began its slow ascent, rising over the city, buildings and cars in the Loop twinkling like stars beside the lake's empty darkness.

"It's a beautiful night," the woman said. "A beautiful evening for a wedding."

I hoped it would stay that way. But I didn't feel better when we exited on the seventeenth floor and proceeded down the hallway to a lone door at the end where a man and woman, both human and both in black, flanked the door. They were security contractors who regularly guarded the House gate.

I hadn't known they'd be here—that Luc or Ethan had assigned guards just for this. They probably hadn't wanted me to worry about the possibility of a threat, but that didn't make me feel better about it.

I glanced at Lindsey, and she must have read the expression

on my face. But before I could inquire, the double doors opened. My sister, Charlotte, stood in the doorway in a BRIDE'S CREW T-shirt and pink seersucker shorts.

"About damn time!" she said, dragging me into the room, squeezing me into a hug. "I can't wait to see your dress!" Charlotte closed the door behind us, rubbed her hands together gleefully. "And it's time to get started."

The room was enormous—a long rectangle with a wall that faced the river, and three separate sitting areas. There was a dining room table at the far end, topped with portable lighted mirrors. On a low buffet on the wall beside it were more bottles of champagne, crystal flutes, and a silver tray of chocolate-dipped strawberries.

"I'll open the champagne," Charlotte said, heading for the buffet on bare feet with pretty pink toes. "Shay, we're ready when you are!"

A woman entered from a doorway at the other end of the room. Curvy and dark skinned, with a cascade of spiral curls that reached her shoulders and a black camera around her neck. She looked at me, smiled. "Shay Templeton. I'll be your photographer for the evening."

"Shay is the best wedding photographer in Chicago," my mother said. "We practically had to get into a bidding war to get her."

I glanced at Shay, who looked faintly embarrassed, but also a little proud, at my mother's raving. I figured that was probably the right response.

I smiled. "It's nice to meet you, Shay. If I could just have one minute?" I held up one finger, then took Lindsey's arm and pulled her into the suite's bedroom, which was as amply appointed as the lounge, with thick blankets and pillows atop a sleigh bed on a carpeted pedestal. I bet the honeymoon suite was insane.

"The guards?" Lindsey asked, closing the door behind us.

"The guards," I said.

"Just a precaution," she said. "Ethan is taking no chances with his bride."

"He could have told me."

"And what would you have said?"

"That we don't need armed guards outside the bridal suite," I grumbled.

"Yeah, and you'd have fought him on it, refused the guards, and been on your guard the entire night. He wanted you to relax, Merit, and actually enjoy your wedding."

I narrowed my eyes at her. I didn't like that he'd done it without talking to me—which was a classic Sullivan move—or that she was absolutely right.

"Fine," I said. "But I'm only going along with this because I left my katana at the House." I hadn't even thought about it. Which meant Ethan was winning, and I wasn't doing a very good job of mixing security and wedding.

Lindsey grinned. "Ethan made sure I brought it with. It's in the other room, just in case."

And so he was forgiven.

In the interest of keeping Weddingpocalypse somewhat contained, I had a maid of honor, Mallory, and only one bridesmaid, Charlotte. Ethan had Amit as his best man and Malik as his groomsman. Like Ethan, Amit and Malik would wear slim tuxedos. Mallory and Charlotte would wear long dresses of delicate pale green lace.

I'd also nominated Lindsey as my official stylist and dresser. Since she'd seemed very relieved to say yes, I guessed she hadn't been confident in my styling choices. But then again, neither was I. Which was why I'd asked the House fashionista to do it.

She brought one of the black tackle boxes to the dining table, flipped the latch, and opened the top, revealing a dozen trays of lipsticks, eye shadows, blushes, and mascaras.

I blew out a breath, nodded. "Okay," I said. "Let's get to work."

Lindsey took the statement seriously. She pulled my hair into a ponytail, scrubbed my face, and then attacked me with brushes and tweezers, sponges and serums, highlighters and contouring powder.

While she worked, Shay moved silently around the room, sometimes standing, sometimes crouching, while taking photographs. It was . . . unnerving.

"When was the last time you were this poked and prodded?" Mallory asked.

"Last night!" Lindsey squealed, leaning forward to click her glass against Mallory's.

"You're both incorrigible," I said.

"We do have that in common." Lindsey cocked her head. "I like the look of the makeup so far. Romantic, but not too 'windswept on the moors.'"

I smiled. "Possibly the title of the first romance novel I ever read."

Lindsey snorted, dabbed lipstick on the back of her hand, then dotted it across my lips. "Mmm-hmm," she said, nodding at me, then added a coat of clear gloss. She screwed the gloss's applicator back into the jar again, then looked around the room.

"I think that will do it. Everyone?"

Everyone moved in behind me, began cooing over Lindsey's work.

"Very elegant," Helen said, which I figured was as good as a girl could get.

"Now that you're extragorgeous," Lindsey said, "are you finally going to let us see the dress?"

Anticipation fell over the room like a fog, silencing everything.

No one had seen it yet, not even Mallory. I hadn't looked forward to drinking champagne while spending four hours at a bridal store—that really seemed inefficient—but I had accepted that I'd have to do it. I'd imagined Mallory, Charlotte, and Lindsey giving thumbs-down to taffeta, circle skirts, and poufy shoulders. It just hadn't worked out that way. I'd fallen for the first dress I'd tried on. And since we were on a tight schedule, I'd snapped it up, giving the staff just enough time to get it altered before the big day.

It was the most expensive article of clothing I'd ever bought. Jaw-droppingly expensive, but if I was going to spend money on a dress, I figured this was the one. And the price still probably paled in comparison to the dresses Ethan had bought for me. The fact that I'd used hardly any of the House stipend I'd been collecting for a year helped ease the guilt.

"Sure," I said, and they moved aside to let me rise to the dress bag. When I turned around again, they were watching me.

"I can pick my own clothes," I said sheepishly.

"This isn't just clothes," Mallory said. "It's your wedding dress." She held up her hands. "But the bridge has been crossed and I'm not taking it personally."

"You are a little."

"I am a little. But I will live. So let's see it."

I unzipped the bag, unexpectedly nervous about whether Mallory would like the dress or not. I needed her to like it.

"Oh," Mallory said, barely a sound, her eyes welling at the sight of it. "Oh, Merit. That's just . . ."

"It's very you," Lindsey said, reaching out to squeeze Mallory's hand.

That was why I'd grabbed the first dress I'd tried on. Because it was absolutely me, and I felt like me when wearing it. Me, but maybe something more. Me-*plus*, if the plus was a kind of elegance I'd never really felt. But an elegance I imagined my mother would be proud of.

It was a slender dress, overlaid in delicate French lace. There were short cap sleeves of the same lace, and a bodice with a sweetheart neckline. The lace continued through the waist, where the underlying bias-cut silk draped to the ground and pooled in a short train of more lace. It was delicate and romantic and old-fashioned, and it fit my tall frame to a tee.

"It really is," Mallory said, tears falling in earnest now. She stood up and wrapped her arms around me in a fierce hug that made me teary, too.

"There's no crying in baseball or vampire fashion," I said.

"There will be tears at the wedding," Lindsey said. "From those of us happy that the two of you found each other—and those jealous that both of you are off the market."

I almost snorted, until I remembered the fact that Lacey Sheridan, head of San Diego's Sheridan House, had been sufficiently in love with Ethan to try to push us apart. Vampire etiquette demanded we invite her, but I wasn't sure whether she'd RSVP'd. Not that I was worried overmuch about it now. If anything, watching him say "I do" might help her move on. And it would probably piss her off a little. Which was fine with me.

"You will knock his socks off," Mallory said, using a tissue to swipe at her eyes. "I mean, he is totally crazy about you, but if you didn't have him in the palm of your hand before, you will now."

Makeup was followed by dress, which was followed by hair. By the time Lindsey had finished rolling, teasing, pinning, and spraying my hair, my scalp felt like it had nearly been tugged off my head.

I winced as she adjusted a final pin, which poked right into the skin behind my ear. Across the room, Helen smiled. I decided to give her the benefit of the doubt and assume she liked the hair, not the pain.

"Here we go," Lindsey said. "Mirror time."

"Oh, here!" Mallory said. "For full effect." She opened a glossy white box on the counter, pulled out my bouquet.

"Oh, that's beautiful," I said, taking it. There were enormous frilled white peonies and pale green hydrangeas, with sprigs of white lily of the valley. The stems were wrapped in white satin. "And it's heavy," I said as Mallory passed it over. "How does yours look?"

"It's mini-Merit!" she said, and pulled hers out of a second box. Same flowers, smaller size.

"Can I see now?" I asked, holding the flowers obediently in front of me.

"Voilà!" Lindsey said, and rotated the chair.

I stared.

My makeup was, just as Lindsey had said, soft and romantic. My skin looked luminous, my lips bee-stung and just the right shade of warm pink, my pale cheeks prettily flushed. My eyelashes looked a mile long; I'd have to get that secret from her later. There was something a little bit antique in the look—a softened version of a movie star's makeup from the forties.

She'd found the same balance with my hair. She'd waved it into soft curls, then arranged it in an elegant loose knot at the back of my neck. Delicate white flowers that matched my bouquet were pinned into the top of the knot.

"It's *amazing*," I said, looking back at her. "Seriously—you could do this professionally."

She winked. "One of my many talents. And I did, for a very brief time in the forties. So many pin curls and pompadours."

That explained that.

*　　*　　*

Harold Washington Library sat heavily in the middle of the Loop, built like a fort to guard the knowledge held inside. It was watched from above by well-patinaed bronze owls and was edged by a sharp crown of the same bronze, which made the building seem more regal.

I'd stepped off that railing once upon a time, when Ethan was gone and Jonah was teaching me how to jump. Oh, how times had changed.

There were guards outside the building, along with a few dozen humans with smiles and cameras and CONGRATULATIONS! posters. They screamed as we walked toward the door, and I offered a quick wave between very tall security agents as we were shuffled inside. Ethan hadn't spared any expense with the security.

Heels clicking on stone floors, we were escorted to an elevator, which rose slowly and quietly to the Winter Garden that topped the building. The doors opened, revealing Jeff and Catcher standing in front of the doors that led into the space where we'd hold the ceremony.

"You look beautiful, Merit," Jeff said as Shay moved silently around us, capturing the moment. "Like a *Final Fantasy* character come to life."

"Thank you, I think."

"A moment, ladies," Lindsey said, sticking her clutch under her arm while she gave me a final look. She scanned hair, makeup, dress, bouquet, and hem, before nodding with approval. "This House is clean," she said.

"That bit doesn't really work here," I said. "Which means you've been spending too much time with Luc."

"Can't help it," she said, squinting as she leaned forward to tuck in an errant lock of my hair. "I'm crazy about the guy." She glanced back at Jeff and Catcher. "It's time for me to take my seat. Which one of you handsome lads would like to escort me?"

"It's my turn," Jeff said, offering Lindsey his arm as Catcher opened the door so they could slip through.

When they had, I gestured toward the door. "Can I peek in there?" It was time to face the music—and the possibility of doves.

Catcher pointed a warning finger at me. "Don't let them see you, and don't make a scene. We just got everyone into their seats."

"Not a problem," I said as he pulled open the door a skinny inch.

"Oh," I said, eyes widening as I took it in.

It looked like a fairy tale. The garden was swathed in pale, gauzy fabric as delicate as clouds, illuminated by what must have been a thousand candles that reflected off stone floors, glass walls, and rows of lacquered white chairs.

The air was cool and crisp with the scent of flowers—more densely ruffled peonies and pale green hydrangeas bundled together with Lindsey's "branches" in tall crystal stems and swags gathered at the corners of the rooms, and covered an arch at the end of the aisle.

And in front of that glorious arbor stood the man I'd marry. He wore a black two-button tuxedo with a black bow tie that fit his long, lean body perfectly. His shoulder-length hair was brushed back, a smile hinting at the corners of his lips. His hands were crossed in front of him, but his shoulders were straight and proud. He looked powerful, happy, and very content with his lot.

My favorite human, my grandfather, stood behind him in a very smart suit, his hair slicked and combed back, his hands clasped around a small leather book. The mayor had given him authority to conduct the wedding as a thank-you for Towerline and an apology for letting Sorcha slip through her fingers when it was over.

Just to the side, Cadogan vampire Katherine sat behind a cello in a black gown, and her brother, Thomas, held a violin. They played soft classical music as people settled into their seats.

It was beautiful and happy and seemed like a fairy tale. And I made myself forget that most fairy tales had dark endings.

I stood up again as Catcher closed the door, and glanced back at Mallory. Joy bubbled up into a nervous laugh. "Holy shit, Mallory. I'm about to get married."

She straightened her skirt, checked her earrings, gave me a sidelong smile. "You're about to get married to Darth Sullivan. It's a good thing I made you face him down that night, oh so long ago."

"I think I was perfectly willing to do the facing down. But yeah, you definitely egged me on."

"I'm an agitator," she agreed. "You two have been through a lot. But there's no one else I'd trust you with, Merit."

"If you make me cry and mess up Lindsey's makeup, she will probably stab you. Or at least give you a good Cadogan beat-down."

We turned at the sound of footsteps. Malik, Amit, and my father walked toward us. All three wore dark tuxedos similar in styling to Ethan's, crisp white shirts, and pale green pocket squares. My father carried Olivia, who looked adorable in her sleeveless dress, with a pale green bow at the waist and tulle skirt. There was a small bow in her blond curls, and a white basket clenched in her tiny fist.

My father put her down, and she ran to her mother. My father immediately pulled his phone from his pocket, began checking his messages. I guess he couldn't be bothered.

"You will knock his proverbial socks off," Amit said, pressing a kiss to my cheek.

"Good," I said with a smile. "He needs to be kept on his toes."

Charlotte crouched in front of Olivia, adjusted her bow, pointed at me. "Livvie, did you see Aunt Merit? Did you see how pretty she looks?"

Olivia turned to me, held out her basket. "I toss flowers!"

"And you're going to do a wonderful job of it," I said.

She reached in, pulled out a chubby handful of white petals, and threw them into the air, eyes closing as they caressed her face.

"Baby, remember you're going to wait until you get inside?"

It was late for humans, and particularly for a child. She was probably tired and sleep-deprived, and her eyes grew wide, her upper lip wobbling. "Now."

Fortunately, it became "now" quickly, as the door opened, Jeff returned to his post, and "Pachelbel's Canon" began to ring through the air.

"Now it's time," Charlotte said, kneeling to straighten Olivia's skirt. "You ready, kiddo?"

"Flowers!"

Charlotte nodded to Jeff and Catcher, and they opened the doors as people turned in their seats for better views.

"Go for it!" Charlotte whispered, and Olivia took off at a run through the doors. But she stopped in the middle of the aisle, turned nearly a full circle as she stared at the people around her.

"Livvie!" Charlotte whispered. "Throw the flowers!"

While the crowd chuckled, Olivia turned and looked at her mother. "Okay!" She ran down the aisle, flinging petals as she moved. Then stopped again and looked back at the door, where Charlotte and Malik had taken their positions.

"Mommy!" she called out. "Mommy! I do it!"

"You're doing so good," Charlotte said, giving her a thumbs-up as the crowd laughed in appreciation. "Keep going!"

Olivia nodded, and she kept walking, throwing petals with wild abandon. The men and women who sat beside the aisle brushed them good-naturedly from sleeves and laps.

"Oh dear God, that might be the cutest thing I've seen all year," Mallory said as Charlotte and Malik followed Olivia down the aisle.

"She takes after her aunt," I said with a grin.

"You're saying she's cute, or bad at following instructions?"

"Har-har-har," I said, but I appreciated that Mallory was keeping it light. There was so much love in the room, so much anticipation, that I felt like I was standing on an emotional cliff. And if I fell off—if I let one tear fall—I didn't think I'd be able to hold the rest of them back.

Mallory cast a glance at Amit. "Sir, I believe it's time for you to do your duty."

He smiled, offered his arm. "My lady."

She took his arm, blew a kiss at me over her shoulder. "See you in the funny papers!"

And then there were three, I thought, as I stood beside my mother and father and waited for Amit and Mallory to make their walk.

We'd decided my father would escort my mother down the aisle. Instead of being escorted, I would walk to Ethan on my own, stand beside him as his partner and friend and lover. That was how I wanted our relationship to begin.

My father put away his phone and took my mother's hand, then looked back at me with pale blue eyes that so clearly echoed my own.

"Go meet your husband," he said, and they walked through the door together.

I guessed those four words were the only ones my father could spare, as he didn't wait for a response but walked down the aisle and helped my mother to her seat. Then he turned back to Ethan, shook his hand with businesslike speed—the deal finally done—and sat beside her.

The brush-off felt dagger sharp, but I wouldn't let it hurt me. Not tonight. Not now, when the members of the wedding party were in position, and there was only Ethan and me. There wasn't time for regret. Not here. Not now.

Through the open door, the Winter Garden bristled with anticipation.

Katherine and Thomas began to play again, their strings dancing through an arrangement they'd created just for the wedding. The crowd rose to their feet. Ethan and the others turned toward the door as Thomas's notes rode along the waves of Katherine's cello.

I stepped onto the threshold, hands gripped around my bouquet like it was the handle of a precious katana. And then I took a breath, and took the step.

I knew the wedding was as much about friends and family as it was about us. The spectacle was for them; the vows—a different kind of oath taking—were for us.

But the look on Ethan's face when he saw me for the first time, that was just for me.

CHAPTER SIX

I WANT IT THAT WAY

Ethan's eyes widened and went hot, his gaze full of love and pride, possessiveness and wicked promise.

As I walked toward him, my Master and friend, I thought of the first moment we'd talked, when I'd blamed him for making me a vampire without my permission, even though he'd saved my life. He'd asked me if I believed he was a monster, if I believed he'd made me a monster. At the time, I wasn't sure—about either of us. And then he gave his life for me, and by some chance miracle, I got him back. And I couldn't be more grateful for it.

I meant to glance at those I passed, smile or nod, accept their hand-blown kisses. But while I could feel them smiling beside me, I couldn't take my eyes off him. I reached him, had to look up to meet his gaze, even in the heels.

You are the most beautiful thing I've ever seen, he silently said, the words just for me.

I smiled up at him. *In your long and illustrious life?*

In every single moment of it. There is no sunset, no creative master-piece, no aria or symphony as beautiful as you.

You don't look so bad yourself, I said with a grin wide enough that it made my cheeks ache.

I glanced at my grandfather, who winked at me. "If you're ready to begin?"

"I absolutely am," I said, and offered my bouquet to Mallory, who'd given up completely on holding back the tears. Amit reached over, offered her a handkerchief.

"Allergies," she whispered with a laugh, and pressed the handkerchief to her cheeks.

"Ladies and gentlemen," my grandfather said, drawing our attention again. "We are gathered here today to witness the union of Ethan Sullivan and Caroline Evelyn Merit in holy matrimony."

"Woo-hoo!" I didn't see who yelled it, but given the crowd's chuckles, they appreciated the sentiment.

"My thoughts exactly," my grandfather said. "Only a few short months ago, many of the men and women in this room were in very dire circumstances, including our groom. But fate is a crafty woman, and just as we have grieved at times in our recent past, so we have joy tonight, as these two brave and kind and stubborn individuals join together, stand together against fate's future whims." He smiled at the crowd. "Let's help them seal that union in matrimony."

He glanced at Ethan. "Do you, Ethan Sullivan, take Caroline Evelyn Merit to be your lawfully wedded wife, to have and to hold from this night forward, until death do you part? Again, I mean."

The crowd chuckled, but Ethan's expression was set and serious. "I do."

"And will you love and honor her for all of your days, whether rich or poor, in sickness or in health, for as long as you may dwell on this earth?"

"I will."

My grandfather nodded, turned his eyes to me. "And do you, Caroline Evelyn Merit, take Ethan Sullivan to be your lawfully wedded husband, to have and to hold from this night forward, until death do you part?"

I turned my gaze to Ethan, enjoyed that instant frisson of nerves in his eyes. Ethan, Master of Cadogan House, wanted me to seal the deal. It was easy enough to obey that one, as there wasn't a doubt in my mind.

"I do."

"And will you love and honor him for all of your days, whether rich or poor, in sickness or in health, for as long as you may dwell on this earth?"

"I will."

My grandfather nodded. "You have the rings?"

We reached back to our dutiful assistants, who handed us the rings.

"Ethan, place the ring on Merit's fourth finger."

I glanced down, my lips parting as light glinted on the ring. It was a worn silver band, inscribed with a circle of forget-me-nots. An antique, but not the type you could buy in a store.

This had been my grandmother's ring. Tears welled again, but refusing to cry, I looked up at my grandfather. He smiled at me, nodding.

He'd given the ring to Ethan for me because he wanted me to wear it, because I'd loved my grandmother with all my heart, and because he had, too.

"She'd want you to have it," he said with a nod, his own eyes red rimmed.

My heart so full of love I feared it might burst, I looked back at Ethan, at my Master and warrior, who knew exactly how to honor what I'd known of love, and had generously agreed to share it here.

"Repeat after me," my grandfather said. "I offer you this ring, Merit, as a symbol of my love and commitment."

"I offer you this ring," Ethan said, voice as clear as the emeralds of his eyes, "as a symbol of my *eternal* love and commitment." He smiled at the addition and slid the ring onto my finger.

"Merit," my grandfather prompted, and I opened my palm, showed Ethan the ring I'd had made for him.

It was a platinum band, inscribed with the tiny oak leaves of his original family crest, taken from the shield that still hung in the House's training room.

"Well," he said, emotion bare on his face. He looked up at me, awe shining in his eyes.

"Place the ring on the fourth finger of Ethan's hand," my grandfather said, and I slipped the ring onto his finger.

"And repeat after me: I offer you this ring, Ethan, as a symbol of my love and commitment."

I looked up at him. "I offer you this ring, Ethan, as a symbol of my eternal love and commitment." I slid the ring home.

My grandfather smiled. "By the power vested in me by the state of Illinois, I now pronounce you husband and wife."

Forever, Ethan said, just for me.

Forever, I agreed, and could all but feel his love, powerful and strong, like a blanket around us both.

My grandfather smiled, lifted his arms. "You may kiss the vampire."

Ethan wasted no time. His eyes gleaming with power, with pride, he slid a hand around my neck and moved in for the kiss, which was powerful and deep, and singularly possessive.

Our family and friends stood, applauding and catcalling, but Ethan ignored them.

He let the kiss get just heated enough to singe before pulling back again.

The silver in his eyes glowed. "I love you," he said. *Mrs. Sullivan,* he added in silence, just for me.

Mr. Merit, I offered back.

He smiled. *You are mine and I am yours, whatever the titles.*

"Ladies and gentlemen," my grandfather said, "a Sentinel and her Master."

"That works," I whispered, as Mallory handed back my bouquet, Ethan took my hand, and the audience cheered.

Katherine and Thomas began their music. Together, we walked down the aisle, among friends and family and lumps of rose petals, and into our future.

The spare elegance my mother and Helen had managed for the service had been abandoned for the reception.

It was held on the other side of the divided space and featured a parquet dance floor and plenty of cocktail tables and round tables with seating, all of it draped with tropical flowers. There were pots of palm trees, birds-of-paradise in clear cylinders on every table, and floral swags hanging from the ceiling.

My mother insisted we not enter the reception proper until Shay had photographed us in every possible position around the exterior of the room with every possible group of individuals. Family groups, friend groups, House groups, business associate groups. (A ticket to the Merit-Sullivan wedding was apparently a hot one.)

You spared no expense, I silently said, smiling as Ethan shook the hand of one of my father's business associates. He'd paid for the bulk of the wedding from his own personal savings.

You're worth it, he said.

When every photographic box had been checked, Shay released us, and the leader of the band stepped to the microphone.

"I am thrilled to present, for the first time, Mr. and Mrs. Ethan Sullivan!" He hadn't gotten the naming memo, but then, he also probably hadn't played a wedding for supernatural creatures who didn't generally use last names. We were a particular bunch.

We'd survived the wedding and made it to the reception. For the first time, I felt myself relax. Felt that knot of tension in my gut finally loosen.

Vampires came forward. They came to pay homage to Ethan, to greet and congratulate us. Nicole Heart, with dark skin and serious eyes, hair waving gently at her bare shoulders in a dress of pale peach. Morgan Greer, head of Chicago's Navarre House, with pale skin, dark hair, and dreamily good looks.

There were more Masters, more humans, more captains of finance, industry, and academia whom Ethan had come to know in his many years as a vampire. Supernaturals of most peaceful varieties, which left a few humans staring at the nymphs, trolls, and broad-shouldered shifters.

Saxophones filled the air, and the singer did a pretty good impression of Al Green as he began to croon "Let's Stay Together."

Ethan held out his hand, crooked his finger to beckon me forward. *Need I call you, Sentinel?*

I grinned at him. *Why don't we save that for the honeymoon?* I offered my hand, and he pulled me against the long, hard line of his body, to the enjoyment of the crowd, which hooted in appreciation.

One of his hands in mine, the other at the small of my back, we swayed to the music while the crowd watched.

The happiness in the room was literally palpable, magic bubbling into the air from supernaturals who nursed champagne, chatted and caught up, or otherwise enjoyed a good party.

"It looks like everyone's having a good time," I told him.

"I believe you're right," Ethan said, and, when I looked back at him, tipped up my chin for a kiss. He got catcalls for the effort that I'm pretty sure came from Luc's direction.

I love you, he said. *Truly, madly, fiercely. So much that I'm nearly drunk with it.*

Part of that may be the very good champagne, I said. *The French may make irritating vampires, but they make very good bubbles.*

Ethan smiled. *So they do.*

And I love you, too. And I think you will very much enjoy the trousseau I've put together later.

His brows lifted with interest. *I'm enjoying even knowing that it exists.*

Just you wait, I said, and gave him a wink.

We danced, and the world around us disappeared. There were only Ethan and me and the sweeping melody among the glow of those thousand candles. No politics, no drama. Just love and hope, and the fact that this incredibly sexy and powerful man belonged to me.

When the song ended, Ethan spun me around and dipped me low to more applause and amusement.

"You are really working the crowd tonight."

"It's my party," he said with a smile.

The sound of ringing crystal was a welcome interruption. We looked back, found Amit on the small stage, microphone in hand.

"Ladies and gentlemen," he said, "for those who don't know me, my name is Amit Patel. And I have had the dubious honor of knowing the groom for more than a century."

There were well-timed chuckles.

"I have seen him at his worst, and this wouldn't be a very good wedding toast if I didn't share at least a few of those embarrassing anecdotes with you."

"Good Lord," Ethan whispered beside me, as my smile spread.

Embarrassing anecdotes about my gorgeous husband seemed like the perfect cure for family-related blues.

"Yes, please!" I yelled out.

"Well, there was the time the only mount we could find was a very sad-looking donkey. So close your eyes, if you will, and imagine Masterful Ethan Sullivan riding Eeyore. Until Eeyore decided he wasn't interested in being ridden, and chucked him into the street. The look on his face—even then." Amit stopped to laugh. "He was shocked—absolutely shocked—that a donkey would dare." His smile was warm when he looked at Ethan again. "He was a Master even then. And then there was the time in a certain house of ill repute . . ."

There were salacious whispers in the audience, and Ethan cleared his throat. "Pay him no mind, Sentinel."

"Oh, I'm paying him all the mind. Please continue!" I called out.

"Ethan, of course, did not partake of the less honorable offerings. But he was running from a human who suspected Ethan of demonic leanings. So, of course, Ethan pitched out the window. Landed in a horse trough, to the amusement of all."

I snorted, glanced at Ethan. "Why do you always end up on the ground?"

"He's choosing selectively," Ethan said, shaking his head at Amit.

"But there is more, of course," Amit said. "More stories, good and bad. Because while I have seen Ethan at his worst, I have also seen Ethan at his best." He glanced at me. "And he is at his best when he is with you. That, I think, is the best kind of love. Love doesn't guarantee happiness or wealth or success. But if you're willing to commit to it, to work at it, it guarantees partnership. So that no matter the trials or tribulations, no matter the joy or loss, you are not alone." He raised his glass. "To Ethan and Merit."

"To Ethan and Merit!" the crowd responded, punctuated with more clapping and the ringing of crystal, which hopefully distracted them from the tears I swiftly wiped away.

Amit handed the microphone to Mallory, then stepped down and moved to us. He shook hands with Ethan, then pressed a kiss to my cheek. "Congratulations and Godspeed."

"Appreciated on both counts," I said with a smile.

"My turn!" Mallory said. "I wanted to do a skit, but our illustrious wedding planners ixnayed that idea. I also proposed to learn how to play the ukulele and honor our Merit and Ethan with a song, but that was a no-go. So I guess I'll have to use my words."

"You can do it!" Catcher yelled out.

"Thank you, honey," she said with a chuckle. "I debated how much detail I should get into on this stage, whether I should embarrass her completely, or just a little bit. I'll probably take the high road." She put a hand on her hip, getting into the speech. "But I will note for the record that she has an unparalleled love of chocolate, and she was, for a brief time, obsessed with the Backstreet Boys."

"Oh God," I murmured, and covered my face with a hand.

"What's a Backstreet Boy?" Ethan whispered.

"Never you mind," I said. "Never you mind."

"There's the 'vacation' to DC, in which she spent three full days in the Library of Congress, the one time I took her bowling. One time," she repeated, with a dramatic eye roll and headshake. "And the incident involving the marathon she basically ruined when she tripped the front-runner."

"It was an accident!" I insisted. "He ran into me."

"Mmm-hmm," Mallory said. "Our girl, our bride, is a little bookish, obsessed with chocolate, and prone to become obsessive about the weirdest things. *Newsies*," she added through a fake cough.

"But most of all," she said, settling her gaze on me again, "there is Merit. There is joy and curiosity and bravery that's almost ridiculously terrifying. And there's loyalty. There was loyalty at a time I didn't deserve it, which probably makes it the best possible loyalty of all." She sniffed, looked away, obviously holding back tears. And when she'd composed herself, she looked at Ethan.

"You have that loyalty now, and I don't have any doubts that you feel the same way about her. We may call you Darth Sullivan, but you're really her knight in shining armor. You let her see a side of herself that she didn't know existed, and it's a pretty kickass side. For that, the world is forever grateful." She raised her glass. "To Ethan and Merit!"

There were more cheers, and then Amit helped her step down again. She wrapped her arms around me, squeezed me tight enough to bruise ribs.

"I love you."

"I love you, too, Mallory. And I will get even for the *Newsies* comment."

She pulled back, thumbed a tear away from my cheek, winked at me. "Do your best, vamp."

"Looks like you're having a good time."

I glanced back, found my grandfather smiling at me, hands in the pockets of his suit jacket. Both the gray jacket and pants were a little too big for him, the pants bagging a little over his thick-soled shoes. It was perfectly grandfatherly, and just made me love him that much more.

"It's been a pretty good night," I said.

"It's been a beautiful night," he said. "A beautiful wedding, a wonderful couple, and some damn good food."

My stomach rumbled. I could smell steak but hadn't had a chance to try it.

I glanced over the crowd, happened to catch sight of my father, who was walking across the room with my mother. No, not just across the room, I realized. Toward the door. His hand was at her back, her wrap over her arm.

They were leaving. They waited just long enough for pictures and toasts, and that was apparently enough. I guessed there'd be no father-daughter dance.

My grandfather must have realized what I'd seen, and sighed heavily. "I'm not sure why he's leaving so early."

"Business deal," I said. "Conference call . . ."

"He is a busy man."

"He's a man with skewed priorities," I said. "And that doesn't make it feel any better."

"No. It doesn't. I'm sorry."

I nodded, feeling my buoyant mood slip away, and grasping at the thin tendrils of it. "Robert didn't even show up." Robert was my older brother, and very much my father's son. He'd been injured at Towerline while courting Adrien Reed for a new business deal. That had been a bad move on many levels, but he'd put the blame on "supernaturals," or so I'd heard. He hadn't spoken a word to me since.

"I don't know why I expect otherwise," I said, but that was a lie. I expected otherwise, at least from my father, because there'd been glimmers of hope recently.

"Because you expect more of him, and rightly so. You expect a lot of your friends, of your family, of yourself." He glanced at the door, gaze narrowed. "It's not unreasonable to expect your father to be a willing and complete participant in your wedding.

"If it helps," he said after a moment, "I don't think he disappoints you for the sake of disappointing you. He has known loss. And in response, he tries to control what he can, by whatever means he can." He looked at me. "Your immortality being a prime example. I'm not trying to make excuses for him. I'm just trying to explain what he might be thinking."

"That helps, actually," I said after silence had filled the air. "Do you really believe it?"

My grandfather smiled. "I believe it's possible. But I'm not sure there's anyone on earth entirely sure what's in that man's head, Merit."

That wasn't much of a surprise.

I refused to let circumstances I couldn't control affect my mood. Mallory, Lindsey, Margot, and I danced until my feet were numb with it, and I'd had more champagne than I should have, and not nearly enough food.

"Well, well," Mallory said, sidling next to me as we took a breather between songs. "Looks like you managed it."

"What?" I asked, and turned in the direction of her pointing. Jonah and Margot stood in a corner, nearly hidden by an enormous potted palm. He was taller than her by nearly a foot, his auburn hair and chiseled face interesting contrasts against her sleek black bob and curvy figure.

Margot laughed at something he said, touched his arm in a gesture of camaraderie. It was a simple, easy move, something she'd probably done a thousand times before. But they both seemed startled by the contact and looked away, both with secret smiles. Smiles full of hope.

A woman walked by, offered a tray of hors d'oeuvres. Jonah held up a hand to decline, but Margot laughed, took his arm, pointed to the tray, began explaining the snacks arranged there while Jonah looked on. He looked suspicious when she pointed to something, but agreed to try it, popped it into his mouth.

And then closed his eyes in obvious satisfaction.

"I told you," she mouthed, the words easy enough to read on her smiling face, and nudged him with her elbow.

I wanted to rub my hands together and cackle in satisfaction. But gloating seemed like bad juju at my own wedding.

Mallory put an arm at my waist. "You know what's amazing?"

I let my head drop to her shoulder. "What's that, kid?"

"We've made it through a wedding and reception without supernatural drama."

"If you just jinxed us I'm going to be so pissed."

"Jinxing isn't a thing. Charming? Yes. Hexing? Absolutely. But not jinx. That's just coincidence."

"What, supernaturally, did you expect to happen?"

She snorted. "Anything and everything? You know how it is—life for the Real Cadogan Housewives."

"That should never be an actual thing."

"Au contraire," Mallory said. "I would watch the shit out of that."

I bet she wasn't the only one.

———— ❧ ————

CHAPTER SEVEN

DELUSIONS OF GRANDEUR

When hunger got the best of me—there'd been no time to even sample the beautiful food Margot had put together—I grabbed a spiraling cheese straw from a basket and ducked into a corner to munch it.

I wasn't officially sure if Margot had put crack in it, but it was good enough that I instantaneously wanted another. I carefully dusted off my hands, trying not to get Parmesan-scented crumbs on my dress, and emerged from behind a potted palm.

"And there's the beautiful bride," Gabriel said. He was tall and tawny, with golden skin and blond-brown hair streaked by the sun. He'd traded his usual jeans and leather jacket for slacks, a button-down shirt, and a blazer, but the clothes just made him seem more feral. Tarzan, newly emerged from the jungle, disguising muscle beneath a suit.

"Merit, you look lovely. And it was a lovely wedding. I hope your husband proves himself worthy."

"I don't think that will be a problem," I said with a smile. I glanced around, didn't see Tanya. "Where's your lovely wife?"

He gestured across the room, where Tanya—slender and delicate, with brown hair and blue eyes—sat at a table with my grandfather. He was talking animatedly while she scribbled something on a small pad of paper, smiling as she wrote.

He smiled. "She's borrowing your grandmother's meat-loaf recipe."

"Excellent choice," I said with a nod. My grandmother had been a fantastic cook.

He pulled a hip flask from his coat pocket, offered it as Ethan joined us. "May I offer you a congratulatory drink, Kitten?"

Ethan's smile looked pleasant, but there was steel behind it. "I'll thank you not to call my wife 'Kitten.'"

Gabriel grinned. "Wondered when you'd get around to saying that."

"And now you know."

"So I do."

"Drink," I requested, and took the flask from Gabe's hand, sipped it suspiciously, and was pleasantly surprised. It was Scotch, or so I thought. Dark and oaky, but still as smooth as honey, and with the same citrusy sweetness.

I handed the flask to Ethan. He lifted his eyebrows but took a drink, and surprise crossed his face, too.

"Well," he said, and took another. "It's like . . . drinking sunshine."

Gabe took back the flask, capped it. "This is a little something we've been working on." His smile went sly. "We're happy with the first results."

Ethan slipped his hands into his pockets. "Are you looking for investors?"

That sly smile went positively wolfish. "Shifters in bed with vampires? That's a dangerous game."

"Too dangerous for the Apex of the North American Central Pack?"

"Didn't you once say we were family?" I teased.

At the word "family," a shadow crossed his face, and the dread in his eyes chilled my blood. I didn't like seeing that emotion on Gabriel Keene, who was as fearless as they came.

"What is it?" Ethan asked.

Gabriel shook his head. "It's your wedding." He uncapped the flask he hadn't yet put away, took a drink of his own before tucking it away.

"It's our life," Ethan said. "And our city. If you know something . . ."

Gabriel had prophesied Ethan and I would have a child—the first among vampires. Historically, three vampires had been conceived, but none were carried to term.

There'd been a caveat to our possible miracle: We'd have to face some unspecified test before it happened, and even the drama of the last year hadn't filled that horrible quota.

Gabriel turned and looked at me, seemed nearly to look through me in that shifter way of his. "You need to be on your game." He looked at Ethan. "Both of you."

"Meaning?" Ethan asked, a thread of concern in his voice.

"Meaning . . ." He paused, seemed to grapple for words. "There's something in the air. Something I don't like. Something uncomfortable."

The chill grew stronger, lifting goose bumps on my arms as I thought of my conversation with Mallory . . .

"What kind of something?" Ethan asked.

Gabriel just shook his head. "That's the problem. I don't know."

"Is it a general unease?" I quietly asked. "A malaise?"

He looked surprised, then suspicious.

"Mallory said the same thing," I explained. "That she had a sense of dread and didn't know why. Couldn't identify a reason for it. Catcher didn't sense anything, and she didn't want to talk to you because she was afraid she was just being paranoid."

Gabriel shook his head. "I don't like this."

"Why do you think it's happening?"

"I don't know," he said, and looked back at us. "You know prophecy isn't exact. I get senses, images, but I don't know details."

"But?" I said.

"But it feels like the world is shifting. And with it, the future. Your future." He glanced down at my abdomen. "His or her future."

I hadn't taken the idea of a child for granted, or hadn't meant to. I knew the future was uncertain. But that didn't ease the fear that clutched at me, that made me feel preternaturally protective of someone who didn't even exist yet.

Ethan moved a step closer, as if to bring me within the sphere of his protection. "You've already said we'd be tested."

"And you will be." Gabe lifted his gaze again, and the sympathy in his eyes nearly brought me to tears. "But that may not be enough."

"Meaning?" I said, but the word sounded hollow, far away. As if I wasn't actually part of the conversation, but hearing it. Trying to live through it.

"Meaning there is no guarantee," Ethan said.

Gabriel pushed a hand through his hair, his frustration obvious. "I'm sorry. I didn't intend to talk about this here. It's not the time or the place."

"If there's danger out there, it's exactly the time and place."

Gabriel grunted, an acknowledgment of Ethan's protectiveness.

"What do we do?" I asked.

"Don't live in fear," Gabriel said. "Just live. Keep your people close; keep your eyes open. That's all any of us can do."

A few feet away, Tanya turned back, beckoned Gabriel to her. His attention shifted, narrowed on his wife, like a man too accustomed to the possibilities of danger and loss.

He pressed a hard kiss to my forehead. "Be careful, Kitten," he said, then strode to his wife.

Ethan and I stood quietly together for a moment.

"I told him not to call you Kitten," he muttered, probably just to make me smile. Which worked.

"Yeah, well, we can't always get what we want."

The words were out before I'd thought about them, and I reached out, squeezed Ethan's hand, made myself lean into the uncertainty.

"I don't want him to be right. I don't want Mallory to be right. I want the world to spin like it has for these last few months, when my toughest decision was picking out a bridesmaid dress for Charlotte."

"And perhaps dealing with the ghost."

"And the ghost," I said with a nod as our friendly neighborhood necromancer, Annabelle, swirled on the dance floor with her husband, looking radiant in her signature pale pink.

Ethan put an arm around my waist, pressed his lips to my temple. "We take each night as it comes, just as we have before. That is all we can do, and the best we can do."

I nodded, let myself have a moment to lean against him, be still beside him, at least until my stomach grumbled.

"Let's also take in some food."

I would not argue with that.

By the time the early hours of the new day approached, just as Mallory had predicted, my face hurt from smiling, I'd ditched my shoes, and curls were slipping loose from the updo Lindsey had worked so carefully to achieve.

Supernaturals, used to the late hour, still danced to the band, which had been playing for hours. A few hearty humans danced, but the rest sat droopy-eyed at tables, yawning as they waited for an opportunity to leave.

"Ladies and gentlemen!" Lindsey said from the stage, microphone in hand. The crowd quieted. "We've reached the end of our evening—literally, because the sun will be up in a few hours, and we still have to get Ethan and Merit to their very special bridal suite."

The crowd hooted.

"But before we go, it's time for one last tradition. Merit, if you'll join me onstage, it's time for you to throw the bouquet!"

Good luck, Sentinel.

I glanced back at Ethan, who winked rakishly. This was the last moment of our wedding, and therefore the last moment before our wedding night began. Uncertain future or not, there was no mistaking the desire in his eyes.

I stepped onto the stage, accepted the bouquet Lindsey offered me. And a good thing, too, as I'd lost track of it hours ago.

A number of women and a handful of men gathered in front of the stage, laughing as they prepared for the ritual. "Everyone ready?"

The screams were high-pitched and energetic. I glanced at Lindsey. "You want to get down there, too?"

"Oh, hell no. My cowboy and I are not contract people."

"You do you," I said, and turned around, took the bouquet in both hands, and launched it.

There were shrieks as the bouquet went airborne and the sound of scrambling behind me as high heels and taffeta and manicures battled.

And then a gasp . . . and silence.

I turned around.

A girl with the same tawny hair as Gabriel's but who was dressed in edgy head-to-toe black stared down at the ribbon-wrapped flowers in her hands, her gaze wide and a little bit horrified.

I'd thrown the bouquet a little too hard, pitching it over the crowd of writhing brides- and grooms-to-be, and landing it in the hands of a woman behind them.

I bit my lip to keep from laughing at her expression. However much she loved Jeff Christopher, marriage did not look to be in Fallon Keene's immediate plans.

"Oh, now, that is ironic," Lindsey said behind me. "Congratulations, Fallon!"

The ladies who'd missed gave good-natured applause, but you could tell their hearts weren't in it. For his part, Jeff walked to Fallon with a wide grin on his face. Suspicion in her eyes, he pulled the bouquet from her hands and kissed her hard. And whatever he whispered to her after that had a smile curving one corner of her mouth.

Yes, there was something about weddings.

"Before the wedding party disperses and you two head off to Paris," Shay said, "let's go outside and get some city shots with the bride, groom, maid of honor, and best man."

"Is that necessary?" I whispered. "She's taken seven thousand pictures already."

Mallory feigned shock. "Seven whole thousand?"

I poked her. "Smart-ass."

Ethan reached out, took my hand. "Outside is fine," he said, making the decision for both of us. "I'm thrilled to have more time with my beautiful wife."

That was a powerful word, and on his lips, nearly seductive.

Just you wait, Ethan silently said, echoing the implicit promise I'd made to him earlier.

Eagerly, I promised him. *I have plans for you, Sullivan.*

The bright flash of his answering magic lifted goose bumps across my skin.

"We'd better get this done as soon as possible," Mallory said, grinning at us. "Before they start vamping each other among the stacks."

Ethan's smile left little doubt that we'd already explored that particular activity, albeit in the House's library, rather than this one. "We'll manage," he assured her.

I squeezed my feet into my shoes again, let Lindsey stuff rebel tendrils of hair back into my updo. Catcher came out with Mallory, and when Lindsey was done, Amit offered her a gentlemanly arm.

"You're becoming an expert escort," I told him as the elevator whisked us back down to the first floor.

"One of my many skills," he said, leveling his deep brown eyes at Shay's camera when she tried to snap a shot.

We walked out of the library's big brass doors, went down the street to the El train trestle that rose above Van Buren.

"Here," Shay said, pointing to either side of the steel trestle supports, lit from above so light pooled on the sidewalk. "Ethan on that side, Merit on the other."

"And we're doing this," he said, and stepped on one side, leaned a hand against the steel structure.

"Give me a pose, Merit," Shay said.

I curled my hands into claws and bared my teeth, heard the responsive *click* of a camera shutter. I guess she liked it.

"Ahem," Ethan said, and I glanced at him. He gestured toward the trestle. "Waiting for you, wife."

"Don't get huffy, husband," I said, and mirrored his pose.

Shay took pictures, then gestured to the stairs that rose to the

El station. "Go up to the tracks," she said. "Then look down over the railing."

We did as she requested. Shay walked into the middle of the street, aimed her camera up at us.

"Do something romantic!" Lindsey called out, and before I could respond, Ethan's hands were on my face, and his lips were planted on mine. He snaked an arm around my waist and pulled me against the solid length of his body, and the arousal that hardened between us as he deepened the kiss.

Soon, he said to me, the word echoing around my head like a marble in an empty box.

"I believe it's time to get the honeymoon started," he said when he finally pulled back again. Since my body was molded to his, my mouth swollen, I wasn't really in a position to argue.

"Sure," was all I managed to say. And weakly, at that.

"Let's switch positions!" Shay called out.

"Not in this lifetime, sister," I murmured, and kept a grip on Ethan's hand.

Ethan chuckled with masculine satisfaction. "No worries, Sentinel. You're the only woman for me."

Damn straight.

We did more El shots, a few shots in Pritzker Park, a few shots in front of brick walls, and then the same shots with a variety of people. Shay offered to walk us down to Buckingham Fountain, but Ethan's looks were becoming increasingly incendiary, and I was losing my immunity to their heat.

"We could take—," Shay began, but I cut her off with a hand.

She'd been taking pictures for hours. And my mother had long since departed the wedding, so she'd forfeited her right to complain.

"I believe we have adequately captured the moment," I said, and glanced at Ethan. "Unless you disagree?"

"There is one I'd like to get," he said with a smile so sly I was afraid he'd suggest she follow us back to the hotel. But instead, he took my hand, and we walked back to the library and the entrance on Van Buren. We reached the arched brass doors, CHICAGO PUBLIC LIBRARY etched into the glass in the arch.

"Here," he said, and, without bothering to explain, picked me up. I squealed, wrapped my arms around his neck as he centered our bodies beneath the sign.

His smile held cool confidence. "Proof that I managed to get her out of the library."

I rolled my eyes during the first shot, smiled during the second, and pressed my lips to his cheek during the third. "Thank you for indulging me," he said, when he put me down again. He pressed his lips to my forehead. But even that chaste act sent frissons of excitement and anticipation through me.

"Thanks, guys," Shay said. "It was a great event. I'll be in touch." But her gaze was on the display on the back of her camera, fingers busily working the controls.

"I bet she says that to all the girls."

"She probably does," Ethan said. "But we're done, so let's take our leave."

"Your limo is around the corner," Amit said with a grin that told me he and Malik had done some decorating.

Hand in hand, we walked around the building to South Plymouth, where the library's red brick gave way to dark glass and sleek steel. The limo sat at the curb, JUST MARRIED in white block letters across the back window, white balloons affixed to the fender and trunk, blue and white ribbons and streamers spilling out from beneath the back bumper.

"And I guess that's our ride," Ethan said dryly.

My first thought was that Amit had been offended by the comment, had made the sound that speared the air in front of us. Ethan realized the truth faster, threw a protective hand in front of me as he stared into the shadowed street.

The sound hadn't been an objection.

It had been a scream.

A dozen humans filled Plymouth between Congress and Van Buren, and they were beating the shit out of one another, the sound of flesh hitting flesh echoing through the near darkness. The crowd was a mix of people in street clothes, pajamas, suits, and an assortment of ages, genders, races.

Cars were stopped in the middle of the dark street where people had simply abandoned them, climbed out, and begun pummeling one another, engines running and radios still blasting. Doors to apartment buildings were open, and a paper bag of fast food—someone's late-night snack forgotten—lay tipped over on the sidewalk.

This wasn't a party, wedding or otherwise. It was a fight.

I couldn't tell what had started it. It didn't look like a turf war or victory riot. This was a brawl that had brought people out of cars, out of homes when they should have been sleeping. And there was no obvious cause. But something had driven these people to violence.

"What the hell is this?" Catcher asked.

A man ran toward us, yanking at tufts of his hair. "The voice! Get the goddamned screaming out of my head!"

This man wasn't the only one screaming those words—the same words I'd heard Winston mutter. And he wasn't the only one with panic practically itching across his skin.

I swore, and could feel the blood drain from my face. *There's something in the air,* Gabriel had said. *It feels like the world is shifting.*

Was this what he'd meant?

"Winston," Ethan said quietly, as if raising his voice might have drawn them closer.

I nodded. "Yeah," I said, but the word felt thick on my tongue. And in the back of my throat, the sharp tang of chemicals, just like I'd sensed in the House.

He was only ten feet from us when he suddenly pitched over, and the scent of blood filled the air, adding copper to that sharp tang of magic.

Behind him stood a man in a business suit, tie unknotted and top button undone, dark circles beneath his eyes and five-o'clock shadow across his face. And in his hand, a bloody tire iron. He looked at us, raised his weapon.

"Is this your fault? Are you doing this to me?" The words were demands, his eyes flitting back and forth between us, looking for someone to blame. And since we were the only ones unaffected by the magic—whatever magic it was—he'd picked us.

"Get inside."

Ethan and I gave the orders to each other simultaneously. But when we looked at each other, we nodded acceptance. We'd just taken a vow to stand beside each other. Might as well get started now.

Catcher looked back at Shay. "Get inside and call the cops. Go. *Now.*"

She wasn't a war correspondent. She was a wedding photographer, and horror had her freezing in place, eyes wide and dazed.

"Shay!" Catcher said again, a sharp and decisive order.

She blinked, looked at him.

"Inside. Call the cops. Go."

He must have gotten through, as she turned on her heel and ran for the door.

Unfortunately, Catcher's voice, that protective order, had traveled. More of the brawling crowd realized we were there, and turned back to look at us, their immediate conflicts forgotten.

We condensed into a smaller group, a tighter group, scanning the growing threat.

"Sentinel?" Ethan said. "I believe you're the one with the experience here."

They didn't need killing; they just needed subduing. "Knock them out," I said. "That's the best way to keep them from killing themselves or each other."

"Or us," Mallory quietly said.

"We can distract them, separate them," Catcher agreed, gaze narrowed as he looked over the group.

The man with the tire iron raised it over his head.

Mine, Ethan said silently, and took off his jacket, tossed it on a parking meter.

That was the first act of the offensive. Amit's jacket followed Ethan's. Mallory and Catcher began to gather power; it bristled around us as they prepared magical fireballs.

"Luc is going to be pissed he missed this," Lindsey said, stepping beside me. She'd pulled a dark elastic through her hair, was twining it into a bun to keep it out of the way. It was a practical move that matched the determination in her eyes. Lindsey may have enjoyed her shares of sass and fashion, but there was no one fiercer in battle.

"Probably so," I agreed. "Let's shut this down."

CHAPTER EIGHT

WAR OF WORLDS

There was a rhythm to every fight, a kind of dance between opponents. But the speed, the steps, the music of it, varied. When Ethan and I practiced, it was a fine ballet with careful moves and exquisite precision. This fight was a drunken midnight dance. All elbows and unfocused eyes and stepped-on toes.

I separated two women in nightgowns, slippers still on their feet, who were screaming like banshees between sobbing, terrified wails. Like Winston and the first man we'd seen tonight, they tore at their hair like they might rip the demons away. That obviously didn't work, which seemed to exacerbate their screaming.

It had been unnerving to see Winston struggle. It was exponentially worse to watch the insanity travel its way through a crowd.

The women fought back as I pushed them apart, turning on me instead of each other. I swept the feet of the one on my right with a low kick that put her on the ground. When she went down, I turned to the other, ducking to dodge a ball-fisted slap. She wasn't a fighter. She was an animal, striking back at something that was attacking her. Something predatory.

I came up again, shoulders hunched in case she tried to make another move. That she wasn't trained didn't mean she wasn't dangerous. She windmilled both arms at me, nails bared, a manicure that couldn't have been more than a few days old. I grabbed one of her arms, turned and twisted until she was bent over, wrenched by the shoulder. She wouldn't know how to escape the move, so I used the moment to my advantage. Or tried to. The other woman popped up again. With my free hand, I hitched up the right side of my dress and kicked out, toe pointed.

I caught her underneath the chin, snapped her head back. Her eyes rolled, and she hit the ground.

"Good girl," I said, and turned back to the other woman.

"Sentinel," Ethan said, and I glanced back at the black bow tie he'd extended. His hair was loose around his face, his shirt unbuttoned. "Tie her hands."

I nodded, took the thin panel of silk as he ran forward and blocked the strike of a woman carrying—quite literally—a wooden rolling pin that looked like it was still dusted with flour. And worse.

Focus, I told myself, and pulled the woman's other arm back. By that point, her voice had become one long ramble of throaty pleas. "Make it stop make it stop make it stop make it stop!"

"I'd like to, but you don't want to be coldcocked, so you'll have to settle for second place." I maneuvered her to the bike rack and pushed her to the ground, then pulled her arms through one of the rack's supports and used the bow tie to secure her. "We'll get you unconscious as soon as reasonably possible."

I turned, was pushed backward by Catcher's outstretched hand as a blue ball of fire whirred past me, thrown by Mallory's hand. It hit a man wielding a bloody wooden baseball bat in the chest, sent him flying backward, arms and legs thrown forward by the momentum. He flew ten feet before hitting the sidewalk, arms and legs splayed. And he stayed down.

I looked back at Catcher in horror. "Did she kill him?"

"God, no. It's just force, not fire. Kind of like getting hit by a very large beanbag."

I looked back at the man. Sure enough, his chest continued to rise and fall, but he didn't try to get up. I'd say that hit the mark.

"Shit!" Mallory called out, as a hulk of a woman—easily six and a half feet tall and two hundred forty pounds of muscle—stalked toward her. Two whole Mallorys would have barely covered her bulk. Her Cubs T-shirt was torn and bloody, blood dripped from her nose, and her eyes were wild with fear. And she was much too close for Mallory to use magic.

"Stop screaming!" she said, accusation clear in her eyes. "Stop screaming! Stop screaming!"

"I'm not screaming!" Mallory said, now screaming.

"Later," Catcher said, and went to help his wife.

The gleam of metal in the streetlight caught my eye, and I looked back. A woman walked forward, chef's knife in her hand. She was wearing pajamas and scuff-style slippers, and I'd bet the knife had come from her kitchen.

For whatever mysterious reason was driving them, she'd probably walked right out of her house and right into hell.

Her hair was short and curly, her eyes wild and panicked. She raised the knife in one hand, beat against her temple with the other. "Get them out of my head!"

"I can help you," I said, reaching out a hand while I kept my eyes trained on the knife and its wide, flat blade, with a pattern that looked like *mokume-gane*. If it had been well cared for, it would be sharp and could do some damage.

"You can't!" She screamed it, putting so much energy into the sound her body bowed with the force of it. "They won't stop. I will make them stop! I will stop them!"

She held the knife to her throat, and my heart seemed to stop sympathetically.

"Please don't," I said, trying to draw her gaze back to me. "I promise I can help you. There's a place you can go where the voice won't bother you anymore."

That place might have involved a cell and a drug-induced coma, but it was all I had to offer at the moment, at least until we learned more.

She paused for a moment, shoulder twitching up toward her ear, and I could see hope spark in her eyes. But it was a small spark, extinguished by whatever delusion ripped through her awareness. She grabbed handfuls of her hair, bent over from the waist like the voice had weight and was pulling her to earth.

She screamed and stomped her feet in obvious frustration, and when she lifted her gaze again, there was a horrible desperation in her eyes. "This won't end. It doesn't end. It's the same thing all day, every day, and there's nothing you can do about it or that I can do about it. It doesn't stop. It doesn't stop!"

She regripped the knife so the blade pointed toward her, a new grim determination in her eyes.

"No!" I said, and ran forward, but I was a moment too late. She plunged the knife into her abdomen, dark blood staining her apron. The fingers still wrapped around the blade turned crimson as she fell to her knees, eyes wide. She looked down, horror filling her eyes, and began to shake.

"Little help here!" I called out, and dodged forward. She pulled one hand away, began to beat back at me. I grabbed her slick wrist, wrapped my free hand around the one still on the knife. There was no telling what she'd punctured, or if pulling out the knife would make the situation worse.

Malik hit his knees beside me. "Do exactly what you're doing," he said, and pulled off his jacket. "Keep your hand on the knife. I'm going to apply pressure."

I just nodded, since I was busy trying to keep the woman's

clawing hand away from me. She was still screaming; her plan to kill the noise by giving herself a brutal amount of pain clearly wasn't working.

Malik wrapped the coat around the knife below our joined hands, pressed firmly down. The woman screamed with pain, which made more delusional heads turn our way.

A blue ball whizzed by, sparks jettisoning as it passed like an out-of-season sparkler. I looked up, watched it stream toward a young man in his early twenties in athletic shorts and shower shoes shuffling forward, hands gripping his head like he was trying to rip away a vice. He hit the pavement much the way the first one had.

"Merit," Malik said. I looked back, found him nodding toward my skirt.

"*Shit,*" I murmured, and slapped at the sparks that were eating their way through the silk. But my hands were very much occupied . . .

"I got it," Amit said, slapping out the sparks with a hand. He blew away the ashes, tamped again just to be sure, and then looked back at the woman bleeding on the ground in front of us. There were streaks of blood on his face.

"Cadogan House has a unique way of partying," he said.

I looked back at my hands, covered in blood and around an equally bloody knife, hoping to God I wouldn't lose the woman I hadn't been able to save.

"Yeah. I'd say that about sums it up."

The ambulances arrived first, sirens roaring toward us, lights flashing. Catcher pulled the EMTs to our position, and they worked to stabilize the woman, get her into the ambulance. They must have been experienced with disaster work, as they didn't flinch at the sight of the chaos, or the humans on the ground.

"Keep her guarded and secured to the bed," Catcher said of the woman with the knife. "She did this to herself."

"Suicide?" one of the EMTs asked, crossing himself in the process, two fingers across forehead, breastbone, left, and right.

"Not exactly," Catcher said. "But we don't have time to explain right now. The Ombudsman will be in touch."

They nodded, swept her away and to the hospital with sirens roaring again.

One of the EMTs offered me a bottle of water, and I rinsed the worst of the blood from my hands.

Ethan walked toward me, looked me over, and I did the same to him. Limbs still connected. Filthy and blood smeared, like me, but generally healthy.

"I'm okay," I said, anticipating the question. "You?"

He nodded, looked down at his now-untucked shirt and ripped pants. "The streets of Chicago are filthy. I don't recommend rolling around on them."

I looked down. I'd lost a sleeve, the lace along the bottom of my dress had been shredded, and blood stained the front in ugly vermillion streaks.

"Yeah, my dress is toast."

He glanced down at it. "You and clothing. At least the wedding was already over."

I blanched as I realized what would come. I'd have to take the dress back to the House, where Helen would undoubtedly see it. I could all but feel the lecture taking shape, judgment forming like a cloud over us, never mind that I'd paid for the damn thing.

"Helen," I said, looking up at him, and watched understanding dawn in his eyes.

His gaze went steely. "We'll move. Our bags are already at the hotel. We'll just pick up and leave, and she'll never know what became of it."

Until the dozens of passersby with cell phones and reporters with cameras—all of whom were outside the hastily hung caution tape—shared their images with the world.

"Too late for that," I said, and looked back at the carnage that we'd helped wreak tonight.

There had been more humans than supernaturals, but we had more strength and more firepower, literally and figuratively. Some had been knocked out, some were still squirming, and some were tied to bike racks with more abandoned bow ties. More than a dozen prone humans on the ground while we stood, bloodied and torn, over them—humans who'd come down with some kind of delusional disorder we'd seen in a vampire in Cadogan House.

"It wasn't just Winston," I said.

"No," Ethan said. "It wasn't just Winston. And we need to know why, and how."

In addition to the people on the ground, two trash receptacles were on fire, sending the scents of burning plastic and garbage into the air. Blood spattered and pooled on the concrete, reflecting the cruisers' blue and red lights.

When four uniformed CPD officers emerged from their cruisers, we lifted our hands instinctively. But for the wedding attire, it would have looked like we'd made a breakfast buffet of the neighborhood.

My grandfather and Jeff hustled toward us from the library, both still in their pristine suits.

My grandfather pulled out his identification. "I'm the Ombudsman," he said. "The perpetrators are all on the ground. These are the ones who kept them from killing each other."

We gave the cops a minute to orient themselves, holster their weapons, and for the officer in charge to find my grandfather.

"Oh, Merit," Mallory said, joining us. "Your dress."

"I know. Yours isn't much better." There were small circular burns and ugly red smears across the pale green lace.

She glanced down. "Oh yeah. Got a little singed with that last bombardment. Guess I won't be turning this into a cocktail dress."

"And I guess I won't be getting married again." Not that I'd want a repeat of this evening. Or the latter part of it, anyway.

Accompanied by my grandfather, a detective walked toward us, badge hanging from a chain around his neck. He had a pale, lived-in face, a crop of white hair, and a suit that was turned out, from the sharp lapels to pixel-thin stripes to pocket square. I wouldn't have been surprised to see spats beneath the pants' cuffs.

"One dead, twelve injured to some degree," my grandfather reported. Ambulances were still rushing to and away from the scene, carrying the humans who'd been part of the mob to nearby hospitals.

"I'm Detective Pulaski," said the detective, notepad in hand. "Who wants to start?"

"We stumbled into it," Ethan said. "We were taking wedding photographs, rounded the corner, and there they were. Fighting and talking about delusions."

My grandfather's gaze widened, and he looked at me. I nodded at the unspoken question. "Same as Winston. They're panicked and afraid, and they hear screaming. And because of that, for whatever reason, they become violent."

"Winston Stiles," my grandfather explained to Pulaski. "A vampire who attacked Merit last night in Cadogan House. He's currently in lockup at the supernatural facility."

Pulaski looked back. "Any of these people vampires?"

"All humans," Ethan said.

"So a vampire went crazy, and then a bunch of humans went crazy?"

Was it contagious? he meant. Were the delusions spreading across the city?

"Vampires did not infect humans," Ethan said. But there was worry in his eyes. We didn't know how this had spread—whatever it was. And the only other person we'd seen with delusions had been a vampire in our House.

"Then how did it spread?"

"Maybe it didn't," Mallory said, and we all looked at her.

"Delusions aren't generally contagious, and they don't have any other symptoms."

"So what's the other option?" Pulaski asked.

"They're telling the truth," Mallory said. She pushed back the hair that brushed her face, her pale manicure—the same we'd all gotten for the wedding—chipped at the edges. "They're having the same delusions because they're hearing the same things. They're hearing something real."

Ethan tilted his head. "If the sound—or its origin—is real, why can't we hear it? Why isn't everyone affected?"

"I don't know," Mallory said. "I think that's what we have to figure out. And that doesn't even get to the bigger question."

"Which is?" Ethan prompted.

She looked at him. "Who is screaming? Who wants so badly to be heard?" She spread her gaze across the city like she was looking for an enemy sail.

"Sorcha?" Ethan asked.

Mallory shook her head. "The wards are intact."

"And there's no way for her to get around that?" Ethan asked. "To circumvent it?"

We'd covered this ground before, of course. When the wards were proposed, we'd gone over every detail of the magic, of the wards, of the degree to which they'd give us protection—and fair warning.

"The wards are a circuit. She uses magic, it breaks the circuit, and we hear about it. We haven't heard about it; ergo . . ."

"It's not Sorcha," Ethan concluded.

Mallory nodded. "Besides, she's an alchemical witch. This doesn't feel like alchemy."

Pulaski held up his hand. "I'm not interested in the magical mumbo jumbo. I'll leave that to you. What I want to know is what, exactly, happened here. In detail."

"I'll walk you through it," Catcher said, and led him a few feet away, pointing at the spot where we'd rounded the corner some unfathomably long time ago.

My grandfather followed them but looked back at us, circled a finger in the air. He wanted us to keep going, to keep talking it through.

"So it's someone else's magic?" Ethan asked.

"It has to be," Mallory said. "I just don't know whose, or at least not yet. Although there is that weird metallic thing."

"Yeah," I said, turning back to Mallory. "I sensed the same thing after seeing Winston. I thought it was *because* of the delusions. Like, he'd been sick, which gave his magic a weird scent. But maybe it's a signature of some kind. Is it associated with a certain kind of magic or creature?"

She shook her head. "Not that I'm aware of, but I'll have to check the books."

"Paige is out of town," Ethan said, "or I'd have her look, too." Paige was a sorceress who practically lived in Cadogan House, mostly owing to her relationship with our Librarian. "The Librarian's at an ALA conference in New York," Ethan added. "She's with him."

Paige had been bummed about missing the wedding. The Librarian had been too excited about the conference—and the books—to be overly concerned.

"I can look," Mallory said, glancing at her husband, who stood with my grandfather and Pulaski. "He's going to be tied up with this for at least the short term."

"The mayor's going to blow a fuse," I agreed.

"Yeah. Probably."

Amit walked over to us. "Not the trip to the States I had in mind," he said, and glanced at Ethan, concern in his eyes. "There is something about Chicago, isn't there?"

"Something in the damn water, I'm beginning to fear," Ethan said.

"Or in the air," I said, and looked at Mallory. "Gabe's had the same sense of dread. So whatever you're feeling, you aren't alone."

She looked understandably relieved and concerned by that information.

A reporter had found us, was busily snapping pictures of the carnage, the remains of the wedding party.

"Take this picture," Mallory said to him, moving aside so that Ethan and I stood alone.

"If you want the real sense of Cadogan House, get Merit and Ethan after battle. Get the shot of them together, bloodied because they tried to make a difference. Those are Chicagoland's vampires."

With a somber expression, the reporter nodded and aimed his camera at us.

--- ✦ ---

CHAPTER NINE

BITTERSWEETNESS

W e said good-byes to what remained of the wedding party and climbed into the limousine that would take us back to the Portman.

At dusk, we were supposed to take a specially equipped and sunlight-protected plane to Paris for a week of madeleines and espresso and moonlight reflecting on the Seine.

Except I knew that couldn't be. "We aren't going to Paris," I said, and settled my head on his shoulder.

"No," he said. "And I should request all wedding guests leave Chicago as soon as possible. There's no point in dragging them further into this."

I felt suddenly, unbearably tired. Emotionally exhausted by a long night of prepping and socializing, physically exhausted by the battle we hadn't wanted to find ourselves in. And as much as I knew why we couldn't go, why we couldn't leave the city in the midst of some unknown supernatural contagion, I couldn't shake the heavy grief that settled into my bones.

I'd only wanted a honeymoon. That wasn't so much to ask, was it?

Ethan put an arm around me, drew me closer. I shut my eyes and let myself be calmed by the warmth and nearness of him. "I suppose I was wrong about this not being our problem," he said.

"It became our problem through no fault of yours. Not much we could have done about that. And it's better we were there than not. It wasn't our plan, but if we hadn't stepped in, things would have been a lot worse."

Ethan smirked, drew me closer. "I believe I'm the one who should be comforting you, rather than the other way around. Because my beautiful wife deserves peace and comfort."

"'Wife' sounds weird. I wonder when I'll get used to it."

"You've an eternity," Ethan said, "as I'm not letting you go."

It was nearly dawn, and the Portman Grand was quiet, our footsteps echoing on the marble floor. A woman stood behind the reservation counter, brow furrowed at something in front of her. A man across the room dusted tables in the sitting area, and a lone and exhausted-looking family waited at the bottom of the stairs, all in matching CARTER FAMILY VACATION T-shirts. The parents' gazes lifted to watch us, eyes widening as they took in our torn clothes, scraped bodies.

"Sit down," Ethan quietly said. "I'll check in."

I nodded, walked toward the stone fountain against the far wall.

"Big fight over the bridal bouquet," I said to the parents, with the only hint of a smile that I could manage, and hoped that would be enough to soothe their fears.

Water trickled from a lion's head mounted to the wall in a quatrefoil base. I sat down on the edge, watched koi dart across the water toward me, probably hoping for breakfast.

I closed my eyes and listened to the sound of the water, tried to forget everything I'd heard and seen and felt tonight. Everything except love. Because when all was said and done, that might be the only real thing we had left.

I was tired enough that I didn't know he'd joined me again—hadn't even heard him cross the marble lobby—until his hand was on my shoulder.

"Sentinel, I believe you are nearly done for today."

I nodded. "I think I am, too."

"In that case, let's go upstairs." He pulled me to my feet, kept my hand in his.

The honeymoon suite was even more grand than the rooms in which we'd prepared for the wedding—and not just because of the sleek grand piano that faced a long wall of windows overlooking the city. Like the other, this room had been divided into separate living spaces, including a dining room, an enormous sectional sofa facing the windows, and a library's worth of books on a wall that must have stretched twenty feet to the ceiling. A door in the window wall led to an outside terrace dotted with boxwoods and low furniture.

Several doors led from the hallway at the other end of the room. A floating staircase monopolized the interior wall, leading to what I guessed was the bedroom. And beside the stairs, a suite of suitcases, dark brown leather with the Cadogan "C" embossed across the front in silver, stood ready for Paris.

I'd been prepared to wax poetic about the glory of the penthouse, but the sight of them brought that grief into full focus again.

I walked to the windows, looked out at the city. It seemed dark and peaceful from this height, although I knew that was a mirage. That we'd see more of whatever it was that we'd seen tonight. And until we figured out exactly what that was, we wouldn't be able to stop it. More people would die.

I sighed heavily and with much self-indulgence. "Sometimes I wish our lives were normal."

"We just got married," Ethan said, walking to a standing champagne bucket and checking the vintage. "That's a fairly normal thing to do."

"And we were attacked by a mob of housewives and coffeehouse kids. That is not."

Ethan slid the champagne home again, looked up at me.

"Think of everything that we might have missed, Sentinel. So many full moons. So much magic that others have missed. So many Mallocakes that a slower metabolism might not have handled."

I knew he was trying to make me laugh, and looked back at him. "Now who's comforting whom?"

"I owed you one."

I smiled at him. "I'd like a hot bath. Maybe you could comfort me in there?"

His smile was slow and hot and promising. "I believe I could arrange something." He glanced at the stairs. "Shall we go upstairs, wife?"

I smiled at him. "Let's do, husband."

"Damn," I quietly said.

We'd made it up the stairs, but gaped in the doorway.

The bedroom was enormous, with silvery paper on the walls and pale carpet across the floor. The bed was a pool of blue in front of a wall of windows that faced Lake Michigan and below a chandelier of sculpted glass teardrops that sent soft orbs of pale light across the room. Eucalyptus and lavender scented the air, and soft, chiming music played in the background.

"It is a room for relaxing," Ethan said. "For rest and sleep.

And since tomorrow will come quickly enough—and whatever fallout that includes—we'll rest while we can."

Rest sounded delicious, but somehow defeatist. This was, after all, the only bit of honeymoon we'd get. Paris was a memory. Fallout was our future.

"You may need some assistance getting out of your dress. Or what remains of it."

"Don't remind me."

"Turn around," he said, spinning a finger. I was too tired to argue or make a seductive response, so I turned, waited as he unfastened the hooks, unzipped the back. The dress was ravaged enough that it fell to the floor in a heap of stained silk and satin.

"Well," Ethan said, taking in the ensemble beneath—the thigh-high stockings, garter, and bustier. Part of my wedding trousseau, and an ensemble intended to be seen only by him.

"That is . . . lovely," he said, his voice smoky with appreciation. He skimmed a hand down my back, his touch lifting goose bumps across my body. "You are a beautiful creature, Merit."

"Can you help with my hair?" I asked, pointing to the knot that was now hanging heavily at the nape of my neck.

"Of course."

He walked forward, and began unraveling the curls and braids. It took a solid couple of minutes to pull out the pins. When he was done, I flipped my head over, shook out my hair, flipped it over again, scrubbed fingers through my hair.

"Even better," he murmured.

I looked back at Ethan, his eyes—silver with emotion—tracking my body like a man with a long-denied thirst. "All of this is mine," he said, trailing the back of his hand across my bare arm.

"I love you," I told him, putting a hand on his face. "But I would shove you out of the way to get into the shower right now."

He laughed. "I'm glad to know where I stand, Sentinel. And in this particular case, I won't stand in your way."

The bathroom was nearly as large as the bedroom, with lots of pale marble and a curvy soaking tub big enough for a crowd. Fluffy towels were piled on a bookcase near the door, and a chandelier of glass shards cast pretty shadows across the floor.

"Impressive," I said.

"Only the best for my Sentinel." He turned both faucets, and water and steam began to fill the room.

"I could use a drink," he said. "Keep an eye on the water."

I nodded, pulled the lid from a glass jar of what looked like purple dust dotted with tiny dried flowers beside the tub, sniffed. Lavender and something slightly astringent. Eucalyptus, maybe. "Fancy some bath potpourri?" I called out.

"I'm not entirely sure what that is," he said from the other room. "Although I'd prefer not to smell like a Parisian *parfumerie*."

"I don't think that will be a problem," I said, and scooped some of the salts and sprinkled them over the water. The smell was heavenly, a soothing balm that pushed thoughts of battle and blood out of my mind.

"This is the second time I've found you nearly asleep near water," Ethan said. He'd taken off his shirt, his shoes, his belt. He wore only black trousers, the waistband framing the bricks of muscle across his abdomen, and just skirting the diagonal muscles that marked his hips.

I opened my eyes, took the glass of wine he offered, its color as pale as light. "Not asleep," I said, taking a sip. "Just trying to be somewhere else."

He lifted an eyebrow.

"Not away from you," I clarified. "Just away from that."

He nodded, brushed a lock of hair from my face. "There will

be more questions, more demands. So let's take tonight, Merit, just for ourselves. We may not have Paris, but we'll at least have memories from our wedding night that don't involve violence."

"That sounds good."

He turned off the water, then took my glass, setting both of them on the edge of the tub, then went to his knees in front of me.

"I'm afraid it's too late for a proposal," I said, swallowing hard against rising lust. I didn't have to fight that feeling—not with my husband, not tonight. But the lust was fueled by exhaustion, and I didn't want to rush this. Not our first time as husband and wife.

"It seems you have me on my knees, Sentinel," he said, and ran his hands up one leg. My eyes closed instinctively, my head dropping back. I focused on the sensations of his hands on me, those long and skillful fingers provoking as they slipped, one inch at a time, up my thighs. He unclipped one stocking from the delicate lace garter that held it, skimmed the tips of his fingers against me.

I looked down at him. "I'd say you're tending me again, but I'm not sure that's accurate."

He looked up at me, eyes silvered with emotions. "I have no tending in mind, Sentinel. I intend to make you desperate, and leave you breathless."

As if on cue—as if he mastered my body as well as my House—the breath shuddered out of me.

He slipped down the second stocking, tossed it away as he had the first, and then slipped down the garter, fingers skimming my core. I had to reach out for balance as sensation threatened to topple me.

He rose again, took my hand, placed it against his heart. "This beats for you, eternally."

I nodded, incapable of words, and slid my hand down his chest and abdomen, then found him rigid with arousal and want. He sucked in a breath.

"Who's breathless now?" I asked.

His jaw clenched. "Maybe I should be on my knees again."

I smiled, unzipped his trousers, letting them fall to the floor. The silk boxers he wore beneath did little to camouflage his excitement.

"Turn around," he said, and I did, pulling my hair back from the bustier he hadn't yet unfastened. He slipped one hook, then another, tossed the silk away, and pulled me hard against him, his hands roaming from ribs to breasts, cupping and teasing. He bent his head to my neck, teased with kisses and the hint of fangs that he well knew would drive me crazy.

A bit more silk, and we were naked.

"Water," he said, and helped me into the pool-sized tub.

The water was just shy of scalding, my favorite kind of bath. Lavender steam rose around us, tiny purple buds floating on the fragrant surface.

He stepped in beside me, his long legs rippling the surface of the water. He'd rippled through my life. He sat down and pulled me toward him, long fingers gripped in my hair as he plundered my mouth, taking possession of body and soul. The water lapped my breasts, but I could hide nothing from him. He wouldn't allow it.

Not that I had anything to hide. He knew me better than anyone, better than everyone. Every inch of my body, every mote of bravery and fear. I wouldn't claim knowledge of every mote of Ethan's four hundred years, but I knew the truth of him. I knew the dark and light, understood his secret symphony. He belonged to me as much as I belonged to him.

I settled my body atop his, harbored him, and felt his shuddering response.

"Forever," he said, the fingers in my hair still strong, still refusing to let go, as if he still needed to bind me to him.

"Forever," I whispered against his mouth, and rocked against him, the fragrant water lapping our bodies. The rhythm quickened, Ethan moving faster and deeper, teeth and tongue fighting a similar battle above the water, need quickening inside me like a tangible thing, the union of pleasure and pain and desire.

"Go," he said, and my body responded to the command like a soldier. I gripped his shoulders as my body bowed, contracted, heat and electricity pulsing like a live connection.

"Yes," he growled, his pride and satisfaction giving texture to the word, so it seemed to sharpen the air. "Forever," he said as his body contracted, a sound of beautiful agony slipping from his lips.

"Forever," I said, and put my hands on his cheeks, pressed a soft kiss to his closed eyes, his lips. "Forever."

The wedding had been beautiful. The reception had been great fun, at least until chaos had taken her turn with it. Making love for the first time as husband and wife had been sublime.

And later, after love had been shown and proven and we'd wrestled our own demons, as dawn had begun grappling at the horizon with her rose fingers, we were on the bed in clean pajamas, a room service spread between us, and bottles of Blood4You and Veuve Clicquot on ice nearby.

"I understand the food at the reception was divine," Ethan said, stretched on the bed beside me, scooping caviar onto a toast point. "Not that we had time to enjoy it."

Not being a fan of fish eggs, I scooped guacamole with a blue corn chip. "No, and I am starving. A wedding and mass mob will do that to a vampire."

"So I hear. I noticed Jonah and Margot dancing."

I nodded. "I'm trying to hook them up. I think they'd work well together."

He glanced up at me. "In my experience, playing matchmaker often backfires."

I snorted. "When did you last play matchmaker?"

"Juliet and Morgan."

I stared at him, chip halfway to my mouth, then lowered it again. "You tried to set up Juliet and Morgan." Morgan was finally coming into his own as Master of Navarre House, but even still, I couldn't see him with our pixie guard and fearsome fighter.

"'Tried' being the operative word," Ethan said. "It didn't take." His voice was flat.

"Well, of course not." I frowned, trying to imagine sly Juliet with the previously passive-aggressive Morgan. "Oil and water."

"I don't see why they should be. They're both senior staff, in a manner of speaking. They're both witty and intelligent people, Morgan more so now that he's stepped out of Celina's shadow."

"Wrong personalities. Wrong chemistry."

"There are some who'd say the same thing about us."

"And they'd be wrong," I said with a smile, and bit into the chip. "I help keep your ego in check."

"I am a shy and retiring vampire," he said, with not one bit of sincerity or believability. "And I keep you from running headlong into danger."

I gave him a look.

"Well, I try," he amended. "And is that to be your official Dry Wife Expression? I'd like to go ahead and commit it to memory."

"You're hilarious, husband."

"And you're beautiful, wife. Headstrong or otherwise."

A compliment either way.

CHAPTER TEN

WE'LL ALWAYS (NOT) HAVE PARIS

I woke to the smells of chocolate and sugar, but kept my eyes closed, basking in the fantasy that Chicago's problems had resolved themselves and we'd been whisked away to Paris while we slept. I'd open tall, iron windows to a balcony, a wonderful breeze, and a view of the Eiffel Tower.

"Bonjour, mon amour," I said.

"You're still in Chicago," Ethan reminded me. "And the mayor wants to see us."

Of course she did. I pulled a pillow over my face. "I can't hear you. The sun's still up."

"The sun has set. And the mayor has beckoned. And I have breakfast."

I tossed away the pillow, sat up.

Ethan sat beside me on the edge of the bed, naked but for a pair of silk pajama bottoms. The breakfast tray sat on the bedside table with the promised cup of dark, steaming chocolate, and two perfect-looking croissants beside a bowl of perky raspberries.

"Two delicious choices," I said, leaning up to kiss him. "Good evening, husband."

He smiled wickedly, kissed me back. "Good evening, wife."

I plucked up a croissant, tore off the pointy end. "Did the mayor really summon us?"

"She did, as well as your grandfather. We're all to be at her office as soon as possible."

The croissant was good, but the thought of dealing with drama again made my mouth dry. Launching myself into a fight? Not altogether unenjoyable. Dealing with a mayor who tended to believe the worst of us? Not as much fun.

"We should have invited her to the wedding," I said, crossing my legs and picking off another bite.

Ethan chuckled. "We did. Didn't you see her?"

"No." I grinned at him. "I only have eyes for you."

"Mmm-hmm. And carbs."

"Is she planning to blame us for what happened last night? I don't see how she could. We kept the situation from getting worse." I pointed to the *Tribune* folded beside the food, which featured a shot of Ethan and me in torn wedding clothes, hands linked and staring at the desolation. VAMPIRES STOP RAGING HUMANS was the headline. It was, by far, one of the better headlines we'd seen. Maybe the city was finally beginning to see us as soldiers, rather than perpetrators.

Ethan's gaze slid across the room, to the stained and torn heap of white silk and lace on the floor. "Until we take that to Helen."

"She's probably seen the *Tribune*," I said. "I suspect she already knows."

"And will undoubtedly be stewing about it until we return to the House." Ethan stood up, the bottom half of his outrageous body framed perfectly by draped silk. "Eat your breakfast and get dressed, and let's get this over with."

I'd do both. But since it was still technically my honeymoon, I put an arm around his waist, tugged him back to the bed.

The mayor and the croissant could wait a little while longer.

*   *   *

We dressed and traveled through the lobby of our beautiful hotel, stopping when it seemed everyone else was pressed against the lobby windows or walking around outside.

Something had happened. Something that had drawn the attention of the humans and, from the jittering energy in the room, had made them very skittish.

Take care, Ethan silently said, and we walked through them, whispers in our wake. We stepped outside . . . and into a thick swirl of white snow.

The flakes were enormous, the snowfall heavy enough that I couldn't see the buildings across the street. They muffled the sound of traffic, of pedestrians, of the typical buzz of the city.

"It's seventy degrees outside," Ethan said. "This isn't possible."

I'd paired a thin, three-quarter-sleeved black shirt with jeans and boots and was actually a little warm. This probably wasn't the first time it had snowed in Illinois in August. And while we could see only a sliver of sky between tall skyscrapers, what we could see was dark and clear. Which meant the snow wasn't falling from clouds, but from *nothing*. It was spawning out of literal thin air somewhere above us.

"Magic," Ethan quietly said. "Gabriel said there was something in the air. I thought he meant last night."

"Yeah. I did, too."

Magic buzzed around us, but without the chemical smell that had marked the hallucinations. This was magic, but different magic. I wasn't sure if that was better or worse than the other option.

Our meeting with the mayor was about to get a little more intense.

My phone began to ring, and I pulled it out, checked the screen as Ethan did the same. There were alerts from Jeff and the

House about the weather—and the wards that were screaming across the city.

Sorcha's wards had been breached, which meant this was Sorcha's magic—and she'd somehow managed to control the weather.

That was Official Big Bad territory.

"Let's get moving," Ethan grimly said, and we headed to City Hall.

The Loop's sidewalks were busy with people who'd come out to wonder at the weather, catch snowflakes on their tongues, or take videos to share for the shock and awe of it.

City Hall looked like a lot of government buildings in the US—square, with granite, symmetrical rectangular windows, and lots of ribbed columns. The doors were edged in brass that gleamed like gold, and the lobby was marble, with towering vaulted ceilings and elevators covered by more lustrous brass.

Catcher and my grandfather stood in the lobby, just past the security area, waiting for us. My grandfather had exchanged his usual brown sport coat for a dark suit that was a little baggy in the arms, the trousers a smidge too long. I found both of those things almost stupidly endearing. Catcher wore jeans and a black T-shirt without a smart-ass comment, which was practically business wear as far as he was concerned.

"Good evening," Ethan said.

My grandfather nodded, his expression somber.

"She's in the city?" Ethan asked.

"There's been no report of her yet," Catcher said.

"If she isn't here yet," my grandfather said, "she'll be here soon." He glanced back at the snow falling outside. "She'll want to see this."

"What's the protocol now that the wards have been triggered?" Ethan asked.

"Baumgartner will send a patrol to each sector," Catcher said.

Baumgartner was the leader of the Order, the sorcerers' union. "They'll determine where the breaches occurred, which will hopefully help us locate her and figure out what kind of magic she's using."

"It's about damn time."

Everyone just looked at me.

"Sorcha," I explained. "She's too egotistical to walk away, to be cool about what she would have seen as a humiliating defeat. That's not how she operates. This was inevitable. At least now we won't have to wonder when it's going to happen."

I looked around at all of them, saw the flash of acknowledgment in their eyes. Even if we hadn't talked about it, we'd felt the same. We'd believed she'd come back. And now she had.

"There's no chemical smell," I said.

Catcher nodded. "I noticed that. We haven't tied the voice or the chemical smell to any known magic. But the absence suggests this is something different."

"A different magic, or a different sorcerer?" Ethan asked.

"Either," Catcher said. "Or both."

"How are the humans?" Ethan asked.

"All are stable except the woman with the knife," Catcher said. "Her name is Rosemary Parsons. She's in critical condition, but they're hopeful."

"She's sedated?" Ethan asked.

"She is," my grandfather said. "And still at the hospital. Everyone else is at the factory."

The supernatural prison, he meant. "Why?" I asked.

"Quarantine," Ethan said, and my grandfather nodded.

"We don't know why this is happening, or if it's actually transmittable. So we have to take precautions. The CDC's Chicago field office is doing some testing, just in case. But they don't think this is a biological contagion, either."

"We need to talk to them," Ethan said. "Get more information about the delusions they're experiencing."

My grandfather nodded. "Winston Stiles is awake and communicating. He'd like to see you, to apologize."

"Maybe he can give us some damned idea of what's happening here," Ethan said.

"It can't hurt," I agreed.

"And tonight's meeting?" Ethan asked, gesturing to the elevator.

"We'll report," my grandfather said, "and offer ideas for resolving this thorny little problem."

"And do you have an idea?" Ethan asked.

"No," my grandfather said. "Here's hoping the elevator ride is productive."

If City Hall was built to inspire, the mayor's office was built for business. It was a big open room of golden wood floors and paneling, curtains covering the windows. Mayor Kowalcyzk had settled her dark, curved desk beneath an enormous aerial photograph of Chicago, in case anyone forgot the realm over which she ruled.

The mayor sat behind her desk, her brown hair carefully coiffed and sprayed, makeup still polished, even though she'd probably already been on the job for twelve hours. She wore a power suit in deep crimson, hands crossed in her lap as she watched video on the flat-screen on the opposite wall, which showed footage of the fight, the image shuddering left and right as the camera was jostled.

A man I assumed was her aide—in his forties with a paunchy build and receding hairline—stood behind her against the wall, one arm crossed over his chest, the other holding a small tablet.

When an anchor appeared on-screen again, the mayor pressed a button on a flat remote and glanced at us, fingers now interlaced in her folded hands. She looked at each of us in turn, then settled her gaze on my grandfather. "Mr. Merit."

"Madam Mayor."

"You know my chief of staff, Lane Conrad."

They exchanged nods.

"It's snowing outside for no apparent reason and from no apparent band of moisture," the mayor said. "That is disturbing. And that video, of course, is disturbing in its own right."

He nodded. "Agreed on both counts, Your Honor."

"And their cause?"

"Both phenomena are under investigation. That said, we've just been informed the wards have been tripped."

Both the mayor and her aide went very still.

"*She* is back in my city?" the mayor asked, forcing the pronoun through a tight jaw.

Good, I thought. At least that anger was directed appropriately. That might make dealing with the problem a little bit easier.

"Not that we're aware of, but that's within the CPD's jurisdiction. The wards were tripped when the snow began to fall."

"So she created the snowfall?"

"That's the logical conclusion. The timing suggests either she created it or she caused it to happen by some other magical manipulation. We'll begin investigating that as soon as we leave here."

"And the delusions?" the aide asked, without looking up from his tablet. "Early reports say they're magical, too."

My grandfather kept his gaze on the mayor. "We don't have any definitive evidence one way or the other. But there are indicia of magic."

"Which are what?" the mayor asked.

"Magic has a unique kind of energy," my grandfather explained.

"A buzz that's detectable by other supernaturals, and occasionally carries a particular scent. The vampire that attacked Merit at Cadogan House had that scent. And so did these humans."

The aide lowered his tablet. "The humans had magic?"

"Not precisely. More that it seemed they'd been touched by it."

"By Sorcha?"

"We don't have any evidence of that at this time, Your Honor. The wards weren't tripped until the snowfall."

"You said a delusional vampire attacked Merit?" the mayor asked. "When was this, and why wasn't it reported to me?"

"The vampire, by all appearances, was emotionally unstable," my grandfather said. "He attacked Merit night before last. We had no reason at that time to believe the attack was anything more than the action of a sick man."

She gestured toward the window. "And now the snow. How are they connected?"

"We have no reason to believe they're related at this time."

"They're both magic," Lane said, crossing his arms over his tablet and exuding haughty skepticism.

"We aren't saying they won't ultimately prove to be related," my grandfather said. "Just that we haven't found the common thread yet. The humans' identities were only released to us an hour ago, so we haven't been able to research or interview them completely." He gave Lane a none-too-friendly glance.

"Your office opens at dusk," Lane said, with superior tone.

"Yours doesn't," my grandfather said.

"Gentlemen." The mayor's tone was crisp, her gaze narrowed at my grandfather. "If this is a supernatural activity, it remains under your jurisdiction. Lane, you will provide Mr. Merit with information as it is gathered."

Lane looked prepared to mutter behind her back, but tapped something on his tablet.

"Thank you, Madam Mayor."

"Don't thank me yet, Mr. Merit. That means this remains your problem. Determine the cause and correct it. And if it is that woman . . ." She paused, clearly working to control her anger. "We will deal with her as is appropriate for a traitor, a murderer, a sociopath." Her gaze lifted again. "Is that understood?"

My grandfather nodded. "Yes, ma'am."

"The media," the aide prompted, gaze on his tablet, and the mayor nodded.

"Reporters will, of course, be contacting all of you for comment. For the time being, please direct those inquiries to our public relations staff. We may want you to speak to the public later. But I would prefer for these matters to be investigated and addressed before that becomes necessary. Is that understood?"

"Perfectly, ma'am."

"Then you're dismissed," she said. "Keep us apprised and keep the city safe."

Easier said than done.

It was still snowing when we stepped into the street again. The temperature had dropped a little since we'd been inside, but that was probably due to the cooling night, not any magic by Sorcha— or anyone else. Still not cold enough for the snow to stick, although the sidewalk and streets gleamed with water.

My grandfather held out a hand, watched dime-sized flakes float into his palm, melt. "There are things I wouldn't have thought I'd see in this or any other lifetime. Magical snow is definitely one of them."

"That went better than I'd have thought," Ethan said. "Much less blame assigning than I thought she'd do."

"She's learning," my grandfather said. "And I'll give her credit for that. But it's hard to say how long it will last."

"As long as the city stays mostly safe," Catcher said, pulling out his phone. "If it gets worse, she'll look for someone to blame."

"The aide's willing to hang us now for not having all the answers," Ethan said.

"Lane is an impatient man," my grandfather agreed. "But if our office is to be seriously considered the arbiter of magical issues, it's fair for us to demand we resolve it. That's chain of authority."

"It's politics," Catcher muttered.

"That, too." My grandfather glanced around, settling his gaze on a line of brightly colored food trucks lined up in the Daley Center Plaza across the street: Spotted Dogs, which served gourmet hot dogs, Pizzataco, which served a pizza-taco hybrid, and Coriander Creamery, which served supposedly "gourmet" ice cream that mostly involved chopped herbs and flowers that didn't have any business in hot fudge sundaes or sugar cones. In my humble opinion.

"Is anyone hungry?" he asked.

"I've heard the hot dog truck is pretty good," Catcher said.

"I'm starving," I said, to absolutely no one's surprise. "But I don't have any cash." I rarely carried anything other than my ID and transit card. I glanced at Ethan. "At the risk of sounding anachronistically wifely, can you pay?"

"I can spare some money for you," Ethan said. "Probably. How hungry are you, exactly?"

"You're hilarious," I said, but held his hand as we dashed between cars to the other side of the street.

We all opted for the hot dog truck, joining the line of people who hadn't been fazed by the weather. But that didn't stop them from speculating about it.

"It's the vampires," said the man in front of us, his voice thick with Chicago. He talked with his companion, who wore a Blackhawks jersey that matched his own.

"They work black magic in that House of theirs. Drove past it once, saw lights blazing in the middle of the night. I know what they were doing."

Probably taxes or something equally dull, Ethan silently said. *But who are we to argue?*

Ethan was becoming increasingly frustrated with willing human prejudices.

"No," said the woman in front of him, turning around to join the conversation. "It's the witches. This is witch magic, and I'd put good money on it." She glanced at his jersey, nodded. "Go, Hawks."

"Go, Hawks," the men said. Even if they couldn't agree on magic, they could agree on hockey.

Perhaps we'd better just plan our meal, Ethan said, gaze narrowing at the dry-erase menu on the side of the truck. *What is a "Funyun"?*

The child of an onion ring and a pork rind. You wouldn't like them.

Which means you adore them, he said.

I really do. Which was why I'd settled on the "Garbage Dog." *You should stick to Chicago style,* I told Ethan. *That's your favorite.*

He glanced at me. *A year of knowing me, and you've already figured me out? Am I so predictable, Sentinel?*

That's Mrs. Sentinel to you. And yeah, I have a pretty good sense of you. Good enough that I could have penned the *Novitiate's Guide to Ethan Sullivan*, if I'd had the time. *You enjoy being in charge, fine china, food served on fine china, bespoke suits, twenty-year-old Scotch, and, for reasons I don't understand,* Doctor Who.

He smiled as the line shuffled forward. *He's a Time Lord. I can relate.*

I just shook my head. Ethan had enough honorifics, and certainly didn't need to add "Time Lord" to the list.

When we reached the window, we were greeted by a man with tan skin and dark hair, and broad shoulders beneath his SPOTTED DOGS T-shirt. "What can I get ya?"

"Chicago Dog," Ethan said.

"And for the lady?"

"Garbage Dog," I said.

Ethan gave me a sidelong glance. "And?"

"And . . . fries. And onion rings, too, if we're already throwing stuff in a fry basket."

The man winked. "I like a woman with an appetite."

Probably not my particular appetite, given last night's activities, but whatever. "And a drink."

"I recommend the chocolate shakes. We make the best in town."

My gaze narrowed, and Ethan just chuckled, pulled bills from his pocket, and offered them to the vendor. "You may have started a conversation you don't have time to finish."

"How chocolate is chocolate?" I asked.

But the man was prepared, and his expression was utterly serious. "Our chocolate base includes a syrup made from small-batch beans from a roaster in California, flakes of eighty-five percent dark, and cocoa powder from France."

"Your terms are acceptable," I said with equal gravity.

Shaking his head but resigned to his fate, Ethan peeled off another bill, passed it through the window.

"You two are cute together," the vendor said, passing a foam cup through the window. "You should get married."

Ethan held up his hand, light glinting off his engraved band. "Already done."

CHAPTER ELEVEN

RATIONS

We took our dogs to the nearby picnic table beneath a wide umbrella that had probably been for shade against the sun but worked pretty well for snow, too.

The spread of food was nearly embarrassing in both breading and quantity. But odds were good last night's battle wasn't the only one we'd face in the coming nights, and I wasn't going in unprepared.

Unfortunately, the plastic fork was hardly up to the challenge of a hot dog amalgamation that included mac 'n' cheese, hot sauce, and fried pickles. I managed a bite, chewed, considered. And frowned.

"You look unimpressed," Catcher said, squirting ketchup into a careful circle on a napkin.

"I'm mostly confused." I popped a fried pickle, nearly winced with the wonderfully vicious acidity. "And still evaluating. I'm going to have to work through my feelings."

Ethan just shook his head, amusement in his face. "My intrepid Sentinel, beaten by a Garbage Dog."

Snorting, Catcher wiped his hands to pull his phone from his pocket. He scanned the screen. "Well. That's interesting."

"What?" my grandfather asked, wiping mustard from his cheek.

"The first two humans Jeff checked out were near Towerline the night Sorcha tried to initiate her alchemical web."

"How near?" Ethan asked.

Catcher swiped the screen. "One was an electrical sub doing some after-hours work when the magic spilled. The other lived across the street, was on the roof watching the action. Neither evacuated."

I nodded. "So at least some of the people who hear the screaming were near Towerline when the magic went down."

"The delusions started before the snow," Catcher said. "And the wards didn't sound until the snow started. Therefore, Sorcha isn't causing the delusions, at least not by any active, ongoing magic."

I looked at Catcher. "Could it be some kind of latent effect from her alchemy?"

"We unwound her magic," Catcher said. "It doesn't make sense that any magic was left, latent or otherwise. On the other hand, while it could be someone other than Sorcha, given the connection to Towerline, that's highly improbable. 'Eliminate all other factors, and the one which remains must be the truth.'"

"Sherlock Holmes," my grandfather said approvingly. "The one which remains, in this case, is her alchemy and its lingering effects."

Which meant the delusions, one way or the other, were Sorcha's fault.

Ethan's phone beeped again. He checked it, then looked at my grandfather with a worried expression that didn't give me any comfort. "The *Tribune* interviewed the woman who was on the roof after the fact," he said. "She said there were forty people watching the battle."

"They couldn't evacuate all the high-rises near the battle site," my grandfather said. "There wasn't enough time or manpower."

"What about Winston?" I asked. "Do we know if he was near Towerline?"

"We don't," my grandfather said.

"We need to talk to him about that, and about what he's hearing," I said. "We need to figure out what's happening before anyone else is hurt."

Ethan nodded. "If physical proximity to Sorcha's alchemy is the trigger for the delusions, we have a very big problem. We'll see more delusions, more violence."

Catcher took the last bite of dog, wiped his hands, rolled up his napkin. "We'll cross our fingers that these people were more exposed or differently exposed." He looked at my grandfather. "But we'll have to tell the mayor it's possible there will be more incidents. She'll need to be prepared—and to have medics at the ready, law enforcement standing by."

"I'm less than enthused about giving her those directions."

Catcher chuckled. "That's why they pay you the big bucks, Chuck."

"And give you the title and the van," I pointed out.

My grandfather huffed. "Those are hardly worth it." He glanced at my meal appraisingly. "But a bite of that might be worth it. Is that a Funyun?"

"Damn right, it is," I said with a grin, and slid the leftovers toward him. "Excellent taste is clearly genetic."

"I question several things about that statement," Ethan said. "But considering our circumstances, I'll hold them back."

My grandfather picked up his fork, blew snow off the picnic table before pulling my dinner the rest of the way, began to dig out a forkful of Garbage Dog.

"So," I said, "to summarize, we think the delusions are some kind of latent effect of Sorcha's work at Towerline. And the snow?"

"The wards sounded," Catcher said. "And it's still fifty degrees out here, and not falling from an actual cloud. So it's active magic. Snow-adjacent magic."

"'Snow-adjacent'?" my grandfather asked.

"Too warm, no clouds," I said. "It's falling like snow, but it's not created the same way."

"Exactly," Catcher said.

"So she's not really manipulating the weather," my grandfather said.

"Not in the technical sense, although she is creating a meteorological phenomenon." Catcher put his elbows on the table, linked his hands as he leaned forward. "That's the thing I don't get, don't understand. Why snow? Chicagoans have seen snow before. We've lived through blizzards."

"And yet . . ." Ethan said.

"And yet," Catcher growled.

My grandfather's phone buzzed. He pulled it out, looked at the screen, frowned.

"What's wrong?" I asked.

"Message from Jeff. It just says, 'Look at Towerline.'"

We all looked to the northeast, but couldn't see that far in the tangle of skyscrapers.

"I guess we're going for a walk," Catcher said. We rose, tossed our trash, and set out on our next journey, dread collecting around us.

We zigzagged east and north toward the river. My grandfather was on the phone, having called in the CPD to cordon off the building, just in case.

The temperature was dropping, the snow now beginning to stick on slick roads and sidewalks. It still had no obvious meteorological origin—the sky was clear above the snow—but that didn't seem to matter.

"Does Reed still own Towerline?" I asked. I wasn't entirely sure what happened when you became a supervillain. Were your assets forfeit?

"I don't know if he had a will," my grandfather said. "He died before Sorcha, and she probably would have been the beneficiary of his assets. But since she killed him, the Slayer Statute would likely prevent her from inheriting. They didn't have children, so I'm guessing his parents would be next in line."

"Either way," Ethan said, "Towerline and everything else he owned will be tied up in probate for years to come." He glanced at me. "So your father won't be reclaiming it anytime soon."

I wasn't sure he wanted to. We hadn't talked about it, but I had the sense he considered Towerline a personal failure, even though he'd given it up for good reasons, and that wasn't the kind of thing my father wanted to commiserate about. I wouldn't say the building was cursed, but I wouldn't want to own real estate with that much supernatural baggage.

We emerged from the labyrinth of buildings at the corner of State and Wabash, the State Street bridge in front of us, the corncob-shaped Marina Towers to our right. And to our left, in the prime real estate on the north side of the river at Michigan, was the Towerline building. Or what remained of its structural shell. The missing glass panels in the tall lobby had been boarded over. It was an ugly solution the city didn't like, but until the courts resolved the issue of ownership, there were no funds to repair it.

And given the sight in front of us, I doubted those funds would be coming anytime soon.

A column of clouds rose above the building, bands of swirling white and brilliant purple against a sky otherwise as dark as pitch. It looked like a cyclonic storm, but the snow wasn't coming from these clouds, or any others.

"No snow," I said. "But does anyone else think it's colder over here?"

"The temperature dropped the closer we got to Towerline," my grandfather agreed.

Ethan sighed. "The honeymoon is decidedly over."

I generally tried to be brave, and was certainly more willing to take chances than I had been a year ago as a still-pink vampire. But even I wasn't taking the rickety construction elevator—or climbing dozens of floors of steps—to the top floor to inspect what might be happening on the roof.

We left that to the CPD helicopters my grandfather called in, while we crossed the State Street bridge to the area the CPD had once again cordoned off in front of the building's sweeping plaza.

Michigan Avenue had been roped off with caution tape, CPD uniforms already posted at intervals along the line. Traffic had been rerouted, but that didn't stop the pedestrians who gathered at the edges, just like the last time. There seemed to be fewer tonight, maybe because of the weather, hopefully because they'd learned their lessons the last time, understood that this woman's magic was inherently dangerous.

And in the middle of the street, behind a barrier of police cruisers and vans, stood the SWAT team members who'd coordinate the CPD's response to . . . whatever this was.

There was a buzz around the men and women, but it wasn't magic. It was steel, my body's magical reaction to their weapons, a sensitivity related to my connection with my sword.

"We meet again," said a man with a strong body and short, pale hair.

He'd been in charge of the response on that fateful night

when we'd beaten back Sorcha the first time. That was also the night Ethan had proposed. We returned now as husband and wife, but just as aware of Sorcha's power.

"Pity we didn't manage to hold her," the officer said, and there was apology in his expression. Good. There was no way that could be blamed on us.

"It is a pity," Ethan said. "And you didn't offer your name that evening."

"My bad," he said, and offered a hand. "Jim Wilcox."

"Ethan Sullivan," he said.

"Helicopters on their way?" my grandfather asked.

"They are." He gestured to a comm unit built into the back of a white panel van. "The mayor is patched in, and she's monitoring the situation."

"And she is pissed," said a woman with dark skin and a cloud of curly hair depressed by a slender headset and mouthpiece. She wore slim black pants and a crimson top beneath a dark gray suit jacket, her badge on a chain around her neck. I guessed her to be in her early thirties. "Pierce," she said. "Agent Mikaela. FBI Paranormal Response Unit."

This was the first I'd heard of such a thing, but I wouldn't argue that it was unnecessary. The clouds above Towerline proved its necessity easily enough.

"Agent," my grandfather said, shaking her hand. "Chuck Merit. Catcher Bell, my associate."

She nodded at them. "I'm based in New York, but I've heard a lot about your work in Chicago." She looked at us. "And I've heard a lot about you, Ethan and Merit."

"Do you know Victor Garcia?" Ethan asked. He was the head of New York's Cabot House.

"I do," she said with a wry smile. "He asked me to pass along his good wishes if I saw you, and said you could call him if you wanted to check my bona fides."

Ethan smiled, appreciating that she'd prepared for this meeting. "I'll keep that in mind. What brings you to Chicago?"

"The peace and quiet," she said, without missing a beat. "Should we turn to the magic?"

"Let's do," my grandfather said.

"We've scanned the building looking for heat signals and movement," she said, "and found nothing. Sorcha, if she has returned to Chicago, isn't in the building. The chopper will be reporting momentarily."

Pierce put a finger against her ear as the *thwack* of helicopter blades began to beat the air overhead. "First copter report coming in," she said. "And . . . the roof is empty. There's no indication of movement or activity."

"Is it colder up there?" Catcher asked. "Directly beneath the cloud formation?"

She lifted her brows but repeated the question into her headset. "That's affirmative. Temperature readings are ten degrees colder in the space between Towerline and the phenomenon."

She pushed the mouthpiece away, looked back at us. "What does that mean?"

I looked at Catcher, who seemed to be as flummoxed as the rest of us. His gaze was on the cloud swirling ominously above the tower, hands on his hips as he tried to ferret out its meaning.

"It has to be the source of the weather, but I don't know how or why. The last time I've seen something like this, something meteorological, was . . ."

"Mallory," I finished for him, thinking of the havoc she'd wrought through Chicago during her thankfully brief stint as a dark sorceress. She'd torn the city apart.

"Yeah," Catcher said. "The wards say this is Sorcha. But I'm not sure how she's doing it, or what it's supposed to be doing."

I crossed my arms as the temperature seemed to drop another fifteen degrees instantaneously, my breath turning to pale vapor in the chilling wind.

"She's going to freeze us out," Ethan said.

Catcher rubbed fingers across his forehead. "That's a possibility," he said, but one he didn't look sure of. And Catcher wasn't a man who liked not knowing.

There were gasps of shock behind us. I turned, expecting to find Sorcha descending onto the Michigan Avenue bridge like one of the Horsemen of the Apocalypse.

Instead, people had gathered at the ornate balustrade at the edge of the bridge that overlooked the river.

I jogged over, Ethan in step behind me, and squeezed through the people until I could see the water below—and the thick white scale that was working its way down the river and toward the lake.

"What is that?" he asked beside me. "Some kind of contaminant?"

"No," I said, and the dread that settled into my bones was as cold as the cutting breeze. "The river is freezing."

I'd seen the river flowing, and I'd seen it frozen. But I'd never watched it freeze, never seen ice crystallize on a scale that large, watched water turn opaque and opalescent, its movement stiffening like someone had flipped a switch and turned it off.

It shouldn't have happened so quickly. The river shouldn't have frozen all at once, and certainly not in August.

Screams issued up from the canal.

Notwithstanding the snow, it had been a warm day, and people had taken advantage of the weather—and the chance to experience the weirdness of snow in August. A tour boat, its upper deck full of people, was approaching the Michigan Avenue dock but was still a dozen yards west of it. The water was expanding as it froze, and that force—that volume—was pushing the boat into the concrete bank.

The groan of metal filled the air, then a sound like a shotgun. The boat lurched, spilling people into the narrow gap between the boat and the river. A chasm that was filled with solidifying slush. The ice would crush the boat, and everyone else would be crushed by the pressure or sent into the river.

The CPD was behind us, and they'd get divers out as soon as they could. But we were here now.

I wasn't entirely sure whether vampires could drown or get hypothermia—surely not?—but it didn't really matter. Our chances of survival were higher than theirs. So we had to take the chance.

A look at each other, a confirming nod, and then we climbed onto the balustrade, and jumped.

Vampire and gravity were friends. Maybe not BFFs—we had to plan our falls to keep from being injured—but we made the twenty-foot drop to the boat below without breaking any bones. We still skidded along the ice-covered deck but managed to catch ourselves, stand up straight again.

And we probably should have announced our presence, because two people suddenly dropping into a ship of screaming passengers didn't exactly help calm them.

"I'll help those in the gap," Ethan said.

"I'll take this deck, try to get them down the stairs and closer to the dock."

I'd guessed marriage was going to require divvying up responsibilities. I hadn't expected we'd be dividing jobs in two separate rescue missions less than twenty-four hours into it.

Forever, Ethan said to me, then jumped down to the second deck.

"It's all right," I said, striding forward to the humans who were hanging on to benches bolted to the deck in an effort to stay upright and keep from sliding into the gap themselves. "We're going to get you off the boat. And onto the dock," I added, since getting them off the boat and into the water was a real possibility.

The boat's staff were downstairs, so I looked around, found someone who looked reasonably strong and reasonably calm, pointed at him. He was young, with tan skin, dark hair, and a faint mustache over his top lip that he probably wished was thicker.

"You!" I said. "What's your name?"

"Pham."

"Excellent, Pham. I'm Merit. You're going to help me, okay?"

He swallowed hard, Adam's apple bobbing in his thin neck. "Okay."

I put a hand on his arm. "You've got this." I glanced around, pointed to the closest stairway—or the boat's half-ladder, half-stairway version of one—where people were pushing and shoving to get to the first deck. The stairs were already leaning and slick, so pushing was a recipe for certain disaster. "Go stand at the stairs," I said.

"I can't swim," he said, blinking back tears I could see he was working not to shed. "I don't want to drown."

"Pham, do you know who I am?"

"Vampire," he said with a nod.

"Exactly. I'm immortal, which means this water can't hurt me." Or so I hoped. God, I really, really hoped. "So one way or another, I will be here to make sure you get off this boat. Okay?"

That seemed to be enough to satisfy him. With grit in his eyes, he nodded, then slip-slid down the leaning deck toward the stairway, squeezing his lean form into the line and positioning himself at the access point. "One person at a time!" he yelled out. "One person at a time!"

I found another supervisor, a woman with strong shoulders and a narrow waist. A swimmer's build, I hoped. Just in case. I put her in charge of the opposite stairwell.

"Get the fuck out of my way!"

I looked back, watched Pham work to stop a man in a suit who tried to push an older woman out of the way so he could get to the stairs first.

And that was my cue. I pushed through the throng, grabbed him by the arm. I saw fury fire in his face, replaced by quick confusion, and then anger again when I pulled him back.

"Get your fucking hands off me."

I hauled him closer by the lapels of his very expensive coat. "You will not make this situation worse and more dangerous by being an asshole. You can't follow the rules, you go to the back of the line."

He tried to shove my hands away.

Emphasis on *tried*.

"I'm stronger than you. I could make sure you're the last person off this boat, or I can call the *Tribune* and let them know you just tried to push a woman twenty years your senior down the stairs."

"I'll fry you for this."

"I doubt it. But my name is Merit, Sentinel of Cadogan House. You want to fry me? The House is easy to find."

That put the fear of God in his eyes.

"Exactly," I said. "Get your ass in line."

He moved back into position, stayed there until it was his turn. "*What a piece of work is man,*" I muttered, and turned around just in time to hear a woman scream when the boat shuddered. She lurched forward, hand outstretched, as something disappeared over the side of the boat.

"Shit," I murmured, and ran forward, slipping once and hitting my knees on the slick and icy deck; it took a moment before I could get traction again.

Her son had tumbled off the boat and onto a plate of ice below, screaming in terror. He slid across the ice nearly to the serrated edge, managed to stop himself before hurtling into the dark water.

There were cuts on his cheeks from scraping the ice, and his face was pale with fear. But he was in one piece.

"I'll get him!" I yelled, and looked down at the slick flat of ice, a chunk about the size of a recliner. I couldn't jump down onto it. It still bobbled in the not fully frozen water, buoyant now, but maybe not if I put all my weight and the force of my jump onto it. If it didn't hold, we'd both end up in the drink.

Kid overboard, I told Ethan. *I'm going after him.*

Be careful, he said, but I was already moving, not bothering to wait for a response.

The child had fallen on the side that tilted toward the water, probably having slipped on the snow that was hardening like concrete around the deck as the temperature began to fall. *The ice vampire cometh*, I thought, and went to my knees at the railing. There were ropes that linked one deck to the other on this part of the ship. If I was careful, and really lucky, I might be able to get a toehold.

I was glad I'd worn my boots.

"My baby!" the mom screamed as I stood up, put one leg over the railing.

"What's his name?" I asked her, putting the other leg over, which left me cantilevered backward along the side of the boat. I kept an iron grip on freezing steel with frigid fingers. Too bad I hadn't thought to wear gloves.

"Stephen," she said, kneading her fingers with understandable nerves. "His name is Stephen."

"I'm going to get him and bring him back to you." I looked around for something helpful for her to do. "Grab that life buoy," I told her, gesturing to the white ring with red stenciled letters that hung along the railing a few feet away.

"Keep the rope attached to it, and come stand near the rail. When I give you the signal, throw it down to me."

She nodded, picked her way across the slanted deck with both hands on the rail, and unhooked the ring.

I took a breath and took the first toe off the bottom rail, stretching down and searching for the rope that hung below.

But I was too short, or the rope was too far away, depending on your perspective. I'd have to drop both feet.

"Fingers, don't fail me now," I murmured, and let go of one railing to grip the next one down, then moved hand over hand until I hung from the bottom rail, feet suspended in midair due to the boat's list. My wedding and engagement rings bit into my finger, but I ignored the pain, focused on finding the rope with my toe. The tilted deck put the rope at least a foot in front of me, so I had to swing like a gymnast to bow forward. It took a moment of ungainly scrambling, but my toes made purchase.

I glanced down, fought off the sudden vertigo caused by the bobbing water beneath me. The river was only a few feet down now, a small drop. But his plate of ice had moved a few feet away, driven by the river's current. Another plate of ice had taken its place.

There was no help for it. I kept my gaze on the ice, ticked off the seconds until I could land as squarely as possible, and let go.

I hit the ice in a crouch, square in the middle.

And I should have known better than to get cocky about it.

There was a splash on the other side of the boat, a scream.

Someone else had fallen into the water. And that movement, as slight as it was, tilted the ice. Before I could react, the sheet tilted, sending me sliding backward. The shift in my weight tilted the ice further, and there was nothing to grab, nothing to hold on to.

The woman at the railing screamed, and then I was underwater.

CHAPTER TWELVE

HEART OF ICE

The chill was instantly painful, every cell and nerve screaming simultaneous alerts that something was very, very wrong. That the water was much too cold, the temperature much too low, and I was in too much danger.

I bobbed up, sucked in air, pushed frigid water from my eyes. I grabbed at the closest sheet of ice, looking for a fingerhold so I could claw my way onto it. But my fingers and toes were numbing, and it was hard to grab. And there was no point in it, I realized, my brain logy. If I was in the water, I might as well aim for the ice the kid was actually on.

I paddled through the slush, pushing ice out of the way, my fingers blue with cold, to the ice floe where Stephen lay crying, hands gripping the edge of the ice. He wore a T-shirt and shorts and was probably as cold as I was.

"Hi," I said at the edge of the water, trying not to let him see my teeth chatter. "You're Stephen, right?"

He nodded, his enormous blue eyes filled with terror.

"Excellent. I'm Merit, and I'm going to help you get back on the boat."

"Are you a mermaid?"

"Not exactly," I said, and turned the ice toward the boat, kicking as I pushed us toward it. I was suddenly in swimming lessons again on a kickboard—except those lessons had never been in freezing water in the middle of the Chicago River.

I kicked as hard as I could, and could feel the river freezing around my feet. I was kicking upstream and each kick was getting harder, like swimming in thickening sand.

"Life buoy!" I managed through chattering teeth, and caught it one-handed. "Stephen, honey, let's get this on you, okay?

"Hang on!" I said. "Pull him up!" I yelled, to whoever could still hear me, and they began to haul him over the side of the ship.

"Stephen!" His mother had made it to the lower deck.

"Here!" a man called, holding out a hand to help pull me on board. But that hand seemed so far away, and it seemed to get smaller and smaller. I couldn't understand how that was possible, how the world could shrink. And as his hand moved farther away, the brutal ache of cold that had lodged in my bones like a cancer began to fade.

I slipped under and began to sink like a stone. I wasn't buoyant, my clothes were heavy and waterlogged, and the thickening water slowed my progress toward the surface.

I opened my eyes in the dark water, watched light skitter across the thickening ice. I kicked and pushed up, even as ice shoved me around in the water like bullies in a junior high hallway. But the ice above me was congealing, solidifying into a cap above the water below. I dug at the ice with numb fingers, but it was too solid to dig through, too large to simply push aside. Panic clawed at my throat, my lungs begging for air.

Dark spots appeared in my vision. As I sank into the water again, panic faded to a kind of resigned acceptance.

I hadn't thought to wonder what drowning would feel like, but I wouldn't have guessed it felt like this. There was no panic now, just the realization that I'd gone under, and I'd probably run out of oxygen soon.

Thinking-Me was separate from Drowning-Me, and the first watched the second with dissociative curiosity. *Am I drowning? How strange.*

I hadn't managed to be married for very long, I thought. *It would have been nice to be married, to be the First Lady of Cadogan House, for a little while longer. To be with Ethan for a little while longer.*

Ethan, I thought. *Ethan. Ethan.*

The word, his name, the knowledge of him, was a match strike in a dark room. It snapped me from fading consciousness, from the lethargy and acceptance that aching bones and muscles longed for. Anything to take that pain away.

Ethan.

I kicked up, pushing with every joule of energy my body could spare, hands pointed above me to stab through ice, when a hand appeared in the water, grabbed me by the back of my jacket, like a puppy being pulled from danger by the scruff of her neck.

I broke the surface and gasped for air, the ache of cold slicing through me again like a white-hot dagger.

I let him pull me onto the boat and fell to my side, coughed up what felt like liters of river water.

"Sentinel, I may never let you out of the House again."

I nodded, let him help me sit up. Everything ached, and I couldn't stop the shakes that racked my body. "Not . . . bad . . . idea. Also fix the weather, probably."

He pulled off my wet jacket, wrapped a thermal blanket of shimmering silver around me, then pushed damp hair from my face.

"I heard you say my name," he said.

I'd thought it. I hadn't realized I'd said it or that he'd heard. But thank God for it.

I leaned forward, wrapped my arms around him, and let fly the sob that was trapped in my throat.

Thank God for him.

The crowd was appreciative and grateful when we trudged up the stairs back to Michigan Avenue again. But our clothes were wet and were crunchy in the freezing air, and icicles had frozen in my hair. I felt as if I'd been frozen from the inside, like crystals had actually begun to form in my blood.

"Good work as always," my grandfather said. "Although absolutely terrifying."

"Most of the things she does these days are," Ethan said.

My grandfather stepped closer. "Does she need to go to the hospital? Her lips seem . . . bluish."

"No," Ethan said. "We'll keep her awake and moving, and anything that might have been damaged will heal itself." His gaze went hot. "And when she's feeling one hundred percent again, we'll have a very long talk about diving into a freezing river."

Since that sounded much braver than having climbed into the river and fallen at the last moment, I let him believe it. And yeah, not my best move. But the Patton family was super glad of my recklessness right now, and that was the only outcome that mattered.

Pierce walked toward us. She'd abandoned the headset but added a CPD jacket that was too big for her athletic frame. "The Department of Water Management is sending an icebreaker to keep traffic moving. We're going to keep automotive traffic rerouted on this portion of Michigan until we figure out what's happening." She aimed her direct gaze at my grandfather.

"I hope that's something you can do."

"So do I," he said.

"I think we'll want to talk to Winston," Ethan said. "But we need to go to the House first, get a change of clothes." He glanced at me. "I called Brody. He's on the way, will meet us across the river." He looked over at the police boundaries, the detour signs, the general congestion. "It's best to stay out of this."

My grandfather nodded. "Best to stay out of the Loop if possible. As for Winston, let me know when you're ready, and we'll meet you at the gate."

"We'll do that. Come on, Sentinel," Ethan said, putting a hand at my waist. "Let's go home."

I need to be with my people for a little while, he silently said.

And in his House, I thought, behind the fence, where the Novitiates didn't need quite the same kind of saving.

We walked in silence through the crowd, accepted with nods and polite smiles the thank-yous and pats on the back. We were tired enough that the nods and smiles were the only responses we could muster.

"Sire," Brody said, opening the door of the large black SUV he'd driven to pick us up. It would undoubtedly handle better in the snow than Ethan's current wheels—a sleek sports car that was better equipped for straightaways than freezing roads.

To his credit, Brody had turned up the heat and the seat warmers. I was asleep before we left the Loop, my head propped on Ethan's shoulder.

I woke again as Brody pulled the vehicle to a stop in front of the gate, then climbed out of the car to open the door for us. The gate was closed, but the human guards opened it quickly enough at the sight of us. For the first time, we walked into the grounds of Cadogan House as husband and wife.

Before I could argue, Ethan picked me up.

I put an arm around his neck. "I think it's a little late for this, isn't it?"

"Carrying your wife over the threshold is a tradition. And maybe it will be good luck. We could use a little of that."

No argument there.

"Congratulations!"

The door opened to another cacophony of sound, but this cacophony was a lot better than the last one. Lindsey, Luc, Malik, and two dozen more vampires stood in the foyer beneath a gold CONGRATULATIONS banner hung from the coffered ceiling. They blew gold paper horns and bubbles from tiny gold bottles while Margot passed out steaming cups of hot chocolate and warmed blood.

"You didn't get a honeymoon," Lindsey said, "so we decided you at least needed a welcome-home hello. And a warming-up opportunity."

"You must be frozen through!" Margot said.

"I've been warmer," I agreed. "And the temperature is still dropping."

"You did an amazing job," Malik said.

"It's been quite a night so far," Ethan said, shaking his head at the offer of hot chocolate. "The mayor was concerned, but seems to be directing the pressure at the Ombudsman's office, rather than us."

"He can handle it," Malik said as I took the cup of hot chocolate and sipped deeply. Brody had offered to stop for coffee, but I'd mostly wanted to get home as quickly as possible.

"He can," Ethan agreed. "And we'll help as we can. Seeing the river freeze—that was something altogether different."

"Not a soul lost," Luc said, patting his arm in congratulations. "So that's something else to celebrate."

"It is," Ethan agreed. "But Sorcha's involvement is not. The snow and temperature seem to be her first steps. You've seen Towerline?"

"Most stations are showing live footage," Luc said. "It's hard to avoid. What is it?"

"The source of the weather," I said, and shivered involuntarily.

"Beyond that, we don't know," Ethan said. "She needs to change clothes. Give us a few minutes; then we'll meet in the Ops Room. We'll discuss the details then."

Luc saluted. "Sire." He glanced at me, grinned. "Mrs. Sire."

"Nope," I said, shaking my head. "I'm going to nope that one right there."

We made it to the staircase but stopped when we saw the obstacle that awaited us. Helen stood there, hands clasped in front of her. Waiting.

Steady, now, Sentinel. She isn't so bad as delusional humans.

Easy for him to say. Helen adored Ethan. Although when she looked up, she gave us both hard stares.

"Your suitcases have been taken back upstairs, and the wedding guests have left."

Ethan nodded. "Thank you, Helen." He took a step forward to continue up the stairs, but she held up a hand.

"Your wedding ensembles were severely damaged." She looked at Ethan. "A Turnbull & Asser suit." She looked at me. "A Chanel dress. Both garments would have been important parts of the House archives."

"We were attacked."

"I was entirely prepared to remind you of the importance of maintaining the image of this House, of looking the part. But you did right by those poor, deluded humans. So I will have the garments repaired—to the extent they can be repaired—and placed into the archive."

"Your efficiency is appreciated, as is your concern for the House's legacy."

"Yes, well," Helen said. And with an efficient nod, she stepped out of the way.

I think we got off easy, I silently said.

"Sire. Merit."

Jinx, Ethan said, and we looked back.

"It really was a beautiful wedding. Congratulations to you both." With that, she disappeared down the hallway.

Compliments from Helen? We'd definitely gotten off easy.

The shower at the Portman Grand had been good. But a shower on my home turf—with Ethan scrubbing shampoo through my hair? Even better.

He let me stand under the water until I was warmed through again. The shower seemed to rinse away the night's tension, or at least the bits that weren't firmly dug into bone and muscle. That tension wouldn't be alleviated until Sorcha was under wraps. And hopefully, the CPD wouldn't let her escape their grasp this time.

I debated jeans or leathers, wondering how much more trouble we'd experience before the sun rose again. I decided on jeans. They weren't as good in a battle, but they were more comfortable out of one. I was putting my eggs in the "no more battles tonight" basket, although I knew the odds weren't great.

Jeans, boots, long-sleeved shirt, leather jacket, Cadogan pendant. It was my Cadogan uniform, adjusted for the sudden temperature issues.

"Come here," Ethan said, and wrapped his arms around me. "I need a moment here, with you, in the quiet."

Ethan was strong and usually demanding, and he always walked that particular walk. I guess I forgot that even a Master needed a break every once in a while.

"It has been an eventful first night of marriage," he said.

"Freak magical weather, a river rescue operation, a meet with the mayor, and some questionable food choices." I looked up at him. "We didn't say 'for better or for worse,' but it was implied."

He kissed my forehead. "One of these days we'll have 'better' in abundance. There will be quiet evenings with books and good whiskey, trips to exotic locales, and abundant Mallocakes."

He didn't say there'd be evenings with a child, the joy and exhaustion of that experience. It had been an emotional roller coaster—accepting the fact that being a vampire meant no child, letting hope lift again with Gabriel's prophecy, having that dream dampened by a heavy dose of fear. Between Gabriel's pronouncements, there'd been tentative joy, the possibility that I could walk that line between vampire and human—have Ethan, immortality, strength, and a child. Now that line seemed improbably thin.

I'd never been good with uncertainty. So I pushed it down, focused on what was real, what was certain. Ethan beside me, the House behind me.

"That sounds pretty good," I said, forcing a smile.

Sometimes *what was* had to be enough.

The Ops Room was the House's security hub, with stations to monitor security cams along one wall, a conference table, an enormous wall screen for reviewing data and mapping locations, and computer stations for research.

Informally, the room featured a tub of beef jerky that needed replacing at least every couple of weeks. I hadn't yet heard a salty beef joke, but I had to assume one of the guards had one in the chamber and primed. It was really overdue.

The Ops Room was in the basement, along with access to the

House parking lot, the House's impressive arsenal, and one of my favorite spots, the House training room.

We found Luc in his usual position—at the end of the conference table, ankles crossed on the tabletop. He was flicking a finger across the screen of a tablet, probably geared toward the security app he'd designed for the House. He glanced up when we entered, more hot chocolate in hand, this time with a dash of Bailey's.

"Sire and First Lady," he said, sitting up and kicking down his feet. "The Cadogan House Guard Corps has voted that you're no longer allowed to leave the House. It just seems safer that way."

"For all involved," Ethan agreed, and sat down at the table. "Any developments?"

"Jules?" Luc asked, glancing at Juliet, who sat at the other end of the table, a pile of books and papers in front of her. She typed something onto the built-in tablet, and an image of the cloud snapped onto the screen. "She's patched us into the building across the street, which gives us a pretty good view of the site."

It was a good view—in color and surprisingly clear for a webcam, especially at night. The ferocity and enormity of the cloud came through loud and clear. For better or worse, it didn't look like anything had changed. The cloud continued to spin, like a tornado waiting for a moment to strike.

"No change," Luc said. "Except that the temp continues to drop. It's fifteen degrees out there right now. The river is solid ice."

"How wide-ranging is the effect?" Ethan asked.

"Split-screen it, Jules."

"On that," she said, catching her lip with her teeth as she typed. An isothermal map appeared on-screen, with bands of color showing each temperature change. Outside Chicago, the temperatures were warm, the bands in shades of green. The closer you got to downtown, the bluer each band, and the colder the temperature.

So the temperature effect was limited to Chicago, and it was centered downtown. This wasn't the first time we'd seen this kind of geographic focus from Sorcha.

I looked down at Juliet. "Can you superimpose Sorcha's alchemical web on top of this?"

She frowned, looked down at the tablet again. "I think so? Let me play with this a second . . . I have to find the right image."

She tapped keys, looked up at the screen. A photo of Captain America hovered above the city.

"And that is clearly the wrong file," she said. "Someone has been saving graphics files in the work folder again." *Cough. Cough.*

We all looked at Luc.

"Why would you blame me for that?"

We kept looking at Luc.

"Just doing my research," he said. "Captain America versus a vampire. Who wins?"

That actually was an interesting question, but this wasn't the time or place for it.

"Just a sec," Juliet said. It took more than a few seconds. It took images of Batman, Black Widow, and the Falcon before the bright green grid lowered itself to the map she'd pulled up.

Sorcha had worked her magic over the city in a very specific pattern of alchemical hot spots intended to form a kind of web around the city. Tonight's freezing temps coincided with that web almost exactly, with the coldest point centered over the Tower-line building.

"Well, I'll be damned," Luc said.

"Either Sorcha really likes returning to the scene of the crime," I said, "or she's making use of what she did before."

"Maybe she's taking advantage of something left behind," Ethan said. "Capitalizing on the magic she spilled into the alchemical web during her last trip?"

"Maybe," I said. "Catcher thinks that's what's causing the delusions, after all."

"It would take a lot of energy to freeze the river," Ethan murmured as he peered at the charts.

I wrapped my hands around the mug Margot had filled for me, let my fingers draw warmth from the slick ceramic . . . and realized what was happening.

"*Oh,*" I said.

Ethan turned to me. "Oh?"

I took his hand, pressed it against the mug. "Warm?"

"Yes?"

"Because your fingers are absorbing the heat?"

"Yes—oh." He cocked his head at the map. "*Oh.*"

"Oh," Luc said, gaze darting from mug to map. "Very good, Sentinel."

"The cloud formation is some kind of heat sink," I said. "It's pulling heat from the atmosphere. That's why it's colder the closer you get to Towerline and the formation."

"She's pulling the heat out of Chicago," Luc said. "She's going to freeze the city?"

"Possibly," Ethan said quietly. "Although, as Catcher pointed out, that's not much of a threat in Chicago. We've dealt with blizzards before."

"Maybe she hopes to ring in another ice age," Juliet suggested.

"Maybe," Ethan said, but still didn't sound entirely convinced. "In case that's the plan, ready the House. Check our supplies, the emergency tunnels, the generators."

"On that," Luc said, pointing a finger at Juliet. She nodded, turned back to her computer, began making preparations. As she did that, I sent a message to Jeff and Catcher about the weather.

"The delusions and the weather have Towerline in common,"

I said, and explained to Luc what we'd learned from Jeff about two of the humans' connections to the building.

"But there's no obvious connection between the delusions and the weather," Luc said.

"Not that we can tell so far," Ethan said, and lifted his gaze to the map again. "But Towerline is clearly the key. Perhaps Mr. Stiles can give us some insight about the delusions, and that will give us insight into the rest of it." He pushed back his chair, a signal that it was time to leave. "We'll see what he has to say."

"Before you go," Luc said, rising to meet us, "Linds and I got something for you. She's on patrol but wanted me to give it to you."

"You didn't need to—," Ethan began, but Luc shook his head.

"We wanted to." He rose and walked to his desk, opened a drawer, and pulled out a tub of cashews.

"*Oooh,*" I said, but Luc shook his head.

"Not for you, Sentinel. This one's for both of you." He pulled out a small box wrapped in gleaming foil paper, a silver bow on top.

"Our congratulations," Luc said, and offered the box over his arm like he was presenting a gift to his king. Which I guess wasn't far from the truth.

I put a hand at Ethan's back as he pulled off the paper, revealing a pretty blue box the color of a robin's egg. He opened it, pulled back delicate white tissue paper. His smile blossoming, he showed it to me. Nestled inside the box was a small silver rectangle with SULLIVAN / MERIT etched in elegant capital letters.

I ran a finger along the smooth, glinting edge.

"It's for the door of your apartments," Luc said. "We thought it would be a nice touch—reminding everyone that it's a shared space now."

There might have been chaos outside the House. Magic we didn't understand, and enemies we couldn't yet identify. But here, inside our halls, there was family.

"That is a wonderful thought," I said. "Thank you and Lindsey so much."

"You're welcome, Sentinel. I'll ask Helen to have it installed for you so you can be on your way."

"Thank you," Ethan said, and offered his hand. "It is appreciated."

They clasped hands, the moment full of friendship and feels. And being alphas in every sense of the word, they shook it off quickly enough.

"Get out of here, you crazy kids. And be careful around the criminals."

That was a good life lesson.

CHAPTER THIRTEEN

NIMBY

Chicago kept its supernatural prisoners away from the human population. The factory comprised a dozen buildings, in the same red brick, of course, in a circle around the largest one, where the prisoners were kept.

Brody parked the SUV at the end of the gravel road near the newly installed double fence. If it hadn't been for that fence, and the towers being erected along the perimeter, you wouldn't have known this was a prison. But those towers would probably house guards soon enough. Guards with guns and aspen stakes.

The snow was still coming down, had thrown a pretty white blanket across the factory grounds, which made everything look a little bit cleaner, a little less prisony. It also dampened sound, so we could hardly hear the city's noise from here.

My grandfather pulled his big, boxy sedan next to ours, climbed out of the car. He'd donned knitted gloves and a matching hat against the cold, probably something Robert's wife, Elizabeth, had made for him. She was a knitter. Not that she deigned to talk to me these days, but that was a matter for another day . . .

"That was a good thought," my grandfather said, stepping

toward me at the prison gate. "Seeing if the change in temperature coincided with Sorcha's web."

"Any idea why they match?" I asked.

My grandfather shook his head. "Plenty of hypotheses, but nothing concrete. We may not have anything until she makes her next move." He cast a glance at the sky, which was obscured by the falling snow. "And there's no telling what that might be." He glanced back at me. "You'll be all right?"

He was thinking of Logan, the vampire who'd made me. I wasn't, or hadn't been. That was part of the deal I'd made with myself—I'd let him live, but put him out of my mind. He wouldn't control my life.

My eyes went cold. "If he's smart, he'll stay far away from me."

"He's in a different sector of the ward," my grandfather said. "And the humans are in a different building altogether."

"Then we'll be fine," I said, and Ethan put a hand at my back.

That's my girl.

A guard in a golf cart pulled up inside the gate, climbed out to open it.

"Mr. Merit," he said, then nodded at us.

"I believe this is your ride," my grandfather said.

I looked back at him. "You aren't going with us?"

"I think you'll have better luck if you talk to him alone. He wants to apologize to you"—he looked at Ethan—"and he came to you for help. He might be more open without me there." He smiled. "But ask good questions."

I nodded. "We'll do our best."

I wasn't sure what this building had been used for—kilns, maybe? Storage? It was large and open, with brick walls and a concrete floor dotted by cubes, the pods in which the supernaturals were held. Winston was in a back corner of the room.

The guard escorted us silently to the pod, pointed to the yellow stripe around the box. "Stay on this side of the box," he said, then looked at his watch. "You have fifteen minutes."

He started a timer with a beep, then moved to a station along the wall with a computer and security camera.

Winston Stiles sat on the edge of a metal bed fitted into the wall, a short mattress on top of it. His elbows were on his knees, his hands linked together, his eyes closed. His brow was heavy, his mouth moving in silent speech, as if he was saying a prayer.

He seemed smaller in the pale blue jumpsuit. He looked cleaner, his hair brushed and face shaved. He also looked more alert, and a little less delusional. But his skin was still pale, his eyes hollow, his cheeks sunken.

"Mr. Stiles," Ethan said.

He blinked, turned his head toward us. And his eyes widened, horror blooming there. "It's you." He jumped up, ran to the bars so quickly I stepped in front of Ethan, pushing him back. From the sound, that didn't make Ethan happy, and it unnerved Mr. Stiles.

He wrapped his fingers around the bars that lined the front of his cube, looked at me with pleading eyes. "I'm so sorry. I'm so sorry about what happened." He looked at Ethan. "I'm so sorry. I didn't mean to do—I was overcome. I wanted help, and I couldn't figure out how to make it stop, and I just . . . I just lost it." His face fell, guilt heavy around his eyes as he looked back at me. "I'm sorry."

"It's okay, Mr. Stiles," I said, offering him what comfort I could from behind the yellow line. "We know it isn't your fault."

"You do?"

"You didn't cause the trouble, Mr. Stiles," Ethan said. "You were a victim of it. And we're trying to identify the perpetrator."

"Please, call me Winston. The perpetrator . . ." His voice

trailed off as he considered the word and its implications. "You think someone did this to me? You think I'm not just crazy?"

"You aren't crazy, Winston," I said. "We think you were affected by magic. But we don't know why, and we aren't sure how."

"There was another incident last night," Ethan explained. "Downtown. More people like you heard things that upset them, made them fight each other. Something is doing this to people. But we aren't sure what. That's why we're here."

He nodded, pulled a hand across his jaw. "All right. All right."

"Winston, can you tell us about the voice you heard?" I asked. "What was it saying?"

He scratched his temple. "The only words I remember were 'hello' and 'I am here.' He said those words a lot."

"He?" I asked. "It was male?"

He paused. "Well, yeah. I guess I didn't think about that, but yes. I think it was a male voice. It was deep in that way. I had the sense he wanted someone to hear him. Desperately wanted it. Like he was hurting and confused and needed to be acknowledged."

"He was hurt?" I asked. "He needed help?"

"Maybe, but I don't really know. It wasn't that specific, if you understand me. It was just begging, really."

Ethan nodded. "Could you tell where the voice was coming from?"

"No, other than inside my head, I mean. I know that sounds crazy, but I could hear him—really hear him, like someone turned up the volume on the television. It wasn't like a hallucination, or like I was pretending. It was real, except I was the only one who could hear it."

"Was it only a sound?" Ethan asked. "Did you happen to see anything? Hear anything else?"

"Well, no. It was just the words. Just the same words, over and over and over again. And loud. So very loud." He rubbed his earlobe, winced.

Ah, but it wasn't just the noise, was it? "What about smell, Winston? Did you smell anything?"

He looked confused. "Smell anything?"

"When you heard the voice, or maybe just before you started hearing it, did you smell anything unusual?"

He looked down, gaze slightly unfocused as he considered the question. "Now that you mention it, yeah. Many years ago, I worked at a plant in Skokie—we made certain beauty products—nail polish and the like. There was usually a whiff of solvent in the air.

"When I first started hearing the voice, I guess, I smelled something like that. Not the same, but an industrial kind of smell, if that makes sense."

"It does make sense," I said, and Winston's smile was appreciative.

"Do you smell anything now?" Ethan asked. "Hear anything?"

"Oh no. Not since they put me out. I do get memories, though. The words were so loud that I remember hearing them."

"But the memories are different?" I asked. "I mean, you can tell the difference?"

He nodded. "With the memories, I don't really *hear* it. Not the same way. I'm not sure why it makes a difference, but it does. Still loud, though. Like a flashback."

I looked around the room, the simple desk welded to the wall that held a cup, an apple, and a small notebook. A set of paints in tiny plastic cups along a single spine sat beside it, along with an old and chipped paintbrush. The handle was wide, as if the brush had been made for children.

"You've been painting?" I asked.

Winston blinked for a moment, looked back when I gestured

to the table. "Oh, my notes, you mean? I asked if I could have a notebook, a pen. They offered me a book, but I'm not much of a reader. But I do like to draw."

"Could we take a look at them, Winston?"

He scratched his cheek absently, looked back. "Oh, I don't know. There's nothing particularly good in there. It's just a kind of sketchbook, you see. Just something I do to pass the time. Nights get long. I practice making things look, well, real, I guess. And sometimes I just scribble out whatever comes to mind. Helps clear away the clutter."

Bingo.

"You said you wanted those images, those sounds, out of your head. Did you draw them?"

Understanding dawned in his eyes. "Oh, I see! Of course. Then if it will help, absolutely." He walked back to the table, the hem of his too-long pants shuffling against the concrete floor. *Shush-shush-shush.*

He brought the book back, held it out through the bars.

Most of the pages had been used. Some of the sheets were bare but for a small, precise pencil sketch. Winston's view from his cell, the pots of paint, his hands in different poses.

"You have a lovely hand," Ethan said, looking as I turned the pages.

Winston shrugged. "I find it relaxes me."

Others were painted abstract shapes filling the page from edge to edge, making them thick and hard to turn, the paint chalky beneath my fingers. Most were in shades of gray with streaks or lines of sharp white or black, and a few featured words in the same strong colors. VOICE on one, HEAR IT on another. There were several pages with white and gray blocks that looked like teeth, others with ears and spirals of tiny words.

"What are these?" I asked.

He shrugged. "The mouths, I think, that are saying all those words. The images just kind of come to me, and I draw them."

"Winston, could I borrow this? Only for a little while," I assured him when he looked crestfallen. "I'll give it back, and I'm sure we can arrange for you to have another notebook while we're borrowing this one."

"Why do you want it?" he asked.

I tried to choose my words carefully. "I'd like to look through your pictures again when I have more time. Think about them, I guess. Just in case they give us some clue about what's happening."

"Okay," he said. "But I would appreciate getting a replacement."

"I'll take care of it personally," Ethan said.

I tucked the notebook carefully inside my jacket, to keep it dry in the snow.

"Winston, do you remember the night of the attack at Towerline?" Ethan asked. "When Sorcha used her magic?"

He nodded gravely. "I do. Matter of fact, I wasn't far from there when it went down. I was laid off earlier this year, been working temp and contracts since then, taking what work I could find. I was working about a block from there—helping unload boxes of materials at the Wellworth Hotel for a convention of some sort—when it happened." He shook his head. "Quite a night that was. Never seen anything like it."

Bingo, I thought. Another connection to the magic that had gone down at Towerline. "That might be one of the reasons you're hearing the voice," I said. "We're looking into it."

His eyes widened. "You think I caught something because of that magic?"

"Not a virus," Ethan said. "But there may have been some effects. We'll let you know if we figure out that's what happened."

He nodded, ran a hand over his head as he seemed to consider.

"That's why I came to Cadogan House in the first place. Not Towerline," he added at our surprised expressions. "Employment. It's been hard—not having permanent work—and not easy to find work as a vampire. I was hoping to speak to you about a job." He shook his head. "It seems selfish now, to have caused all this trouble."

"It isn't selfish at all," Ethan said. "That's why we offer the assistance—to help vampires in unusual situations."

Winston sighed. "I don't suppose this will help me in the job market."

"We'll cross that bridge when we come to it," Ethan said. "You won't be here forever. And when we figure out what's causing the delusions, and we put a stop to it, you'll still need that help."

Very deliberately, his gaze on Winston's, Ethan stepped over the yellow line, extended his hand through the bars of Winston's cell.

Winston took a step closer. The movement was tentative, but the handshake wasn't.

"Thank you for listening," he said. "Sometimes you just need someone to listen. Think that you aren't crazy."

No argument there. The question was—which someone had needed Winston to listen?

Before we walked back to the guard, I stopped Ethan with a hand on his arm.

"There's someone else we could talk to. Someone who might have an idea what's happening."

Ethan considered for a moment. "You're thinking about Tate."

Former mayor Seth Tate was the "good" of the magical twin beings created millennia ago, compressed together by magic, and split again due to Mallory's dark magic. He'd confessed to a crime he hadn't committed in order to atone for those he had, and to stay close to Regan, his magically enhanced niece, in order to help in her rehabilitation in prison.

We'd known each other for a very long time, and I think we'd come out as friends. Or some supernatural version of friends.

"Other than talking to Claudia, he's our best—and oldest—source for information about magic."

Claudia was the queen of the fairies. She'd been separated from her homeland in Britain, and had been living in a tower in Chicago for hundreds of years. She led the fairies who'd guarded Cadogan House before they betrayed us. She—and the rest of them—were dangerous.

Ethan considered for a moment. "Okay. And it might be good to show him the ring. Remind him that you're taken."

"Seth isn't interested in me," I said. "Not like that." I'd known him since I was a child; my father had supported his campaigns since he'd been a young alderman.

"Just so," Ethan said, taking my hand. "I've no qualms about a reminder."

I looked back at him, this man with broad shoulders and golden hair, a brilliant mind and rapier wit, and green eyes that were focused on me. No one had ever looked at me the way he did—as if he could see who I was and what I might be simultaneously. And I knew he didn't want to give the reminder because he feared I'd stray or others might have an interest, but because of who and what I was to him.

Because just as he was mine, I was his.

We waited ten minutes while inquiries were made, while our request to talk to Tate was considered by the appropriate parties.

"This way," the guard said. He led the way back to the front row of cubes, where Seth's box was positioned.

Seth Tate might have been an angel, but he had the look of the fallen variety. Hair as dark as midnight around bright blue eyes, generous lips, and a square jaw. He wore a floor-length black cassock, even if there was little that was angelic about his past.

Where Winston's cube had been fronted by bars, Seth's was fronted by a long sheet of glass. There'd be no contact between us.

"Merit," Seth said, rising from his seat at a small table, his robe swirling around his feet as he moved. "Ethan. It's good to see you. Congratulations on your wedding. Although I'm sorry it took a turn for the worse." He gestured to the newspaper spread on the table. "I was reading about the attack."

"That's why we're here," I said. "Something's happening, Seth."

Seth moved a step closer. "What kind of something?"

"You don't feel anything?" Ethan asked.

"In here?" Seth crossed his arms, looked up at the ceiling of his box. "No. But then again, I spend every day in this very warded building. And there have been many of those days." He looked down again. "I've been blocked from magic for many months. Long enough that my ability to sense it has faded, too."

"The humans who attacked us last night are having delusions," I said. "As was the vampire who attacked me two nights ago."

"The *Tribune* suggested it was an illness." Tate's eyes widened. "Are you sick?"

"I'm fine," I said. "We don't think it's a sickness, or anything else contagious, or at least not in the traditional way. We think it's caused by some kind of unfamiliar magic that carries a chemical smell. Does that mean anything to you?"

Seth lifted his brows. "Technically, everything in the world is a chemical."

"Industrial, then," Ethan said.

Seth frowned, linked his hands in front of him. "Not offhand. Each kind of magic, each methodology, has its own characteristics. An industrial smell," he said, looking down again as he considered. "What else does it do?"

"The affected hear a voice screaming at them, over and over again," I said.

"What does it scream?"

"Simple phrases," I said. "'Hello. Help. I'm here.'"

His brows lifted. "They're hearing something, or someone, that needs help? Something that's attempting to contact them?"

"Are those questions or theories?" Ethan asked.

"Yes," Seth said. He turned, walked to one end of the cell, then turned back. "If you believed it was Sorcha, you wouldn't be here, asking."

"Correct," Ethan said. "The city's warded, and the wards weren't breached until the snow."

Seth nodded. "Do the affected have anything in common?"

"At least two of them, and possibly more than that, were near Towerline when Sorcha made her magic the first time. The delusions didn't cause the wards to sound, although the snow did."

"Some sort of latent effect?"

"That's what we're thinking," I said. "What is this, Seth? Who is it?"

"I don't know. Perhaps your first step should be to find out who, or what, needs the help they're asking for."

"I don't suppose you know how I could go about doing that?" I asked with a half smile.

"I don't," he said. "And listening isn't always the easiest thing to do."

Without waiting for an answer, he walked back to the table and took a seat, then ran a hand through his hair. Maybe he needed help . . . or at least someone to listen.

"Ethan, could you give us a minute?"

Ethan didn't look thrilled by the idea. But even if he didn't entirely trust Tate, he trusted me.

I'll be at the door. Be careful.

I will.

I watched him walk back to where the guard waited, then looked back at Seth. "Are you okay?" I quietly asked.

It took a moment for him to answer. "A conscience is a heavy thing to bear." He smiled, brushed away a spot of lint from his right knee. "I'm neither saint nor priest, and I know the scales can never really be balanced. But I do believe everyone is redeemable."

"And how is Regan?" I asked.

"She's still so angry. It's like a fire in her core, even here, where the magic is dampened. I'm not sure if she can lose that anger completely."

"She may not," I said. I knew something of anger and resentment, as I'd been angry at Ethan for a very long time, however unjustified that turned out to be. "But can she learn to manage it? To channel it?"

"I don't know." He drummed his fingers on the tabletop, a signal of frustration. "She doesn't like to talk to me about it. I would be more to her—a father to her—if I could. But she does not want that."

Seth had been a playboy in his pre-Dominic days. Power was alluring to many, especially in a city like Chicago, which had been built on handshakes, backroom deals, and graft. I'd never known him to be a family man, but I guess given the opportunity, he'd discovered he wanted it. And then had been denied.

Seth rose and walked to me, hands gathered in front of him. "I appreciate your asking and listening. But you don't need to bear the weight of my fears, too. You can't save everyone." A sad smile lifted one corner of his mouth. "Much as you might try."

I thought of Gabriel again, of the future that now seemed precarious, of the child he couldn't guarantee, and I lifted my gaze to Seth. "I'll try anyway. I'll keep trying, because that's what I have to do."

The same smile again, edged with sadness. "Go find your magic maker, Merit. And be careful out there."

"I will. Good luck, Seth."

I hoped there was enough to go around.

My grandfather was waiting in his car when we came back, engine running and heater blasting against the cold.

"Report?" he asked, rolling the window down with its old-fashioned hand crank.

"Winston seems quite normal," Ethan said. "Whatever delusions he was experiencing, he doesn't hear them now."

"The doctors suspect the sedation may have 'reset' his brain," my grandfather said. "And besides that, the building is sealed from magic, thanks to the Order. So the magic won't affect him while he's here."

"What if he stepped outside again?" I asked. "Do we think the effect just fades after time?"

"We don't know," my grandfather said. "We haven't tried it yet."

That wasn't an answer I liked. Fading magic meant we just needed to keep the victims from hurting themselves or others until the magic wore off of its own accord. If it didn't wear off, we'd have to keep them separated and safe—and figure out a way to make it stop. That sounded much, much harder.

Our phones—all three of them—began squealing at once. We pulled them out, checked the screens.

"Well," my grandfather said, looking up at us, "I guess you'll be going now."

"Two dozen fairies on my front lawn?" Ethan said, gaze narrowed dangerously. "Yes. I believe that's something we'll need to address." He glanced at me. "It seems you may get your chance to talk to Claudia after all."

CHAPTER FOURTEEN

THE SHADOWED GIRL

Mercenary fairies had once been allies of Cadogan House—or close enough. They were fearsome and fearless warriors, and they'd been the first to guard the House's gate while we slept. But fairies liked gold, and they'd been lured away by the Greenwich Presidium, our previous British masters, and had turned against us. So it wasn't good news to learn they were camped out in the yard.

On the other hand, given the week we'd had so far, it was somehow not entirely surprising.

Brody hauled ass back to the House. He piped in the Ops Room through the vehicle's audio system, so we could commiserate with Luc and Malik.

"What do they want?" Ethan asked, brow furrowed, arms crossed, one leg over the other. He'd switched from investigation to Master mode pretty quickly.

"We haven't even opened the door yet," Malik said. "We called as soon as the gate alerted us. They were allowed into the yard for the sake of supernatural comity."

"Weapons?"

"None," Luc said. "That's reason number two they were allowed into the yard. They've said nothing. They're standing in forma-tion. She's standing in front of them. Waiting, as they all are."

"Suggestions?" Ethan asked.

"I think we hear them out," Luc said. "They aren't allies, but they're also not being aggressive, at least right now. They came to us without weapons, and although she probably won't deign to talk to anyone but you, they do seem very interested in a conver-sation."

"Malik?" Ethan asked.

"Agreed."

He glanced at me. "Sentinel?"

"Agreed. Odds are, she wants to talk about the same things the rest of us want to talk about."

"The weather," Malik said, without irony.

"The weather," I said.

"I concur," Ethan said. "Lock down the House. I want every-one on full alert, just in case. We'll be there in—"

"Two minutes," Brody supplied, meeting Ethan's gaze in the rearview mirror.

"Two minutes," Ethan said with a nod. "Let's be on our toes."

Tires squealed as Brody pulled the vehicle to a stop in front of the House.

"Ready?" Ethan asked Luc.

"Ready as we'll ever be when a few dozen mercenary fairies come to the door."

"Then, let's go," Ethan said, and the audio went quiet.

Brody opened Ethan's door, and we walked to the gate, nod-ded at the guards, who stepped aside to let us enter the grounds. At the same time, Malik opened the House's door, walked out first, Luc and Lindsey behind him, then Kelley and Juliet.

The fairies, uniformly lean, with sculpted cheekbones and

long, dark hair, all of them clad in identical head-to-toe black, stood in a wide triangle, the point facing the gate, the broad side facing the House. They were a striking, graphic contrast to the inch of snow that covered the lawn.

They parted as we approached, splitting with mathematical precision along the sidewalk. And when the last line of them split, she turned to face us.

She stood in front of that line of fairies, an absolute vision. Her skin was milk white, her hair long and wavy and strawberry blond and topped by a delicate ring of white flowers. Lily of the valley, just like the ones in my bouquet. She wore her usually diaphanous white gown, her voluptuous body easily visible beneath it.

But there was a difference. Claudia had always been beautiful, but millennia trapped in a tower had begun to take their toll. Tonight, the age and fatigue that had pulled at her skin had been brushed away, as if by an artist with a very skilled hand.

She was stunningly beautiful. And very, very dangerous.

"Claudia," Ethan said.

"Bloodletter." She slid her gaze, full of peril and old magic, at me. "Consort."

"Wife," Ethan corrected.

She looked dubious at the distinction. Fairies didn't believe in love, or so they said.

"Why are you here?" Ethan asked.

"The world is changing." There was a hint of Ireland in her voice, a trill that hadn't been there before. She held out a hand, watched the snowflakes that settled on her palm, then blew them away. The flakes sparked, dissipated.

"So we are aware," Ethan said. "I've allowed you onto my grounds, Claudia, despite your previous treachery. Tell me what you want, or be on your way."

I wasn't sure that was the best tone to take with a dangerous woman who'd brought her dangerous army. I put a hand on my katana, just in case.

"There is no need for threats," she said, and flicked a hand in the air.

Something brushed across my hand. A thin green vine had bloomed from my katana's lacquered sheath and slunk toward the sword's handle, twining around it to keep it in place. Leaves, small and brilliantly green, split from the vine and uncurled, sending the scents of new spring leaves and powdery flowers into the air.

This was old magic, fairy magic. Magic she'd been able to access before she'd voluntarily given it up. She'd loved Dominic, Seth's literal evil twin, and had given up her magic to save him, even while maintaining that fairies were above such base emotions.

She wasn't supposed to have this magic anymore.

That's new, I said silently to Ethan.

And concerning.

For several reasons, I thought, and glanced up, saw the challenge in her eyes. "Get your magic off my sword."

Claudia's gaze shifted to Ethan as if to confirm I had any authority in the House—or to assess whether getting married had softened his edge. He smiled back at her.

"She stands Sentinel of this House, Claudia, and you know she can fight. For that reason alone, I'd suggest you heed her advice."

Claudia watched him for a moment. Her expression didn't change, but I caught the light flick of her fingers, the rustle of her long red locks. And I didn't need to look down to know the vine was retreating. The tingle of magic receded along with it.

"You've regained power," Ethan said.

Her smile looked pleasant, but there was something behind it. Something old and powerful and treacherous.

The air filled with buzzing magic so quickly I barely had time to recognize the attack before we were somewhere else . . . and some*when* else.

I stood in a meadow, green and lush, and as misty as an Irish shore. A lark sang somewhere in the distance, its voice a melody against the low *thrush* of waving grass, the faraway sound of a beating ocean. I looked down, found myself in a long skirt of soft, nubby fabric, a tunic over it in the same shade of pale blue.

Ethan stood beside me, eyes closed, in leggings and tunic, a heavy iron sword in his hand, streaks of blue across his face.

"There," Ethan said, and lifted his arm, pointing toward the meadow.

A dozen men and women stood in a circle, moving rhythmically to the soft and hollow sound of a leather drum.

I closed my eyes, let the breeze caress my face, as soft as a mother's kiss. There was no buzz of magic here. It was the breeze, the tall grass beneath my fingertips, the swell of the cold ocean tide. It was the salt air, the pale mist, the dancers and their music. It permeated every rock, every hill and vale, every person, every thought in the land of fairy, the place where they made their home. A place that *was* home.

There was happiness here, and pain. Birth and death, and the parade of things that happened in between, the kaleidoscope of experiences that made up a life. But beneath it all, there was contentment, because there was home. Because this was the domain of the fairy. This was fairyland, literally and figuratively.

A sound echoed over the hill, the laughter of a child whom I'd never seen before, but somehow knew as intimately as I knew myself. The giggle echoed across the land, bursting with joy and buoyant silliness.

Ethan's smile widened, his eyes alight with joy and hope as he watched the horizon, waiting for the child to crest the hill. He moved forward to be one step closer to the child . . . But the wind lifted and turned cold. The earth shuddered, and we stood once again in Chicago.

Wherever we'd gone, we'd come back.

I knew it hadn't been real, that nothing we'd seen had been real, so it couldn't have been taken away from us. But that didn't matter. The grief was instant and as deep as an ocean, leaving me empty and aching, and hollowing out a part of my soul I knew would never be filled. Not when I might have stayed in that world forever, waiting for the child to run into our arms.

The child whose existence was no longer guaranteed.

A hand gripped mine, and I looked at Ethan, found that same look of longing on his face. And as the moment passed, that longing faded to understanding. We'd been there in that world for only a moment. And neither of us had wanted to come back. From the expression of the vampires around us, we weren't the only ones affected.

No wonder so many fairy-tale characters disappeared, accidentally (or intentionally) stepping foot into the land of the fae, never to return again. They hadn't been captured by the fae, or not literally. They simply hadn't wanted to return. They'd have lived contentedly in Emain Ablach for an eternity.

I was pretty sure I hadn't even heard the phrase before. But it had been slipped into my thoughts like a secret note, a hidden message that I would remember for an eternity, and a place to which I'd probably never return.

I shifted my gaze to Claudia, saw that she knew at least something of what we'd seen, what we'd experienced, and also saw what looked like arrogance.

Claudia looked at me, and I found myself unnerved by her attention. Her eyes seemed to see too much. "You have seen much."

I shook my head. What I'd seen wasn't for her. And I didn't

have time to dwell on it right now, so I pushed it aside. "What is Emain Ablach?"

"The green land. *Our* land."

"You have access to the green land again," Ethan said, every word carefully spoken.

Claudia nodded. "I can see home, as I have shown you. I cannot physically travel there, but I can see it. That is . . . a change."

"And you're here to show us," Ethan said. "To demonstrate your power."

"Or to flaunt it?" I asked.

My tone hadn't been friendly, and neither were her eyes.

"I chose to sacrifice my connection, however undeserving the recipient of my gift. The deal was done. The power should not have come back to me."

Her eyes, so vividly blue, darkened, like seas beneath a roiling storm. And there was fear in her eyes. Even Claudia, who was as egotistical and dangerous as they came, was worried.

"Why is it happening?" Ethan asked.

Her brows lifted. "I am not here to answer your questions, bloodletter."

Ethan's expression remained implacable. "And yet, you're here. In my territory, without permission, to seek an audience with me."

Claudia growled, anger flashing in her eyes. "You did not stop her when you had the chance."

No question as to the "her" she intended.

"To the contrary. We stopped Sorcha; the humans allowed her to escape. You believe she's the reason your power has returned?"

For the first time since I'd known her, there was uncertainty in Claudia's expression. "There is power in this land. Power the shadowed girl worked to contain."

"The shadowed girl?" Ethan asked.

But I understood. "She means Mallory," I said. She'd been shadowed by dark magic. "Mallory reversed Sorcha's magic. There shouldn't have been anything left of Sorcha's spell."

And that had been bothering me—how could there have been magic left over to create the delusions if the battle at Towerline had eradicated it?

With impeccable timing, and before Claudia could answer, Mallory and Catcher strode through the gate and down the sidewalk.

They stopped when they reached us, and Mallory's eyes grew wide as she took in the spectacle that was Claudia.

Emotions evolved on her face—confusion, curiosity, and, as she probably felt the depth of Claudia's magic, something that looked like lust. Like *need*. Something that probably wasn't good for a woman with an addiction to dark magic.

"Mallory," I said, making her name a quick snap. It accomplished what I needed it to do, and seemed to pull her out of her momentary magical stupor.

"Hello," Catcher said, nodding at Ethan, at Claudia. "We don't want to interrupt."

But he plainly was here to interrupt, to jump in, in case the fairies were a threat. And with Mallory, to contain them.

"You aren't," Ethan said. "Claudia, this is Catcher and Mallory Bell. Claudia is queen of the fairy."

"The shadowed girl," Claudia said quietly. Her gaze had skipped over Catcher, evidently unimpressed. But she looked at Mallory carefully, and for the first time since I'd known her, there was something akin to respect in her eyes. Something that looked like recognition, like she'd finally found someone worthy of her interest, rather than the same old stringy vampires.

"You wrought old magic," Claudia said. "That magic shadowed you."

"I've worked to lift that shadow," Mallory said, straightening her shoulders.

"And turned away from limitless power," Claudia said, clearly unimpressed. "You turned instead to words and chants, herbs and whispers."

"Didn't you turn away from power, too?"

"You would judge me?"

"If you're going to judge first, yeah. Maybe we can skip the rest of the intimidation game and get to the point?"

Claudia's eyes fired—she wasn't used to smart-mouthed sorceresses—but she let the comment go. Maybe she was intimidated by Mallory, which was fine by me. I wasn't comfortable without a check on Claudia's power. We didn't need another Sorcha.

"I felt your magic, your unraveling of hers. It wasn't enough."

Mallory blinked, looked baffled and insulted at the same time. "We reversed the spell successfully."

"Perhaps. But she did not allow the magic to disseminate after it was unraveled."

Mallory just stared at her for a moment. "That's impossible," she said quietly. "That couldn't have worked. We knew her magic—her alchemy. We worked the reversal completely."

She looked at me, at Ethan, at Catcher. "They know the truth."

Mallory's gaze snapped to ours. "They do?"

"There had to be leftover magic," I quietly said. "The delusions were created by magic, and they didn't set off the wards."

"But I was so careful." She reached out, took Catcher's arm. "We were so careful. We did everything right."

I could feel her ire rising, watched her work to control it. Muttering to herself, Mallory walked to the gate, shoes scuffing through the snow, then back again.

"We nailed her alchemy," she said, pointing at each of us in turn. "Nailed it to the wall. But maybe, while we were on the roof, she snuck in some kind of hidden code. A worm or Trojan horse she added at the last minute, something we couldn't detect . . .

"Oh my God!" she said, and thumped her palm against her forehead. "It's so obvious. So freaking obvious." She looked at Catcher. "That's why our spells got stuck—why her magic blue-screened. Because of her little magical Trojan horse. We unwrapped the alchemy, but instead of the magic disseminating across the city, there's—what?—a fog of it stuck here?" She looked at Claudia, who merely inclined her head.

"Why can't we feel that magic?" Ethan asked. "The buzz?"

"Because it's spread over a large area," Mallory said. "Not strong enough to feel, but still there. Still waiting."

"And the wards were created after Towerline," Catcher said, nodding as the pieces fell into place for him. "After the magic had been released. That was the baseline the wards were created against. Only new magic by Sorcha above that baseline would trigger them."

I looked at Claudia, considered the glow of her skin, her new green-land visitation rights. "You've been affected by that magic."

She didn't bother to look at me, but kept her gaze on Mallory. "My tower is magicked; it's how I stay here, and alive. I suspect it has absorbed that power, and I have reaped the benefits."

"And the delusions?" Ethan asked.

"Maybe the magic settled in pockets," Catcher said. "Jeff has confirmed all the humans who fought us last night were near Towerline when the battle went down. And two dozen more—humans and sups—have been arrested in sporadic outbreaks, most of which have been downtown."

"This land is poised at a precipice," Claudia said. "Whether it falls or not I cannot see; that will be for you to determine, your battle to win.

"*Win it*," she said, and with that final demand, she turned and walked through her lines of fairies, who'd stood motionless in the snow for so long that flakes had gathered on their shoulders. They gathered behind her like a train, then disappeared down the walk and through the gate, steps fading into silence.

"Take the House off alert," Ethan said. "For now."

Luc nodded to Juliet, who headed to the basement to make the arrangements.

"Was it real?" he asked quietly, stepping beside Ethan. Luc wasn't the type to have reservations. "Were we there?"

"She took us to the green land," Ethan explained.

Mallory's brow lifted with interest. "Really."

"The green land isn't part of our world," Ethan told Luc, putting a supportive hand on his shoulder. "But it's as real as anything in it."

Luc ran a hand through his hair. "I'd have stayed forever. She could have dropped me off and walked away, and I would have stayed a million years and never wanted anything else."

"That is the power of fairy," Ethan said. "There's a reason fairy tales exist. They are not love stories; they are warnings."

"If she keeps enough magic to visit the green land," Catcher said, "she'll change supernatural power dynamics across the world."

"If she gets the opportunity, she'll use it against us," Ethan agreed. "But for now, we must deal with the present." He cocked his head at Catcher. "Did you come here to help?"

"And to research," Mallory said. "I wanted to borrow your library, do some research on the magic we're seeing. Maybe it will ring some historical bell."

I couldn't help but smile. "Or historical Bell?"

"Naming pun," Catcher said dryly. "Very clever."

"And here's something else clever," I said. Seth's suggestion—and Claudia's visit—had given me an idea. "I think we should go to the source."

"Meaning?" Ethan asked.

I looked at Mallory. "This started with a voice. I think it's time we take a listen of our own."

Ironic silence followed that suggestion.

"To clarify," Catcher said. "There's a voice powerful enough to drive humans literally crazy. And Merit thinks we should tune in to it."

But I kept my gaze on Mallory, watched the interest spark in her eyes.

"If we heard it, we'd learn more about it." She nodded. "Maybe try to figure out where it was coming from—or who."

"That's the idea," I said.

"Could it be done?" Ethan asked.

"It's certainly possible," she said. "It's magical in origin, so theoretically we should be able to use magic to listen in. But I'd have to work out the details, get my kit together. That will take time. This isn't OTC magic."

"Over the counter?" Ethan asked.

"I was thinking 'off the cuff,'" Mallory said with a smile, "but I like yours, too."

"How much time will you need?" Ethan asked.

"Couple of hours, maybe." Mallory grinned. "I suspect you newlyweds can occupy yourselves in the meantime."

"I bet we can," I said. But the gleam in my eye wasn't romantic. It was strategic. "I want to break into Sorcha's house."

- ❖ -

CHAPTER FIFTEEN

B TO THE E

"You're just full of interesting plans tonight," Catcher said. But I kept my gaze on Ethan, watching emotions and considerations move across his face.

"She has to have a workroom, an office," I said. "A place where she preps her magic. I want to see it. Maybe we'll find something that explains what the hell is happening in Chicago."

"And maybe we won't," Ethan said, "and we'll be arrested for breaking and entering." He looked at Catcher. "Didn't you look through the house after she was arrested?"

"We were allotted ten minutes by the crime scene folks," Catcher said, voice as dry as toast. "That didn't give us time to get through the entire house—just the center wing."

"And we didn't get anything out of that," Mallory said, "other than a sense of their atrocious taste."

She had it right. There wasn't much in the Reed house that hadn't been covered in screaming red velvet or gleaming gilt, every nook filled with furniture and statuary.

"Can we even get in?" Ethan asked.

"Reed's estate is in probate," Catcher said, running fingers over his shorn hair. "Since Sorcha's accused of his murder and is still on the lam, the house is being monitored by a security outfit hired by the executor."

Ethan looked at me as if he thought that might dissuade me. I just smiled at him.

"What's the point of being Sentinel of the city's best vampire House if I don't get to break a few human laws?"

Ethan arched an eyebrow. "Working on your brownnosing game?"

I grinned back at him. "If it gets me what I want, yes."

"I could make a phone call," Catcher said, "ask for formal permission for you to go through the house. But if they say no, they'll be on alert, and that will make it harder for you to get in."

"And if you don't make that call," I said, "we may be able to use our considerable skills to slip inside undetected?"

"Something like that. And if she does have a work space, there's a chance she'll be there, that she slipped past the guards and got inside."

"Then she should mind her manners," Ethan said. "Because this won't be a social visit."

"I say skip the call," I said, "and don't put them on alert." I looked at Ethan.

He considered in silence for a moment. "What my Sentinel wants, my Sentinel gets."

"Since I don't have a closet stocked with chocolate, that is literally incorrect," I said. "But good about this Sorcha thing."

"While you're committing crimes, we'll stay here, work on the magic," Catcher said. "And maybe, if you're cool with it, we'll stay the night at the House."

It wasn't the first time they'd done so. When Mallory had been plugged into the House's ward, she'd stayed here to keep it running. She'd since figured out a way to power it with good old electricity; she just had to check the magic to make sure everything was working the way it should have.

"No objection," Ethan said. "I'm fairly certain your manners are better than Sorcha's."

It wasn't a difficult threshold to meet.

We were dressed in black, which wasn't especially unusual for vampires, and had swords belted at our waists. I'd brought along a small, sleek backpack, just in case I found anything worth larceny.

Luc insisted Brody take the wheel of the SUV, giving us at least one more guard in case we got into trouble. But we didn't plan to get into trouble. The steady expression on Ethan's face said that much.

The temperature had grown even colder. Only five degrees above zero, according to the current weather report. The snow had stopped; maybe the heat sink had sucked all the available moisture from the sky.

The Reed house was in a historic neighborhood northeast of Hyde Park, where several Gilded Age mansions had been kept historically pristine. It took up a large chunk of the block; not as large a chunk as Cadogan House did in Hyde Park, but with significantly more attitude. This was old money. Old Chicago money.

The living quarters were shaped like a U, one unified center and separate wings on each end, a private courtyard in the middle. Catcher had been right about the guards. There were two in the front, an additional guard stationed on each side of the house. Possibly more roaming around inside. The heirs to Reed's fortune, whoever they might be, were taking no chances on their inheritance.

"We can't walk in," I said, and narrowed my gaze at an enormous oak that abutted one corner of the house. "So we go up."

We left Brody at the curb, crept in darkness through the old and elegant trees that shaded the block, then slipped to the side of the building. We watched the guard in silence, waited for him to pass, then darted to the tree that stood at one corner of the property. There was snow on the ground, but, since it was August, still leaves on the trees. That would give us some cover, at least until we made our way into the house. But we'd cross that bridge when we came to it.

It's been a while since I've climbed a tree, Ethan said, but he grabbed a branch, hauled himself up easily. Vampire strength was a very handy thing.

A while for me, too, although not the centuries you've probably got on me. I followed him up, and we took one large branch at a time.

Hold, Ethan said, and I stilled, watched the guard pass beneath us, the green light on his communicator blinking in the darkness. I held my breath, like that would keep us hidden in the dappled moonlight, but couldn't stop the chunk of snow that fell beneath my foot and landed with an audible *splat* on the ground fifteen feet below.

I willed my heart to slow, because it pounded loudly enough that I was sure the guard could hear it. But he kept walking, making his slow procession down the block, watching for the sorceress who might steal her way back into her home.

This is the tricky bit, Ethan said, and climbed into a standing position, then edged his way across a limb to the stone parapet that edged the house's second floor. It was only about three feet wide, and would be a very tricky walk. But that was the way in, so no point in bellyaching about it.

Ethan held out a hand, helped me jump across.

Being in the tree hadn't bothered me, but standing on a ledge two stories aboveground did nothing for my appetite. We moved to a dark window, peered inside. It looked like a bedroom, dark and mostly empty. I tried to lift the sash, but it was locked.

Watch for cars, Ethan said, *and let me know when you see one.*

While I nodded, Ethan unsheathed his katana, turned it so the heavy pommel faced the window. And waited.

It took two long minutes for headlights to play down the street. *On its way*, I told him. *Five seconds*.

When the car passed in front of the house, he slammed the katana against the glass. Glass tinkled inside, but the noise was at least partially muffled by the sound of the passing car. We waited in silence for an alarm, for the heavy thump of guards' feet, but heard nothing.

Eyes narrowed in concentration, Ethan reached inside the opening of jagged glass, flipped the lock, lifted the shutter.

He climbed in first, pushed away glass, then offered a hand to help me inside. We left the window open, cold air spilling into the room behind us, and crept to the closed door that probably led to the interior hallway.

I got there first, turned the knob with slow and careful concentration, pulled open the door just a sliver.

The light in the hallway was pale and golden, and there was nothing but silence on the other side.

We're clear, I told him, and we stepped into the hallway.

It was big. Cavernous, as far as houses went. A lot of open space, a lot of marble, and a lot of décor. A museum's worth of portraits and paintings and tables and credenzas.

We crept down the hallway to the junction that led to the long gallery of art, and the main staircase between. The hallway was like a museum of doors—one after another in two long rows.

I guess we start here, I said, and Ethan nodded.

You take this one, Ethan said. *I'll take the other.*

Roger, I said, and we walked to our respective doors.

I got a closet. He got the master bedroom. We scoped it out, found nothing interesting. We followed with another bedroom, a bathroom, and a small home theater.

I hit pay dirt, personally if not professionally, on my third door. The room was small, little more than a nook with a window at the end. But the longest wall was filled with books, with a couple of chairs and a small table in front of them.

Curious, I walked to the shelves, scanned the spines. I'd expected grimoires, celebrity biographies, or true crime stories. I couldn't imagine Sorcha reading anything else.

But they were fairy tales. Volume after volume of them, from countries and cultures around the world. Reference books, books for children, picture books. But all about magical creatures and the worlds they inhabited.

"*Fairy Tales of the Round, Round World*," I murmured, and pulled the book from the shelf. It had been one of my favorite books as a child, and I'd pored over the stories of Camelot and Rose Red, fairies and djinns, dozens of times. As a child, this book had been my companion. I'd lost my dog-eared copy somewhere along the way, and hadn't thought about it in years.

I opened the book, the pages thick and stiff with age, but absolutely pristine. There were no crayon marks here, no drawings or scribbles in the margins. If Sorcha had read this book, she'd read it carefully and left no trace behind.

Something about that made me terribly sad. And, looking back at the rest of her books—the hundreds of volumes of stories in this lush room—absolutely furious.

She had everything, and she'd still demanded more. More power. More fame. Just . . . *more.*

Ethan must have felt the burst of magic. *Sentinel?* he asked, stepping into the room.

She had every opportunity, I told him. *Privilege, wealth, status. She could have done anything with that kind of power. And she chose to destroy.*

He walked toward me, brushed a lock of hair behind my ear. *You are angry because you were not so different, once upon a time. But your paths diverged.*

He knew me so well. *In very different directions,* I agreed.

We'd both been pulled into the world of supernaturals. Me, by an attack. She, presumably, when she learned about her power. And, just like I said, she'd chosen to destroy.

What did you find? I asked him.

Another bedroom, he said. *So nothing. Since Catcher's been through the center wing, let's check the others.*

We walked back into the hallway, made it four feet before the digital *pop* of a communication device engaging broke the monasterial silence.

"Moving up to the second floor," said an unfamiliar voice from the long gallery that led to the main staircase, flashlight beam bobbing as he climbed toward us.

A guard, probably, doing a sweep of the premises.

Here, Ethan said, and pulled me into a rounded alcove, our backs pressed against cold stone as the flashlight swept across the hall in front of us.

The footsteps drew closer until a man in a dark suit with plenty of muscle beneath walked past, flashlight in one hand, comm unit in the other. He paused in front of the alcove, and we held our breath.

"Nothing in zone four," he said, lifting the comm to his mouth. "If she's here, I don't see her."

"Roger that," said the digital voice on the other end of the line. "Proceed to zone five, check in again."

"Roger that," the man said, and kept walking down the hallway. We peeked out as he turned the corner into the other wing of the house.

Let's go, Ethan said, and we crept down the hall in the opposite direction. We found two more bedrooms, three more bathrooms, a sitting room, a game room, and what looked like servants' quarters.

And then, at the end of the wing, we opened the final door, and walked into madness.

"Whoa," I quietly said.

The alchemical symbols Sorcha had drawn across the city had been crazily written, in one case covering walls, floor, and ceiling of a toolshed in a cemetery. I'd assumed there'd been so many— and that they'd been drawn in such a bizarre way—because it had been necessary for the magic. Now I wondered if it wasn't just a symptom of her underlying insanity.

The room was large, at least as big as the other bedrooms we'd seen. Pale walls, wooden floors, no furniture but a wooden table and chair in the middle of the room.

But the walls were almost entirely covered in pieces of paper. There were small handwritten notes, pages with pictures and blocks of text, and long scrolls of alchemical symbols like the ones Sorcha had drawn across Chicago tacked across the room. Origami shapes in white paper hung from the ceiling, and shreds of paper were scattered across the floor.

Ethan walked closer to the wall, brow furrowed as he looked it over.

I walked to the table, looked at the simple stone bowl that sat there. There was a box of matches beside it, and a drying twig.

I lifted it, sniffed. Rosemary, and with the matches and crucible, probably a spot where Sorcha had performed alchemical magic. I looked up. The middle of the ceiling was marked by a large round medallion, its floral shapes covered in soot.

I put the rosemary down, walked back to Ethan. *Alchemy*, I said. *This is her workroom.*

He nodded, gaze tracking the writings and images.

There seemed to be a focus area centered on the wall across from the crucible. Green twine linked pages in other parts of the room back to the sheets here. But if there was a narrative here, or any kind of linear logic, I couldn't see it.

Does this mean anything to you? he asked.

Not even a little. I'm guessing she's working out magic, trying to fig-ure out how to make connections between symbols or spells? But that's my best guess.

Ethan nodded.

Maybe it will make more sense to Mallory, I said, and pulled out my phone, managed to snap one photograph when the alarm split the air, as sharp as a knife.

"Attention," said the voice that rang through the house's ap-parent intercom system. "Your illegal entry has been detected, and the authorities have been notified. Attention," it said again, then repeated the message.

I guess they found the window, Ethan said.

Or saw our tracks in the snow.

Either way, he said with a wink, *let's make a graceful exit.*

I nodded. *I'm right behind you,* I assured him. I darted to the center of the chaos, began ripping papers from the wall, shoving them into my open backpack. I wasn't leaving empty-handed.

Then we moved into the hallway, clung to the shadows, and made our way out again.

Mallory was situated at the conference table in Ethan's office when we returned, books, notebooks, soda cans, paper, and pens spread across the table. It wasn't unlike the mess in Sorcha's office, although it didn't look quite as insane. And I didn't have a single doubt about Mallory's motives.

"We weren't even gone for two hours," Ethan said, gaze wide as he took in the chaos of his usually ordered office.

"Good witches work fast." She looked up at me, gestured to the backpack. "What did you find?"

"Insanity," Ethan said.

"Seriously," I said, putting my backpack on the table. "It was *A Beautiful Mind* in there." I gave her the details. "We didn't find any computers, notebooks, whiteboards. No secret plans just lying around." I unzipped the backpack, pulled out the papers I'd snatched from Sorcha's office. "But I did grab these."

"And they are . . . ?" Mallory asked, eyeing them suspiciously.

"A very small percentage of her notes," Ethan said.

I nodded. "They were all over the room, so I grabbed a couple of square feet before we had to make a run for it."

"They saw you?" Catcher asked.

"No," Ethan said with a smile for me. "They found evidence of our entry. I'm afraid we may have broken a window."

"Should have broken more than that," Catcher muttered. "The assholes."

Mallory pulled off the top sticky note, which read "glizzard," eyed it suspiciously before setting it aside again. "We'll look through them when we get back."

"I take it you're ready?" Ethan asked.

"Ready to listen, and ready to go."

He arched an eyebrow. "And where will we be going?"

"Downtown, relatively near Towerline. It needs to be within the former alchemical web, and preferably quiet." She winced. "And maybe not right next to a residential building. Just in case."

In case things went sideways. Because there was always a chance of it.

"To confirm," Ethan said, "you want to be near Towerline—in downtown Chicago—but not too close to the other million people who live there."

"Exactly," she said brightly.

"Millennium Park," Catcher said. "There won't be anyone at the pavilion tonight. The lawn will give us space. It's not exactly close to Towerline, but it's as close as we can get with that kind of space and privacy."

Mallory pursed her lips. "Interesting idea," she said. "Maybe I can use the trellis as some kind of antenna."

"Let's just take this one step at a time," Catcher said.

Since we'd all be heading back to Cadogan House after our trip downtown, Catcher drove the SUV. He and Ethan landed in the front seat, which gave Mallory and me a chance to talk. Doubly good, because I wanted to keep pushing aside my rising emotions.

"And how are you finding married life?" Mallory asked from her spot beside me on the second-row bench.

"At the moment?" I considered the question. "Treacherous."

Mallory snorted. "Yeah, but in fairness, your dating life was pretty treacherous, too. That's what you get for nabbing a Darth Sullivan."

I glanced at her. "Has he told you his nickname for me?"

"Of course he has."

I lifted my brows. "What do you mean 'of course he has'? Fess up!"

"Oh no," she said, picking a remaining bit of chipped polish off her nail. "I want no part of that. You'll weasel it out of him eventually."

I narrowed my gaze at her. "I could weasel it out of you."

She grinned. "I seriously doubt it, vamp."

"Spoilsport."

"Probably about many things, yes."

The view turned to darkness as we reached Lake Shore Drive, which would take us into downtown.

"And how are you?" I asked.

She frowned. "What do you mean?"

I kept my voice low. "You looked, I guess, kind of lustful about Claudia's magic."

She smiled a little. "For a second, I thought you were going to say I looked lustfully at Claudia. Which, I mean, she is a babe."

"It's that ancient, voluptuous, Irish sexpot thing. Girl crush."

"Total girl crush," she agreed. "I'm all about the boys, and my boy in particular. But she has an appeal that's just—it socks you in the gut. And the dress doesn't hurt. I couldn't pull that off. But damn, does she have the figure for it." She smiled. "I really want to ask her out for coffee to talk about her magic. Maybe she'd take me to the green land, which would be pretty amazing. But with the magic and the dress, she'd either be arrested for lewd behavior or completely swamped by admirers. And I don't know if fairies even drink coffee."

I didn't, either. "And the magic?" I prompted.

Mallory paused. "I'm not going to lie—I felt a twinge."

"A twinge?"

"Want. Desire. It's not dark, Claudia's magic. She doesn't need death and pain to make her magic operate. But it's old. And with magic that old, good and evil aren't nearly so far apart."

"You resisted, so that's good."

She frowned, arranged herself in a cross-legged position on the wide leather seat. "Yeah." She held out a hand, flexed her fingers, made a fist. "And it wasn't easy not to reach out and grab a handful of magic. The memory is so vivid. How it felt running beneath my skin, so much energy, so much potential. That's the hard part of any addiction, I guess. Remembering how good it felt, and saying no anyway. But even if I was going to indulge, which I'm not, this is not the magic to indulge in. Too old. Too different. Too powerful."

"Unless we all want to end up on a direct flight to the green land," I said.

"Seriously. Merit," she said after a moment.

I glanced at her.

"Thanks for asking. For, I guess, engaging me about it. Addiction isn't easy. But it's a little easier when you can be honest about it. When you can acknowledge it, instead of pretending it doesn't exist."

"You're welcome, Mallory." I reached out and squeezed her hand. "That's what friends are for."

"And sharing girl crushes."

"And sharing girl crushes."

"Seriously, that dress, though."

I decided to leave it at that.

Catcher found an on-street spot a block from Michigan, and we climbed out of the car, katanas belted beneath our coats. We also carried supplies for the magic Mallory intended to work downtown, and blankets to spread on the ground beneath her accouterments.

I'd wondered whether we'd see more people outside or fewer: Had they stayed inside to avoid the building danger, or come outside to gape at the gathering snow?

The former, mostly. Even in the chill, people milled about on sidewalks, tourists rubbing their arms in the short-sleeved T-shirts they figured were enough for a late summer, or donning new Bears and Blackhawks sweatshirts they'd grabbed at souvenir shops. Most stared nervously at the sky, cast glances toward the river. Others stared out from hotel lobbies, from restaurants along the sidewalk, watching the city like Chicago might have been a pacing tiger—a danger that hadn't yet struck.

We crossed Michigan into the park, past the few tourists who stared at their reflections in the Cloud Gate, snapped selfies with friends. Danger may have kept many Chicagoans indoors. But it didn't dampen the selfie spirit.

We walked into the stretch of grass in front of the bandstand, its silver plates gathered and arched like armor. Steel beams rose over us, crisscrossing to hold speakers for concerts in the park. Icicles hung down from them, their pointed ends making it appear that we were trapped in an armored cage.

And beneath the spiky beams, a stretch of snow that had clearly been the site of joy and happiness today. There were paw prints, snow angels, and plenty of footprints marring what might have been a perfect blanket of white.

"Any particular place?" Ethan asked.

"Any will do," Mallory said, walking into the middle of the lawn. She put down her bag, pulled a blanket out of it, spread it on the ground.

Catcher followed her. Ethan glanced at me.

"Is this a good idea?"

I looked back at Mallory. "I'm not altogether sure. But what choice do we have?"

CHAPTER SIXTEEN

WHISKEY TANGO FOXTROT

We sat in a semicircle on the blanket, which didn't do much to buffer the snow beneath us.

Mallory opened her bag, pulled out a round sterling silver platter polished to a high shine. She'd borrowed it from Margot's stash of serving ware during her search for magic-making gear. She'd also brought matches, a sprig of rosemary, and a short bottle of champagne.

"What's the bubbly for?" Ethan asked, when she'd set out her equipment and put the bag aside.

"Us," she said with a smile. "It's been a long night already." She handed the bottle to Catcher. "Please to uncork, while I prepare the rest."

She put the platter on the ground between us, the sprig of rosemary on top of it.

"This looks like alchemy," I said. "Minus the crucible."

"It's inspired by alchemy, by what Sorcha did, and by my own style."

I looked at Catcher. "What's your style?"

"You know the answer to that," he said, pulling the cork with his teeth, a whisper of smoke escaping the bottle.

"Weapons," I said. He'd been the first to train me to use a katana, had used magic and my blood to temper the blade, which gave me the ability to sense steel weapons. Not an unuseful skill given the kinds of things we usually faced.

"Weapons," he agreed, taking a swig of champagne and passing the bottle around. "We get to the point that we actually have something to fight, and I'm your man."

"He's being modest," Mallory said, taking a hearty drink and passing the bottle to Ethan. She sat back on her heels. "That he's best at weapons doesn't mean he isn't great at everything else." She looked at him, winked. "All sorts of things."

"We don't need the details," Ethan said, taking a drink and passing the bottle to me, condensation icing over the outside of the bottle. If it hadn't been for the alcohol content, the champagne might have frozen in the achingly crisp air. But that didn't affect the taste, the delicate blossom and bubbles.

Mallory shook her head. "You've already been married to Duchess too long." Then she slapped a hand over her mouth, let out a mumbled swear.

It took me a moment to cue in to what she'd said—to the fact that she'd just given up his nickname for me. I glanced at Ethan, eyebrow arched in perfect imitation of his own favorite quirk. "Duchess? That's what you call me?"

His smile was broad and amused. "Darth Sullivan," he reminded me.

"That particular shoe fit," I reminded him.

"And 'Duchess' doesn't?"

"I'm not the princessy type."

"No, you aren't. But that's not how you earned the name. Recall that on our first meeting you marched into my House, with your pale skin and dark hair, and those hauntingly pale eyes—eyes that were filled with so much pain and anger. You looked like the duchess of some strange and beautiful land. I couldn't take my eyes off you."

I just stared at him. He'd given me compliments before, and obviously I knew that he loved me. But I'd never heard the story of our first meeting in quite the same way.

"And then she challenged you to a duel," Mallory said to him.

"She did. She was very imperious."

Mallory nodded. "And you were like, 'All right, girl. Let's go. Let's see what you've got.'"

I pointed at Mallory. "You aren't helping."

"I disagree, but . . ." She mimed zipping up her lips.

"And she's right," Ethan said. "That's fairly close to my recollection."

"Damn, Sullivan," Catcher said as I offered the bottle back to him. He declined, so I recorked it, set it aside. "Merit's got that Angry Master look down pat. You should probably be careful using that particular moniker."

Ethan grinned at me. "He has a point, Duchess. You are good at it."

I growled. Maybe I needed to challenge him more often, I thought. Just to keep him in line.

Ethan leaned over, pressed a kiss to my lips. "If it helps, you became Sentinel very, very quickly."

I kept my gaze narrowed. "Does the entire House know about this?"

There was amusement in his eyes. "Fewer than those who know about 'Darth Sullivan.'"

"Touché," I said after a moment.

"If you're done flirting," Catcher said, "should we get on with the magic?"

"Let's do," Mallory said, pulling a match from the box. "I'm ready to get started."

"What should we do?" I asked.

"Seem friendly. We don't want to scare it." With that, she flicked the match against the side of the box, spark and sulfur following in its wake. She put aside the box, carefully applied fire to the stick of rosemary. The herbal scent filled the air, made me hungry for baked chicken. But I put that aside.

Silently, Mallory opened her notebook, scribbled something on a page, tore it out. She folded the page into a complicated arrangement, held it over the smoldering rosemary until it caught fire, too, and dropped it into the platter.

"For ambience and explanation," Mallory said, then sat crosslegged, hands on her knees, and straightened her back. And she began winding up her magic.

Catcher had once told me that sorcerers didn't make magic—they funneled it. They were capable, for genetic or paranormal reasons, of funneling the universe's magic, redirecting it for some purpose of their own. That was what Mallory did now, pulling in magic that was warm enough to make steam literally rise from the top of her head.

She cupped her hands together, blew into them.

"Is she blowing out the magic?" I quietly asked.

Catcher clucked his tongue. "She's warming up her hands, noob."

Logical, but how was I supposed to know? I didn't spend many nights with Mal in public parks trying to contact unseen magical creatures.

Hands apparently warm enough, Mallory cupped them in front of her. A spark appeared, which grew larger and brighter as she concentrated, lips moving and head bobbing in some silent motion. I'd have guessed she was singing a favorite Muse song, but that would probably also be wrong, so I kept it to myself.

The spark blossomed to the size of a golf ball, then a baseball, then a softball, the light bright enough to shine blue through her hands, like when I'd held my fingers over a flashlight as a child.

When the orb of light, the same pale blue as a summer sky, was large enough, she opened her eyes. "Carefully," she murmured to herself, and leaned forward, placed the ball on the platter. It hovered there, vibrating with power, casting pale light on our faces.

I glanced around, hoped no one was watching us. Sorcerers were out of the closet, but that didn't mean it was a good idea for humans to watch this little experiment. Considering the weather, they might have called the CPD first, asked questions later.

Mallory sat back again, cleared her throat. "We've created a receiver. We'll see if we can dial it in." She put a hand over the fireball, fingers extended, and slapped the air on top of it.

The motion created a dull, round sound that rippled the air, just like she'd dropped a pebble in a lake. The circles moved out from the orb, to us, through us, until they diffused a few yards away.

Hand over the orb, ear cocked to the sky, Mallory waited. "We're here," she said. "And we're looking for you."

She hit the orb again, making another dull sound and sending another wave rippling.

But there was still no response. Not that I was entirely sure what kind of response we were supposed to receive.

"What are we hoping to hear?" Ethan asked.

"Acknowledgment," Mallory said. "I know it can hear me. The messages are bouncing back."

"Like radar," Ethan said, and Mallory nodded.

"The concussion finds something, the message comes back. I can sense it." She lifted her gaze to Catcher. "You?"

He nodded. "Faintly, but yeah. There's something out there."

"Then we try it louder," she said. She resituated herself, blew out a breath, and positioned her hand over the orb again. She gave the orb another *whack*, then a second, and a third.

The sounds seemed to grow louder, deeper, with each hit, until it felt like the vibrations would stop my heart.

This time, the greetings made it through. And the voice didn't like our intrusion.

Lightning ripped across the sky, thunder cracking like the shot of a rifle at point-blank range. Power burst across the field like a slapping hand, and then I was flying, the city lights blurred with movement.

I hit the ground on my back, my diaphragm seizing with shock, head rapping against the ground, my fingers and toes tingling with heat and energy.

I lay there for a moment in the grass, looking up at the few stars that had managed to pierce the sky. Each was surrounded by a halo of light, and bees buzzed in my ears.

Slowly, I pushed up on my elbows, looked around. Ethan, Catcher, and Mallory were on the ground, too, all blinking up at the sky. We'd fallen perpendicularly to one another, our bodies aligned like the points of a compass. And between us, the orb still glowed.

"Well," Mallory said, pushing hair from her face.

I sat up, put a hand on my forehead, as if that would stop the world from spinning. "That was not a success. That was some kind of magical grenade."

"It was a success," Mallory said, and we all looked at her.

"How?" Ethan asked, brushing snow from his sleeves.

"We know it heard us. And we know it can fight back." She moved to her knees, poked at the rosemary with a finger, then sat back on her heels. She looked up at the sky, closed her eyes, the breeze blowing her hair across her pinked cheeks. After a moment of silence, she looked at us. "We need to try again."

"No." This time, Ethan said it. "Absolutely not."

"Agreed," I said. "When you poke the bear and it tries to tear your face off, you regroup and replan."

Ethan rubbed the back of his head. "Or perhaps you can try again solo and give us the report later. While we're several miles away."

Mallory sat up but looked back at the ground, frowning. "Look, even if the answers are somehow automatic, if the delusions are just emotions trapped in the magic, and no *thing* is actually asking for help, we can still learn from it. If we keep asking questions, maybe we can get a sense of its spread, of its size, from the answers we get back."

"Like echoes," I offered.

"Like echoes," she agreed. "We're running out of time. She's getting ready for something big, and that big is going to happen very, very soon. If we aren't prepared for it, it's going to be worse than Towerline."

Towerline had been half success and half disaster, with plenty of injuries and destruction.

Ethan opened his mouth but closed it again and glanced at Catcher, who was rolling his head, then his shoulders, as if trying to loosen a stubborn ache. Then he looked at us.

"We're all in one piece," Catcher said. "I'm not suggesting you're cowards if you don't try again, but . . ."

"But you're subtly implying it," Ethan said.

Catcher grinned. "This is magic, friends. It's a dangerous game. Maybe vampires can't hack it."

Ethan's eyes blazed silver. "Is that a dare?"

"If that's what it takes." Catcher looked at me. "We have to try something. This is currently the only thing we know to try."

I couldn't argue with that logic, so I looked at Mallory. She'd pulled a small kraft-paper notebook from her bag, was thumbing through it. "Just give me a minute."

I narrowed my gaze at Catcher. "Beer and pizza after this, and you're paying."

His lips curved into a smirk. "You're a cheap date."

"That is one of her finer qualities," said my husband.

I elbowed him, and we settled back into our positions.

"It's getting colder," Catcher said. "We should probably move this along while we can still function."

I made a sarcastic noise. "Go swimming in the river and then talk to me about cold."

"My little mermaid," Ethan murmured, as Mallory positioned a hand over the orb again.

This time, a single tap. "We're here to listen," she said, "not to harm you."

We sat in the cold darkness, ears perked for any response. But there was none.

Mallory shook her head, wet her lips, and hit the orb again. "If you talk to us, we can try to help you."

She nearly squealed when the orb pulsed with light, and jumped backward.

It started as a whisper, a faint and faraway call. And with each percussion the sound lengthened, heightened, grew.

help.

Help.

HELP.

HELP.

The voice was masculine. It was one sound and many, a singular cry and a million voices. That was probably the "depth" Winston had mentioned.

"Whiskey Tango Foxtrot," Mallory murmured, as we stared at the thrumming orb.

HELLO. HELP ME.

The volume was huge, as if the sound was a room that had suddenly enclosed us, sucking out the air and leaving behind only the fear, the terror. It wasn't just a cry, but a demand for attention. Not just a plea, but an order.

This was panic and anger and frustration and grief, a cocktail of hopelessness. And it wasn't the kind of emotion that dulled the senses but the kind that heightened them. The kind that made every noise seem a timpani drum, every caress a blinding burn. Irritation began to itch under my skin, the emotion weighted with despair.

This had to be what the delusional had been hearing. Little wonder they'd been terrified, Winston and the others. Little wonder they'd begged for help, and had considered death to stop the pain.

"They weren't delusional," Catcher quietly whispered. "Not even close."

"Hello," Mallory said to the orb. "We are here in Chicago with you. Where are you? How can we help?"

HELLO. HELP ME.

"It sounds like a recording," Ethan quietly said. "Just reflected thoughts."

HELP ME. HELLO. HELP ME. HELLO. HELP ME. HELLO.

The words became faster, seemed more insistent, as if they carried more emotional push—and more magical baggage.

"We're here," Mallory said. "Can you tell us where you are? Can you tell us how to help you?"

Silence.

I AM . . .

The orb throbbed with each word.

I AM . . .

"It's sentient," Mallory quietly said.

"That's not possible," Ethan quietly said. "Latent magic isn't alive."

The magic disagreed. *I AM!* it screamed, loud enough that we clamped our hands over our ears.

I AM! The orb exploded, shooting the silver platter into the air.

Ethan threw an arm over me, pushed me to the ground as magic splintered the air around us. The concussion of sound echoed across the bandstand, back and forth across the buildings near us like a bomb.

And then, just as suddenly as the explosion had happened, the world became quiet again.

We sat up cautiously, looked around us. The orb was gone, and with it the platter and rosemary. And there was a hole in the middle of the blanket, the edges still marked by smoking char.

"Dibs on not telling Helen about the platter," I said quickly, before Ethan could object.

Ethan growled his displeasure. "Everyone okay?"

"Fine here," Catcher said, helping Mallory sit up. There was a streak of smoke on her face, but her limbs were still connected, which she confirmed by patting down each arm and leg.

"Well," she said, then huffed. "The source of the city's delusions is kind of an asshole."

As if that source were insulted by the statement, a gust of icy wind sliced across the lawn, carrying with it the same chemical scent that had marked the others who'd heard the delusions. The smell surrounded us like a fog.

And this time, as we sat in the middle of downtown Chicago on a blanket in the snow, I realized how familiar that smell was.

No, I thought. Not smell. *Smells.*

It wasn't really industrial, or chemical. It was industrial and chemical. It was exhaust and people and movement and life. It was river and lake and enormous sky. It was Chicago, as if the city had been distilled to its essence, to an elixir that carried hints of all the things that existed inside its borders.

Or inside the alchemical web Sorcha had created, the one that had stretched out from Towerline like a spider's.

I thought of what Winston had painted in his small, tattered notebook, and the painting of what even Winston thought had been rows of teeth—jagged and uneven—from the mouth that had screamed his delusions.

They weren't teeth, I realized, looking back at the uneven line of buildings to the east. He'd drawn the skyline. He'd drawn Chicago.

He'd heard *Chicago*. Somehow, because of magic I didn't understand, he'd heard Chicago.

"Merit?" Mallory asked, head tilted as she studied me.

"Winston Styles painted images that came to him when he heard the voice. He drew the skyline," I said. "He heard Chicago. The smell isn't the magic, or a chemical. It's Chicago. Squeezed down and distilled, but Chicago all the same."

None of them looked convinced. "Close your eyes," I said. "Close your eyes, and think about the scent."

They looked even more skeptical about that idea. But they did it.

"Traffic," Mallory said after a minute. "Exhaust."

"And beneath that?" I asked.

She frowned.

"Smoke. And the lake. And the wind blowing in from the prairies. Hot dogs and hot beef and summertime grills. Bodies and sweat and tears." She opened her eyes. "It's like someone made a perfume of Chicago—all of it together."

Ethan and Catcher inhaled deeply, held the air in their bodies as if to measure its contents.

"Pizza," Ethan said.

"Yeah," Catcher said. "I mean, a lot of exhaust and smoke, but there's a thread of sausage, maybe?"

"The delusions aren't delusions," I said. "They're hearing *Chicago*."

"The voice is sentient," Catcher said. "Chicago isn't. That's not possible."

"There shouldn't be snow on the ground in August," Mallory said. "There shouldn't be people trying to harm themselves to alleviate their delusions. We don't have the luxury of 'possible' right now. But," she added, "I think you're right about the city—Chicago is a really big place. *If* it was possible a city could be sentient, and *if* Chicago was that lucky, one-in-a-million city, I'm pretty sure there'd be more than a single voice and some stink."

"Like dancing Chicago dogs?" Catcher asked.

"Something. Unfortunately, that doesn't help us say what it is." Mallory's gaze narrowed dangerously. "But I aim to find out."

We were less than an hour from dawn, so we skipped the previous food and beer plan, opted to head back to the House. The ride was silent, all of us thinking, wondering what was happening in Chicago. Catcher parked on the street, and we walked silently into the House.

Mallory yawned hugely but rolled her shoulders as if to shrug off exhaustion. "I need time to read and think," she said. "I'm going to hole up in the library for a little while if that's okay with you."

"It's fine by me," Ethan said. "But don't forget to take care of yourself, to sleep."

She nodded. "I'll sleep when I feel better. When I've conquered this."

"I'll tell Chuck what we've found," Catcher said.

"Will he want to tell the mayor?" Ethan asked, closing and locking the door behind us.

Catcher tugged his ear. "Not yet, I think. Not until we can really tell her what it is. But that will be his call."

Ethan nodded. "Let's meet at dusk. And no magic in the House."

"Trust me," Mallory said. "I want no more of this magic until we have some information."

"A good plan for all of us," Ethan said, and we headed upstairs.

"There is not a Margot basket big enough for this day," I said when we were alone again. I pulled off my boots, let them drop heavily to the floor.

The voice had been so sad, so angry, so frustrated, and it felt like those emotions still clung to me. And when that door was opened, the other emotions I'd pushed aside—the grief I still felt from our visit to the green land—rushed forward again.

Gabriel, Claudia. The messages about the possibility of our child were getting grimmer, and the possibility of having a child seemed to slip further and further away.

Ethan grunted, walked to the desk, looked over the basket she had assembled. And then smiled. "I believe you may want to reconsider that statement, Sentinel."

I doubted reconsideration was necessary, but indulged him with a look at the basket.

"Mmmph," was the closest approximation to the sound that I made. "I'm not really hungry."

I walked to the window, pushed back the heavy silk curtain with a finger. The world outside was dark and cold, frost already gathered on the glass.

"Not hungry?" Ethan joked, pulling his shirt over his head. "How is that possible?"

When I didn't answer, he moved closer, turned me toward him, and frowned down at what he saw. "You're troubled," he said, stroking a thumb along my jaw.

I paused, fearing I'd sound ridiculous, but remembered he was my husband, my partner, my confidant and friend, so I trusted him with it.

"I was thinking about the green land, and the child we saw there. It hurt. Seeing her, and having her taken away."

"We weren't really there," he said kindly, "and she wasn't really taken away."

"It felt real. It hurt like it was real, and Gabriel said nothing was guaranteed. What if that's really our future? In our time, instead of Claudia's, but the same kind of loss?"

"It wasn't our future," Ethan said. "It was an illusion."

But sadness had gripped me, wrapped fingers around my heart, and wasn't ready to let go. "And even if it was," I began, and turned back to the window. "Look at the city, Ethan. This is our legacy: violent sorceresses, enemies on our doorstep, humans driven mad by magic. Why would we even want to bring a child into this world? Into Sorcha's world?"

"It's not Sorcha's world," Ethan said, his tone as sharp as a knife. "It is *our* world. She is intruding, and we will handle her as we always have."

I shook my head. "Even if we could have a child, children are fragile."

"Children are resilient, and our child will be immortal."

"So we assume. But we don't know that. Not really. We don't know anything about the biology, how it would work. And if she's the only one—the only vampire kid? What kind of life would that be? What kind of life would she have?"

"Where is this coming from?"

I flung a hand toward the window. "From out there. From in here. From every night we have to fight to stay alive. From wondering if that will ever end."

"It's not like you to be afraid."

"It isn't every night that I'm facing down a city that is somehow possessed with magic. Only an idiot wouldn't be afraid."

"Merit, it's been a long night punctuated with fear and anger and magic. You just need sleep." His voice was soft and kind, and that nearly brought me to tears again. I didn't want pity or consolation; this sadness, this near grief, demanded my full attention.

"I don't need sleep." My voice sounded petulant even to me. And that only made me feel worse.

"Then perhaps I might have said that it's not like you to back down in the face of fear."

"Is that what we'd be doing? Backing down? Or just being logical?"

This time, his tone was firmer. "Nothing you've said is logical."

"Don't be condescending."

Temper flashed in his eyes. "I am not condescending. I am expecting bravery from you. If you're afraid, we'll work through it. But we will not back down because of her. We will not let her destroy our family before we have a chance to begin it."

"Nothing is certain," I said, thinking of Gabe and Claudia. "And maybe I don't want any more risk."

"Then maybe you aren't acting like the Sentinel of this House."

I had no words for him, no possible response. I didn't like feeling afraid, and certainly didn't like showing that fear to him. But that didn't seem to matter. The fear still gripped me, dark and icy, just as winter had apparently gripped the city.

We stared at each other in silence until automatic shades descended over the windows, until the sun breached the horizon.

We slept because the sun demanded it, but there was a cold gap between us.

CHAPTER SEVENTEEN

SNOWBALL

I'd planned to go for a run at dusk, hoping the chill in the air would clear my head—and some of the tension that still lingered between Ethan and me.

Wondering what I should wear—how bundled I'd need to be against Sorcha's chill—I pushed back one heavy curtain. And stared at the canvas of white that glowed beneath a clear, dark sky.

"Ethan."

He was already dressed, was flipping through the *Tribune*. He moved behind me, and I heard the catch in his breath when he realized what we were facing.

It looked like the city had been dipped into liquid nitrogen—or dropped into an ice age. There was a foot of snow on the ground, and every surface above the ground—trees, fence, the houses beyond it—was covered in gleaming, blue-white ice or hanging with icicles as sharp as stilettos.

The street outside, usually busy into the early hours of the night, was empty of cars. The vehicles that had been parked on the side of the road were coated in snow and ice so thick it looked like rubber. If the entire city was like this, she'd have brought the city to a standstill.

Dread settled low in my gut.

"I hadn't checked my phone yet," Ethan said. "I was giving myself—us—a chance to talk first."

I looked back at him, saw the same worry in his eyes. "There will be messages galore. My grandfather, the other Houses. The mayor." I looked back at the window. Hell, if the rest of the city was like this, the Illinois National Guard would probably be beating down our door.

"Everyone," he agreed. "This is not the type of thing we can push aside or ignore. This will require a response."

There was a pounding on the door.

"And I guess we won't have the luxury of that talk," he said, and looked at me for a moment before turning for the door.

He opened it, found Luc with fist raised, ready to knock again. Luc wore a Cadogan House Track T-shirt with jeans and scuffed cowboy boots, his hair more tousled than usual.

"Sorry for the interruption, Sire, but I'm guessing you hadn't checked your messages." He met my gaze, nodded. "Mrs. Sire."

"I hadn't clocked in yet," Ethan said. "What's wrong?"

"If you'd come downstairs? Mallory and Catcher are already down there."

Ethan nodded, glanced back at me, saw that I still wore pajamas. "We'll be down in a moment. As soon as Merit's dressed."

Luc nodded. "We're in your office."

Snow or not, I wasn't going for a run.

We were downstairs in three and a half minutes, and walked into Ethan's office to find Catcher, Mallory, Malik, Lindsey, and Luc already assembled. All of them were standing, and all had their gazes on the television built into one of the shelves on the far wall.

Catcher and Mallory were still in pajamas—Cadogan House T-shirts and plaid bottoms they'd probably borrowed from Helen for the night. They looked like they hadn't slept much.

The television was tuned to a news station, where a male reporter stood in front of the Towerline barricade. He wore a coat, scarf, gloves, and hat, and he still looked cold. Behind him, the street was empty and slicked like an ice rink.

"I'm here in front of the Towerline building," he said as we moved into the crowd, closer to the television, "where moments ago, the sorceress Sorcha Reed appeared to deliver a chilling ultimatum to the city of Chicago. Let's watch that footage again."

Cold fear snaked down my spine.

The shot switched to the previously recorded footage—Sorcha, with the golden light of dusk around her—standing in the snow that covered Towerline square. Either she was ignoring the cold, or she'd magicked it so it didn't affect her. Weather be damned, she wore an emerald ball gown. It was long-sleeved and fitted on the top, a voluminous skirt on the bottom, all of it covered in geometric lace over mesh in the same deep green. Her hair, thick and blond, curled prettily over her shoulders.

She stood with perfect posture, her hands behind her, the dress's glass beads and sequins sparkling in the spotlights and camera flashes. The smile on her face was contented and only a little smug, like a student showing off her first-prize ribbon at the science fair.

"Good evening, citizens of Chicago. I hope you've enjoyed this bracing taste of my powers." She looked around, pride gleaming in her eyes. "It took remarkably little effort on my part, although it was, of course, helped along by the sophomoric efforts of the sorcerer Mallory Carmichael."

Mallory cursed under her breath.

I didn't like the way she used "sorcerer" like a title, like we were characters in a spaghetti Western, and she planned to take care of us at dawn on a dusty, sun-bleached road between worn wooden buildings.

"Rest assured that this is only the beginning—a sample of my practiced powers. And I intend to use them. I had a plan for this city, one that would bring us into a new era. That plan was ruined by your supernaturals, your law enforcement officials, because they are too shortsighted, too stupid, to see the virtue of it."

Some of that calm and collected visage, the debutante-trained smile, faltered, like a mask slipping away.

"You have debts to pay. I will collect them. I will take back what you've taken from me, and I will take what I am owed."

She smiled, and it was chilling. It was a predator's smile, amoral and sharp.

"I will take this city in payment of your debts, or I will take the traitors. If Merit of Cadogan House and Mallory Carmichael are delivered to me by dawn, I will release Chicago."

There was a gasp in the room—maybe it came from me?—and a few heads turned to look at Mallory and me before staring at Sorcha again.

"If you do as I've asked you—this one small thing that I've asked you—the ice will melt, and the temperatures will climb, and you can have your city back." Her eyes darkened, like storm clouds passing over. Although she smiled pleasantly, there was nothing pleasant in her eyes. "If you do not, if you deny me what I am owed, you will learn how vindictive I can be. It's such a small thing to ask, don't you think? Two lives, in exchange for three million?"

She waited, as if allowing the entire city to gasp, and slid her hands into pockets tucked into the voluminous skirt. "You have ten hours. I hope you're smart enough to make the right decision."

There was a movie-worthy swirl of smoke—green, of course—and she disappeared, the scuffed snow the only evidence that she'd been there.

"Okay," Lindsey said into the intervening silence. "I'm going to cut the tension by saying she's a stone-cold bitch. But it truly pisses me off how gorgeous she is. Can I have a fashion crush on my mortal enemy?"

"Yes," Mallory said, gaze narrowed on the screen. "Unrelated issues."

"Good. Because that dress was *sick*. I hate her."

"Because of fashion or mortal enemy?" I wondered.

"Yes," was Lindsey's answer. "Because of that."

"She's bluffing," Catcher said, his voice low and dangerous, like fury only barely bridled. "She doesn't have that kind of power— not to destroy the city." But he didn't sound entirely certain.

"She only needs our fear," Mallory said. "And she has plenty of that to do this. Enough to extort the mayor and everyone else. At least she's not passive-aggressive."

"She's aggressive-aggressive," Catcher said. "And I want a chance at her this time."

"She didn't ask for you," Mallory said. "She asked for us."

"She won't get you," Ethan said. I looked at him, found his gaze on me, eyes full of flashing heat. "Under no circumstances will you be handed over to Sorcha Reed."

"Seconded," Catcher said, a deep timbre to his voice, as if he'd imbued the word itself with magic.

Like me, Mallory looked ready to argue. Not that I wanted to hand myself over to Sorcha—I'd seen what she could do. But nor did I want to sacrifice Chicago—and every person in it—to her sociopathy. There had to be a middle ground between giving in and giving up.

And both of us were smart enough to pick our battles. Mallory and I exchanged a look and the smallest of nods. We'd do what we had to do, to protect our city, our people, and our men.

"We took her out once," she said, with a long look at her husband.

"And she'd have stayed that way if the CPD hadn't lost her. We'll take her out again."

The phones started ringing, the modern-day warning siren, and we pulled them out. "Jonah," I said, reading mine. "Letting us know Gray House has our back."

"Your grandfather," Catcher said. "He and Jeff are on their way; the mayor wants a strategy meeting in two hours." He looked up. "We won't be able to avoid it."

"And the *Tribune* asking for a quote." Ethan growled the words, then tossed his phone into an empty chair, where he apparently planned to ignore it.

"It wouldn't be a bad idea to talk to them," Luc said.

The fury in Ethan's face made him seem as much wolf as vampire. "She has asked for my wife's life in exchange for this city. They have no right to justify that demand with questions about whether I'll accede to it. Whether I'll turn Merit over to satisfy the whims of a woman who is certifiable."

Ethan, I silently said, and put a hand on his arm. *This won't help. And he isn't our enemy.*

The room was heavy and silent for a moment, the tension as thick as fog, and then he nodded and took a step back.

"You should tell them what you think," Luc said, and held up his hands before Ethan could argue. "I know you don't like press conferences. But we should consider getting our side of the story out there."

"In less than ten hours, I turn over my wife, or Sorcha destroys the city. Getting my story out there isn't a high priority."

"You are a stubborn man."

"I am," Ethan said. "And I'll be damned if my city is brought down by the Wicked Witch of the Midwest."

Cut and print.

*   *   *

We took time to get organized, get food, and for Mallory and Catcher to get showered. We gathered again in Ethan's office, where the screen now displayed the dossier Luc had put together about Sorcha Reed.

"If we want to beat the Wicked Witch," Luc said, "we have to predict her magic. And if we want to predict her magic, we have to know how she ticks."

"Wicked Bitch, more like," Lindsey muttered.

"No objection there," Ethan said.

Luc nodded. "First, Mallory and Catcher have an update."

Mallory, who'd gotten dressed while we'd gotten ready for the meeting, rose from the couch. Her blue hair was in a high bun today, her petite body swamped by a Cadogan House sweatshirt. She looked a little like a sophomore during finals week. It was a look she pulled off pretty well.

"Thanks to Merit," she said, "we've made quite a bit of progress."

Hope made my heart beat faster. "You found something in the notes?"

"We did," Mallory said. "Kind of. So, the notes are basically ramblings, which is probably not surprising given how they were ordered around the room. It looks like tidbits of spells she was interested in, ideas for projects, stuff like that. It was basically a really obsessive bulletin board. Together, the pieces don't make much sense. So you have to consider them individually. And individually, they didn't make much sense, either. Until I got to this."

She offered me the piece of paper. It was a photocopy of what looked like a book or journal page. The top half of the page was filled with handwritten words in the small script of gilded medieval manuscripts. The bottom half of the page bore sketches drawn in a thin, scraggly line. What looked like a globe near what looked like a star, with two-dimensional renderings of humans.

"It looks old," I said. "But not particularly familiar."

"Nor to me," she said. "Especially the completely whacked-out language. But I did a little sleuthing. It's a page from the Danzig Manuscript."

"You're kidding," I said, but gave the page another look.

"And what is the Danzig Manuscript?" Luc asked.

I hadn't actually seen the Danzig Manuscript, but I knew enough about it. "A book written in the seventeenth century," I said. "Drawings of plants and animals that didn't exist and writings that weren't in any identifiable language." Mallory was right—the letter forms weren't entirely clear on this photocopied page, but it wasn't a Latin alphabet, or Cyrillic, or any alphabet I recognized.

"There are a few dozen theories on what the book's supposed to mean," I said. "Whether it was encoded or encrypted, the last writing in a lost language, the ramblings of a madman, a very old practical joke."

"And Ethan happens to have a facsimile of the book in his magnificent library."

Mallory reached out a hand to Catcher, who offered her a large, dark leather book. She opened the book to the page she'd marked with a ribbon. It matched the page from Sorcha's office exactly.

Ethan looked at the book over my shoulder. "And no one has conclusively determined what it means?"

"Not in four hundred years," I said.

Mallory smiled slyly. "Well, not until tonight."

I looked up, stared at her. "What?"

"I translated the Danzig Manuscript."

"You're joking."

Her grin was huge, proud. "I am not joking. It took me a good hour to figure out the trick," she said with a wink. "But I have skills most academics lack."

"Skills?" I asked, then looked down at the page again.

"Abracadabra," Mallory said, and drew a symbol in the air above the text.

Bright magic spilled into the air, and with it the slightly musty scent of old books, of dark and cool library aisles. The letter forms stretched and shifted like they were animated, then reassembled themselves into Latin letter forms and English.

I flipped to the next page, then the next. All of them had been translated by Mallory's magic.

"Holy shit, Mallory." I looked up at her. "You translated the Danzig Manuscript."

"I know, right?" She blew on her fingernails, buffed them on her shirt. "I'm a badass. Fortunately, the magic is contained in the manuscript's words, not the pages. That's why this little translation works on Ethan's facsimile."

"So what is it?" Lindsey asked. "And what's the significance here?"

"As it turns out, the Danzig Manuscript isn't a joke or ramblings, although it was encrypted. It's a grimoire."

"A spell book?" I asked.

Mallory nodded. "Of a sorcerer named, I kid you not, Portnoy the Ugly. The words are in English, but they're in Portnoy's magical shorthand, which is taking time to translate. We started with the page you found in Sorcha's office."

She pointed to the globe, the circle of crudely drawn humans. "The text describes a group of humans with powerful emotions. Strong emotions that are cast off into the world." She traced a finger to the starlike figure. "Magic unites those emotions, gives them a spark. A creature is born from that collective spirit. It is alive, and it is sentient."

She lifted her gaze to us. "It's called an Egregore. That's whose voice we hear."

The room went silent.

"How?" Ethan said.

"Sorcha's Trojan horse," Mallory said. "The magic that didn't dissipate after Towerline."

Catcher leaned forward. "Think about the emotions people were feeling around Towerline when the battle occurred. People were freaked out by the fight, the supernaturals, the river, the possibility of the building falling over. The city was in crisis, and that was in addition to all the other things they normally worry about. All that fear, anger, and worry was gathered together by Sorcha's magic."

"It was distilled," Mallory said. "Just like the scent of that magic is the distilled essence of Chicago."

"We're hearing the Egregore," Ethan quietly said, studying the picture, then lifting his gaze to Mallory. "Magic creating life?"

"A form of it, anyway."

"And why would she do all this?" Ethan asked. "Create this collective magic? Work to create this Egregore? To foster the delusions? To use them as a weapon?"

"I think the delusions are a side effect," Catcher said. "There were thousands of people near Towerline, but the delusions have been relatively rare, sporadic, and geographically focused. That's probably because Sorcha's magic didn't disseminate evenly."

"The fact that she's never been trained hurts her," Mallory said, nodding. "She's got skills, sure. But it's raw power, untrained."

"And that's much more dangerous," Ethan said. "Not to mention the fact that she's narcissistic and unpredictable. She has changed the weather. Endangered the lives of millions. Brought the city to a standstill because she could." He glanced at Mallory. "Because you didn't let her have her way at Towerline."

"She's acting like a hormonal teenager," Lindsey said. "She is basically the worst *Sweet Valley High* novel ever written."

"Based on what we know about her," Luc said, "that's how

she operated her entire life. She gets what she wants, usually because someone paid for it."

I nodded. "She doesn't even fight her own battles. She used alchemy to control sups so they could do the fighting for her. She wants to win the war, but she doesn't want to fight it. She wants power with impunity."

"She wants a *weapon*," Catcher concluded, nodding at me. "Just like we were supposed to be."

"The Egregore is sentient," I said. "If she can control it, it can fight us on her behalf."

Mallory nodded. "We think that's where she's going, too." She gestured to the book. "But we haven't had time to get further in the book, so we don't know what she'll try next, or how the weather relates to it."

"Another question," I said. "If the Egregore is going to be her weapon, why does she want us? Why the ultimatum?"

"Revenge," Ethan said, and the word hung in the air, heavy and dangerous.

"I'm sure that's part of it," Mallory said. "But that can't be all of it. She's creating a spectacle, sure. But she's also giving us a chance to prepare, to be ready. To be armed. We're missing something. Something involving the Egregore and us together. I just can't see what it is. I either need more time to work through the Danzig"—she turned to Catcher—"or I need to go to the source."

Catcher glared back. "Don't even think what you're thinking. Jumping into her arms won't change anything."

"I love you, but you don't even know the half of what I'm thinking right now." Mallory's teeth were gritted with anger, every word bitten off like a bitter seed.

"He's right."

We looked back at my grandfather in the doorway. He walked in, Jeff by his side.

"How much of that did you get?" Catcher asked.

"Enough," he said. "We'll get the details later." He sat down beside Mallory, clasped his hands together. "Even if you and Merit walked right up to her, offered yourselves, do you think it would make a difference? Do you think it would change anything?"

"Probably not," Mallory admitted. "But if there's a one percent chance she'd back down? That if we go to her, turn ourselves in, she takes her ice and her couture and walks away? Isn't that worth taking to save the city?"

"Mallory," Catcher said, "you know the math doesn't work that way."

"It's just an example," she said, and rubbed a hand over her face.

It might have been an example, but she had a point. I didn't want that many people on my conscience, weighing it down.

"I need more time," she said. "We all need more time."

"I'm sure she realizes that," Ethan said. "Which is why time is a luxury she isn't giving us." Ethan looked at my grandfather. "What's the situation outside?"

"The city is frozen and, because of it, quiet. The governor has called in the National Guard, and they're helping those who've opted to evacuate. There've been two more instances of humans having delusions, which sent four people to the hospital. No fatalities, thank goodness. And there are protestors on your lawn."

"Protesting?" Ethan said, gritting out the word. "Protesting what?"

My grandfather looked at me. "They demand Merit and Mallory immediately surrender for the safety of the city."

Protestors were nothing new. Much like the House's fans, their numbers waxed and waned, usually depending on the weather and our news coverage. But that didn't much matter to Ethan.

His magic flared like a burst of energy from the sun. "They

CHAPTER EIGHTEEN

—◆— ⚎◆⚎ —◆—

MERE MORTALS

We followed him down the hall, reaching the foyer as he pulled open the door with enough force that it bounced against the wall, leaving a dent in the plaster.

There were vampires in the hallway, in the foyer. Vampires bundled against the chill, and their gazes slipped away as we moved past them. There was guilt in their eyes—either that Mallory and I had been the unlucky ones called out, or that they'd thought accepting Sorcha's proposal was a good idea.

I bit my tongue, kept my eyes on Ethan. Ignoring the snow, the ice, the chill, Ethan strode down the sidewalk like a warrior heading into battle, then through the gate to the sidewalk outside.

We trailed him, stopped behind him on the sidewalk, where he stared down at the thirteen humans who'd taken up positions on the strip of snow between sidewalk and street. They were bundled up against the weather, and they'd brought camp and lawn chairs, blankets, mugs of hot chocolate.

They looked cold and a little bit pitiful, but Ethan didn't seem to care. Defenseless or not, he gave no quarter.

His shoulders were back, his feet planted, his hands fisted at his sides. The wind blew back his hair, the lapels of his expensive jacket, so he looked like an ancient raider come to claim his prize.

"You're here, in front of my House, drinking coffee and cocoa, and advocating murder. Can you be so casual about it? So callous?"

"They're immortal," said a large, pale woman in a camp chair, her gloved hands around an insulated mug. "So turn them over. What's the worst thing that could happen?"

"Mallory isn't immortal," Ethan said. "And being immortal doesn't mean you can't be killed. It means you don't age." I could hear *dimwit* as the unspoken punctuation to his sentence, but he managed not to voice it. "They are vulnerable."

"We're more vulnerable," said a thin, tan man a few seats over. "We're human. Look what she's already done to our city."

"It's our city, too," Ethan said.

"It was ours first." A large man in a ball cap, puffy Cubs jacket, and jeans pushed aside his blanket and stood up, knocking over his lawn chair in the process. "If it wasn't for you, we wouldn't be in this situation."

Slowly, Ethan turned his gaze on the man. "How, exactly, is this our fault?"

"You riled her up. Pissed her off." He looked around, nodding at the others, trying to get them to throw their hates into the ring. "This fight doesn't have anything to do with us. It's between you supernaturals, and you need to work it out for yourselves."

"This fight has nothing to do with *us*," Ethan gritted out, frustration obviously rising. "A madwoman wants to use magic to put the city under her control, under her power. She is a demagogue with no conscience, and through no fault of ours. But we're the only ones who seem interested in trying to stop her." He looked at the humans again. "If she'd asked for your wives, your husbands, your children, would you be so eager to hand them over? And yet, here you are, talking about things you don't even try to understand."

"You think you're better than us," said the man in the ball cap. "That's the thing, right?" He gestured toward Cadogan House. "You live in some big House, wear your fancy suits. You don't know what it's like to be out there, working every day, and have magic throw your whole world into a spin. The world would be better off without magic in it."

He'd said so many incorrect things, so many absolutely wrong things, that Ethan looked momentarily dumbstruck. "Get off my lawn," he said through bared teeth.

"We got constitutional rights."

Ethan took a step forward. He was a good five inches taller than the man, with all the muscle and power of vampirism.

"I doubt you understand what that phrase actually means, given the context you've used it in. But if you want to protest, do it across the street. Better yet, instead of sitting here, chatting with your friends and complaining, go do something about it. Go to the Ombudsman's office and volunteer. Go to a charitable organization and donate your time." He spread his gaze over all of them, covering them in furious disapproval. "But don't you dare think that sitting here and advocating my wife's murder is something I will allow. You have two minutes until I take things into my own hands. I suggest you use it wisely."

He stared at them, this ancient raider, and waited for them to flinch.

And of course, they did. It didn't take bravery to advocate that someone else throw their family to the wolf.

The man with the ball cap muttered insults, but he picked up his chair. The rest of them looked at least a little chagrined, and three climbed into waiting cars, deciding either the weather or the vampires weren't worth the trouble.

"They'll come back," my grandfather said, when the last one had decamped to the strip of grass across the street.

"They will," Ethan acknowledged. "But perhaps a few of them will think before they demand our blood in exchange."

He looked back at me, his gaze locked to mine for a very long time. *You promised me eternity, Sentinel,* he said. *I intend to collect.*

Because the snow and ice would make getting downtown more difficult than usual, our two hours was something more like seventy minutes. And then it was time to head downtown again and talk to the mayor about Sorcha's threat.

"Are you nervous?" Mallory asked as we walked through the foyer to the front door and the SUV that waited outside. Catcher would drive us to the mayor's office. Everyone in the House would stay here, gates shut, with the House on high alert. My grandfather would drive separately, meet us there. In the meantime, Jeff would work with Luc to apprise the other Houses, our supernatural allies, about the situation.

"Nothing to be nervous about," I said. That was mostly a lie, because I didn't trust human politicians—with the possible exception of Seth Tate. But she looked nervous. That wasn't a common emotion for Mallory, but this particular debacle mixed powerful sorcery, old magic, and extortion, and she hadn't gotten much sleep. I could be strong for her. "This is just a strategy session."

"A strategy session," Mallory said, dipping her chin inside her thick scarf. "Right. Just going to talk a few things over with the mayor."

"That's precisely what we're going to do," Ethan said, putting a supportive hand on her shoulder and giving me a look behind her back, a nod that said we were in this together.

Good. Because that knot of worry was back. I didn't like being worried. I'd come far enough as a vampire and Sentinel that I preferred a good old-fashioned fight to magic wrangling.

A few hardy and wrong-minded souls still sat on the strip of snow across the street, clearly convinced of their rightness, the rationality of Sorcha's two-for-three-million calculation. Would it be the same, I wondered, if she'd asked for one of their wives or husbands or children? I seriously doubted it.

Once we were in the SUV, the going was slow, and Catcher took his time driving through the alternating mix of crusty slush and snow-covered ice. Beyond Hyde Park, the world was mostly quiet. The El wasn't running; icicles hung from the elevated platforms, as sharp as sharks' teeth. Few vehicles braved the roads, and then only snowplows, Guard vehicles, and cars headed out of Chicago, hoping to get clear before things got worse.

There were no people downtown. Those who were still in the city had stayed indoors, because of either the chill in the air or the fear that hung with it.

We parked in front of the building and headed inside.

The mayor asked that we meet her not in her office, but on the roof of City Hall. We went through security, then were escorted up an elevator and into a long hallway.

Lane stood at the end, gaze on a phone, fingers skimming and sliding along the screen. He looked up, nodded. "She's waiting for you," he said, then opened a heavy door beside him, sending a gust of cold air down the hallway.

We stepped outside and onto the building's roof—and into a frozen world. The city spread out around us, most of it gleaming with the ice and snow that Sorcha had managed to dump in less than twenty-four hours. The cold had a boundary; we'd seen it on the map last night. But the parts of the world that remained green weren't visible from up here.

To the northeast, clouds still swirled over the Towerline building. They didn't look any bigger or fiercer than they had the night before, but until we figured out exactly what Sorcha was doing, I wasn't sure that mattered much. How much colder could Chicago get?

Apparently, very cold. The wind on the roof was a thousand ice picks, harsh enough to make breathing feel like fire. Snow was bundled over what looked like planter boxes, with rows between for walking.

The mayor, bundled in a long, baffled down coat, was crouching near one of the piles of snow, sweeping the crust of it back from the plants beneath. Three guards in black suits stood around her, each of them gazing in a different direction, as if waiting for a threat to descend from the air. We walked toward her.

"There was a garden here last week," she said without glancing up at us, rising and wiping the snow from her gloved hands. "Tomatoes, corn, beans. They were thriving in the heat, the rain we've gotten." She looked around. "Part of the effort to 'green' the city and cut our heating and cooling costs. And it was working, until now."

I didn't know much about gardening, but I doubted much would survive the snow and the cold.

The mayor crossed her arms, tucked in her hands. "I've lived in this city for fifty-three years. And I'd never have imagined seeing something like this. Or not in August, anyway." She sighed heavily, her breath crystallizing instantly in the frosty air.

She looked back at us. "I asked you to come up here because I wanted you to get a good look at it, to see what she's done. The lengths she is willing to go to get what she wants."

It wasn't hard to guess that we were being set up for something.

"We drove in from Hyde Park," my grandfather said. "We saw much of the city along the way."

"A portion of it," she agreed. "But not the whole. Not the reach of what she's done. The sheer enormity of the problem she has created, and the suffering she has caused by it."

"Why are you telling us this?" Ethan asked.

"Because I have a request. And you're not going to like it."

The mood wasn't any less somber in her office. Worse, since Ethan and Catcher were nearly vibrating with anger, and Mallory didn't look much better. I wasn't sure how I'd become the calm one of the four of us, but I'd have to use that to our advantage, if I could. That depended very much on what the mayor had to say.

Lane was back in the office, and when we came in he glanced up at us from the tablet that seemed to absorb most of his attention.

"Mr. and Mrs. Sullivan," he said by way of greeting, gaze still on the screen.

"'Merit' is fine," I said.

He slid me a glance, looking me over with distaste, like the fact that I'd declined the name made me suspect.

The office door opened. Jim Wilcox and Mikaela Pierce walked in, the man and woman from the SWAT and FBI units who'd been behind the barricade at Towerline. Pierce wore a suit again; Wilcox wore dark fatigues. They nodded at the mayor, at Lane, at us, before moving to the other side of the room to stand alone and apart. If anything, it said we weren't on the same team.

"Status?" the mayor asked.

Mallory and I stood beside each other, Catcher and Ethan on the outside edges like guards.

"Stable, for the moment," Pierce said. "The clouds above Towerline continue to spin, but the temperature is holding. There's been no precipitation in the last two hours."

"The Guard has units in the designated emergency zones," Wilcox said. "They're working to keep people calm, but with the city frozen over, people who would normally be working are home. They're home, and they're thinking." He slid a glance to me, to Mallory. And for the first time, I saw guilt in his eyes.

They were going to ask us to turn ourselves over. There might be some pretty words about not negotiating with terrorists, apologies about the sacrifice, but the question would be asked.

I reached out, squeezed Mallory's hand in support. She squeezed back, and her expression had gone stony. Whatever fear she might have felt, she was pushing it down, too. Pride blossomed, raising goose bumps along my arms. She was my sister in all the ways that mattered. And tonight, we were in this together.

"They're thinking about the money they're losing, the loved ones they can't check in on, the property damage they're likely suffering."

"In fairness," Pierce said, "some of them are probably happy about the snow day." She looked at me, tried for a smile. I appreciated that she was trying to keep the mood light, but that telltale guilt was in her eyes, too. And I didn't give guilt a whole lot of credit these days.

Screw this, I thought, and released Mallory's hand, took a step forward. She did the same thing, moving to stand beside me.

I felt Ethan's magic prickle with concern, but I ignored it, settled my gaze on the mayor.

"We are all aware of the situation, Madam Mayor, and of the deadline we're under. And we all know what you're about to ask. In the interest of time, perhaps we could get to the point?"

I could feel my grandfather's concern, too, about the fact that I'd just made demands of the mayor. It certainly wasn't the usual way of things. But there was no point in waiting.

Lane made a huffing sound of disapproval. He finally put down the tablet, looked at me with more irritation. But when I slid my gaze back to the mayor, there was something different there. A kind of respect I hadn't seen before.

"I appreciate your candor," she said.

I nodded, accepting the compliment, while Ethan fumed behind me. But there was no help for it.

She looked at Wilcox, nodded. "Lieutenant."

"Sunrise is at five forty-eight a.m.," he said. "In order to make the operation seem as realistic as possible, we propose Merit and Mallory present themselves to Sorcha shortly before that time. We move in, take Sorcha down, and end this."

"No," Ethan and Catcher simultaneously said.

I reached back, put a hand on Ethan's arm. "Where?" I asked.

"Northerly Island," Wilcox said, looking at me. "It was her idea, but it's a good one. There's plenty of open space in the park, good visibility, room for a helicopter on standby to land."

"How will you neutralize her?" Mallory asked.

"We're working with Baumgartner," he said.

"You went to Baumgartner instead of us?" Catcher's voice was barely controlled fury.

"And the tone of your voice proves that decision was correct," Lane said. "You aren't neutral."

"Damn right I'm not neutral. You're talking about using my wife."

"Catcher," Mallory quietly said, but didn't turn around.

"Baumgartner and several sorcerers of his choosing will take positions on Northerly Island. When Sorcha arrives to meet Merit and Mallory, we'll move in and take her down, move her to the supernatural holding facility."

He said it so simply, with such confidence, that it was easy to understand why the mayor had believed him. I wasn't sure if he believed his own words—his poker face was impressive—but the chance he'd pull off that plan without a hitch was approximately zero.

"By 'take her down,' you mean kill," Ethan said.

The room went silent.

"Because you certainly know she does not intend to discuss the situation with Merit and Mallory. She doesn't intend to 'take' them, or to question them. She intends to kill them."

"And we intend to prevent that from happening," Wilcox said.

"With all due respect, your intentions are worth nothing to me. My wife's life is worth something to me. Mallory is worth something to me. And your plan is literally a bait and switch," Ethan said. "She will not fall for it."

"She doesn't need to fall for it. She only needs to believe it's possible we would give them up."

"Which sorcerers?" Mallory asked, interrupting the byplay.

Wilcox closed his eyes, as if to improve his memory. "I believe he said Simpson, Tangetti, Morehouse."

I glanced at Mallory, who met my gaze, shook her head just a little bit. They weren't strong enough to take her, I presumed. I wasn't sure if that was an assessment of anyone Baumgartner might have chosen, because any sorcerer he allowed in the Order was necessarily weaker than him, or because these particular three were weak, and he'd chosen them as bait for a battle he knew he couldn't win.

Neither was especially comforting.

"And how are you going to get to her without her noticing?" Mallory asked. "She'll see a SWAT team coming."

"The sorcerers will handle that," Wilcox said. "They'll arrange for cover for our folks, and neutralize Sorcha when she arrives."

"And who will be protecting Merit and Mallory?" Ethan asked.

Lane made a sarcastic noise. "You're saying they can't protect themselves?"

"I'm saying they should not be thrown to the wolves with no regard for their safety."

"We're a little more worried about the safety of every other citizen in this city, Mr. Sullivan. All three million of them."

"And what's two lives in exchange for so many?" Ethan asked.

"I wonder if your math would change if she'd demanded someone you loved."

"But she didn't, did she?" He glanced at Mallory and me. "This is a supernatural problem with a supernatural solution."

Ethan took a step forward, teeth bared, and Lane flinched back instinctively. Probably his first smart move of the night.

"Say that again to me," Ethan said. "Tell me again this is a supernatural problem. Show that ignorance one more time, and I will . . . educate you."

There was little doubt his education would be fierce and physical. Sensing the same thing, the mayor held up a hand. "I understand your concerns, Mr. Sullivan. And I don't take with negotiating with terrorists."

"All evidence to the contrary," Ethan muttered.

The mayor's brows lifted. "While I am willing to give your people some leeway considering the circumstances, do consider in whose office you are currently standing."

Ethan didn't respond, but only a human could have missed the angry energy he pumped out like heat shimmering on asphalt.

Evidently satisfied with his silence, she looked at me. "We need a solution to this problem. You and Ms. Bell are that solution. We cannot allow her to destroy Chicago if a solution exists."

"She won't stop," I said. "This won't appease her."

"Of course she will." Lane stepped forward, arms crossed. "She's been silent for four months. She heard about the wedding, became enraged, and used her magic accordingly. Or do you think it's a coincidence the river froze the day after your wedding?"

That thought hadn't even occurred to me, because Sorcha simply wouldn't care. I thought she might have interrupted the wedding for the purpose of causing us pain—not because she cared whether we were married. We were irritants to her. Tools to be used. Nothing more, nothing less.

"She wasn't silent because she was happy or growing a conscience," Mallory said. "And she didn't suddenly snap because Merit made it into the *Tribune*. Again. She's been working on her magic." She pointed to the window. "Case in point. This isn't a card trick, and it's not something you just whip up with a few pretty words. Sorcha's an alchemist. That takes times, preparation, and practice."

"And you are absolutely certain what type of magic she's using? What she intends to do with it?"

Mallory had no response.

"Precisely," the mayor said. "You can presume she's planning something magical, but until you have something concrete, it remains supposition. For now, we cross the bridge in front of us—a very concrete deadline—using the tools at our disposal." She settled her gaze on us. "I realize, ladies, that we are asking a lot of you. But you're both longtime residents of Chicago. You were born here, raised here. Your friends and families are here. Consider what you love about this city, and whether the risk is worth saving it."

When all else failed, go for the guilt.

She glanced at me, at Mallory, surmising we were the deciding votes here. We looked at each other, nodded.

The mayor was visibly relieved, which meant she really thought this plan had a chance of working. She sat back in her chair, which creaked beneath her. "Good," she said. "Good."

"We'll prep for the op at the planetarium," Wilcox said. "Oh four hundred hours. We'll tell her the delivery will take place at oh four thirty hours. That gives us time to grab her, and you time to get somewhere dark before the sun rises again."

"We'll be there," I said.

That gave us four hours to come up with a plan that didn't suck.

⊷ ⊷⊟⊷ ⊶

CHAPTER NINETEEN

GIRLS ON DEADLINES

C atcher and Ethan were both furious. They managed to hold in their anger in the elevator down to the ground floor, until we walked into the dark street, empty of cars.

"I believe we all have things to say," my grandfather said. "Perhaps we could find someplace warm to say them?"

Ethan gestured to the small hotel across the street, its front entrance squeezed between a chain doughnut shop and a shoe store, the windows dark in both of them. "They'll be open despite the weather," he said, "since they'll already have guests in the rooms."

We nodded silently, trudged through unplowed snow— thicker here than in Hyde Park, probably because we were closer to Towerline—and into the lobby.

The reception desk was empty, but light and sound blared from a small room beside it. Canned laughter echoed out from a late-night sitcom.

We dusted off as much snow as we could, walked to a seating area on the other side of the room. The hotel was small, the lobby prettily decorated but showing signs of wear—chipped baseboards, threadbare furniture, worn floors.

My grandfather took a seat first, gestured to us. "Why don't you four talk through what you need to talk through, and then we'll discuss the details?" Nonplussed by the possibility, he pulled out his phone, began scanning the screen. "I'll just do a little reconnaissance."

We left Mallory and Catcher to their own conversation. I was going to have a hard enough time dealing with Ethan; I certainly didn't need two alpha males in a single argument.

We stood in the elevator bank, the doors of three of four elevators opened like maws waiting to be filled.

Ethan paced to one end of the short hallway, then back again, his gaze focused on me like a predator scenting prey. "You will not hand yourself over to a monster."

"Ethan—"

But he took a step toward me, emerald fire in his eyes. "I am your husband, and your friend, and your lover. And I am also a soldier. I am a vampire. I am a monster, in no small part." The emerald shifted, transmuted to quicksilver—one element battling another. "And if I must show them that in order to protect you, I will. Should it come to that, God have mercy on their souls. Because I will have none."

"You know that I have to do this." I lifted my chin. "And you know that I can do this."

"She will kill you."

"She will try. I won't let her. Mallory won't let her. She's a supernatural, just like the rest of us. And she is a narcissist." I lowered my voice, trying to make him understand. "She will destroy Chicago if she gets the chance, Ethan. Even if worse came to worst, my life is a small price to pay for that city."

"There are other options."

"Name one."

Heat flared in his eyes again, and he took a step backward, put distance between us. "I want to both throttle you and lock you away."

"You could try it."

He looked back at me, eyebrow arched imperiously, a challenged king. "You think I couldn't best you?"

We'd fought each other before, battled too many times to count. We'd both won battles, lost them. But that didn't matter now. I walked away, giving myself some room, then looked back at him. "I know you're torn, and I know why, because I know you."

His face was still drawn with irritation, but he lifted his brows.

"On the one hand, I'm your family, your life. You love me, and you're drawn to protect me. That's who you are. And on the other, I'm your Sentinel, and your partner. You know that I'm skilled because you trained me, and you wouldn't have allowed any other result. And you've helped me be brave, and that makes you proud."

He still looked irritated, but I thought that was because he knew I was right. And I was.

"That's our dynamic," I said. "That's our life. You're going to be proud, and you're going to be worried. And the same goes for me, because if you'd had your way—and the voting hadn't been rigged—you'd be King of All Vampires, and I'd have to worry about coups d'état and assassinations."

A corner of his mouth lifted. "If the voting hadn't been rigged?"

"Obviously it was rigged. You scored higher than Nicole, and you saved her life. Little wonder, since she's the one who set up the voting in the first place."

He just stared at me.

"Did you think I hadn't figured that out?"

"You never mentioned it."

I shrugged. "I didn't want you setting yourself up for assassination. But look at the evidence—vampires decide to leave the

Greenwich Presidium and she wants to be their leader, so she sets up an 'election' that pits you against her. And yeah, you have enemies, but enough to decide to vote her, a weaker vampire, into a position of authority? No. She wins, which is what she wanted all along. But she made it look like a democratic process, and then says the vote was close. So everybody thinks the vote was fair and that she was the democratic choice. She wins both ways."

Something flashed in his eyes. "She rigged the votes. She was required to hold the electoral data, which we obtained. Jeff analyzed it for me."

"And didn't spill a word to us."

Ethan smiled. "He's good and reliable."

"So she stuffed the ballot box." I nodded, thinking it through. "We'd wondered how it was done."

"We?"

"The guards."

Ethan blinked. "Luc knew?"

"Of course." I smiled at him. "You hired canny vampires, Ethan, unless you forgot. And to come full circle, you'd have been head of the GP, and I've have worried about you more. Instead, I worry about you the usual amount, and I know you're capable of handling yourself—at least when you aren't stepping in front of stakes for me."

"Well worth it," Ethan said, inching closer and wrapping his arms around me. The tension had left his body, but the magic still prickled. "You are uniquely skilled at diffusing my anger. Malik, as well, but with a very different energy."

"I should hope so, as your wife and his would likely object." I leaned up, pressed my lips to his. "I love you, Ethan. And I appreciate that you worry, that you're concerned enough about me to do so. I won't tell you to stop—as that wouldn't be fair. But we have a good team, and you've trained me well. The rest of it—life, immortality, safety. None of that is guaranteed, even if I was House Librarian."

He chuckled. "You'd have grown bored, Sentinel. Books should be your respite, not your prison."

It had taken time for me to understand that was true, but I understood it now. "You're right. And kicking bad-guy ass is so much more satisfying. If we're going to survive, if Chicago's going to survive, we have to do what scares us."

"Last night, a lot seemed to scare you."

"Yeah, it does. But that's life, right? Isn't that what you taught me? To be scared, but do the thing anyway?" I paused. "This doesn't change anything about our conversation last night. If anything, doesn't it prove I was right? That we'd bring a child into a world that's not only dangerous for her, but everyone she cares about?"

"I could throttle your father," he said, teeth bared. "I could throttle him for what he did to you."

"The fact that you were assassinated in front of me doesn't help."

He growled, put a hand on my chin. "I intend to have you both."

I didn't mean to smile, didn't mean to make light of the fire and emotion in his eyes. But the sheer "alphaness" of it tickled me. "The child isn't even here yet, and you're already overprotective."

The mask of anger dropped incrementally.

"Does it matter that I said I wouldn't hand you over to her?"

I put a hand on his cheek. "I'm not anyone's to be handed over, or to be accepted. Mallory and I are volunteering for an op that might end Sorcha's reign tonight. That's not an opportunity I intend to pass up. And look at it this way: We are inherently more capable than the mayor and her cabal of bureaucrats."

"So I shouldn't consider you prey—I should consider you hall monitors?"

I grinned at him. "Exactly. But minus the teacher's-pet over-tones."

"I believe we've just crossed into some personal territory."

"Possibly." I smiled at him. "Now that we've gotten the ego and bravery parts done with, can we talk about how truly and terribly bad this plan is?"

As expected, Ethan smiled, just a little. "It's truly and terribly bad." He leaned down and moved his mouth over mine, a whisper of a kiss. "I love you."

"I can tell," I said with a grin. And then yelped when he pinched me.

"I love you, too, you tyrant."

Ethan snorted, took my hand. "That's Darth Sullivan to you, Duchess."

I just shook my head.

The hotel's clerk had some questions about why vampires had gathered in her lobby. Because of that, because of the fact that we wanted to be out of downtown, and because we had better snacks at the House—or maybe that was just my reason—we headed back to the House to get into the nitty-gritty.

And because this fell under the banner of actual operational planning, we choose the Ops Room for our HQ.

Jeff came downstairs with bottles of beer in hand. "I'm not sure of the appropriate beverage for a freezing night in August before you mock surrender to a crazy sorceress. IPA? Lager? Red wine?"

"Blood works," I said, and snagged a bottle, grimacing only a moment at the label. How, exactly, did one bottle blood that was "shade grown"?

It didn't matter. I popped the cap, took a drink, appreciated the sudden and fulfilling comfort of it. *Blood to a vampire*, I thought, *like mother's milk.*

When we were gathered around the table—Luc, Lindsey, me, Ethan, Catcher, Mal, my grandfather, and Jeff—we ran through our understanding of the magic she'd created thus far: alchemy, Egregore, and heat sink—used for some purpose we hadn't yet figured out, but she probably intended to use it against us.

"The plan," Luc said, pointing at the downstairs whiteboard with a laser pointer no one should have let him have, "is not great. Northerly Island isn't a horrible choice for this particular op. The line of sight's pretty good, and it gives you a bit of a buffer between magic and residential areas. On the other hand, there are only so many land forces you can line up on the island itself if she escalates. And we will be pushing it very, very close to dawn. We're going to need evac options, but we'll get to that." He looked at Mallory. "The people Baumgartner has lined up?"

"None are strong enough to counter Sorcha."

"Bigger issue," I said. "We're assuming she really wants Mallory and me. Isn't it just as likely this is a showcase for whatever magic she's been working on? A way to force us to watch it? To be the forced audience at her little magical display?"

"It is," my grandfather said.

"Or to get us away from Cadogan House," Luc said.

"I'll talk to Grey, Greer," Ethan said. "Maybe I can convince them to offer vampires to protect the House while we're gone, just in case. As to the rest of it—the risks—the plan is what the plan is," Ethan said. "The mayor won't change it now."

"Agreed," my grandfather said. "She'll be preparing a statement, if she hasn't issued one already, about how she's working with us on a plan for the cool and collected handling of the situation."

"She'll probably hint that she intends to turn Merit and Mallory over," Jeff said. "She's savvy, or Lane is. They may be smart enough to lead Sorcha into believing they really are going to hand you over."

I looked at Mallory. "If you were Sorcha, would you really believe it? If she said she was demanding we offer ourselves in sacrifice?"

"The demand is what the demand is," Mallory said with a shrug. "The fact that she made it says she at least has a hope the mayor will pull through. Her arrogance helps—she thinks she's scared the city senseless, so they'll have no choice but to act. And she already sees us as Goody Two-shoes, although probably incompetent ones. Even if the mayor didn't make us, she'd expect us to show up like sacrificial lambs."

"The question, for us, is how we deal with that," my grandfather said, leaning forward and linking his hands on the table. "How we layer our plan atop the mayor's."

"The floor is open," Ethan said. "And no idea is a bad idea."

"We could call in vampires," Luc said. "Request the Houses send people out, surround the island to help in case she pulls something, and make sure she can't get away."

"After the puff-of-smoke trick she pulled at Towerline, she may not leave on foot," Catcher said. "And more people means more casualties if she does pull something."

Not a comforting point.

"We don't know precisely what she's planning until we know it," Mallory said. "In the meantime, we plan for what we can. If Sorcha's working alchemy, knocking out her crucible would be a good start, if it's there."

"Northerly Island is within the wards," Catcher said. "So she can't arrive magically without our knowing it."

"And in case she tries to come into the city some other way, sneak behind us?" Luc asked.

Jeff nodded. "I've tied the wards into a visual monitor, so if she breaches them, we'll know where and can plan accordingly."

"That won't give us much advance notice," Ethan said, "but it's better than nothing." He leaned back, hands linked in his lap, and closed his eyes. "We'll know when she arrives. We'll have six sorcerers on the ground to battle her, plus Mallory and Catcher. At least a few vampires with the SWAT members, all of whom will have weapons. We'll make sure the House is protected in the interim." He was quiet for a moment, then opened his eyes, looked around at us. "What are we missing?"

"Allies?" Luc asked. He'd crossed his arms over his chest, rocked back on his heels. "She might bring someone else."

"Is there anyone she hasn't made an enemy of?" Catcher asked, glancing at my grandfather.

"Not that I'm aware of," he said. "The fairies might be the best option, simply because their allegiance is always, apparently, for sale. But I don't think Claudia would allow that here. Not after what she said to you. She may like her new power, but it doesn't sound like she's comfortable with the power Sorcha has."

"We need escape routes," Ethan said. "The SWAT team will have mapped out ingress onto and egress off the island, but I don't think we should take for granted the possibility that they'd help us get away."

I thought of Lane's words. "Not if we're just 'supernaturals' involved in a feud."

"And not if they want to leave Sorcha with something to work on while they get away," my grandfather said. "I don't like to think of CPD officers as being that cowardly. But their training didn't prepare them for this. Not for Sorcha and her magic."

Ethan nodded. "We'll want alternate means off the island." He glanced at my grandfather. "A helicopter would be useful."

My grandfather nodded. "I'll check on that."

"I might know someone with a boat," I said, thinking of Jonah and the speedboat the RG used to get to its HQ—the lighthouse in the marina near Navy Pier. I'd have to give him a call. I wasn't on the best of terms with the RG right now, as I'd given them a pretty tough lecture about being a little more walk, a little less talk. But maybe we'd finally catch a break—and maybe the ice would break enough to make it useful. "I'll check."

"If we're separated, get back to the House." Ethan looked at Luc. "Suggestions for an extraction point downtown?"

Luc pulled up a map of Chicago, zoomed in to the Museum Campus, looked around, aimed the laser pointer at Soldier Field. "Here," he said. "Easy foot access, easy car access. And if we run this thing tight to dawn, there's shade."

"Agreed," Ethan said. "Put Brody there in the SUV. Contact the security company, get a blackout vehicle ready just in case we need a daylight extraction."

"Roger that," Luc said. "If we cut this close, get to the stadium and into some shade. They'll find you, bring you home."

I didn't like that option—the vulnerability of being carted out of downtown Chicago unconscious during sunlight hours—but there was no help for it, so I nodded. Sorcha had probably done this on purpose, I realized. Made the deadline dawn, to create the possibility the sun would take us out without any effort on her part, and make us more nervous about the entire thing.

"And we have egress," Ethan said, looking around. "Me, Catcher, Luc, Lindsey, and Juliet on the ground. Brody in the vehicle. Kelley at the House, in charge of security."

"On that," Kelley called out from her spot across the room at one of the security monitors.

Ethan looked at Jeff and my grandfather. "You want to be stationed in the van, I assume?"

"It gives us eyes, ears, and movement," my grandfather said. "That would be my suggestion."

"And quick access to research, information," Jeff put in. "Just in case we need something."

"Google Magic?" I asked with a smile.

"That's actually a thing," Catcher said dourly.

"But he hates it, and don't get him started," Mallory said. "We don't have near enough time for that conversation right now."

I was glad to see the smile on her face, particularly when it was directed at teasing her husband.

"Anything else?" Ethan asked.

"We'll have to be prepared for this to go tits up," Luc said. "Because I'd say the odds are pretty good of it. I'd suggest our goal is the absence of casualties. Anything beyond that is a blue ribbon."

"On a pig," Lindsey agreed.

"I'll suggest again," Luc said, "that you consider putting your own spin out there. We have a PR staff."

"We do," Ethan said. "And the House will provide a statement as it always does."

"Sire, it's time to do more than that. You need to be out there, out front, the face of the Chicagoland Vampires." He cleared his throat, as if preparing himself. "Celina did it."

Ethan's jaw worked. "I recall what Celina did. And I appreciate the suggestion. But that's not the focus I want for the House right now."

"*Sire*," Luc said, but his tone clearly said that he thought Ethan was making the wrong decision.

Ethan checked his watch. "We leave here at twenty after three. That gives us time to get to the rendezvous point on the island, do our own look-see before the op."

"We'll get the van," my grandfather said, looking at Jeff. "Get things set up on our end. We'll meet you there."

Ethan nodded.

"I'll keep working on the manuscript," Mallory said. She glanced up at the clock, which ticked down ominously. "I don't know if I'll find anything in a couple of hours, but I'll try."

"I'll help you," I told her. "We don't have much time, but maybe our luck will hold."

"Do the best you can in the time you've got," Ethan said. "I want everyone wired and downstairs, ready to go by then." He looked at Luc. "You'll handle the details."

"Always," Luc said.

Ethan rose. "In that case, I think we're done for now." He began to move toward the door, but turned back. "Relations with humans have improved, undeniably. But they still don't see us as subject-matter experts on supernaturals. We will hope that is neither their downfall, nor ours. But we should be careful and vigilant. We must be on our toes, and we must take care of each other. Our lives depend on it."

Portnoy the Ugly could have easily been called Portnoy the Inarticulate. Portnoy the Obfuscating.

"Portnoy the Jerkface," Mallory muttered, flipping another page in the manuscript. Since we had only one copy of the document, she sat on my right, reviewing the manuscript's right-hand pages as I reviewed those on the left.

With a groan, she rose from the chair, stretched arms and neck. We hadn't gotten any further in the hour we'd been squinting at the pages, trying to find something that related back to the Egregore, explained how it might be used—or how it might be used against us. We'd found charms, potions, a few recipes (for "Gud

Bredde," among others), ramblings against kings, descriptions of plants and animals. And nothing else about the Egregore.

Mallory lay down in the middle of the floor, arms and legs spread. "I'm giving up."

"You aren't giving up. You're just taking a break."

I flipped another page, found another recipe, this time for a meat pie heavy on organ meats, rendered fat, and "chicken foot jelly," which I didn't want to think too closely about.

I blew out a breath as I pushed off with a toe and spun the chair around.

"Maybe we need to go back to the beginning."

"Towerline?"

"Too far back," I said, turning back to the table. "Back to the Egregore page." I paged through the book until I reached the now-familiar globe, spark, and people, and stared at it, willing insight to come.

I started at the top of the page, working my way line by line toward the bottom. And my gaze nearly passed over what I found there—the pale, faint lines at the bottom of the page.

"Huh," I said, and flipped to the page before, and then the page afterward. Nothing on either about the Egregore, or anything else.

"What are you seeing?"

"I'm not sure. I need a magnifying glass," I said, and rose, went to Ethan's desk. We might have been in a digital age, but Ethan liked his old-fashioned tools. His fountain pens and letter opener—and the large tortoiseshell magnifying glass beside them.

"Here we go," I said, moving back and centering the circle of glass over the fuzzy lines I'd seen at the bottom of the page. "What does this look like to you?"

Mallory leaned in, frowned. "It looks like the bottom of the page was folded up." Like I'd done, she flipped back and forth. "But I don't see any continued pages here. Hmm," she said, and slid over a tablet, pressed keys. She read the information on the screen, then flipped to the front of the book, checked the title page.

"Damn it," she said, and looked up at me. "The manuscript has foldout pages—bigger sheets of illustrations that were folded up to fit into the manuscript. Like you might find for advertisements in a magazine. But they were removed from the original manuscript so they could be sold separately. They weren't found until 1987, which is more than a hundred years after this particular copy of the Danzig was printed."

"Which explains why they aren't in there. Do we know what was on them?"

She looked at the screen again, shook her head. "They haven't been digitized." A slow smile spread across her face. "And you are not going to believe where they are." She looked up at me. "They're at the University of freaking Chicago."

The U of C was my almost alma mater, the place where I'd been working on my Ph.D. in English literature the night I'd been attacked. The night I'd been made a vampire.

"Probably in the Special Collections Research Center. It's where they keep the old stuff."

She checked the tablet again, nodded. "You're right. How do we get a look at it?"

"Normally," I said, thinking back to my grad school days, "we'd make a formal request to the center to view the documents. We show up with ID, and a staff member brings it out. But even assuming the library's still open given the evacuation, that would take time." And require daylight.

Mallory swore. "So that's it? We're out of luck?"

No, I thought. Not if I was willing to go back there. Not if I was willing to open the door I'd closed more than a year ago, and hadn't reopened since then. But what choice did I have?

"No," I said, and pushed back my chair. "We're not out of luck. Not yet."

—✦—

CHAPTER TWENTY

TRIPLICATE

I told Mallory where I was going, asked her to let the others know. I needed to do this, and I was afraid I'd lose my nerve if I talked to Ethan first. If I acknowledged the fear I'd have to face down.

This would be a homecoming, and not an altogether good one. I'd come face-to-face with Logan Hill only a few months ago. And even though the university was barely a mile from the House, I hadn't so much as walked into the library where I'd spent so many nights a single time since my attack. I hadn't talked to my professors, my advisers. Hadn't talked to my friends in the English department. I'd needed a clean break.

That didn't keep guilt from forming a hard, cold weight in my chest.

The man, tall and thin, with dark skin and short hair, was waiting in front of the library's entrance, its imposing concrete walls rising on either side of us. "Merit," he said with a smile. "Long time no see."

"Hey, Pax."

Paxton Leonard hadn't been a colleague; not exactly. He'd been a gatekeeper, one of the few men and women trusted with the literal keys to the most precious documents at the University of Chicago. I'd spent enough time in the center reviewing manuscripts for my dissertation that we'd become friendly.

He reached out, and we exchanged an awkward hug. "You don't call. You don't write."

"I know," I said. "I'm sorry."

"Not that we did any better." He paused. "We felt . . . awkward about it."

I nodded. "Me, too."

"But we've kept up with you—watched the news. You've come quite a long way. From books to swords."

"It wasn't a transition I figured I'd ever have to make," I said, and let a smile touch my lips. "But it kind of worked out."

He smiled. "I'm glad to hear it."

"How's your family?"

"Good!" he said with a bright smile. "Mom and Howard finally tied the knot."

"Oh my God! When?"

"In June," he said with a grin. "He kept asking, and she finally said yes." He leaned forward conspiratorially. "Said she went to Dad's grave, talked to him about it, finally got his approval, so she felt okay about it again. And Amanda finished her first year of medical school."

"That's great, Pax."

"Thanks, Merit." Then he waved it away. "I know you're in a rush, so let's get going." He fished keys from his pocket. "Hell of a lot easier to get into a library when you're the only person left in Chicago."

He unlocked the door, and I slipped inside behind him. The library smelled, as it always had, of paper. Books, maps, notebooks, manuscripts. Including the one I needed to see.

"You want to tell me why we're doing this?" he asked, when he'd pressed buttons on the alarm and we'd moved into the elevator.

"I want to look at the Danzig Manuscript foldouts."

His dark eyebrows lifted. "The Danzig Manuscript? Why? That's just mumbo jumbo."

"It's not mumbo jumbo. It's real, and it's encrypted. Magic rearranges the letters."

He blinked. "You're serious?"

I nodded. "I absolutely am. Long story short, we think Sorcha's using the Danzig Manuscript as a kind of magical guidebook. And if you can help me get it, I can introduce you to the woman who figured it out." I grinned at him. "And you two can write up her groundbreaking discovery."

The light in his eyes was very familiar—the excitement of academic discovery.

"Merit, you have a deal," he said, and swept out a regal hand when the elevator door opened again.

Unfortunately, the deal had limits. He didn't allow me into the space where the documents were kept. So I waited impatiently, pacing the center's hallway while he found the pages.

Finally, he came back with a large box of cream paperboard, which he carried to a table. He pulled cotton gloves from his pocket, slid them on, and lifted the box's lid.

Inside, nestled in undoubtedly archival tissue paper, were several folded sheaths of cream paper. "The Danzig Manuscript foldouts," he said. "As you requested."

I smiled. He'd said those words—or words like them—many times during my tenure here, and probably many times since.

"I don't suppose you'll let me copy these."

"Hell no," he said. "Don't want to expose them to that kind of light." But he smiled and pointed to a small room. "But we can

digitize and print them. They're in line anyway, so I'm really doing the university a favor."

That was good enough for me.

Ethan was pacing the office when I walked in, the rest of the crew
settled around the conference table, looking through manuscript
pages. He turned toward the doorway at the sight of me, and relief flooded him.

He strode toward me. *You should have told me where you were
going.*

I nodded. *I know. But I was afraid I'd lose my nerve.*

He smiled, pushed hair behind my ear. *And did you?*

I held up the folder, smiled cockily. *I did not.*

"You got them?" Mallory asked, coming toward me.

"All forty, just in case." I handed her the folder. "I haven't even
looked at them yet—just rushed there and back. And when this is
all said and done, you have a rendezvous with a research librarian."

She smiled. "Did you set me up on an academic date?"

"I did. You'll like Pax."

"Just don't like him too much," Catcher said from the conference table.

She clutched the folder to her chest. "Never fear, Mr. Bell,"
she said, squeezing my arm before heading back to the table.
"Good job, vampire."

"Thank you, witch." I looked back at Ethan. "I should probably go get dressed." I was still in jeans, and I'd need something a
lot more substantial for tonight's events.

Ethan checked his watch. "You've got twenty minutes."

Immortals with so little time. Wasn't that ironic?

I opted for my leathers. Good boots. Hair in a ponytail, to keep it
out of my face. My dagger tucked into my boot, my katana belted

around my waist. My wedding ring was a new weight on my hand, and I looked down at it in the mirror, smiled at the gleam of metal, the reminder of my grandmother. The reminder of family, and things worth protecting. It was time to do a little protecting of my own, and this time with my family by my side. Or the supernatural members of it, anyway.

I walked downstairs, found Ethan at his desk, Mallory and Catcher at the table. There was a faint buzz of magic in the room, which I hoped was a good sign.

Ethan was on his phone, nodding. "Thank you," he said after a moment, and put it down again. He looked up, looked me over. "Well, Sentinel. You look fierce."

"I am fierce," I said. "Do I look ready to take on a crazed and possibly magic-addicted sorceress?"

He cocked his head, gave me a serious appraisal. "Absolutely. Although you may want to work on a ferocious scowl."

I gave him a look. "How's this one?"

"Keep working on it," he said, then rose, walked around his desk, tipped up my chin with a finger, gazed at me carefully. *You're okay?*

I'm fine, I promised him. *I'll be better when she's wrapped up. Who was on the phone?*

He leaned back against the desk, crossed his arms, smiled. "It was Morgan, my nosy Sentinel. He's offered whatever help we need."

"Good," I said with a nod. "What did you tell him?"

"He'll put a dozen vampires in Grant Park, just in case. Another dozen vampires here, just in case." Ethan smiled. "And he's going to be with them, sword in hand."

"Good boy," I said. "He may make a decent Master after all."

"Fingers crossed," Ethan said. "Were you able to find a boat?"

He hadn't known that I'd meant to ask Jonah—and didn't

know where the Red Guard's HQ was—but there was still a gleam in his eye.

I shook my head. "Couldn't connect. Unless I get a quick response, we're going to be boatless."

"We have other evac plans," Ethan said. "Even if we have to swim, we'll make our way off that island."

"If the harbor's frozen, we could probably just walk across the lake. But I take your point."

Mallory's triumphant yell cut through the room like a knife through frosted cake.

"Oh yes!" she said, jumping up to high-five her husband.

We moved to them. "You figured it out?" I asked. "Already?"

We moved to the table, where Mallory had spread out the pages into groupings of two rows of four or six sheets each.

"It took very nimble finagling and rearranging," she said. "When the foldouts were separated from the main text, they were also separated from each other, so we had to reorganize them." She pointed down at the six pages directly in front of us. "This is the foldout from the Egregore page."

Ethan and I frowned down at the pages. Unlike the main body of the manuscript, these pages consisted mostly of line drawings, the paper and ink having long since faded to sepia, even on the center's excellent color copies. But if the drawings were supposed to represent something, I didn't get it. They looked like random squiggles, without the recognizable globe and human form we'd seen on the main page.

"I get nothing beyond Portnoy's horrid penmanship," Ethan said, hands on his hips as he surveyed the pages.

"He's not going to win any handwriting awards," Catcher agreed.

"Portnoy clearly didn't want anyone futzing around with his grimoire," Mallory said. "The illustrations work on the same principle that the words did; they need the same kind of translation. But you've got to get them into the right *position*."

"My turn," Catcher said, then shook his hands, preparing himself. He reached out, turned the page in the top right corner ninety degrees clockwise. Then he turned the page in the bottom left corner ninety degrees counterclockwise, made a symbol in the air above the set of images.

Just like with the text, the line drawings began to reorganize themselves—not just the discrete lines changing size and position, but the entire drawing rearranging, reassembling itself into a different whole as magic vibrated softly in the air.

And what was pictured there left us in silence.

The spark from the Egregore's page was there, and beside it what looked like a complex arrangement of alchemical symbols. And after that, presumably created from the working of alchemy on the Egregore magical spirit, was a large animal-like form that loomed over a sleepy village. The Egregore's spark was barely a dot in the middle of its broad and jagged forehead.

"She's going to give the Egregore a physical form," Mallory quietly said.

"We said she wanted a weapon," Catcher said. "Someone to fight her battles for her. We were right."

"How could she do this?" Ethan's voice was tight with concern.

"That's the really clever bit," Mallory said. She moved to the next set of images, moved these into different positions, and made another symbol. This time, the lines rearranged themselves into a mass of clouds over the same village.

"She did it with the weather?" I asked, confused.

"Not weather," Mallory said. "That's coincidental." She looked back at us. "We thought the clouds over Towerline were a heat sink—that she was pulling all the heat out of the city, and that's why the weather turned, the lakes froze, whatnot. But what is heat, really?"

Understanding widened Ethan's eyes. "It's energy."

Mallory touched her nose. "And the vampire gets it. It wasn't a heat sink, or not as its main purpose. It's an energy sink, because that's what heat is—the effect of solar radiation and whatever. She wanted all that energy"—Mallory pointed back at the animal—"because she's got big magic to do."

"This is good work, Mallory," Ethan said. "This is damn good work. She wants the Egregore to be physical, and she's pulling energy to make that magic. What form will she pick?"

"That," Catcher said, "we can't tell you. The spell doesn't specify a form. She could pick whatever she wants."

"Narwhal?" I asked.

"Or swamp monster, wooly mammoth, polar bear, griffin," Mallory said. "She just needs something that can hold the Egregore's magic, and its sentience."

"So we're going to meet her at Northerly Island," Ethan said, pacing to the bookshelves, then turning back, "and she's going to bring a monster to fight us."

"Or she'll manifest it then," Mallory said. "She may want to work the magic in front of us—show off a little. And if she does that, I've got a little something that may help."

She reached over, picked up something small and round.

"A Color Bomb makeup compact?" I said, reading the gold script on the top.

"It's a governor. Like on a car. I mixed it up while Merit was on campus."

"A governor?" Ethan asked. "As in the elected official?"

"As in speed governor," Mallory said. "Like on a car, except this is for magic. I didn't have much time, but it's supposed to limit how much power she can use at one time. It might keep her from gathering up enough power to manifest the Egregore."

Even Catcher looked impressed. "How did you come up with that?"

She smiled. "You don't want to hear the full tangential train, but I thought of it on the way to the bachelorette party. Well, kind of. I was thinking about being chauffeured, and I wondered if Ethan put some kind of governor on his car so that Brody could only drive a reasonable speed, like, for safety. And then I thought, no, that might hamper things if he needed to get away in a hurry, and that's no good. And then I started thinking about other kinds of governors, or things that operate like governors—like how ovens can only go up to certain temperatures, and planned obsolescence, and why pencils are exactly the length that they are, instead of some other length, because they'd last longer."

"Your mind is a weird little labyrinth," I said.

She grinned. "Sometimes the randomness comes in handy. Not always, but sometimes."

"Good thinking," Ethan said. "Very good thinking. That gives us another line of defense." He looked at Catcher. "You need to tell Chuck, and he needs to alert the CPD."

"On it," Catcher said, pulling out his phone.

Ethan looked at the clock, something we'd been doing a lot of lately, then glanced at me. "A moment, Sentinel?" he asked, then drew me back to the other side of the room. When we got there, he looked down at me, silence between us, full of words unsaid. But this wasn't the time to say them, to talk about futures that seemed so suddenly uncertain. Not with half a dozen people in the room.

"You will take no chances with your life."

"I will take no *irrational* chances with my life."

An eyebrow lifted.

"That's as good as you're going to get considering what we're about to do. And I say the same thing to you." I pointed a finger at him. "There will be no sacrificing of self for others."

"Isn't that exactly what you're doing?"

"No. Because Mallory and I are both going to walk away. And hopefully, Sorcha will not. Not this time."

"Sire. Sentinel."

We looked back. Malik stood in the doorway, a sly smile on his face. "I think you'd better get out here."

We didn't bother to ask questions, but followed him to the front door, Mallory and Catcher behind us.

A dozen vampires stood on the lawn, every single one of them in Midnight High School T-shirts, a dozen members of the Red Guard. They wore the shirts to identify themselves on an op.

As far as I knew, the RG members themselves were the only ones who knew what the T-shirts symbolized. Although that might change if the House saw them all here together. And particularly the vampire who stood in front of them, auburn hair blowing in the wind.

"Holy shit," I murmured, as Jonah walked toward us, then nodded at Ethan, at me.

"Jonah," Ethan said.

"Ethan."

"What are you doing here?" My voice was a whisper. "This isn't exactly secret agent–type activity."

Jonah's smile was sly. "We're doing our jobs," he said as calmly as if we were discussing the weather. Maybe not this particular weather, but weather generally . . .

"We're here to help."

"To help?" I was having trouble processing this entire situation. "You got my messages?"

"We did. Sorry for not returning the call." He smiled. "I figured it would be faster if we just showed up."

"We are the Red Guard," Jonah said, loud enough for every vampire in the House to hear him. "We exist to guard the Houses and their vampires, to keep them safe, healthy." He glanced down at me. "And it's time we come out of hiding and actually live up to our reputation."

I was staggered. I'd given them a pretty solid lecture on making their organization mean something, instead of paying a lot of lip service to high ideals and secret meetings. But I hadn't actually expected them to follow it.

"You've rendered her speechless," Ethan said.

"A nearly impossible task," Jonah said. He stepped forward, offered Ethan a hand. "We're at your service."

"We're glad to have it," Ethan said, then looked at the rest of them. "Your organization is brave and honorable, and you're doing a brave and honorable thing here."

A few of the vampires looked appreciative at the sentiment, like they hadn't been sure this would be a good idea, or that Ethan wouldn't send them running from the yard. Others looked skeptical. Understandable, given that the entire point of the RG was to be suspicious of Masters, to keep them from oppressing their Novitiates.

Jonah nodded, smiled at me. "I understand you were looking for a boat."

Luc stepped forward to shake Jonah's hand. "Let's discuss the details."

I was still staring as Luc led him into the yard, began talking with animation. The other Guards—including those who hadn't been especially fond of me the last time we'd met—gave me acknowledging nods. None looked as angry as they had been when I'd lectured them. None looked especially friendly, either.

It didn't matter. Right now, we didn't need friends. We needed allies. And those were very different things.

* * *

I'd met only six sorcerers in my time: Mallory, Catcher, Paige, Sorcha, Baumgartner, and Simon, another bad egg. They'd generally been young and attractive, up-and-comer types.

The men and women standing in the lobby of the Adler Planetarium looked to be an entirely different breed. Average, middle-aged midwesterners. Men and women with dark skin and light, who wore puffy jackets against the cold, khakis, and very practical shoes. I felt overdressed in my leathers and steel.

"Bureaucrats," Mallory whispered as we moved toward them.

That explained that.

The SWAT team had moved an e-screen into the marble lobby, which was lit with golden light from the chandeliers above us. They were gilded and old-fashioned, not unlike the lights in the first floor of City Hall. Vestiges of a different era in Chicago.

"Ah," said a pale man of average height with silvery hair and a paunch above his belt. He wore khakis and snow boots, and a puffy jacket that looked warm, but not conducive to fighting. "You're here."

This was Al Baumgartner, the head of the Order.

He walked toward us, the others in the room taking the opportunity to look us over. Their glances, from what I saw, weren't flattering. I saw at least one pair of rolling eyes, wondered if they saw us as too "obviously" supernatural, in the same way they all appeared to be very "plainly" human.

Baumgartner stopped, looked at Catcher. There'd been bad blood between them, and while those wounds were healing, they still looked at each other with wariness.

"Bell."

"Baumgartner."

"If everyone would gather round?" Wilcox asked, gesturing us toward the screen. "We'll get this under way, and get this closed down."

Does he really think it will be that simple? Ethan silently asked. *Or does he say it because he has to?*

My grandfather told him what Sorcha's planning, I said. *So probably a little from Column A, little from Column B.*

The screen showed Northerly Island, the planetarium at the north end to the lagoon at the south. An "X" marked a spot near the south end atop one of the flattened hillocks the Army Corp of Engineers had sculpted out of dirt and rock. "This is the location she's agreed to meet us."

Baumgartner pulled at his bottom lip. "You think she'll follow through with that?"

"If she wants action, she'll come where we are," Wilcox said. "And that's where we'll be." He looked at me, at Mallory. "Where you'll be."

"And you will be where?" Ethan asked.

He pointed to a position along the concrete trail that circled the lagoon, a spot in the water. "Here, and we'll have snipers atop the planetarium, just in case." He looked at Baumgartner. "Your people will be here, and shielded?" He pointed to spots at the base of the hill.

Baumgartner nodded. "She won't know we're there."

"Be careful," my grandfather said. "She's more powerful than she seems."

One of the other sorcerers stepped forward, and her tone was catty, which pretty much matched the expression on her face. "We know who and what she is. We set the wards. Just because you aren't trained to deal with her doesn't mean we can't handle it."

"It's not an issue of training, Simpson," Mallory said, and there was no anger in her voice. Just fatigue. "You've heard what she's planning to do?"

"What you think she's planning to do," Simpson said, rolling her eyes. "The Danzig Manuscript isn't a grimoire. It's nonsense, and you're reading too much into it."

"Sorcha isn't even trained," Baumgartner said, as if that were a defense against magic. "Even if the manuscript was legitimate, there's no way she could accomplish magic on that scale. The delusions, the weather, the ultimatum—it's all for show. She's acting out."

I looked at each of them, the sorcerers who refused to believe the world wasn't exactly as they imagined it, ordered in exactly the way they believed. Fury rose, that they refused to see the truth and face the coming danger. And pity accompanied that anger, that they lived in worlds so simple, so defined by their own prejudices.

"Even if I'm wrong," Mallory said carefully, her eyes narrowed to dangerous slits, "would you rather prepare for the worst and be pleasantly surprised, or walk in with your arrogance, and be blown out of the water?"

The sorceress rolled her eyes. "Always drama with you, Bell."

"Simpson," Baumgartner said. "Focus."

Simpson bit her tongue, but rolled her eyes again.

"I've got a governor," Mallory said. "A small spell that will ratchet down her magic, keep her from being able to give the Egregore physical form. I just need to get close enough to use it."

"Take the chance when you can get it," Wilcox said. "Let's bring her down." He pointed to a spot at the music pavilion near the park. "The vehicle to take her in will be here. It's been warded and sealed, and it's ready."

"And you'll actually contain her this time?" Baumgartner asked haughtily, as if he'd been the one to put out all the effort at Tower-line. In fact, he'd put out none. My opinion of him before walking into the room hadn't been high. That didn't help matters.

"The wagon team assures me they will. You'll help us get her in?"

"We have containment expertise," Simpson said.

I doubted that was true, too, and that she'd ever "contained" anything larger than a random bird or field mouse. But I wouldn't be petty aloud.

"Then let's take our positions," Wilcox said, and we walked to the door, outside again into freezing temps.

"Well," I said. "That went about as well as I expected."

"Fucking bureaucracy," Catcher said. "But yeah, not entirely unexpected."

"What is it with supernaturals and bureaucrats?" Mallory asked.

"Something in the DNA, I suspect."

"I've done what I can," Mallory said, then looked up at Catcher. "Right?"

"You did. You can lead a bureaucrat to a better idea," he said with a wink. "But you can't make him use it."

Mallory chuckled, which had been the point, stepped into his arms.

Ethan put a hand on my face. "I love you. Be careful."

"Ditto that," Catcher said to Mallory.

We exchanged brief kisses, and then looked at each other.

"You ready for this?" I asked Mallory.

She held out her arm. "Let's follow the yellow brick road," she said. And we set out to find the Wicked Witch.

We followed the island's main road toward the park, the sorcerers in front of us, at least until they split off to take their positions. Ethan and Catcher would come in from other directions, hopefully surreptitiously. Luc, Lindsey, and Juliet would stay near the planetarium and closer to shore, in case Sorcha made a run for it. Brody would stay with the vehicle. Thankfully, the CPD had thought ahead, made sure the snow and ice had been mostly cleaned off. The asphalt was still slushy and slippery, but we didn't need skis and snowshoes.

"How are you feeling about the governor?"

"'Confident' is a word. It's not the word I'd choose, but definitely a word."

She slipped a little in the slush, and I grabbed her elbow before she could go down, helped her straighten again.

"And what word would you choose?" I asked her.

She thought about it for a moment. "Encouraged?"

"I'll take that. How close do you need to get?"

"As close as possible." She pulled the compact from the pocket of her coat. "It's a spell-alchemy hybrid. I'm a spell kind of girl; she's an alchemy kind of girl. Without getting into the gory details, it's like Spanx for magic. Sucks it all in."

"You are a wonder. And you've come a long way in a year."

"Just need an endorsement deal and I'm good to go. I'm going to need to concentrate—both on finishing the spell and keeping her from knowing about it. So I need you to handle her."

"That will not be a problem," I said. My blade and I needed a good workout.

She nodded. "I'll give you a signal when I'm ready."

As we reached the hill, she cleared her throat nervously. "Do you want to bet on how bad this gets?"

I grimaced. "Like the number of people who die?"

"No, that's just morose. More like, will Baumgartner blame us when this thing goes to shit?"

I'd spent ten minutes in a room with the man, and I already knew the answer to that. "He absolutely will. No bet."

"Hmm," she said, and crossed her arms. "Other obvious predictions—Sorcha will wear a completely inappropriate outfit. She'll blame something on someone other than herself. Baumgartner's sorcerers will either completely fail to make a dent, or screw up out of some misplaced sense of ego." She paused. "The mayor will refuse to take responsibility."

"You're basically laying out the Supernatural Debacle bingo card," I said. "And you're right about all of it."

We reached the loop around the lagoon, scoped out the place we were supposed to wait for Sorcha.

"You think she'll come down in a puff of smoke?"

"Wicked Witch," she reminded me.

One more square on the bingo card.

The sky was clear, and the air was frigid. We stood atop the snow-covered hill in utter darkness, in the middle of a plateau about forty feet across. The hill wasn't very tall—maybe twenty feet above the lake—but it was elevated just enough so the wind whipped around us.

It was August in the Midwest, and the island should have been alive with sounds—the chirp of crickets, the croak of frogs, the rhythmic humming of cicadas. Waves should have bumped against the shoreline, and wind should have rustled spent and browning grass. Instead, the world was silent.

"She's coming," Mallory quietly said, at an hour until dawn.

She didn't need to tell me. The wind picked up, magic prickled the air uncomfortably, and there was an electric crack in the air, like the sound of crinkling static electricity.

She's here, I told Ethan, unsure whether he was close enough to hear.

We're ready, came his answering call, and I felt immediately better. I trusted Ethan with my life—and had done. I was glad to know he was here and ready, just in case . . .

"The wards are breached," said Jeff's voice through the comm unit. "She's coming in nearly on top of you, so keep an eye out."

"We will very much be doing that," Mallory said, and we stepped back together.

It started as a bit of fog, a smear in the air in front of us, as we watched it thicken and grow in three dimensions, like a storm cloud gaining strength. But this didn't just swell in size—it moved in streaks and jerks, pushing forward in one direction, then swelling, pushing back in another direction, swelling.

For a moment, I was afraid we'd completely misapprehended the situation. That Sorcha hadn't come at all, and instead she'd created some new, diaphanous monster that would kill us in secret silence, like the antagonist of a King novel.

But as quick as a finger snap, the fog dissipated, leaving Sorcha standing before us, her expression haughty and her eyes wild.

She'd picked a pantsuit this time, another of her favorite looks. Emerald green silk with an asymmetrical bodice that looped around one shoulder, leaving the other bare. Her hair fell onto her shoulders, with slender brass bobby pins arranged in "X's" at her temples.

I wondered if she had a stylist, someone who helped her prep before she dropped in to destroy more of Chicago. Or if she sat alone in her secret hideaway, wherever it was, with a closet full of clothes and a trunk of accessories, and prepared herself in silence. Prepared herself to do havoc and murder, a woman with no god to answer to.

"Lindsey is going to freak about the jumpsuit," Mallory whispered.

"Probably. And isn't she freezing?"

"Could be magic," she said.

She smiled at us, took a step forward. "Well, well, well. I guess the city of Chicago made its choice. Not that a skinny vampire and a little bitch of a sorcerer are worth much."

I glanced at Mallory. "I guess I'm the skinny vampire?"

"And I'm the little bitch." She clucked her tongue. "Resorting to crass language, Sorcha—really?"

"Very gauche," I agreed, then looked back at Sorcha. "We're here," I said, beginning the rough script we'd outlined with the SWAT team. "You said you'd release the ice if we showed up."

Her smile was thin. "You think it will be that easy? Especially with a field full of cut-rate sorcerers out there waiting for me? At least you've got a little pizzazz."

"And what do you want?" I asked.

"You two begging for mercy would be a good start. You embarrassed me. I had a plan, which I've now had to change!"

Sorcha had the emotional development of a teenager. Which made her that much more unpredictable.

She took a step forward in sandals that gleamed gold beneath the hem of her jumpsuit. "Do you have any idea how long I worked on that alchemy? Months. And you ruined it in one single night." She smiled her catlike smile, the one that said she was gearing up for the bad news.

"But that's fine," she said. "I have a new plan. I just need a little more power." She leveled her gaze at Mallory, her eyes intense and seeking. "You'll do very nicely."

She wants Mallory to finish whatever she's started, I told Ethan.

Acknowledged. The sorcerers have begun their magic. She's been using her.

Mallory's gaze narrowed. "You're the reason I've been so tired! You've been using me. Draining me, just like a . . . ."

"Vampire," Sorcha finished, sliding her gaze to me. "A little something I whipped up. Because I'm just that good."

"It didn't trip the ward."

Her smile was thin. "Because it was already there."

Part of the Trojan horse, I thought. Part of the magic already at Towerline when the wards were created.

"But it's not enough," Mallory said, glancing back at the clouds that loomed above Towerline, visible even as far away as we were.

"That's why I'm here. Because long distance wasn't doing it. You need me here, now. Why?"

"Because there's work to be done."

"On the Egregore? On manifesting it?"

Sorcha's smile faltered. She hadn't expected us to get that far.

"Yeah," Mallory said. "We got to the Danzig and your little plan. Creative, as things go, if not entirely elegant. Too many steps. Clunky."

Fury rose in Sorcha's face, putting hot color across her cheeks. "I will finish this, and you will help me."

"Oh, I don't think so."

Sorcha slid her cold gaze to me. "You will help me, or I will kill your vampire friend."

Tell them to hurry, I told Ethan. *Because I'm Mallory's incentive.*

But that didn't mean I couldn't enjoy myself. I flipped the thumb guard on my sword, unsheathed it, and spun it around. It felt good in my hand, and good to hold it again.

"How about me and you take a few turns at each other, Sorcha? Unless you're afraid?"

"I'm not afraid of you."

I winked, crooked a finger at her. "Come on, then. Let's see what you've got."

The first fireball *whizzed* by so quickly I hadn't even seen her throw it.

Damn, she's fast, I told Ethan, and barely dodged out of the way, hitting the ground as the chartreuse blaze flew above me. It hit the snow ten feet away and exploded with a ground-shaking thud, sending snow ten feet into the air.

Fast and strong, I amended.

I popped up again, blade in front of me to shield her next volley. Sorcha just rolled her eyes and sent another volley my way. I spun and sliced through them, my arm singing when a spark penetrated leather, stung with needle-sharp pain. The fireballs dissipated but left greasy marks across the blade of my sword. I ran the flat of the blade against my pant leg to wipe it away.

"Come on," I said. "You aren't even trying."

"I hate you," she said, taking a step forward. I moved to the left, trying to bait her into turning a full circle and putting Mallory at her back.

"Yeah, I'm not super fond of you, either," I said, and struck forward, just catching the fabric at the edge of one knee, and ripped a four-inch hole in the silk. I nicked her pale skin, scenting the air with her blood. Powerful blood that I had to force myself not to think about.

Sorcha screamed and turned, hair flying around her face in an arc. She whipped another fireball at me—how much magic was she carrying?—her eyes now wild and dilated. She was too close for the shot; I sliced through it with my katana, but the movement sent an explosion of sparks into the air, hitting us both.

Pain exploded through me, like I'd taken fire-hot shrapnel in every bit of skin, muscle, and bone. The force of it pushed me down, and I hit the ground on my back, eyes squeezed closed as magic pulsed over my skin with a million painful pricks.

"You bitch!" Sorcha cried out. She was still on her feet, but her pantsuit was now a dodgy mess of burns and holes.

She took some of her own, I told Ethan. *This would be a good time for them to strike.* Hopefully Mallory would do the same thing.

Nearly there, Ethan said.

"Hey, you," Mallory said, and Sorcha's head whipped toward her. Mallory smiled, tossed the compact at her.

At the same time, a fireball lit the sky on its way toward us, sending light in an arc over the hill and heading right toward Sorcha.

I looked back. At the origin point, where sparks still faded in the darkness, Simpson stood in the glow of her own magic, preparing another round. Her expression was determined, mixed with the ego of a woman who hadn't been battle-tested and believed she was stronger than she actually was. And because of that, she'd let Sorcha see her—and her position at the bottom of the hill.

"No!" Mallory called out, gathering up her magic and preparing to lunge down the hill toward Simpson, already gathering magic for a shot to intercept whatever Sorcha might throw.

But it was too late.

CHAPTER TWENTY-ONE

WEIRD SCIENCE

Attention drawn by the light, Sorcha moved toward Simpson. The compact hit the ground where Sorcha had been a millisecond ago and shattered open, the spell spilling impotently across the ground, a haze of golden light. Sorcha was already five feet away, heading toward Simpson's position.

"Simpson!" Mallory called out. "Move!"

Too stubborn to obey, Simpson threw another volley. Sorcha batted it away like an irritating insect, and then sent a fireball toward Simpson. Mallory tossed hers at the same time, but finishing the compact had taken a toll on her magic, and it fell short.

Simpson might have had some magical skills, but she wasn't quick on her feet. Instead of dodging, she turned around as if to run away. The fireball caught her square in the back, sending her flying into the snow. She hit with a sickening sizzle, and didn't move.

"She killed her," Mallory said. "Killed her."

And when she did, the sorcerers' concealment magic faltered, making visible the now-triangle-shaped wire of blue magic that vibrated above them. It looked like liquid neon and scattered blue light around them. Now they were all visible to us . . . and to Sorcha.

We're going to need Plan B, I told Ethan, stepping beside Mallory so we stood in a line together against Sorcha. But her eyes, and her rage, were focused at the moment on the trio of sorcerers who raised the wire into the air, began moving it toward the hill. I guessed it was supposed to be a lasso, a very literal way of roping Sorcha into police custody.

Mallory's compact seemed much simpler and more elegant by comparison.

"Do they think she's going to stand still for that?" I asked.

"They thought it would be invisible," Mallory said. "But yeah, it's too cumbersome. Which I could have told them, if they'd shared any of it with me." She gathered up another round, tossed it into the air. Short again.

And she wasn't the only one. Blue shots began to pierce the air from the other side of the lagoon. *Catcher*, I thought with relief.

Sparks flew over the lagoon as the sorcerers battled, magic spilling into the air each time the shots collided, so the sky over the entire island began to glow from the haze of it.

Sorcha was focused on the sorcerers, and she kept moving forward through waist-high snow on the other side of the hill, into the valley where the lagoon reflected back magic. She was moving closer to the lasso the sorcerers still managed to hold aloft, but they were having trouble keeping it stable. It jolted and jerked between them, more live wire than lasso.

Sorcha aimed a fireball at Baumgartner, who fended it off with a shot of his own. But he lost hold of the lasso, which sizzled and disappeared into the air.

"The containment field is down," Mallory called into the comm.

The immediate threat minimized, Sorcha turned back to us,

began tramping up the hill. I pushed Mallory, obviously exhausted, behind me and bared my sword—and my teeth—at Sorcha.

"I'll throw down my sword if you throw down your magic," I said. "And we'll have a good old-fashioned free-for-all."

"You couldn't just give me what I wanted," she said, gaze narrowed at us, her hair spread and lifted in the air as she rallied for one more volley.

My skin still firing with nerves, I took a step toward her. Anything to keep her gaze off Mallory. "I'm not in the habit of handing my city over to self-centered sorceresses."

"I will show you self-centered," she said, and flicked a hand in the air.

Such a fickle gesture to have so much power in it. Energy burst through the air. I shielded Mallory from it, took the blast full-on. I hit the ground on my knees, limbs shaking with the new round of shocking pain.

Light bulleted past me, a shot of blue fire that sliced across her arm, propelled by Mallory. Sorcha slapped a hand over the wound, screamed out with pain that seemed to shake the earth. Thunder cracked like a gunshot as lightning split the sky in the same sickly green shade.

"I am owed!" she screamed into the sky. And when she looked down at us again, her lips were moving in some silent chant. She pulled a fat bundle of what looked like sage from her pocket, touched a fingertip to the end, and it began to smoke. She drew it through the air in front her, lips still moving, and that same greasy magic gathering around us.

"Magic incoming!" I said into the comm over the static, my voice hoarse with pain, and hoped someone could hear me. "Prepare yourself." For the magic and the monster it might create, I thought.

Mallory screamed and crumpled to the ground, clamping her

hands over her ears. And the air around her began to glow, to buzz with magic. It looked like steam was rising from her body. But it was magic—magic that Sorcha was pulling out of her with the power of her filthy song.

"Mallory!" I said, and put my arms around her, shielding her body with mine, and covered her hands with mine in case it helped block the sound.

Mallory cried out again.

"I'm here!" I called out over the crackle of Sorcha's power. "And I'll help you. Just concentrate! Don't let her use you!"

Mallory's entire body was rigid, and she began to shake from the effort.

I didn't know what else to do, how else to help her in the war she was waging with herself, to block out the magic and the sound of chanting. I began to sing the only tune I could think of.

"I'm sorry!" I called out, and screamed out words I hoped I'd never have to repeat. *"Never gonna give you up! Never gonna let you down!"*

"We've found the crucible," Jeff said, his voice crackling in our ears. "Going to destroy it!"

They were a moment too late.

Sorcha kindled the magic. Thick swirls of sickly green power began to compose themselves in the air, spinning and blossoming, and obscuring her completely behind them. The air filled with the chemical scents of the city.

Mallory shuddered. "No," she said. "No, no, no, no, no!"

"Get out of there!" called a voice over the communicator.

"I'm here, right here," I said, and she curled into me. "You're stronger than she is. *Never gonna run around and desert you!*"

"Merit!"

"Here!" I called out, leading Catcher and Ethan to us. They scrambled up the side of the hill.

"Sorcha's been draining Mallory," I said as Catcher lifted her into his arms.

Ethan offered a hand, helped pull me to my feet. "I'm okay," I said. "Just a little unsteady." The earth shuddered, sending ripples across the lagoon's surface. "And that is not helping."

"To the evac point!" Ethan yelled, as another concussion shook us, and the cloud of smoke and magic blossomed larger yet.

Catcher scrambled down the hill, snow flying as he tried to keep his balance. We followed suit, hands linked together, my vision not quite focused, and slipping every few feet in snow that was becoming slushier.

A hot and hazy wind blew across the island, carrying the scents of sulfur and smoke, and warming the air by at least twenty degrees. Cracks echoed across the island as the ice in Burnham Harbor began to split with the sudden temperature increase.

"The snow and ice are melting!" I said. "Be careful!"

We made it back to the looping trail around the lagoon when a sound cut through the darkness, something hard and sharp, a blade meeting stone, that sound bouncing against the city's glass and steel and echoing back again.

It was loud. It was close. And it sounded very, very angry.

It screamed again, and we clapped our hands over our ears, but the scream still pierced through, furious and cutting. The sound wrapped claws around my heart and squeezed, and for a moment I couldn't find my breath.

Sorcha had made a monster of the Egregore. And her monster was coming for us.

"I hope to God that is Chris Pratt riding a velociraptor," Catcher said.

"I don't think we're that lucky," I said.

"I honestly wouldn't be surprised to see the Four Horsemen

of the Apocalypse right now," Ethan said, gripping my hand with steel force.

There were two more pounding concussions. And one more minute of silence—the horrible silence of anticipation, the blissful silence of not yet knowing what monster awaited us.

The ground shook as it lifted off the hilltop, screaming furiously.

It moved on four legs, had a long and serpentine neck, was covered in gleaming black scales. Or I thought they were black. They were so dark it was hard to discern a color, but they gleamed in a shimmering rainbow of luminescence that shifted as the creature moved.

Its wings were thin and veined, mottled dark and red, with claws at the ends of the supporting bones. Its body ended in a long, whiplike tail, and steam rose from its length like it had ascended directly from the depths of hell. Its tongue, long and black, was forked like a swallow's tail.

I stared at it, my brain trying to catch up with my eyes, trying to process what I was seeing.

Catcher got there faster than I did.

"Holy shit," he said. "She made a dragon."

There was no breathing of fire, at least as far as we could see. No medieval maidens in pointed caps, no armor-wearing knights. But the thing Sorcha created sure looked like a dragon.

We just stared at it, trying to comprehend what we were seeing.

"Get them!" Sorcha screamed.

Like a newborn fawn still getting used to its feet, the dragon lumbered forward, tripped on the curb, crumpled. It stood again on wobbling feet and stretched its wings, flapping them awkwardly and out of rhythm, still learning the syncopation of flying.

The hollow sound of an outboard motor drew our attention,

and we all turned around. Jonah steered a boat to the south end of the island, negotiating through slabs of ice. He sent waves over the shore as he moved in, then gestured us forward. "Let's go!"

"That's our ride!" Catcher said. "Run!"

"Get everyone off the island," Ethan yelled into his comm as we ran. "She manifested the Egregore into a dragon. Yes, I said dragon," he repeated, in case anyone hadn't yet seen the monster flapping its way across Northerly Island.

We hauled ass toward the boat, splashed through mud at the shoreline, and climbed into the boat.

"Where am I going?" Jonah asked.

"Back to shore," Ethan said. "And step on it."

Jonah steered back into the harbor, moving as quickly as he could through the chunks of ice that still floated in the water, ignoring the NO WAKE signs and sending the other boats swaying.

It had become suddenly and swampily August. I pulled off my jacket, stuffed it beneath my seat.

"What the hell was that?" Jonah asked.

"Dragon," Catcher said. "She made a damned dragon."

"Quit saying that," Mallory snapped, lifting her head from Catcher's shoulder. "Dragons aren't real."

"I'm pretty sure that was a dragon," I said.

"Dragons aren't real," Mallory insisted, gaze narrowing at me. "It is absolutely not a dragon."

"You can call it a fluffy bunny if that makes you feel better," Catcher said. "But it's not gonna change what we just saw."

"Dragons aren't real," Mallory said again. "Also, batteries just about . . ." Her eyes rolled back.

Catcher caught her before she could hit the deck. "Empty," he finished.

The dragon lifted, wings sending snow and ice and mud into

the air, and went airborne, made it forty yards before touching down again, scrambling for another running start.

"Advantage," Catcher said. "It's not great at being a dragon."

It tried again, this time made it to the top of the planetarium. The dome burst as the dragon settled atop it, talons grabbing at the steel structure between the panels. It had to work to stay balanced, and flapped its wings for support, their tips slamming against the dome and sending more glass shattering.

"Although that may not matter," Catcher said.

"At least we know which form she picked," I said. "Maybe we can use that—look through the Danzig, see if Portnoy left us some clue about taking it out."

Jonah pulled up to the dock. Ethan jumped out first, took the rope Jonah offered him, tied up the boat. We all scrambled out of the boat, Mallory in Catcher's arms, and ran back toward Solidarity Drive, the street that bisected the peninsula, toward the aquarium and Northerly Island.

We reached the street, found the Ombudsman's van and a mess of people running away from the aquarium—probably the skeleton crew who'd stayed behind to care for the wildlife.

Luc, Lindsey, Juliet, and Red Guard members in their Midnight High School T-shirts were hustling people off the peninsula and into the city, including a limping Baumgartner, who'd given up any pretense of helping out.

"What the hell happened?" Jeff asked, running toward us.

"Simpson," I said. "She got a wild hare and threw a fireball at Sorcha, which broke the concealment spell. Oh, and then Sorcha manifested the Egregore into a dragon."

"You all right, Mal?" he asked, tilting his head at her.

"Sorcha's been stealing her magic," I said as Catcher handed her off to Jeff. "Get her into the van, and keep her there until we're done."

Jeff didn't bother to answer, just nodded and ran back toward the van.

I looked at the sky, my watch, calculated we had half an hour before the sun rose and we were all fried to a crisp.

The dragon launched again, this time managed to stay airborne on the flight between the planetarium and Shedd Aquarium. As it landed, I could just make out the silhouette of Sorcha on its back, planted at the base of its neck like a cowboy, her blond hair flying.

The dragon landed atop the aquarium's pointed dome, sending tiles streaming down the sides, where they crashed on the ground.

And then it turned our way.

"I got this," Catcher said, pulling in enough power to make sparks fly across his skin. "Come at me, you asshole."

It pushed off, buckling the dome and sending stone and steel flying. Water splashed into the air as it burst the tanks below. The dragon shrieked and trained its reptilian eyes on us, squawking as it dipped into a deep descent.

After a moment, Catcher held out his hand, the blue spark glowing into an orb. He wound up, pitched it forward, and it streaked like a star across the night. It hit the dragon's driver's side haunch. But instead of wounding him, digging into scales and flesh, it rebounded at an angle, launching back at us nearly as quickly as he'd thrown it.

"Hit the deck!" Catcher yelled, dragging the hem of my shirt to pull me to the ground.

The fireball flew above our heads, exploded behind us. We looked up at the smoke pouring from a window in the aquarium building.

"Shit," Catcher said. "I guess that's not going to work."

"What the hell happened?" I asked.

"The scales are reflective," Catcher said. "Magic bounces off."

It may not have been hurt, but the fireball didn't do anything for its attitude, either. *YOU CANNOT HURT ME.*

It was less a sound than a rumbling in the air, a deep bass note somehow split into words that we could understand.

"Holy shit," Lindsey said, staring openmouthed at the flying lizard that was circling above us, looking for a spot to land. "Tell me someone else heard that."

"Say hello to the Egregore," Ethan said, and glanced at Catcher. "What do we do now?"

"Maybe we can't hurt the dragon with fireballs," Catcher said. "But we can hurt the rider."

I could tell he was getting tired. His form wasn't as good, his shots not quite on target. But the dragon, even if protected from the fire, was skittish enough. It shrieked at the exploding sparks, turned directly into one of Catcher's blasts.

The shot hit Sorcha in the leg, and she screamed in furious pain. The dragon screamed with her, and we covered our ears at the horrible, grating sound. Then it flapped its wings, lifted into the air, and disappeared into fading darkness.

CHAPTER TWENTY-TWO

SCALES OF JUSTICE

We'd rushed the dawn, made it back to the House in time to seal the door before sunlight speared across the yard.

We woke to find the city had thawed, and no reports of further delusions, at least according to the *Tribune*. On the other hand, in addition to temporarily freezing the city, Sorcha had killed a sorcerer. She'd created a dragon that had killed two humans and injured five downtown, not to mention the near destruction of two of the city's favorite buildings.

We hadn't managed to do anything but goad Sorcha into finishing what she'd intended to do all along—create her brand-new flying weapon.

Ethan's office at dusk looked like the losing team's locker room. No smiles or champagne. Just supernaturals, blood, black coffee, and dour expressions.

"Well," my grandfather said from the doorway, "this is a rather grim room." Jeff walked in behind him in an Ombudsman T-shirt.

I looked up from my spot on the floor, where I'd been cleaning my sword with oil and rice paper. Sorcha's magic had done a number on it.

"We're feeling sorry for ourselves," Mallory said from the couch, where she lay with her feet in Catcher's lap.

"Because?"

"Check the papers," Mallory said.

"I'll agree last night was not what you'd call a victory," my grandfather said, taking a seat in one of the club chairs in the sitting area.

"Drink, Chuck?" Jeff asked, then glanced at Ethan, gestured to the fridge in Ethan's bookshelf. Ethan, who'd been reviewing contracts at the conference table, nodded, walked toward us.

"Water would be appreciated," my grandfather said. "It's gotten sticky out there. So much humidity." He took a long look at Mallory. "How are you feeling?"

"I've been better," she said, and held up her wrist, where she'd tied on what looked like a friendship bracelet with a small gold charm.

"Ward," she said. "Not unlike Merit's apotrope. Keeps the bad juju away."

"Keeps Sorcha from draining any more of her magic," Catcher said. "Although it will be a while before she's in top form again."

Mallory gestured to the green drink on the coffee table. "And in the meantime, he's making me drink grass clippings."

Catcher rolled his eyes. "It's kale, and it's good for you."

"I don't see how it could be," she said, and I grimaced on her behalf. It did look like grass clippings.

"Any signs of the dragon?" Ethan asked, as Jeff took a bottle of water out of the fridge, brought it to my grandfather.

"No," my grandfather said. "There've been patrols across the city. No sight of it here, or in Wisconsin, Michigan, Indiana. They're running patrols across Lake Michigan, and there are copters in the air over the city."

"She'll bring it back," Catcher said.

"Undoubtedly," my grandfather said, uncapping the water and taking a long sip. There were beads of sweat on his forehead. "Let's debrief," he said, and we walked him through what we'd seen on Northerly Island.

"You think you were there so she could use your power?" my grandfather asked Mallory.

Mallory nodded. "Even with the power sink, she didn't think she had enough power to manifest the Egregore." She looked at me, eyes full of emotion. "And Merit was the incentive in case I didn't play ball."

I nodded. "She was working that theft magic pretty hard last night."

She paused, blinked, then looked at me. "Did you Rick-Roll me?"

"Yeah," I said. "To block out some of her chanting. You were sweating it out pretty bad. Did it help?"

She considered. "I think, yeah, a little."

"Then sorry, not sorry."

"So she gathered up all that energy, and waited for her moment to give the Egregore physical form—to manifest it into the dragon," my grandfather said.

"Yeppers," Mallory said.

"Magical Trojan horse to Egregore," Ethan said. "And Egregore to dragon."

"Pretty much," Mallory said.

"And the dragon," my grandfather said. "What do we know about it?"

"At the moment, not much," Mallory said. "We know it's theoretically under her command."

"Theoretically?" my grandfather asked, and worry came into his eyes.

"It's a monster created from the collective unconsciousnesses of lots of Chicagoans. It's angry and ornery, and she finished the magic in a hurry. I'd say it's unpredictable, at the least."

"So we have a dragon in Chicago, and a rider with an attitude," my grandfather said.

"It's a shitty time to be a Chicagoan," I said. "But a great time to be a medieval scholar."

They all looked at me. "I'm just saying," I said, and hunched my shoulders a little. "We read manuscripts about dragons—fearing them, fighting them. There are dragons painted in the margins, gilded with gold. Dragons everywhere. You work assuming they're fictional, trying to figure out what they represent. Turns out, they may not be so fictional."

Ethan smiled. "You've been fighting monsters for more than a year, and you only just thought of that?"

"I've had my mind on other things," I pointed out. "Including those monsters I've been fighting."

"And speaking of manuscripts and fighting," my grandfather said, looking at Mallory, "I don't suppose your manuscript has anything to offer?"

"If Portnoy wrote about how to deal with a rampaging Egregore," Mallory said, frustration souring in her voice, "we haven't found it yet. Maybe that's because it's not in there; maybe it's because we haven't arranged the damn foldout pages in the damn right positions to trigger the damn magic. Screw Portnoy." She pointed her index finger in the air angrily, like she could stab it into his chest. "Screw him and his manuscript."

"And Sorcha," Jeff said.

"And screw Sorcha!" Mallory agreed, pointing again.

"Have more lawn clippings," Catcher said, handing her the drink. "You're getting hangry again."

She just growled.

"Although I don't disagree with the sentiment," Ethan said,

walking over to squeeze Mallory's shoulder, "we've got the complete text now, and two of the best damn sorcerers in the country, if not the world. You can do it, and we are at your disposal."

It was the Master in him, the leader in him, that filled his voice with confidence. And I hoped he was right.

"In the meantime," my grandfather said, "is there any chance we can reason with it?" It was precisely the kind of tack he'd prefer. "It can think, communicate, right?"

"We can talk to it," Catcher said. "But can we change its mind? That seems unlikely, especially if she's got power over it."

"And we know the fireball juju doesn't work," I said. "So what will?"

"The world's largest bear trap?" Mallory asked. "Extra-large elephant gun? Freeze ray?"

"Excellent ideas, Wile E. Coyote."

Mallory growled.

"Maybe you should switch her from kale to chocolate," I suggested.

"Could we unmanifest him?" Jeff asked. "Turn him back into the Egregore?"

"Even if we could," Mallory said, "we'd still be left with a very pissed-off Egregore, which puts us back to where we were yesterday—with too much magic in Chicago. We need to eradicate him completely."

My grandfather's phone rang, interrupting any follow-up questions.

"I really don't want you to answer that," I said, knowing what he'd be called about, what monster was awaiting us again.

"That's the job," he said, then rose and walked to a corner, spoke quietly into the phone. And when he came back, his expression was grim. "It's back."

* * *

It wasn't just back. It was perched atop the Water Tower, according to the photos that were already making their way across the Web, from humans who'd been either unlucky enough to be downstairs when the dragon returned, or stupid enough to seek out the dragon so they could take pictures.

It hadn't been the mayor who'd called my grandfather. It had been Arthur Jacobs, a detective and friend on the force. "Eighty percent of the city has been evacuated," he said. "The mayor has ordered everyone who remains to shelter in place. The CPD is enforcing that order. She's handing the 'situation' to the Guard."

"She learned nothing," Catcher said, words tight with anger. "She tried to apply human strategy to a supernatural situation, and it failed. She was bamboozled by the Order, and they failed. All due respect to our men and women in uniform, but what is the Guard going to do? They can't use jets. The dragon can fly and walk. It can evade anything they send at it. They put a plane in the air, and she'll blow *it* out of the sky, and kill everyone unlucky enough to be standing beneath it. They'll end up setting missiles on the city, and destroying it in the process."

"They'll use armored vehicles, I suspect," my grandfather said. "Try to get it on the ground in order to contain the collateral damage, at least as much as they can."

"So they'll roll tanks down Michigan Avenue? Shoot mortars at Willis Tower? She'll destroy more of the city that way, too, and for what? That's not going to take down the dragon. They need pinpointed magic."

"She'll have decided—or the polls will have decided for her—that a joint human-supernatural approach wasn't effective. That last night was a failure because we were involved."

"Last night was a failure because she involved the wrong people."

"She had a magical problem, and she sought a magical solution," my grandfather said. "The problem has only gotten bigger—"

"And scalier," Jeff put in.

My grandfather nodded. "So it was a failure, and she's going in the other direction."

"We stay home," I said, "and she gives the city to the men and women with guns."

"That's about the way of it," my grandfather said. He rose, water bottle still in hand. "I suppose we should be going."

"Going?" Jeff asked. He looked crestfallen, bummed we wouldn't be joining the fight.

My grandfather's smile was grim, but determined. "If we're going to step in and try to fix this nonsense, we'd better hit the road before the CPD comes." He looked at me, Mallory. "She'll do as much damage as she can as quickly as she can, because she'll want your attention. Give it to her, and take her down."

He walked to the door, leaving all of us staring after him.

"And that's where your wife gets her moxie," Catcher said, rising.

"Apparently so," Ethan said, and glanced down at me. "Sentinel, is your sword ready?"

"And eager," I said. "Let's go."

Luc, Lindsey, and the rest would stay at the House in case Sorcha tried a direct attack. My grandfather would take Catcher downtown in the van. They were official, so the odds they'd be stopped by the CPD were low.

And as for us . . . we had speed. Ethan, Mallory, and I squeezed into the Audi R8 I was still pretty sure Ethan had purchased because he idolized Iron Man. Whatever the reason, she was beautiful, and she was fast. The odds the CPD would attempt to stop us were high. The odds we'd be caught? A little less.

We wanted Mallory—and her magical know-how—on the ground with us, so Jeff volunteered to stay at Cadogan, futz with the foldouts. Mallory had pretranslated the pages, so he was tasked with rearranging them like puzzle pieces until the magic clicked into place. It wasn't a perfect solution, but it was the best option we had.

With the snow's melting, the city was humid, but the streets were dry, the night clear. It was a perfect night for a sports car with six hundred horses under the hood. People were wary enough of the dragon that the streets were relatively clear (for Chicago), and we made it downtown in a reasonable amount of time (for Chicago). Still, we avoided main roads and opted for backstreets, and didn't see a single officer or soldier.

We found them downtown, creating a barrier around Michigan Avenue north of the river, so we parked a few blocks away, met my grandfather in front of the Carbide & Carbon Building, with its dark granite and gold touches that gleamed beneath the streetlights.

"Keep your weapons sheathed," he said, "and let me do the talking."

We crossed the bridge to the barricade at Ohio Street, where he communed with the two soldiers stationed behind camouflaged vehicles.

Beyond them, Michigan Avenue had been cleared of vehicles—except for the tank parked in the middle of the avenue a few blocks down, its barrel pointed at the monster that was, sure enough, balanced on a crenelated turret atop the white stone Water Tower. The dragon had found its castle.

He showed his badge, and there was quiet discussion before he gestured to us. Then more discussion, and my grandfather walked back.

"We in?" Catcher asked.

"We are not," he said, frustration in his eyes. "No supernaturals allowed in the vicinity, for fear that Sorcha will use them as she used the sorcerers last night."

"Sorcha didn't use Simpson," Mallory said. "She bested her."

"I believe that's a detail they aren't currently interested in. Their job is to bring down the dragon, and they're going to do it the way they know how."

"They haven't fired yet," Ethan said.

"They're negotiating with Sorcha. They don't want to start destroying property, and the rounds in that tank will bring down buildings."

Catcher shook his head. "It won't work. It's too much weapon for downtown Chicago. If they're hoping she has a conscience, or will be moved by that weapon, they're doomed for disappointment."

"They have to try," my grandfather said. "That's the paradigm—"

His next words were drowned out by the loudest noise I'd ever heard, a boom that echoed all the way down Michigan Avenue and had my heart hammering inside my chest like it was trying to beat its way out.

Smoke poured down the street, along with the sound of falling rocks and glass. Everyone near the barricade went still, staring into the smoke for confirmation that the tank had hit its target.

My ears rang for the five seconds it took for another concussion to rip through the air. By that time, the world was hazy, and we couldn't see past the end of the block.

There was a thud, the screech of metal, and the whine of something moving toward us.

"Out of the way!" Ethan said, pulling my grandfather and me back as the tank barreled past us, landed upright in the plaza in front of the Tribune building, smoke pouring from the turret.

The dragon had thrown a tank half a mile down Michigan Avenue.

The soldiers at the barricade ran forward to help the soldiers still in the tank, worked to pry open the turret hatch.

"Did the tank miss?" Catcher quietly asked. "Or did that hundred-twenty-millimeter round have no effect?"

When very human screams began to echo through the streets, we decided it wouldn't matter. Ethan unsheathed his sword, streetlights catching the polished steel.

"There's a good chance the sword can't do what a tank can't do," my grandfather said as we prepared to help whoever was screaming.

Ethan's expression was grim. "It's not for the dragon. It's for the rider." He looked at Catcher. "How much magic do you have?"

"I've got plenty of energy," Catcher said. "The question is what to do with it."

Ethan glanced at Mallory.

"Less energy than he does," she said. "Last night wore on me. And the same question about what to do with it."

Ethan nodded. "Go for Sorcha. She can be hit—we saw it last night."

"And she's probably even more pissed off."

"Then maybe she'll make a mistake," Ethan said. "Because we could certainly use one."

My grandfather nodded, looked at me. "Be careful," he said, then went to talk to the soldiers.

I'd seen plenty in my year and change as a vampire, death and joy and destruction and rebuilding. But I'd never run through a war zone. I'd never seen Michigan Avenue—the Magnificent Mile—smoking and strewn with gravel and glass, empty of people beneath streetlights.

This is how the world will end, I thought. With destruction and chaos, and except for the screaming of humans we couldn't yet see through the smoke, a silence that seemed almost impermeable. The Guard had moved in the other direction, chasing the dragon across the city, looking for a better shot; the emergency vehicles hadn't gotten here yet. There were undoubtedly humans in these buildings—they were full of condos, apartments, hotels. But they'd taken the shelter-in-place order seriously. That, I guessed, was the effect of Towerline.

We were nearly on top of the Water Tower before we could see it—and the thin tower had been toppled like toy blocks. The dragon was gone, but the screams grew louder.

How was it fair to bring a child into this? Into a world that could be so easily broken down, torn apart? Into a world that *had* been torn apart?

Figures emerged from the haze. Two men and two women working to free a girl from beneath a pile of twisted steel and brick. Either the dragon or the tank had taken out a chunk of the building on the next block up, leaving a ragged hole where the corner of the building had been.

They caught sight of us, gestured us over with waving flashlights. "There's a kid trapped over here! Can you help?"

"It's my Taylor," said an obviously frantic woman, tear tracks in the grime on her face and a squirming white dog in her arms. "We were going to the bomb shelter, like they told us, but Tootsie got loose, and Taylor went after her, and that's when the bomb went off. She's in there, somewhere."

It hadn't been a bomb. It had been a gun fired by humans to kill a monster they didn't understand. But that didn't matter. The girl mattered, so we ran toward the pile, joined the others in moving rocks and shards of glass and steel.

"Let us try," Ethan said, gesturing to me. "We've got the

strength." We handed Catcher our sheathed katanas. "Keep watch," he told Catcher. "Sorcha's shown herself to draw us out. She'll come back, and she'll be looking for us."

"Eyes peeled," Catcher confirmed, turning his back to us and scanning the street.

We climbed onto the pile, rocks shifting beneath us, and began hefting stones away. The stones had been blown apart, the edges as sharp as glass, and shards scraped into tender flesh with each rock we moved. I'd done this before—had dug through rock in darkness to search for Ethan, not sure he'd still been alive.

Now he was my husband, my partner, fighting the good fight on the other side of the rubble pile.

I heard a chirp of sound, turned toward it, climbing across the mound to the spot on the other side.

"Help." The word was weakly spoken, but it was still a word. Taylor was alive.

"She's here," I said, and pulled rocks faster, tossing them behind me onto asphalt already littered with the detritus of battle.

"Taylor!" her mother screamed, going to her knees in the rubble, the dog now in Mallory's arms. She stretched out an arm, grazed the girl's hands. "Baby? Can you hear me?"

"I'm stuck!" Taylor said. "I'm okay but I'm stuck. There's a bar down here. Some kind of big bar on my leg. I can't get it off."

Ethan dropped to his knees, accepted the flashlight offered by one of the humans, and peered into the hole where Taylor was wedged.

"Steel bar," Ethan said.

Can we move it? I silently asked.

Ethan pulled back, looking over the mountain of debris we hadn't yet moved. We'd moved a lot of rubble, but the concrete on top of the cavity where Taylor lay was at least five feet long.

It's not the bar, he said. *It's the concrete that's pinning it in place.*

I wasn't giving up.

"Mallory," I said. "We need some of that good magic."

She passed the dog to one of the humans, dusted grit from her hands, pulled out a small, worn notebook from her pocket. "Okay," she murmured. "Okay." She walked to the rubble, grabbed a broken rod of rebar, began scratching in the sheet of concrete.

"Jesus, is she doing magic?" One of the humans who'd asked us for help walked toward Mallory, looked ready to snatch the rebar out of her hand.

Catcher pushed him back. "She's my wife, and she's on our side. You lay a hand on her, and you'll answer to me."

Whatever he saw in Catcher's eyes had the man reassessing his position, his desire to start a fight.

"She's on our side," I confirmed to the man, stepping up to them. "Focus on Taylor, and don't worry about the magic."

I took my sword back from Catcher. "Help her," I said, and unsheathed it. Because I had a bad feeling I knew what was going to happen when Mallory fired up her magic. And sure enough, the wind shifted, and suddenly there was heat and sulfur on the air, a burning zephyr through downtown.

I think Mallory just dialed Sorcha's number, I told Ethan.

We're moving as quickly as possible, Ethan said.

Move faster, I said, scanning the street, the air, with narrowed eyes, trying to pierce through the veil of dirt that still clung to the humidity in the air. Too bad dragons didn't have headlights. That would have made the spotting easier.

"Jesus," the human said, and I jerked my head around.

Mallory stood in front of the block of concrete, arms shaking as she reached toward it, palms out, lips moving in that quiet cadence sorcerers seemed to prefer. Catcher and Ethan held up opposite sides of the slab, which was now four feet off the ground.

"Not Jesus," Mallory quietly said, eyes closed in concentration. "Just futzing with some testy Higgs bosons. Oldest trick in the book."

"Quit staring," Catcher snapped to the other humans who stood by, dumbfounded, as he and Ethan held up the concrete, "and get Taylor out."

Snapped out of their haze, they dashed forward. One began tossing aside the rest of the debris that pinned Taylor; the other took her hands, began to pull her free.

And then we heard the sound of a voice in the sky.

Sorcha and the dragon.

I took a step forward, trying to nail down their position, but the sound echoed across the buildings. "Ethan," I said, a warning.

"I hear it. Nearly there, Sentinel."

"Taylor!"

I glanced back as the humans pulled a slender and dirty girl from beneath the rubble.

As Ethan and Catcher returned the concrete to earth, Taylor's mother screamed and pulled the girl into a fierce embrace, both of them crying, the tears carving more streaks in the soot that marked their faces. "Taylor, Taylor, Taylor," her mother sang, rocking the girl, who sobbed in her arms. "My baby girl."

"It's because of Tootsie," Taylor said. "Where's Tootsie?"

"She's right here," said the human who'd held the fuzzy dog, walking it to the pair, at least until it leaped into Taylor's arms. Taylor sobbed and hugged the dog, and her mother embraced them both.

This is why, Sentinel.

I looked up, looked across the mound of debris, and met Ethan's gaze.

This is why you take chances, with love, with life . . . with children. Because sometimes you lose them . . . and sometimes you don't.

The dragon's scream interrupted the thought—angry and shrill. "Incoming!" Catcher yelled.

"Inside!" Ethan said, guiding the humans back through the hole and into the remains of the building, where at least they wouldn't be visible.

We stepped into the street: Sorcerer. Sorcerer. Vampire. Vampire.

"Just four crazy kids against the world," Catcher said, warming up.

"They should make a Lifetime movie about us," I said.

Mallory snorted. "It's cute you think he hasn't already written to the company with a proposal."

The dragon burst through the haze like a rocket. And even after what we'd seen last night, the shock of seeing a dragon fly past the tony shops on Michigan Avenue was nearly visceral.

They came in low and trailing blood. The dragon was wounded, bleeding from a gaping hole in its back driver's side flank. The Guard had hit their target; it just hadn't been quite enough. In fairness, I didn't know who manufactured tank rounds, but I was pretty sure they hadn't calculated the effect on a giant flying lizard.

"Attack!" came Sorcha's demand, followed by a greasy pulse of magic.

The dragon turned, swooped back, but it was whipping its head from side to side, as if trying to dislodge the magic and its creator.

PAIN.

It dove toward us. Ethan and I dodged, rolled, and came up with katanas lifted, scraping swords against the dark, wide scales on its abdomen. It sounded like we'd slid metal against metal, the friction throwing sparks into the air.

I didn't think we'd done any damage, but the dragon shrieked again as it flew forward, arcing toward the sky to get space enough to make the turn. But it misjudged.

Its wings brushed the building, and it lost its balance and pitched to the right, throwing Sorcha to the ground. Ethan held out a hand, holding me back as she climbed groggily to her feet.

She'd changed her ensemble today, exchanging the jumpsuit for an emerald dress with flowing silk sleeves, her hair loose again. I imagined she'd tried to pick an outfit appropriate for the Busy Dragon Rider on the Go. Bummer she hadn't added a pointed hat.

"You are mine!" Sorcha said. "Under my control and within my sole power. You will bow to me and do my bidding."

"Girl takes her role as DM a little too seriously," Catcher murmured. "Details at eleven."

I couldn't take my eyes off the rise and fall of its wings, the rainbow of color that spilled across its scales with each rhythmic movement. It was graceful in its way.

The dragon lifted into the air.

YOU DID NOT CREATE ME.

Sorcha's smile was immense, her pleasure obvious. Her arrogance now physical. "Oh, I created you," she said. "I brought together the disparate consciousness of all touched by my magic, and I created you."

YOU DID NOT CREATE, it said. *I EXISTED. PAIN AND RAGE EXISTED. YOU BROUGHT ME INTO THIS FORM.*

"You're here now!" Sorcha yelled impatiently, lifting her hands to the sky. "And I am in control. *Come to me,*" she ordered, and pointed at the street in front of her, like a human might order a stubborn dog to sit.

There was magic behind the order—the buzz of magic that pulsed through the air, the stain of the darkness that surrounded it.

The dragon swooped in front of her.

Tremulously, just as a girl might have taken her first cautious step toward a quarter horse, Sorcha took a step forward, green silk undulating around her body with each flap of the dragon's wings.

—◆≡◆≡◆—

CHAPTER TWENTY-THREE

MIDNIGHT RUN

We stared in shock and silence for a full ten seconds, gazing at the spot where Sorcha, our feared enemy, had stood. Now our enemy was being crushed and crunched with horrible liquidy sounds while the dragon mawed on her remaining bits like a cow chewing its cud.

"She was our enemy," Mallory said. "But . . ."

"But we would have incarcerated her," Catcher said. "Not made her dragon kibble."

We all looked at Catcher. "I won't apologize for wishing her dead, although I'm guessing 'chewed up' isn't a very pleasant way to go."

We all looked back at the dragon, which coughed, then spat out one of Sorcha's heels.

"Why do I want to laugh?" Mallory asked.

"Because this is horrible and uncomfortable and the best dark comedy ever written," Catcher said.

"Yeah," Mallory said.

But the comedy ended. Done with its snack, the dragon lifted its head, narrowed its reptilian eyes at us.

It had been born of pain and anger and fear—of those bitter, cast-off emotions of human and supernatural Chicagoans. And it had no love for those who'd filled it with agony.

ENEMIES, it said. *PAIN*. And then it lunged.

"Lead it back to the guns!" Ethan ordered, and we ran together down Pearson, then turned back to Michigan, leading the dragon back to the Guard units.

The world began to bounce as the dragon found its feet, began hauling down Michigan Avenue after us. And then the shuddering stopped, replaced by the whipping wind of the dragon's wings.

It was airborne, with plenty of room to spread its wings on Michigan. And we made for a nice, wide target.

"Split off!" Ethan yelled, when we were in sight of the barricade. "Take Mallory and head for the river. We'll head toward the lake, try to draw him away from you. Get back to the House."

I nearly stopped running, nearly pulled Ethan to a stop to tell him not to be ridiculous, that I was his Sentinel and I'd guard him, and not the other way around.

I love you, I told him.

Forever, he said, a gleam in his eyes. *Take care, Sentinel.*

I nodded, grabbed Mallory's hand, and dragged her off Michigan, the dragon's hot breath literally on our heels. We ran down a side street, pressed ourselves against the wall of a building while the sound of gunshots ricocheted off skyscrapers.

But then I glanced at Mallory. Ethan, Catcher, and I were trained in combat. Mallory wasn't, and she was still fighting exhaustion—and had just used magic to help Taylor. She was lagging behind me, so outrunning the dragon didn't seem like a realistic option.

I pulled her into an alley and behind a Dumpster. It could fly faster than we could run, so a foot chase wasn't going to do either of us any good. But I didn't think it was small enough to fly into an alley.

We crouched on the ground behind the steel garbage box. The ground shuddered as the dragon moved, sending liquid sloshing and lifting a foul scent into the air.

"This is not how I thought things would end," Mallory said, her fingers digging into my knee. "Crouching in garbage on the run from a lizard."

"We'll make it," I whispered. We had to make it. I wasn't going down like Sorcha, literally or figuratively. "We'll wait it out, then find a way back to the House. Maybe you could conjure us up some wings."

"No problem," she said, but covered her mouth with a hand as the dragon moved past the alley, its heavy movements sending showers of dirt and grime and brick dust raining over us.

The footsteps grew quieter, but we waited until silence had fallen again. "I'm going to check," I said, and stood up, pulling her clawed fingers off my leg, and peeked past the Dumpster.

The world was dark and silent, the dust from the dragon's footsteps still settling on the street.

"That was close," I whispered. "But I think we're okay."

"Merit!" She screamed and I looked back. The dragon's claw—four armored black toes with two-foot-long black talons—speared into the alley, inches from my face, the talons curled and grasping.

Trying to find us, it slammed against the wall, sending the sound of brick shattering over Mallory's scream. It found the Dumpster, pushed it backward.

Mallory scrambled to her feet to avoid being crushed, and jumped out of the way, into the middle of the alley, where it clawed again, trying to reach us with the tips of its gleaming red-black nails. The plating was different, I realized—the armor different on its toes than on the rest of its body. Slimmer, smaller, probably because flexibility was needed. And maybe, just maybe, vulnerable to a sword . . .

I WILL DESTROY.

"You most certainly will *not* destroy," I said, and raised my katana, sliced down. Blood welled, the scent of it as foul as the garbage in the alley.

The dragon screamed, reared back and pulled up its injured foot, stumbled backward and fell against an SUV parked behind it, crushing the vehicle.

I knew a chance when I saw it. I grabbed Mallory's hand and dragged her out of the alley.

"Bridge!" I said, scanning the neighborhoods on the other side, and spotting the stairs that led down to the El platform. There was no way it could fit down the concrete stairs into the tunnel. We'd be free of it. And with luck, we could make it back to Cadogan House.

PAIN.

We tore across the street, were steps onto the bridge, when the dragon found its footing again. It reached the tower at the end of the bridge, long nails gripping the stonework as its wings flapped, sending brick and gravel flying.

Fear speared through me, regret at the possibility I'd led Mallory the wrong way, made the wrong decision. But there was a dragon behind us, and water beneath us. We had to keep running. We had to get to the stairwell.

"Run!" I told Mallory, and we pounded pavement across the bridge.

And then the lights began flashing ahead of us, and the entire roadway began to vibrate. I glanced back at the river, where an icebreaker—one of the ships sent out by the city to keep the river flowing—was heading out to the lake.

It took me a moment to realize what was happening.

This was a bascule bridge, a roadway that could actually be opened in the middle to let tall ships through, each side lifting into the air, weighted by huge blocks on the shore.

They were raising the bridge.

The ship couldn't stop without ramming the bridge. Which meant, between us and the bridge, the bridge won, even though we were still on it.

I looked ahead at the growing gap between the decks, and the rising incline of pavement above the water. I didn't know how wide the river was here—a hundred feet? more?—but the gap in the road between the bridge's decks would soon be nearly that wide, and the decks nearly vertical.

The dragon's scream cut through indecision. It pushed off the tower, its claws throwing off stones as it lifted into the air. The stones fell like meteorites onto the asphalt.

We couldn't help them, or we'd put the dragon's attention right on them. Jumping into near-freezing water didn't sound much better. That left only one option.

"Mallory, we need to haul ass right now."

"Oh shit!" she said, pumping her arms as we took off, and she settled in beside me, breath huffing.

But with each step the incline grew, the deck slowly rising, so that we had to run with bodies angled forward, nearly on our toes. And all the while, the gap widened.

"Oh, this is gonna be close."

"I can do it," I told her. "Just stick by me." I grabbed her hand. "Whatever happens, don't let go."

Vampires and gravity are friends, I told myself, heart racing, feet pounding pavement. *Vampires and gravity are friends.*

Forty feet.

The dragon's wings beat ferociously behind us, so dust and

rocks beat at our backs like tiny bullets. It was drawing closer, the heat of its magically manifested body bearing down on us like a cruel sun, the chemical smell burning in the backs of our throats.

We were beating the rise, making progress toward the gap. I could feel Mallory slowing—she didn't have my biological advantage—but I kept my grip firm around her wrist, tugging her along as I stared determinedly at the finish line, and the empty space that was growing in front of it.

We were going to have to jump.

If we got that far.

"Shit!" Mallory cursed, her weight dropping. I lost my grip, turned around; she'd hit a patch of wet pavement, was on her knees trying to regain her traction, trying to find purchase with the toe of a sneakered foot.

"Mallory!" I reached out my hand, but she waved me off.

"I'm getting up!" she said. "Keep going!"

I turned my head back to the rising bridge—to check the incline I was fighting against—for only a second. And then she was moving past me, screaming. The dragon had caught up to us and snatched at her; she'd evaded its teeth, but the tip of one wing snagged Mallory's shirt and was pulling her forward.

"Mallory!" I screamed, reaching out a hand as ice chilled my blood.

And then she disappeared over the edge.

Panic ate at me, cold fear its own dragon in my belly, but I pushed it down, focused on inching my way up the incline, now nearly vertical.

I was sweating when I reached the edge of the roadway. I slung an elbow over the end, and spied her rainbow-painted fingernails. She hung by her hands from one of the bridge's structural beams.

"Mallory!" I screamed, and stretched out my hand as the dragon reached the other end of the bridge, banked hard to avoid the buildings on Wacker, and turned to take another shot at us. We were going to have to be fast. "Give me your hand."

Mallory shook her head, staring at her fingers, as if she could strengthen them by sheer force of will. "I'm slipping."

"I won't let you fall." But she was a good two feet beneath me. I had to get closer, and that meant climbing toward her.

I made the mistake of looking down, watching light shimmer across the water so, so far below us. I could make a planned fall from a pretty tall height—at least onto land. The river's eddied surface was something else entirely.

Eyes gleaming in the darkness, the dragon bulleted toward me.

I forced myself to ignore the void, ducking under the roadway just in time to hear the creature's nails screech against asphalt, the thunder of its wings as it lifted again.

"You ever wonder why they call it a death grip?" Mallory asked, as I moved down among the steel beams.

At least the bridge gave us some protection from the dragon, which screamed somewhere above us, furious that we'd spoiled its fun.

"I mean, you hold on because you're gripping life, right?" She blew bangs from her eyes. "Shouldn't it be a life grip?"

"Anyone ever tell you that you get a little loopy when you're in mortal danger?"

"I'm gonna be honest," she said in a hysterical tone. "This isn't the first time."

My foot slipped on wet steel, but I caught myself, squeezed my hands so hard the knuckles were white against the railing.

"Merit, oh Jesus, Merit, I'm slipping."

"I'm nearly there, Mallory. You're doing great."

"Hurry, Merit. Please."

Her fingers disappeared as I pitched forward—and just managed to wrap fingers around her wrist.

She managed to bite back the scream, but I could see the terror in her eyes.

"Oh God, Merit." Her feet dangled above the river. "Oh God."

"You're going to be just fine. Remember how strong I am," I said, keeping a pleasant smile on my face. But strength wasn't the issue. Water was the issue. The slip of my boots on steel wet from melting snow, the slip of her skin in mine from the resulting humidity.

"*Shit. Shit. Shit.*"

"I'm going to pull you up on three," I said. "One, two . . ."

I didn't wait for three. I dug my heels into the frame and dug my nails into her skin, convinced that if I managed to get us out of this, she'd forgive me for the pain. I yanked her up with every ounce of strength I could muster, pulling until she was beside me.

She rested her head against mine. "I thought that was it. I thought that was the end of me."

"You think I'm going to just let you go? No, thank you."

She kissed the side of my head, then spat out grit. "You need a shower."

"You don't look so good yourself, friend."

"Rude."

"It's going to get ruder." I gestured up. "We have to climb back to the roadway."

"And then what?"

The dragon roared, and the bridge shook with it.

"And then we get the hell underground."

We waited until the dragon banked again, then scrambled back onto the road, where we sat for a moment with legs dangling over the asphalt. The lights were still flashing at the end of the bridge, but the ship had passed through. They'd be closing the bridge again soon.

"Suggestions?" Mallory said.

"Yes," I said as the creature turned back toward us. "I'm not going to be taken out by a lizard." I put her arm around my neck, put a hand around her waist. "We're going down the easy way."

"The easy way?" She looked over the rail to the Riverwalk that lined the bank of the river some hundred feet below. "Oh no."

"Oh yes."

The dragon was pissed that we'd survived, its wings beating angrily against the sky, its scream a symphony of fury.

"Hold on," I said. "And you might want to close your eyes."

She huffed out three hard breaths like a woman in labor. "Go. Just go and do it before I change my mind."

I held on to her, took a breath, and took the leap.

Time passed weirdly in midair, so it felt less like we were jumping than like we were simply stepping down. Except for the screaming in my ear.

When we landed with a soft bounce, Mallory slitted open one eye, glanced down at her legs.

"Completely intact," I said. "Unlike my eardrums."

Mallory opened both eyes and looked at me. "Merit," she said a little breathlessly. "You're kind of a badass."

"About damn time you figured that out," I said, and I didn't wait for her retort.

The dragon flew along the river and tried to snap at us, but couldn't get close enough. We ran up the steps and flew across Wacker, where I dragged her into the stairwell as the dragon crashed behind us, teeth snapping as it tried to push its way underground, breaking off concrete and tile with every movement.

We kept running until the stairway was out of sight, stood

huddled together until the dragon stopped screaming. The earth above us shook as it searched us out.

"I hate lizards," Mallory said, wiping brick dust and grime and tears from her face.

"Yeah," I said, glancing up at the blocked stairway. "I do, too."

We were bloody, dirty, and torn by the time we walked back toward Cadogan House. And unlike the last time, a Guard vehicle was parked outside the House, and soldiers with very large guns stood beside the humans we'd hired to guard the gate.

"I could guess they're providing security in case the dragon comes here. But that seems . . . unrealistic," Mallory finished.

"Yeah," I agreed.

We walked inside, found Ethan in his office in a clean shirt, tidy jeans. He, Catcher, and Malik were checking their phones, probably wondering where we were.

They looked up when we entered, expressions shifting from gratitude to bafflement.

"How do you look so clean?" I asked Ethan.

"We found a gypsy cab and got a ride home." He stared at Mallory and me, took in another day of torn and dirty clothes. "Why do you *not* look clean?" he asked, putting away his phone and walking toward us. "What the hell happened to you two?"

"We were chased by a goddamn dragon through the streets of goddamn Chicago," Mallory said, pushing past the men toward the beverage area. I had a sense she was headed for booze.

Ethan arched an eyebrow. "Long night, Sentinel?"

I handed Ethan my sword, my scabbard, and followed Mallory to the bar. "Bite me."

Mallory snorted as she poured liquor into glasses.

"What's with the guard at the door?" I asked.

"Yeah," Mallory said. "They keeping the dragon out, or the vampires in?"

"The latter," Catcher said. "Part of the mayor's efforts to work with the Guard and keep the 'situation' from escalating. There are soldiers posted at Grey and Navarre, too."

There were tunnels beneath the House that would get us past the guards if necessary.

"So a useless gesture to mollify the haters," I said. "What would happen if we tried to go back out there?"

"We would be rebuffed and told to stay indoors," Luc said. "Grey House tried. When they were threatened back at gunpoint, he called us and let us know the state of affairs."

I lifted my eyebrows. "And Grey was okay with that?"

Ethan smiled. "Grey is planning his next move."

"And Jeff?" I asked, realizing that he wasn't in Ethan's office, and neither were the manuscript and foldouts.

Catcher smiled. "He's in the Library. He's scanned in the folio pages, and he's making a program that will compute all possible arrangements and make predictions about which ones are most likely."

"He's a smart one," I said as Mallory came back, offered me a glass. I finished it in a single gulp.

"And what do we do now?" Mallory asked.

"Now," Ethan said with a heavy sigh, "we watch. And we wait."

Mallory and Catcher joined Jeff. The rest of us gathered in the ballroom with the rest of Cadogan's Novitiates to watch the dragon's progress through the city.

The Guard kept firing, trying to drive it closer to the Lake, maybe hoping it would fly north for the remains of the summer and become Canada's problem. But it hadn't worked. The dragon wouldn't be led; it flew where it wanted to go.

So the Guard took to the sky, sent F-16s against the dragon.

That had been another mistake.

Bravery and tactics were no match for a sentient monster that could fly, land, run, hide, and lift off again. Humans had been out-maneuvered, and Chicago had borne the brunt of their failure.

Novitiates around me wept softly as images of the city filled the screen.

Concrete, steel, and glass replaced the snow that had covered downtown Chicago, toppled from buildings. Towers of smoke rose from a dozen fires through downtown. The Navy Pier Ferris wheel had fallen—or been thrown—into the soaring glass of the Shakespeare Theater. An exterior section of the Hancock tower had been gouged away, a tangle of steel and wires hanging from the scar that remained. The top of the Wrigley building had been sheared away, and the lions in front of the Art Institute had been tumbled into the street like broken toys.

The battle had wreaked destruction through the city.

And still the dragon flew.

The dragon had been injured, so blood smeared its body and the trail it left throughout Chicago. But that hadn't stopped it. Its wings remained intact, which was enough to keep it airborne. The dragon had roosted on Towerline roof. Since it hadn't gone any deeper into the city, Mallory speculated the creature was tied to the building—and its magical origin point.

The dragon—the Egregore—had gotten the worst of Chicago, its anger and fear and hopelessness. But it had also gotten some of its perseverance.

Ethan offered to provide transportation for any vampires who wished to leave Chicago. None of them did. Leaving would have felt like giving up. Not that staying was any easier.

Watching our home be destroyed by a monster we didn't know how to kill, a monster that seemed impervious to human weapons, was miserable. Ethan tried to give us hope, bolster our courage, but watching one image of destruction after another filling the screens drained away hope, left grief and numbness behind.

I wasn't sure Chicago would survive this.

I wasn't sure any of us would.

"Do you think they'll figure out this isn't working before or after Navy Pier's in the water?" Catcher asked.

The coverage split-screened to a news studio.

"Sorcha Reed has been neutralized, and the National Guard is working to lead the creature out of the city," the mayor said, "and is very optimistic about their progress to date. In the meantime, the vampires remain in their Houses and are not involved in current containment efforts."

"Public Enemy Number One ate Public Enemy Number Two," Luc corrected. "Maybe it's just me, but I don't think that means the mayor neutralized jack shit."

Pundits tended to agree with him. They blasted the mayor for failing to keep the city safe—and causing more destruction in the city's efforts to kill the dragon—and us for contributing to the chaos.

"I'm not saying this was the vampires' fault," said one woman with big hair and a pinched face. "But these are the dangers of living in integrated communities—that humans will be dragged into their internal struggles. Into their violence."

Angry magic roiling off him in waves, Ethan looked back at Luc. "Schedule a press conference. It's time we did some talking of our own."

CHAPTER TWENTY-FOUR

IMPRESSED

We waited until a couple of hours before dawn, hoping that even if the National Guard didn't scare off the dragon, it would take its leave during the day like it had before.

This time, our hope wasn't futile. Its movements had begun to slow, each flap of its wings seeming heavier than the last. After a final flight over the Chicago Lighthouse, the dragon disappeared in the direction of the sunrise. But the mayor didn't remove the soldiers outside Cadogan House.

It was late for us and early for humans, but it didn't matter. The first press conference held by Navarre House more than a year ago had pulled them in. And now, this first time he'd agreed to hold a press conference, the city would finally hear from Ethan Sullivan.

Representatives of magazines, Web sites, radio and television stations, and newspapers—including our shifter friend Nick Breckenridge, who wrote for the *Tribune*—weren't going to miss this. They gathered on the Cadogan House lawn. Ethan stood on the front steps in his suit, strong and powerful, his attitude completely different from the supernatural eroticism Celina Desaulniers had worked to project at her press conference.

Ethan didn't need to work at it. His power was nearly tangible, his confidence unwavering. He'd played the political game in the interest of peace. Now he would fight back.

He wore a trim, black suit, button-down, and tie in the deepest crimson. Malik, Luc, and I stood in suits behind him, swords belted at our sides. We were the representatives of Cadogan House. And tonight, we would have our say.

"Ladies and gentlemen," he began, and a hush fell over the crowd so quickly he might have used magic to make it happen. But that wasn't necessary. The crowd was rapt.

"My name is Ethan Sullivan, and this is my House. Last night, Sorcha Reed used magic to manifest the creature that has been terrorizing the city. Due to, we believe, a complicated sequence of magic initiated by Sorcha with the financial and political assistance of her human husband, Adrien Reed, she was able to make physical a distillation of magical energy. That energy caused the delusions which affected Chicagoans; the freeze was caused by her gathering of magic as she worked to condense that energy into the dragon that has attacked downtown Chicago."

Probably surprised to get answers to the magical questions that plagued the city, the reporters began shouting questions at Ethan.

Utterly unperturbed, he ignored them.

The three of us all bit back smiles. This was our imperious Master at his political best.

"Do not be mistaken," he said. "The dragon was created by Sorcha Reed to terrorize this city. And though she may be gone, she has succeeded at that. The city is destroying itself in an effort to kill a creature that clearly has defenses to human weapons.

"Unlike others, we will not discuss blame. We will not talk about failures or missteps, because that solves nothing, and because it takes the focus away from where it should be—on the perpetrator of these crimes. On a woman whose self-centeredness and egoism have wrought destruction over the city. We will note that destruction, in part, was caused by this city's willingness to believe human over supernatural, to give deference to humans with wealth and power, and to blame others for their failures. That attitude must change.

"Chicago is not perfect. But Chicago is ours, and it has been ours for a very long time. We have protected it as we've been able, and we will continue to do so. We are not the city's enemy. We are Chicagoland's vampires. Human solutions to this problem have not worked. When you're ready to discuss a real solution, you know how to reach us."

With that, he turned on his heel and walked inside, leaving reporters yelling questions in his wake.

Ethan's phone rang before he'd even made it back to his office. He answered it, eyebrows lifting. "Madam Mayor." A pause. "Yes. We will."

The call lasted less than a minute, and then the phone was put away again. But the smile on his face looked pretty damn good.

"The mayor has formally requested we step in and handle the dragon in the manner we feel most appropriate. The CPD and National Guard await our instructions."

Now we could begin. And a good thing, because we had a lot of work to do.

We assembled the Ombuddies in the Ops Room again, and the energy was much different from the last time. Lindsey picked "Bad Blood" as our preparation music, and the vibe made us all feel pretty vindicated.

Scott Grey and Jonah showed up, as did Gabriel and Morgan. I'd wondered if Claudia would put in an appearance, but she wasn't the helping type. Besides, we didn't yet know what Sorcha's death had done to her newly replenished power; she might not have been interested in destroying the dragon.

"And so," Ethan said as everyone gathered coffee and filled seats at the conference table, "we find ourselves here again."

"And with authority," Scott said, raising his mug to Ethan. "Kudos."

Ethan nodded. "This is a rare and important moment, and we need to capitalize upon it. That's why we're here—to create a plan for dealing with Sorcha Reed's creation once and for all."

"Hear, hear," Gabe said, and lifted his mug. I guess even shifters with flasks needed coffee sometimes.

"In that case," Ethan said, "I believe our Ombuddies have an update. And one honorary Ombuddy," he said as Mallory, Jeff, and Catcher stepped to the front of the room.

"Clicker?" Jeff said, and Luc tossed the screen remote to him. Jeff caught it handily, turned on the large view screen.

"So, Mallory and Catcher figured a sorcerer who's taken the time to explain how to manifest an Egregore is also going to explain what to do when things go bad."

"When the Egregore acts out," Gabe said.

"Exactly. Since we're short on time, we'll skip the programming details. Suffice it to say, while we snoozed, the program worked through the many, many combinations of arrangements that would explain how to, basically, dismantle the Egregore."

"Like a Lego pattern in reverse," Mallory said.

"Kind of like that," Jeff said with a smile. "At Northerly Island, we learned magic pretty much bounces off the dragon's scales, and they're very hard to permeate. At least part of that is because of its nature, the fact that it's a creature born of magic. Like you have immortality and shifters have strength, the Egregore has a certain resiliency."

"So we're out of luck?" Morgan asked.

"Not entirely," Jeff said, and held up the remote. "Because of this."

A blocky white sword filled the screen.

"A Lego sword?" Scott Grey asked, eyebrow cocked.

"Not Lego," Jeff said with a smile, and zoomed in. "Just reordered."

It wasn't a sword made of blocks; it was a sword made of paper. Each "block" was actually a page of the Danzig foldouts, carefully organized into this new shape.

"Computer hit on this arrangement after about seven long hours," Jeff said. "And when you look at the illustration unlocked by this magic and the arrangement, you get this." He held up the remote again.

This time, the pixelated sword was replaced by a line drawing of a sleek, two-handed broadsword with a gleaming jewel in the middle of its hand guard. Below the sword lay the split body of the manifested Egregore.

"It explains how to enhance a sword to increase its potency against the Egregore," Jeff said, beaming with pleasure. "Long story short, each hit will do more damage than it ordinarily would."

"As we fight with swords," Ethan said, "a very handy solution."

"Handy," Catcher agreed, "but not infallible. Presuming the magic works the way Portnoy has laid it out, you'd still be facing a magic monster with increased, as Jeff said, resiliency. It won't be easy to bring down even with a magic sword."

"I'll wield the blade," Ethan said.

I gave him my most Masterly look. "You most certainly will not. I'm Sentinel of this House. I'll wield it."

There was nothing especially pleasant in Ethan's eyes. "I don't doubt your prowess. I do have concerns about sending my wife into a battle with the only sword."

"So I'll enchant more than one."

We looked back at Catcher, whose lips were curved with amusement.

"You could do that?" Ethan asked.

He shrugged. "I don't see why not. We've got Portnoy's instructions and plenty of steel."

I looked back at Ethan, brows lifted.

For a moment, he breathed silently, looking not unlike a dragon himself with his fierce and angry eyes. But acceptance eventually filtered through.

"You'll be careful. And I'll go with you."

It was my turn to frown, to deal, to accept, but we'd sworn we would be partners to each other. Of course, that didn't mean we couldn't use another partner.

"How about four swords?" I asked Catcher.

"Four?" Ethan asked.

"One for me, one for you"—I looked at Jonah—"and two for him, because he's very good with dual blades."

Jonah smiled. "I'm game, subject to Scott's approval."

Scott nodded. "Permission granted."

"Then it sounds like we've decided on a sword battle with a dragon," my grandfather said. "We need to minimize the damage to the city while it's under way, preferably to zero. No injuries, minimal collateral damage."

Luc nodded. "We need a space big enough to contain a dragon, but contained."

"I don't think there's a dragon arena in Illinois," Jeff said with a grin.

"Actually, I've got an idea," Jonah said, then looked at Scott, smiled. "A place that's already big enough to contain Bears."

My grandfather snorted. "You're either thinking the Lincoln Park Zoo or Soldier Field."

"Soldier Field," Jonah confirmed. "Plenty of space on the

inside—more than a hundred yards of it from end to end. But it's contained, at least in two dimensions."

"And the parking lot and lake are buffers," my grandfather said. "So that would help contain damage."

"I doubt the Chicago Park District would be stoked about letting us use Soldier Field for a dragon battle," Mallory said.

"It won't be a problem."

We all looked at Scott.

"We have certain contacts in the sports community," he said. "We'll make it work, ensure the lights are on."

"And how do we lure the dragon into our little trap?" I asked.

"Simple," Mallory said with a smile. "We bring bait."

"You will not be bait," Catcher said.

"Oh, hell no," she agreed. "I've already seen one sorceress get chewed up this week." She waved it off. "The dragon doesn't want me anyway, not really. Remember—it's the manifestation of the Egregore, of a very angry Chicago. With a little creative spell casting, we can create an offer it won't be able to refuse."

I glanced at Mallory. "When we make that offer, and it shows up, and we kill it, what happens to the Egregore, to the magic? Would we release that back into the world again, and just set ourselves up for more drama? For another round of this in the future?"

"There's a risk," Catcher said with a nod. "The magic doesn't dissipate cleanly, just spreads out over downtown again, and we have more delusions, more violence."

"That would be an unacceptable risk," my grandfather said.

"We need to nail that down," I said. "We can't risk letting the magic spread again, or having six or seven tons of dragon fall onto downtown Chicago. We need to take the dragon down, and we need to keep that magic bound together."

"Actually," Mallory said, "Portnoy thought of that, too. Jeff?" she requested, and he panned the zoomed image on-screen to another corner of the arranged pages. There, the Egregore spark was enclosed in some kind of orb.

"He trapped it," Ethan said.

"Technically," Mallory said, "he bound it into quartz. But yeah, same effect."

"So what do we use to bind it?" Gabriel asked with a grin. "World's largest piece of Tupperware?"

"Could be anything," Mallory said with a smile. "As long as it's strong enough to hold the magic without breaking."

"Maybe we can keep it simple," I said. I unbelted my katana, placed it on the table, brilliant red scabbard gleaming beneath the lights. "We'll already have our swords. Can you trap it in steel?"

Catcher opened his mouth, closed it again.

"Is that possible?" Ethan asked. "To bind magic in steel?"

"Like Mallory said, it just needs to be capable of holding magic, and we know it can. The tricky bit would be the size differential. The sword is not literally large enough to hold a dragon's worth of magic. But we might be able to finagle it." Catcher nodded as he considered. "You'll need a protocol. Words, steps. I'll let you know."

My grandfather nodded. "In that case, we've got the place, the weapons, the bait, the binding."

"And tomorrow at dusk," Ethan said, "we finish the job."

As dawn approached again, the Ombuddies returned to their offices, the vampires to their Houses. Mallory and Catcher returned to Wicker Park to ready the magic. We returned to our apartments. Ethan closed and locked the door, emotions heavy around us.

"This could all be over tomorrow," I said.

He looked at me. "I'm not sure if you're saying that with relief or regret."

"Both, I think."

He walked toward me, put a hand on my face. "How are you?"

"I'm managing. How about you?"

"Things feel . . ."

"Precarious," I finished, and knew by the relief in his eyes that I'd captured it exactly. "I've had the same feeling. But, then, we talked about that."

"So we did," he said, careful not to let emotion peek through his voice.

"And I was wrong."

His brows lifted, and a smile crossed his face. "Unfortunate that Nick Breckenridge isn't here with his recorder."

"I assume you mean that metaphorically."

"I do," he said. "What, precisely, were you wrong about?"

I put my arms around him, rested my head against his heart. "About family." I thought of the terror and joy, equally matched, in the faces of Taylor and her mother. "There will always be fear. The possibility of loss. But that's life. And what's the point of living if you don't take a chance on love?"

He went quiet. "And a child?"

"If we're lucky enough, then yes."

"Then yes," Ethan said, and wasted no time. I was pressed against the door, his mouth frantic and possessive, as if each kiss might seal our connection to each other, brand his taste and scent onto me.

He pulled off the suit jacket I still wore with strong and questing hands, dropped it to the floor, and pressed his body against mine.

I only managed to slip one of his buttons before he threw away his jacket, pulled his shirt over his head, and pulled the tank over my head. And then his hands were on my breasts, and I dropped my head against the door, eyes closed as nimble and skilled fingers lit and tended the fire heating in my core.

And then I was in his arms, and he was carrying me effort-lessly to the bed, placing me onto cool sheets with the care used for a priceless antique.

"I'm not delicate," I reminded him, and crooked a finger at him. "Come here, husband of mine."

His smile was slow, masculine, and very satisfied. He stripped off the rest of his clothes, his arousal heavy, and crawled to-ward me.

I reached for him, but he captured my hands, brought them together over my head.

He traveled down my body, removed the remaining scraps of clothing, and touched me until I was quivering with pleasure.

His own body quaking with restrained power, he covered my body again, shifted inside me with a thrust that was equally force-ful and tender. We moved our bodies together, legs intertwined and hips rolling, pleasure building like a wave banking over us.

I tilted my neck toward him, offering him the intimacy, the connection, that only vampires could share. "Take," I said to him, and, when his fangs pierced tender skin, and lightning bowed my body, called his name.

Forever, he said, our new mantra. Our love spell.

Forever, I agreed, and gave over to sensation.

CHAPTER TWENTY-FIVE

DRINK WITH ME

At dusk, the dragon was back, perching on the Chicago Lighthouse, where the Red Guards that inhabited it stayed silent and monitored its activities.

The mayor and governor were eager to move. But we were waiting on our sorcerers and their magic.

Mallory's text messages, which she sent me throughout the day when she should have been sleeping, and the rest of us were allayed by the sun, told quite a story:

BEGINNING WORK ON WEAPON MAGIC.

WEAPON MAGIC IS WEIRD.

SNACK BREAK! CREAM CHEESE DOUBLE BACON!

CB NEEDS "BACKGROUND NOISE." TV MOVED INTO BASEMENT 4 LIFETIME MOVIES. HE IS ALSO WEIRD.

MINORISH BASEMENT FIRE.

. . . IS NOW BIGGISH BASEMENT FIRE.

FIRE CONTAINED. WE DIDN'T NEED THOSE NAT'L GEOGRAPHICS ANYWAY.

YAWN

I'D LIKE TO SEE ICELAND.

PROGRESS!

APPEARANCE BY MINORISH BASEMENT FIRE'S ANGRIER, MORE FIREY
COUSIN.

FIRE CONTAINED TO CHAGRIN OF FIRE.

WEAPON MAGIC IS STILL WEIRD.

The later it got, the loopier the messages. Mallory and Catcher
had been awake for thirty-six hours, refusing to sleep so they
could figure out the binding magic.

They were still going at dusk. Being that we were vampires,
and because we were headed into battle, there were of course
ceremonies to be had while we waited.

According to the *Canon of the North American Houses, Desk Reference*, it was a tradition of Cadogan House, a tradition established
long ago by Peter Cadogan, the House's first Master, at dusk before a big battle. All the vampires of the House would gather together with mutton and ale, and the Master would give a rousing
speech that called the House to victory.

The cafeteria was full, each space at each table taken, and
vampires shoehorned into corners wherever room enough for a
plate could be had. Someone had brought in folding chairs from
the storage room, and the rest stood around the edge of the room,
yawning and waiting for the ceremony to begin.

We'd been ready to go into battle before, when we thought
we'd be facing down Sorcha, getting an opportunity to knock the
smug smile from her face and close that particular chapter of our
lives. Tonight, the mood was somber.

Ethan sat beside me at the table, a pewter stein in front of him.

"The Master's chalice?" I asked.

Ethan smiled, reached out, turned the mug so I could see the
neat inscription on the opposite side: CADOGAN HOUSE BOWLING
LEAGUE, FIRST PLACE, 1979.

"Why haven't we had a bowling league since I've been here? I can bowl."

"You're the social chair," Ethan pointed out. "So that's technically your fault."

Tough, but fair. "I didn't know you bowled."

"I don't," he said with a smile. "But it's my House, and to the sponsor goes the spoils." He pushed back his chair and rose, buttoning the top button of his impeccable suit. Even before battle, Ethan would lead his people. He would Master them, and then soldier them.

A hush instantly fell over the room. "Novitiates."

"Master," they said in unison, as if responding to a pastor's call-and-response.

I didn't say it, because I hadn't known it was a thing. I should have perused the actual *Canon* instead of just the *Desk Reference*. Not that I'd had a lot of free time.

"There have been many battles in the previous days. Many acts of bravery among our people, and many acts of treachery by those outside our House, including the woman whose name will no longer be spoken in its halls.

"In those other battles, we followed the dictates of others who believed, however wrong they were, that they knew what was best for the city. Tonight, we strike out against a monster plaguing the city in our own manner, in our own way." He paused, leaving every vampire on the edge of his or her seat. "Tonight, we fight with steel."

There were *whoop*s of approval.

"Whatever happens here tonight, know that I am proud to be your Master, and proud that you are my Novitiates." He raised a cup. "All hail Cadogan House!"

"Cadogan House! Cadogan House! Cadogan House!" Hands slapped tables in time with the chanting, as Ethan drank from his stein and toasted the room.

* * *

"It was a good speech," Malik said, when Ethan sat again. "You will stay alive, or I will be monumentally irritated."

"Hear, hear," I said, and raised my cup.

Because hungry vampires were dangerous vampires, carts were rolled around the room by Margot's staff, and food was dished out to hungry vampires. She brought the cart to our table herself.

Margot placed dishes in front of us. "Breakfast du jour," Margot said, and lifted the silver dome.

On a plate big enough to serve the entire table was an enormous amount of food. Eggs, bacon, sausage, ham—in case the bacon and sausage weren't porky enough—sliced tomatoes, neatly cubed potatoes, toast, a muffin with a suspicious absence of chocolate chips, a cup of fruit, and a pile of what I thought were grits. I hadn't tried grits before. Although that was beside the point. There was also something black and vaguely sausagelike that I didn't want to think too much about.

"I don't think I need all this."

"You have a battle to attend to. Meat for protein, carbs for energy." She pointed at the tomatoes. "Lycopene and vitamin C for improved healing." She pointed to the bottle of Blood4You that another vampire had placed beside my plate. "The blood is self-explanatory. Because you're a vampire," she explained anyway.

"Yeah, I figured that one on my own." I poked the black blob with a fork. "And black sausage because . . . ?"

"Because it's delicious. It's blood sausage, and an old family recipe."

I believed the second, doubted the first, and poked at the rubbery cylinder with my fork.

Eat your breakfast, Sentinel. Or I'll tell everyone why you're especially hungry this evening.

I forked a potato obediently.

*　　*　　*

Like the mayor, Ethan was ready to move the moment Catcher arrived. But Catcher insisted on training first, on careful preparation for the magic we'd have to face.

In our fighting gear again—but minus shoes—we met in the House's training room, where dark wood walls reached down to floors covered in tatami mats.

Catcher wore jeans and a Hawkeye T-shirt today, while Mallory opted for jeans and a Black Widow T-shirt. They looked exhausted, but managing it.

Catcher carried a black canvas bag to the middle of the floor, began to unload scabbards from it as vampires filed into the balcony that ringed the room to watch. My scabbard was red, Ethan's black. Jonah's scabbards were bright yellow, the wrapping on each handle vermillion red. All four were absolutely gorgeous, and undeniably deadly.

"If Portnoy's got it right, you'll be able to do more damage with each blow than with a nonmagicked sword. But like I said, you don't want to get too comfortable. This is still a monster, and a supernatural one."

"Don't let him step on you," Jonah said.

"Pretty much," Catcher agreed.

"The armor on his toes was relatively weak," I said. "That may also be the case on his underbelly. Slipping the blade between the plates of armor might work."

Catcher nodded approvingly.

"And how will the binding work?" Ethan asked.

"Similar to tempering the blades," he said. "Blood on the blade, then say the magic words." He pulled out his phone, typed something, and ours beeped a second later. We pulled them out, scanned the lines of text.

"Those are your charms," Catcher said. "Memorize them, and don't forget."

"I was an English lit student. I can recite a four-line poem like a boss."

"It's true," Mallory said. "I used to make her recite Shakespearean sonnets. I threw popcorn at her when she got the lines wrong."

"You two have a complicated relationship," Catcher said, gaze narrowed.

"Besties," Mallory said with a shrug by way of explanation.

"What comes after the words?" Jonah asked.

"The dragon has to be mortally wounded, with that sword." Catcher looked at us. "So whoever of you kills it also binds it."

"Roger that," Jonah said.

Catcher looked at us. "And you should know—there could be side effects."

Ethan's gaze narrowed. "What kind of side effects?"

"It's hard to say, because we're dealing with a creature made of magic, which adds an unknowable element. But my concern is that you'll be affected by the very magic you'll be casting."

"In other words," Ethan said, "because we'll be holding the sword when we bind the dragon to it, we could be bound, too."

"I don't know," Catcher said. "But, yeah, that's my concern."

My grandfather looked at each of us, his gaze settling on me. "Your call whether to proceed knowing that. If this won't work, we'll try something else."

There wasn't really a call to make. This wasn't like the issue of children, of facing the possibility of love and loss. There was only one option here—keep the dragon from killing anyone else—so there was no point in fear or worry. There was just the doing.

"I'm in," I said, and looked at Jonah and Ethan. They nodded, too.

"If that's what we have to do," Jonah said, "it's what we have to do."

"Good," my grandfather said. "Good."

"Okay," Catcher said with a smile, clearly proud of our determination. "Let's test them out."

I wasn't bashful about swordcraft, so I stepped onto the mats, picked up my scabbard.

"It's heavier," I said, and flipped the thumb guard, released the blade with a ringing *whish* of sound.

I hadn't expected it to look different. I hadn't expected the katana to have a soft glow, like a little CGI had been added to its edges so it gleamed.

"Hello, beautiful," I said, and slipped a finger down the top of the blade, felt the answering call that sent a shiver down my spine.

"If only she looked at me that way," Ethan said, then unsheathed his own sword. "My, my, my."

Jonah's reaction was pretty much similar, except that he kept getting distracted by glances at the gallery, where Margot sat with Lindsey and Katherine. And to my eye, she looked like she was working very hard to ignore him.

Catcher picked up a *bokken*, a wooden practice sword, tapped it against his hand. "You can take practice swings at me," he said, "so you can get a feel for how they move."

"I was kind of hoping you'd be wearing a dragon costume," I said, extending one hand above my head and the other behind me. "With head and tail and the whole shebang."

"That would probably make for a better simulation," Catcher agreed. "But let's use what we've got."

The sword moved like air was, on its own, something to be cut through. But after half an hour of swinging it around, it started to feel natural.

And those scanty thirty minutes were all we could afford—all the time we could take to prepare ourselves for the coming battle. For the dragon hadn't been content to sit on the lighthouse long. And it left destruction in its wake.

"Mallory's got the bait," Catcher said as we rode to Soldier Field. She was in the van with Jeff, my grandfather, and the crucible she'd use to lure the dragon toward us.

"I'll be standing by, in case the weapons need a boost, or we need to use fireballs to keep the dragon inside the stadium. Mallory will set the bait and join me, and the field will be yours."

Ethan nodded. "Let's finish the mission and win the game."

CPD cruisers and National Guard vehicles formed a perimeter around the stadium parking lot to keep curious humans away from the battle, and deflect the dragon, if necessary, back toward the stadium, at least when the dragon arrived.

In the meantime, it had roamed as it pleased. The National Guard had held its fire this time, fearing that loosing more mortars and missiles on the city would only wreak further destruction. I wasn't sure they could have done any better.

The stadium glowed with light, sending up a yellow haze over the city. I wasn't sure whether the dragon was attracted to light, but it couldn't hurt in getting him to the right place.

Brody pulled the SUV up to the service entrance, where CPD officers waited for us. We climbed out with our quartet of magicked swords. The Ombudsman's van pulled up behind us. Mallory hopped out, took the pitted ceramic pot that Jeff handed her, followed by Jeff and my grandfather.

Pierce and Wilcox walked toward us. For a moment, I was afraid the mayor had reneged on her promise, and we'd have to arrange our battle within their rules and parameters. That fear dissolved quickly enough.

"Everything should be ready," Wilcox said, offering Ethan a hand. "The ops plan looks good."

"I have a very capable team," Ethan said, returning the greeting.

The rest of us exchanged the appropriate hellos.

"The helicopter's waiting in case anyone needs an evac," my grandfather said.

"Good," Wilcox said. "We're on standby out here, with guns ready in case the dragon needs to be pushed back toward the stadium." He looked at my grandfather and Jeff. "You'll be coordinating that from the van?"

"We will," my grandfather confirmed.

Wilcox nodded and looked at our swords, brow lifted. "You sure that's enough firepower?"

Ethan's smile was thin. "We're sure. You let us do what we do best, and we'll end this tonight."

"Understood," Wilcox said.

"And if this doesn't end tonight," Pierce began, "what's the backup plan?"

"There is no backup plan," Ethan said. "We fight the dragon until it's dead, or we are. It's that simple."

Her eyes widened, but she nodded. "Then I'll leave it to you."

"Good," he said. *If only they'd done that in the first place . . .*

I put a hand at his back. *They've done it now. So we'll do what we can.*

The law-enforcement types stayed outside the stadium. We walked through the dark tunnel toward the playing field, and I bet our sense of anticipation wasn't much different from what the professional athletes felt on their way to a game. Excitement, nerves, adrenaline, and a killer instinct.

"You ready?" Mallory asked me.

"I absolutely am." I felt calmer than I had in days. I knew how to use my sword, my sword had been charmed for extra power, and I had two very good fighters at my side. This was, literally and figuratively, what I'd trained for.

"Get it," Mallory said, and we bumped knuckles.

We walked onto the field, the lights glowing above us, the seats stretched in an oval around us.

"Lions in the coliseum," Catcher murmured.

"Better than gladiators facing lions," Ethan said. But he held back when Catcher, Mallory, and Jonah walked into the middle of the field, turned to me.

"This is my last opportunity to request that you don't fight tonight."

I lifted my brows at him, irritated that he was going to start an argument before a battle.

"But I won't make that request," he continued with a smile before I could object. "Because I know you. And because I cherish who you are." He put a hand against my cheek, rubbed his thumb along my jaw. "You will fight for the city, for the people who cannot fight for themselves. There is no better reason to fight fiercely."

I smiled at him. "You're a pretty good reason."

He smiled, touched his forehead to mine. "I love you beyond reason."

"Same goes for me. Otherwise, I'd have locked you away in the House a long time ago." I leaned up, kissed him on the lips. "Go make me proud, Sullivan."

"Same for you, Sentinel. Stay safe."

I'd never been in Soldier Field without people. It was odd, to be in such a large and empty space. It wouldn't be empty for long, and I had a sinking suspicion it wouldn't feel very large with a dragon in it. But we'd cross that bridge when we came to it.

"Mallory," Catcher said as we unsheathed our swords, left the scabbards by the entrance tunnel. "You're up."

She blew out a breath, nodded, and carried her pot into the middle of the field, right on the fifty-yard line.

She put it down, then looked back at us, held up a finger. "One thing first," she yelled as we walked toward her, and then leaned down and did a tidy cartwheel across the grass, followed by a front handspring.

When she came up, she pulled down her shirt, pushed her hair out of her eyes. "I've always wanted to do that," she said with a grin. "Figured I'd get it in now in case I don't get another chance."

"You are medal ready," Ethan said with a grin.

We took the positions we'd agreed upon—four roughly cardinal points around her, fifteen feet away.

She pulled out a can of white spray paint, grinned as she shook it up, the metal bearings rolling around inside.

"I've always wanted to do this, too," she said, and began to spray white symbols around the crucible, symbols of alchemy.

When that was done, she tossed the can away, pulled a vial from her pocket, and emptied it into the crucible.

"What is this, exactly?" Ethan asked.

"A little river water, a little scraping from Sorcha's alchemy, a smidge of grass from Wrigley Field, and sand from Oak Street Beach, and a few other odds and ends, combined with a little magic of my own. Like calls to like," she said, straightening again. "Or at least that's the theory."

She pulled a box of matches from her pocket and took one out, holding it up while she waited for our nods.

"Ready," Ethan said, and she nodded.

"And away we go," she said, and whipped the match against the side of the box, sparking sulfur into the air.

She dropped the flame into the crucible. Almost immediately, thick white smoke began to rise from the vessel's top, streaming upward in a column toward the sky and spilling the Egregore's scents into the air. Smoke, earth, and water, carried by magic.

The smoke rose like a signal fire over the stadium and seemed to glow orange in the lights. Mallory took a seat on the ground.

"While we have a moment," I said, "how's Margot?"

Jonah looked startled by the question. "I'm not— Why do you ask?"

I gave him a bland look.

"That was a setup?"

"It was supposed to be. No spark?"

He rolled his eyes. "I'm not going to discuss this with you."

I narrowed my gaze at him, but the harsh look didn't work. I'd have to talk to Margot later.

"The dragon's moving," said Wilcox in our ear. "He's off the lighthouse and headed your way. ETA three minutes."

"Lighthouse still intact?" Jonah asked.

"It is."

"Good," Jonah said with a nod. "That's something, anyway."

Some nights, you took the victories you could get.

CONSEQUENTIALLY

The dragon circled once, then twice, around the tower of smoke, screaming wildly. Like called to like, and I couldn't help but wonder what it said. Was it hopeful there was another like it, or angry at what it might have believed was the origin of its anger?

"Swords up!" Ethan called out, and we lifted our blades.

It dove like a waterbird and came in fast, moving within twenty feet of us before banking again, rising along the bleachers, and turning for another pass.

It dropped again, and this time aimed for Mallory.

Jonah jumped, spun his katanas against the dragon's right wing, managed to nick the tendon.

I ran beneath the dragon, sliced at its leg, in a spot with scales thicker than those on its toes.

The sword was strong, and Catcher's magic made it stronger, but it was still tough going, felt like cutting through concrete. Each millimeter forward took a disproportionate amount of effort.

I managed to slice a wound into its thigh. The dragon shrieked and ascended again, trailing blood into the sky. And then it turned and headed in for another round.

"Second volley!" Catcher said, and Ethan rolled his blade around his body, gaze set on the creature arrowing toward him.

The dragon reached him, snapped its teeth, and roared with pain and anger. *ENEMIES*.

Ethan dodged gnashing teeth and swung the sword in an arc, catching the plates on the underside of the dragon's neck. They cracked with a snap, like tiles breaking against concrete, blood welling in the cut beneath them.

The dragon hit the ground, rolled, leaving a trail of blood across the grass, and scenting the air with blood and chemicals. Ethan ran toward it, sliced its leg. I did the same with the other, then darted away when the dragon roared with anger, rose to its feet.

Our magicked swords were working. We actually had a chance at this.

And wasn't that always when pride got in the way?

The dragon climbed to its feet. It was nimble in the air, but not on the ground, so I expected it to amble forward. Instead, it darted to the side, head snapping. Its teeth—serrated and sharp—scraped against my arm, leaving a trail of pain and heat.

I cursed and dodged away, and the dragon screamed as a katana lodged in its foreleg only inches away from my head.

I looked back at Jonah, hand still lifted in perfect follow-through form.

"No throwing swords near a vampire's head!" I called out. "New rule!"

"Saved your ass, didn't it?" he said, running forward and hopping onto the dragon's foot, snatching back his sword before flipping away again.

Little wonder he was captain of the Grey House guards.

"Your arm?" he asked.

"It's fine." It actually burned like fire, but that didn't much matter now.

Ethan and Catcher went in for another volley; Catcher tossed fireballs while Ethan spun forward, going in low and catching slices across the dragon's abdomen. The dragon pushed Ethan away, sent him sailing onto his back.

You good, tiger?

Fine, he said, climbing to his feet again, cheeks pinked with anger. *But now I'm pissed.*

With what I'd swear looked like fury in his eyes, the dragon slapped its tail at the fireball, sending it flying through the air. Catcher dodged, but not fast enough. It caught him across the thigh, searing his jeans and the skin beneath.

"Shit!" he said, and fought for control.

FIRE, the dragon said.

It was learning, had figured out how to use its scales' resistance to fireballs to launch them back at us.

Ethan got another shot at its abdomen, and the dragon turned, wings flying around it. "Jonah!" I called out, but a moment too late. The swipe caught Ethan, sent him sprawling forward into the grass.

He didn't get up immediately, and I had to tell myself he was a vampire and could take care of himself, that he'd just had the breath knocked out of him.

I needed to bind the dragon now, before it hurt anyone else.

I put my palm against the katana's cutting edge, pulled. Pain shot through my hand as blood beaded at the edge of the steel.

I turned the blade on its side, watched the drops of blood roll down the blade as if with purpose and into the inscription Catcher had etched there. Blood met magic, and fire burst across the blade, which quickly spread from handle to tip.

"With blade and blood I bind you," I screamed, yelling the words that Catcher had composed.

YOU CANNOT BIND ME. I AM EVERYTHING.

"You are pain and death."

SHE GAVE ME LIFE, POWER.

"And you killed her, so don't lie to me. With this blade and blood I bind you!"

The dragon screamed and flapped its wings and began to ascend straight out of the stadium. I wasn't sure how intelligent it was, but I was pretty sure it wouldn't fall for Mallory's bait twice. That meant this was our one and only chance to take it down without more injuries, more deaths.

I'd either have to give up, or go with it.

If I didn't stop it now, it would destroy more of Chicago. More people, more sups, would be injured and killed. More homes and businesses destroyed. The apocalypse would continue.

But if I jumped, if I took flight with it, I'd have to face my fear of heights, and I'd have to face it alone. I'd have to fight the dragon without Mallory, Catcher, Jonah . . . or Ethan. I'd have to fight him alone—just me and my steel—in a place of his choosing. And then I'd have to find my way back.

I'd have to face the risk of losing, of dying on whatever field it chose for the inevitable battle.

For a moment, I was back in the green land, with the child's laughter echoing across the hills. The laughter, I thought, of a happy little girl.

Yes, I thought, as tears blossomed again, we might never know her. Or worse, we might know her and lose her, as my parents had done with their first Caroline. But if there was a chance I was to be a mother—her mother—she deserved more than fear and bravery. She deserved a Sentinel of her own, someone who would fight for her father, her family, her city.

Gabriel's test, I realized, wasn't about triumph or victory. It wasn't about winning. It was about bravery. It was about trying, and persevering. It was about staying the course even when things seemed desperate, even when all seemed lost.

That left me only one choice.

I ran toward the dragon and jumped, gripping for purchase with my nails one of the ridges that lined his spine and climbing up his leg.

NO, it screamed, furious at the contact, but didn't have enough rotation in the limb to shake me loose.

Its scales were pitted and cracked, giving me handholds to climb the relatively short distance from leg to neck, then throw a leg over its side, settling between two ridges on its back.

Our fates were bound together now. Either the dragon would live and die by my sword—or we both would.

"Merit!"

I wasn't sure whether Ethan screamed the word aloud, or silently for me. But it ran through the air on a current of fear and grief and fury that I'd offered myself up.

Too bad. I was Sentinel of my goddamned House.

I love you, I silently said, and hoped that he could hear me.

The dragon banked sharply, lifted, and I pressed my face into its scales, the scent of chemicals and city, of tears and anger, of sweat and fear.

"Don't fire!" Ethan yelled, his voice in the earpiece Luc had handed out before we'd left the House. "Don't fire! Merit's on the dragon."

The dargon turned and banked toward the heart of downtown Chicago.

I considered my options. I didn't think I could finish the magic in the air. I had to wait until it landed and we were both on solid ground. Otherwise, it would disappear beneath me, and I was pretty sure falling a thousand feet wasn't the same as jumping a few hundred.

So I held on, and felt guilty about the exhilaration of soaring over Chicago, soaring over glass and asphalt as the wind whipped my hair into tangles. I shouldn't have reveled in the feel of flight, shouldn't have closed my eyes in the warm breeze. But it wasn't often that a girl who loved fairy tales, who spent her childhood dreaming of princesses and haunted woods and dragons, got an opportunity like this.

But the exhilaration faded as we moved closer to the river, as I saw what the dragon had done to the city of my heart.

It was an apocalypse. Limited to Chicago, but severe enough that it would take months, if not years, before the city was the same.

The dragon plunged down, zeroed in on the top of the Towerline building. But then again, it was hurt, it was angry, and it felt it had been tricked and betrayed. The magic that created it had begun at Towerline. It had apparently decided this was the place to heal.

I screamed into my comm unit but wasn't sure if they could even hear me this far away. "We're heading to Towerline!"

The building's large roof, still scarred by the magic we'd used before, grew larger and larger in front of us, and I closed my eyes against the rising vertigo.

The dragon hit the roof hard, skidding across the gravel and debris and throwing me off. I made my own sliding roll across rock and asphalt, my momentum only stopped by one of the building's remaining HVAC units.

What was a little concussion between friends? I thought, closing my eyes for a moment to give my head a chance to stop spinning.

The roof shook beneath me, and I reached for my sword before opening my eyes.

The dragon's foot—as big as a hubcap—loomed above my head.

"*Shit!*" I said, and rolled just before the hubcap came down and smashed a divot into the roof. I climbed to my feet, but the dragon caught my foot with a talon and brought me down again.

He began dragging me backward across the gravel, and then its breath was on my back.

"This is not how the story ends!" I said, and spun my sword blindly over my head.

The dragon screamed and reared backward in pain. I rolled away and scrambled to my feet, gravel spraying beneath my boots, and put distance between us before looking back again.

Like the scales on its foot, those on its neck were small and easier to penetrate, and I'd etched a gash on one side.

PAIN! it screamed, the sound cutting the air as sharply as my sword.

"It doesn't have to be pain!" I said, and lifted my sword. "Surrender now, and I won't have to kill you!"

I AM ANGER AND PAIN AND FEAR. I AM HATRED AND REVENGE AND AGONY. YOU CANNOT STOP ME.

The only dragon in existence, and it had to be a sociopath. "This sword in my hand says different."

PAIN WILL EXIST EVEN IF AM GONE. THERE WILL ALWAYS BE MORE.

Now it was just pissing me off. I let my eyes silver, let my fangs descend. "Anger and pain and fear are part of life in Chicago and everywhere else. But so are joy and love. And I'll be damned if you take any more of that away."

Katana in front of me, nearly perpendicular to my body, I strode toward the dragon. *"With blade and blood I bind you!"*

It roared, swiped out, one nail catching a gap where rock had shredded leather and striping a slice across my ribs. The pain was outrageous, fire searing across my skin. But I didn't have time to worry about that now.

I dodged and ran beneath its leg. *"With darkness and steel I bind you!"*

FEAR WILL ALWAYS EXIST. The dragon's tail whipped to the side, and I jumped up to avoid it, hit the ground and rolled, sword in hand. I came up bruised and scraped again, but the sword was still in my hand.

"Maybe so," I said. "But fear doesn't have to be the only thing that exists." I blew out a breath, narrowed my focus, and stared him down.

"With water and wind I bind you! With hope and fear I bind you!"

The sword heated in my hand, the blade going white-hot with the force of the spell. I ignored it, gripped it harder, and ran toward the dragon.

It opened its mouth and snapped, trying to pull the same trick it had pulled with Sorcha. I ducked beneath its mouth and thrust the sword up with both hands between two of the scales in the dragon's neck.

Magic exploded.

Light shot from the katana as the dragon bucked, screamed with the pain of a million souls.

I let go of the sword, tried to scurry back from its thrashing legs and tail, from the magic that bloomed, huge and white, an unfolding flower of supernatural energy.

The dragon bucked as the flower enfolded it, then froze as if captured in glass, just like Portnoy's drawing. But the flower kept growing.

I tried to run, slipped in blood and gravel and hit my knees again—and was too late. The blooming magic covered me. I instinctively braced against the impact of it, of the power I was sure would incinerate us both.

But unlike the Egregore, this magic wasn't violent, and it

wasn't angry. It was familiar, because it arose from the connection that already existed between me and the katana, born when I'd tempered the steel with my own blood.

Even while the dragon was frozen, the magic moved through me, strengthening my bond to the sword . . . and the bond between me and the life that had only just begun to grow. A life I hadn't known existed until the magic firmed its connection to me, binding it inside me, just as the magic bound dragon to blade.

Hope welled so powerfully that tears immediately spilled over. I moved my hand through thick magic, put a hand on my abdomen, felt the flutter that I'd been afraid I'd never feel, but which now seemed undeniably real.

"Hi," I said with a silly grin. "Hi."

Suddenly, with a high-pitched whine, the blossom began to retract, to shrink back toward the captured dragon, the bound dragon. I remembered I was still midbattle, inside a spell, and mere feet away from a magically petrified dragon. So, immediate priorities first.

When the magic freed me, I crawled back, putting space between us and the spell that folded itself over the dragon like a budding flower in reverse, condensing itself more and more until there was nothing in the darkness but a spear of light around my spinning blade, the dragon, the Egregore, condensed inside it.

One final flash of light, the sword white-hot with energy, and it stilled in the air, dropped to the roof with a heavy *thud*.

I fell to my knees, my body still buzzing with magic, the slice along my ribs burning outrageously. But I was alive, and we were safe, and Chicago would go on.

That was enough for tonight.

My blade had cooled, the steel going gray again, by the time everyone else reached the Towerline roof.

I felt the footsteps before I heard them, shudders across the roof. Ethan moved into my vision first, gaze searching frantically. Mallory and Catcher appeared behind him.

"The dragon is bound," I said, "and I survived." But my head was still spinning.

"Merit," Mallory said, falling to her knees beside me. "You're *glowing*."

"Looks like you got a good dose of magic," Catcher said, running a hand along my arm. "But I don't see any lasting damage." He looked back at the sword, and a grin pierced the fear on his face. "And there's a helluva lot of magic in that sword."

"Yeah. There's a dragon in there. And I feel . . . kind of purple." I looked up at Mallory, then Ethan. "Is that a thing? Feeling kind of purple?"

She smiled, pushed hair from my face. "It absolutely is a thing, you crazy vampire."

"My crazy vampire," Ethan said, and scooped me into his arms. "Who I very well may handcuff permanently to the House."

"Not leaving anytime soon," I said, and dropped my head to his shoulder. "Glad you found me. I got the bad guy."

"So you did," he said, and there was no mistaking the pride in his voice. "For now, be still."

He'd said his magic words, and the lights went out.

‣‣ ⧱ ‣‣

CHAPTER TWENTY-SEVEN

CRAVING

Winters in the Midwest were fearsome things, and summers often weren't much better. But early fall, with clear skies and temperatures as crisp as autumn apples, was undeniably beautiful.

Two weeks after the dragon's demise, when the wounded had been attended to and the city had begun to right itself again, we enjoyed that gorgeous autumn weather from the stage at Pritzker Pavilion—the place where we'd first heard the Egregore speak—while thousands of Chicagoans looked on.

Microphone in hand, Mayor Kowalcyzk stood in jeans, boots, and a windbreaker, her power suit abandoned for clothes better suited for walking Chicago's broken streets and helping pick up the scattered pieces.

We stood behind her—vampires of Cadogan House, my grandfather and his staff, Mallory, CPD officers, and the men and women who'd served at Soldier Field.

"Not once," the mayor said, "but twice, have supernaturals saved this city in clear and obvious ways, and at great cost to themselves and their loved ones. And at the head of that effort were the staff of the Ombudsman's office, the vampires of Cadogan House, and sorcerer Mallory Carmichael. And those are only the efforts of which we are aware. How many more times have they acted in the dark of night, in the quiet, when we weren't aware? Or when we didn't believe them?"

She paused, hands at the edges of the podium, gaze downcast and contemplative. "Like you, I've had doubts and concerns. Supernaturals have wreaked havoc upon this city. But supernaturals have saved us, too." She glanced at Ethan. "We owe those supernaturals a debt of gratitude. And to ensure that, in the future, we pay attention to their advice and their warnings, I am pleased to announce the Ombudsman's office is hereby established as a permanent department of the city of Chicago."

She walked back to my grandfather, offered her hand. "Thank you, Mr. Merit."

He nodded gravely, well aware of the responsibility she'd placed on his shoulders. "You're welcome, Madam Mayor."

She shook Jeff's hand, then Catcher's, then returned to face the crowd. "Let's hear it for the Chicagoland Vampires!" she said, and led the crowd in a roaring round of applause.

I looked at Ethan, saw the pride and contentment in his face. And beneath that, hope. He'd shepherded his vampires through many storms in his time as Master, and undoubtedly would again. But for now, there was peace, and there was acceptance. Both had been a long time coming.

Ethan looked at me and smiled. *We did good, Sentinel.*

I nodded back. *We did good.*

When the crowd finally died down, Kowalcyzk lifted the microphone again.

"Chicago has been saved from a most terrifying threat," the mayor continued when she turned back to the crowd again. "But the rebuilding begins now. Let us begin it together. For now, and for the future, let us be one Chicago."

* * *

Because it was Chicago, my grandfather took us for pizza after the event. And then we returned to Cadogan House for the movie night I'd arranged in the House's ballroom. There'd be food, alcohol, and ridiculous comedies, which, as the House's official social chair, I thought was just the thing to reward the House.

But before that, before relaxation, there was one more bit of business. So I stopped Ethan on the steps of Cadogan House, kept my fingers entwined with his, and looked up at him.

"Sentinel?"

"There's something I want to tell you."

Predictably, he lifted an eyebrow. "All right."

I'd waited until a doctor confirmed with science what I'd believed was true on the roof of the Towerline building. And even then, I'd waited until after the mayor's commendation; I wanted to be sure of Chicago.

I steeled myself and said the words that would change everything.

"I'm pregnant."

Ethan simply stared at me. His eyes went saucer-wide, then dropped to my abdomen, my face again. "What?"

"I'm pregnant."

"You're—how do you—how?"

"Well," I said, thinking of the way he and Mallory had both teased me, "when a man and a woman—"

"*Sentinel.*" There was a joyous and impatient edge to his voice, like a child who can't wait to open a Christmas present.

I smiled at him. "It was at Towerline. The binding magic."

Ethan was as smart as they came, and realization dawned quickly in his face. "The side effect. It didn't bind you inside the sword; you think it bound the child to you."

I nodded. "That's the theory. The binding magic made her

stick, at least until she's ready to pop. And 'her' is just a guess," I said, before he could ask. "I don't like saying 'it.'"

"Some magical side effect," he said after a moment.

I grinned at him. "Seriously. Nine months and eighteen years of side effect, give or take."

"The test," Ethan said. "The one that had to be passed. What was that?"

"I haven't talked to Gabriel, but I have a pretty good feeling it was related to the dragon—facing down my fear of the monster, and the possibility of what he'd done, and could do, to Chicago." I smiled up at him. "She'll be the only one of her kind—the only vampire born as a vampire. I think she needed me to prove that I could be as brave as she'll need to be."

Ethan pulled me toward him, wrapped his arms around me, nestled my body against his. "My wife. My child."

"Yep. Probably in May."

"In May," he said, wonder in the word. And then he froze, looked down at me with horror in his face.

My heart sped in answer. "What? What is it?"

"You'll be eating for two."

I slapped his chest. "Don't do that. I thought something was really wrong."

"Something *is* wrong. Do you have any idea how much this is going to cost me?"

I just shook my head at him. "You want to keep going? Just get it all out at once?"

He grinned with the delight of a child. "Can you imagine what your cravings will be like?"

I smiled at him. "Can you imagine bottle-feeding a vampire?"

His mouth opened, closed again. "I cannot. We will literally be writing the book."

"We will. Although I'm sure there will be plenty of people—

supernatural and otherwise—with sage advice to offer. My mother being the first in line." I grinned at him. "And she's going to want to throw a baby shower, probably with you in attendance."

"I already did the wedding shower."

"This is a separate thing. And attendance is mandatory."

Ethan smiled slyly. "I may be sick that evening."

"Vampires don't get sick."

"In fairness, they aren't supposed to be pregnant, either."

He had a point, so I smiled at him. "We'll figure it out."

Just as we'd done before, and just as we'd undoubtedly do again.

He caught my face in his hands, pressed his mouth to mine, and, on the steps of Cadogan House, kissed me madly, deeply. "I do love you, Sentinel."

"I love you, too, Sullivan."

We walked into Cadogan House. And this time, I hoped I wouldn't need my sword, if only for a little while.

THE REMAINS OF THE CAKE

Twenty-one Months Later, Give or Take
Chicago, Illinois

Hands on my hips, I looked down at the year-old girl who bounced on chubby thighs, her tiny fingers gripping the edge of the coffee table. Her golden curls moved as she did, bouncing up and down around her cherubic face, punctuated by emerald green eyes.

This beautiful little girl was stuffing Cheerios into her mouth with wild abandon, bouncing up and down on plump little legs that poked out beneath a blue dress sprigged with tiny white flowers. "Ree!"

It was her favorite sound, the word that meant "Yes," "Cheerios," "Here," and every other phrase she couldn't quite manage to articulate.

I nodded. "Like those, do you?"

Brow furrowed as she worked, she scooped a handful of Cheerios from the coffee table and offered them to me. "Ree."

I walked to the coffee table, went to my knees, and slurped Cheerios out of her unsurprisingly sticky hand. She squealed happily, jogged in place on unsteady feet, and grabbed more Cheerios. Then she lifted the few she managed to corral to my mouth. I obliged her and munched them. Tasty, but five or six were more filling for a toddler than for a thirty-year-old vampire.

"Are you ready?" her father called out from the next room.

"Almost," I said, and pulled a barrette from my pocket, used it to clip back one side of Elisa's hair. It would keep her curls out of her face—and her sticky hands from getting tangled in the thick blond locks.

"Dress!"

"I know, sweetheart," I said, smoothing out the skirt of her blue cotton dress. She was a rough-and-tumble girl, and she'd destroy the dress by the end of the evening, but she looked lovely in it now. I tucked her into white Mary Jane shoes. "Do you like your dress?"

"Pretty," she seriously said.

"Yes, it is. Are you ready to go see Aunt Mallory and Baby Lulu?"

She nodded seriously. "Baby."

Ethan stepped into the doorway, eyes glowing green with pleasure. "How's my birthday girl?"

Elisa squealed, raised her chubby arms.

With the pride of a lion, Ethan walked forward, lifted her up. She wrapped her little arms around his neck, then kissed his cheek. "Ree! Ree! Ree!"

Ethan arched a brow at me. "Did she have coffee for breakfast?"

I patted her little bottom. "Not that I'm aware of. She's in a really good mood, though. Probably because you're so pretty."

Elisa nodded solemnly and patted his face with one hand, the other hand wrapped tightly around his House medal. "Pretty."

Ethan chomped at her hand, and she laughed wildly, swinging her head around.

"Not as pretty as Elisa or Mommy," he said.

I grinned, always amused to hear a four-hundred-year-old vampire call me "Mommy." And still awed that it had happened. That we'd conceived her, that my body had been able to nurture her, and that we'd brought her into the world.

It hadn't been a perfect journey. The "morning" sickness (albeit at dusk) had been horrific, the cravings completely bizarre, and, at the end, labor that had to be halted twice when the sun rose. And there'd been a moment of complete and utter terror when we'd thought we'd lost her. Even now, when she was healthy and happy and *here*, the memory made my body clench with fear.

She was the first vampire child in history—the only vampire born of vampires. But more important, *most* important, she was ours. She had been born of love, and born into a House of vampires who loved her nearly as much as we did. She was part of me, and part of Ethan, and so much her own person. I loved her more than I'd have thought possible.

I owed my life to Ethan, and I gave him my heart. And now Elisa held them both.

We headed to the House's first floor with a diaper bag; the House was big enough that it was faster and simpler than traversing it every time Elisa needed a diaper or clothes change. Which was often. I liked to joke that she was the only person who could throw up on one of Ethan's expensive custom suits and live to tell the tale. There wasn't a vampire in the House who wasn't wrapped around her tiny little finger.

As far as we could tell, she hadn't been negatively affected by the magic that made her. She was usually hungry, and had a quick temper, but those seemed perfectly explainable by biology and genetics, no magic required.

Mallory, Catcher, and Lulu sat on the couch in Ethan's office, Lulu nestled in her mother's arms. She was a tiny pale doll of a thing, except for the head of thick dark hair she'd been born with. Mallory had put a tiny polka-dot bow in it today.

"Hi, Elisa," Catcher said.

"Catch!"

Elisa didn't have a shy bone in her body.

I walked over, pressed a gentle kiss to Lulu's forehead. "How's the World's Tiniest Yeti today?"

"Uninterested in sleep," Mallory said with a yawn. There were circles under her eyes, and Catcher didn't look much better. "I'll give her to you for a dollar."

"I will take you up on that temporarily," I said, carefully taking the tiny package and sitting on the floor at their feet. Every newborn was tiny, but there was always something surreal about holding a creature so tiny, so delicate. She looked up at me, blinked Mallory's blue eyes.

"Hi, baby Lulu."

She blinked again, her lashes nearly as thick and long as her hair.

"You're going to be on the porch with a rifle when she's old enough," I told Catcher, brushing her hair back.

"Like he's going to be any different," Catcher said, gesturing to Ethan, who was kissing the palms Elisa held out to him.

"Aspen stakes, but probably, yeah. Although I'd think you'd have to be pretty brave to call on the daughter of a Master vampire."

"Especially the only daughter of a Master vampire," Mallory said. "Her suitor is gonna have to come correct real quick."

"That's a good girl," Ethan said as she squirmed in his arms. "Do you want to say hello to Lulu?"

Elisa nodded, and Ethan put her down. She waddled toward me, reached out a hand to touch Lulu's hair. But before she made contact, she looked up at Mallory, who nodded.

"You can touch, Elisa."

"Elisa," I said, "do you remember how we said to love the baby?"

She nodded solemnly, her blond hair bouncing. "Careful."

"That's right." I put my hand over hers, helped her softly touch her.

"Soft," Elisa quietly said, raising her emerald green eyes to mine. "Baby soft?"

"Yes, she is. Like your baby?" Her baby was a floppy-eared, floppy-legged rabbit nearly as tall as she was that she'd dragged around by an ear as soon as she started walking. It had been a gift from Mallory, her first stuffed animal.

Elisa nodded gravely. "Baby," she agreed. "Soft."

"Good girl," Mallory said. "You're really good at that, Elisa."

"Hep."

"She likes to help," I translated. "Ethan let her put a book on the shelves in his office yesterday, and she was pretty sure she'd earned her own House."

"So she got his looks and his attitude?" Mallory said, glancing up at Ethan.

"And my charm," he said.

There was a knock at the threshold. We looked back, found Margot in the doorway. She smiled at us. "We're ready if you are."

"I think we're ready." Hands on his hips, Ethan looked down at Elisa. "Would you like some cake?"

She just blinked up at him, gaze blank. This would be her first experience with cake, which made it special for both of us.

Ethan held out his hands, and she abandoned Lulu and me, practically jumped into his arms. He situated her on his hip again. "Let's see if you can hold as much sugar as your mother does."

Mallory snorted, climbed to her feet. I did the same, and carefully handed Lulu back to her. "I'm not sure that's possible."

"Says the woman who out-ate me at my own bachelorette party."

"That was more than a year ago. When are you going to stop bringing that up?"

"When it stops serving my purpose."

Mallory just shook her head. "Never change."

"I'll do my best."

Some children might have shied away from a room full of dozens of humans and supernaturals, from the cheery music and the bundles of balloons that filled the House's cafeteria. Those children probably hadn't grown up in a House of vampires, loved within an inch of their lives.

Those children were not Elisa.

"Happy birthday, Elisa!" they called out when we entered. She screamed and clapped her little hands together, tried to wiggle out of Ethan's arms.

"Okay, my little lemur. Hold on." He put her on the floor and she dashed toward a rainbow-hued column of balloons that reached to the room's high ceiling. She reached out a tentative hand and touched the column, watched it wobble beneath her touch.

She shrieked with joy and touched it again, then tried to drag it away from its column.

"Just to touch, honey," my grandfather said, gently taking her free hand. Her face screwed up into angry lines before she realized who'd touched her. And that smile blossomed again.

"Give your Papaw a kiss?" He bent down to her, leaning on the cane he'd been using more frequently these days.

Elisa squeezed up her little face, closed her eyes, and leaned in, pressing her lips to his face.

"She got that expression from you, you know," Ethan said, putting a hand at my waist.

I humphed.

"Good kiss," my grandfather said. "I hear it's your birthday."

"Ree?" She looked back at me, her official translator.

"It's your birthday," I said. "And do you know what birthday girls get?" I pointed to the giant sheet cake—chocolate with emerald green icing—that sat on a table near the rest of the food, a high chair posed next to it, ready for the birthday girl. Elisa's eyes went huge.

"*Ree,*" she said reverently.

Ethan smirked at the sound, and settled Elisa in the high chair. And she started immediately squirming for a better view of the cake.

She was definitely my kid.

"Ladies and gentlemen, people and . . . *other*," Ethan said, glancing around.

The crowd knew their cue and chuckled just when they should have.

"We're here today to celebrate the first birthday of the most amazing girl on the face of the Earth. And we wanted to take this opportunity to thank all of you for the support you've given us over the last twelve months. We couldn't have managed it without you, without your love and support. Without your gratuitous diaper changings and willingness to experiment with pink milk."

Pink milk was the concoction of blood and milk it had taken us nearly three months to work out. Elisa was a vampire, but she was also a child. We were writing the book on baby vampire nutrition. In the unlikely event anyone else might ever need the book . . .

I looked at Elisa, who stared happily around the crowd. "But I'm sure you'll agree that she was totally worth it."

"Hear, hear!" said my grandfather.

"To Elisa Isabel Sullivan," I said.

While the crowd repeated her name, which amused the tiny

blonde to no end, I lit the candles on the cake. Elisa's eyes went astoundingly round.

"Ree," she quietly said.

"And that's all for you, Elisa," Ethan said. Margot cut a piece of the cake, handed me the plate. Ethan fastened on a bib—much good it would do—and I put the cake slice on the high chair table.

Elisa stared at it. Gently, I dipped her finger into the green icing, then brought it to her mouth. She grinned and looked at her now-green finger, then dug her other hand into the icing and brought a sticky handful of it to her mouth. But before she dug in, she looked at me.

"Go ahead," I said, nodding at her.

Elisa pushed icing into her mouth, giggling all the while, then dug both hands into the cake again.

"And that cry of joy at the taste of chocolate pretty much confirms she's your daughter," Mallory said, slinging an arm over my shoulders. "I mean, in case the labor wasn't proof enough."

"You just wait until Lulu's a toddler," I said, putting an arm around her waist. "There's plenty of fun in store for you, too."

We eventually said good-bye to our guests, and the Remains of the Cake (the lesser-known British novel) were finished off by a descending horde of hungry Cadogan vampires. It took two baths to remove Elisa's skim coat of chocolate, and we were inching toward dawn by that point. She slept like a vampire—lights out at dawn, fully awake at dusk—with naps sprinkled during her waking hours.

We'd just given her a late bottle when Malik found us in Ethan's office, sitting on the couch as we perused one of Elisa's favorite books.

"Meek!" she said, clapping her hands together when she saw him.

"Ms. Sullivan," he said, and she squealed with delight. Probably didn't know what it meant, but she enjoyed it all the same.

"There's someone here to see you," he told her, then glanced at us. "Of the shifter variety."

Together, we walked into the foyer, found Gabriel with Connor in his arms. Connor's head was on his father's shoulder.

Connor's hair was as dark and curling as his mother's, his eyes as blue as a spring sky. His fingers were clutched around a plastic giraffe, and he watched us with baleful eyes and the poked-out lip that said he was unhappy about his trip to Cadogan House.

"Sorry we missed the party." Gabriel's gaze narrowed at his son. "Someone had a tantrum."

"He looks displeased," Ethan agreed.

"Yeah," Gabe said. "I offered him a cup of water."

"A parent's worst betrayal," Ethan said soberly.

Gabriel's mouth twitched. "I love my son. God and Pack willing, he'll lead the NAC someday. But if there was a pill that would get him to adulthood that much faster, I'd take it."

"Probably a good thing you missed cake time," I said, imagining Connor smearing green frosting down the hallway. "But there's plenty left, if you'd like a piece to go?"

"Let's see how it goes." He looked at Connor, brushed a dark curl from his face. "Would you like to say hi to Elisa, kiddo?"

In response, Connor buried his face in Gabe's shoulder.

"We'll get things started," Ethan said, and carried Elisa to the front parlor, put her down on the rug in the middle of the floor, where she promptly sat down in her footie pajamas. It had been an exhausting night, evidently.

"Here we go," Gabriel said, and put Connor on the floor in front of Elisa, giraffe still firmly in hand.

They hadn't actually met yet. Scheduling vampire-shifter playdates hadn't been the easiest thing to do, especially given the sheer number of people who'd wanted to lay eyes on Elisa, assure themselves that Ethan and I had actually managed to make her.

None of them, curiously, wanted to deal with her when she had soggy diapers, pureed carrots in her nose, or Spaghetti-Os in her hair.

For a long moment, Elisa and Connor just looked at each other.

"Doggy," Elisa said.

I stared at her. "Did you just call him 'Doggy'?"

Ethan lifted a brow at Gabriel. "Do I even want to know how she knows that?"

Gabriel grinned. "Magic is magic."

"Doggy!" Elisa said again, this time with more force, and bounced on her butt.

Connor blinked at her, then looked up at Gabriel for support.

"She's not wrong, son. Technically."

Elisa looked at the toy in his hands, her eyes widening. "Doggy?"

Connor frowned, hugged the toy to his chest. But much like her father, Elisa was bound and determined to get what she wanted. She scooted forward on her bottom, touched a finger to the giraffe, and lifted those big green eyes to his. "Doggy?"

Connor's eyes narrowed, a toddler not quite ready for sharing— or a shifter trying to distinguish enemy from friend.

"Doggy!" Elisa said, clapping her hands together. Then she laughed like she'd told herself the world's funniest joke, and tossed her head around. "Doggy doggy doggy."

"Not a dog," Connor said with a burgeoning smile, and held out the giraffe. "Giraffe!" He said it with a hard "g," so it came out more like "graph." But close enough for Elisa's eyes to widen with the thrill of a new word.

"Graph!" she said, and took the toy, mashed it against the rug like it was running. "Graph! Graph! Graph!"

"And I apologize for that," Gabriel said.

"Graph!" Connor said with a grin, and they took turns march-ing the giraffe up and down the rug, Elisa occasionally laughing in that utterly selfless, completely happy way.

"The beginning of a beautiful friendship," Ethan said with a smile.

Gabriel made a rough sound. "*Now*," he said, gold and amber swirling in his eyes. "But you just wait—"

I knew where he was going, so I cut him off with a pointed finger. "*No*. No more prophecies unless you've got a time and place I need to be to keep my daughter safe. Barring that, she lives her own life, 'tests' or otherwise." I didn't want the pressure. Not anymore.

Gabriel went quiet, and for a moment I was afraid I'd pissed him off. But he was watching Connor and Elisa, brow furrowed in contemplation. "No one's future is written completely. Not in stone. There are always choices to make, roads that could be taken. Life is in the choosing of them."

Ethan reached out, put a hand at my back. "And they have to make their own choices, just as we did. Just as we do."

Gabe grunted. "This got philosophical quickly," he said, then glanced at me. "You sure you don't want details?"

I narrowed my eyes at him. "Just tell me this—is there a happy ending?"

Screams erupted from the floor, and we all looked back again. Elisa had made the unforgiveable mistake of putting the giraffe on top of a plastic dollhouse. Because toddlers.

We all sighed.

"I guess that answers that," Ethan said, and we went to separate our screaming children. "On the other hand, I'm pretty sure our first meeting looked fairly similar. And look what we have now."

I glanced at the crying child, plastic giraffe in her mouth, now kicking at the shifter who was trying to take it back from her. It didn't get any more real than that. Or any more perfect.

"Everything," I said. "We have everything."

Don't miss the first novel in
Chloe Neill's Heirs of Chicagoland series!

WILD HUNGER

Coming in 2018 from Berkley

As the only vampire child ever born, some believed
Elisa Sullivan had all the luck. But the magic that
helped bring her into the world left her with a dark
secret. Shifter Connor Keene, the only son of North
American Central Pack Apex Gabriel Keene, is the
only one she trusts with it. But she's a vampire and the
daughter of a Master and a Sentinel, and he's prince of
the Pack and its future king.

When the assassination of an ambassador brings old
feuds to the fore again, Elisa and Connor must choose
between love and family, between honor and obligation, before Chicago disappears forever.

The French Quarter was thinking about war again.

Booms echoed across the neighborhood, vibrating windows and shaking the shelves at Royal Mercantile—the finest purveyor of dehydrated meals in New Orleans.

And antique walking sticks. We were flush with antique walking sticks.

I sat at the store's front counter, working on a brass owl that topped one of them. The owl's head was supposed to turn when you pushed a button on the handle, but the mechanism was broken. I'd taken apart the tiny brass pieces and found the problem—one of the small toothy gears had become misaligned. I just needed to slip it back into place.

I adjusted the magnifying glass over the owl, its jointed brass wings spread to reveal its inner mechanisms. I had a thin screwdriver in one hand, a pair of watchmaking tweezers in the other. To get the gear in place, I had to push one spring down and another up in that very small space.

I liked tinkering with the store's antiques, to puzzle through broken parts and sticky locks. It was satisfying to make something work that hadn't before. And since the demand for fancy

French sideboards and secretaries wasn't exactly high these days, there was plenty of inventory to pick from.

I nibbled on my bottom lip as I moved the pieces, carefully adjusting the tension so the gear could slip in. I had to get the gear into the back compartment, between the rods, and into place between the springs. Just a smidge to the right, and . . .

Boom.

I jumped, the sound of another round of fireworks shuddering me back to the store—and the gear that now floated in the air beside me, bobbing a foot off the counter's surface.

"Damn," I muttered, heart tripping.

I'd moved it with my mind, with the telekinetic magic I wasn't supposed to have. At least, not unless I wanted a lifetime prison sentence.

I let go of the magic, and the gear dropped, hit the counter, bounced onto the floor.

My heart now pounding in my chest, the fingers on both hands crossed superstitiously, I hopped off the stool and hurried to the front door to check the box mounted on the building across the street. It was a monitor with a camera on top, triggered when the amount of magic in the air rose above background levels—like when a Sensitive accidentally moved a gear.

I'd gotten lucky; the light was still red. I must not have done enough to trigger it, at least from this distance. I was still in the clear—for now. But damn, that had been close. I hadn't even known I'd been using magic.

Boom.

Already pumped with nervous energy, I jumped again.

"Good lord," I said, pushing the door open and stepping outside onto the threshold between the store's bay windows, where MERCANTILE was mosaicked in tidy blue capitals.

It was mid-October, and the heat and humidity still formed a miserable blanket across the French Quarter. Royal Street was nearly empty of people.

The war had knocked down half the buildings in the Quarter, which gave me a clear view of the back part of the neighborhood and the Mississippi River, which bordered it. Figures moved along the riverbank, testing fireworks for the finale of the festivities. The air smelled like sparks and flame, and wisps of white smoke drifted across the twilight sky.

It wasn't the first time we'd seen smoke over the Quarter.

On an equally sweltering day in October seven years ago, the Veil—the barrier that separated humans from a world of magic we hadn't even known existed—was shattered by the Paranormals who'd lived in what we now called the Beyond.

They wanted our world, and they didn't have a problem eradicating us in the process. They spilled through the fracture, bringing death and destruction—and changing everything: Magic was now real and measurable and a scientific fact.

I was seventeen when the Veil, which ran roughly along the ninetieth line of longitude, straight north through the heart of NOLA, had splintered. That made New Orleans, where I'd been born and raised, ground zero.

My dad had owned Royal Mercantile when it was still an antiques store, selling French furniture, priceless art, and very expensive jewelry. (And, of course, the walking sticks. So many damn walking sticks.) When the war started, I'd helped him transition the store by adding MREs, water, and other supplies to the inventory.

War had spread through southern Louisiana, and then north, east, and west through Alabama, Mississippi, Tennessee, Arkansas, and the eastern half of Texas. The conflict had destroyed so much of the South, leaving acres of scarred land and burned, lonely cities. It had taken a year of fighting to stop the bloodshed and close the Veil again. By that time, the military had been spread so thin that civilians often fought alongside the troops.

Unfortunately, he hadn't lived to see the Veil close again. The store became mine and I moved into the small apartment on the third floor. We hadn't lived there together—he didn't want to spend every hour of his life in the same building, he'd said. But the store and building were now my only links to him, so I didn't hesitate. I missed him terribly.

When the war was done, Containment—the military unit that managed the war and the Paranormals—had tried to scrub New Orleans not only of magic but of voodoo, Marie Laveau, ghost tours, and even literary vampires. They'd convinced Congress to pass the so-called Magic Act, banning magic inside and outside the war zone, what we called the Zone. (Technically, it was the MIGECC Act: Measure for the Illegality of Glamour and Enchantment in Conflict Communities. But that didn't have the same ring to it.)

The war had flattened half of Fabourg Marigny, a neighborhood next door to the French Quarter, and Containment took advantage. They'd shoved every remaining Para they could find into the neighborhood and built a wall to keep them there.

Officially, it was called the District.

We called it Devil's Isle, after a square in the Marigny where criminals had once been hanged. And if Containment learned I had magic, I'd be imprisoned there with the rest of them.

They had good reason to be wary. Most humans weren't affected by magic; if it was an infection, an illness, they were immune. But a small percentage of the population didn't have that immunity. We were sensitive to the energy from the Beyond. That hadn't been a problem before the Veil was opened; the magic that came through was minimal—enough for magic tricks and illusions but not much else. But the scarred Veil wasn't as strong; magic still seeped through the rip where it had been sewn back together. Sensitives weren't physically equipped to handle the magic that poured through.

Magic wasn't a problem for Paras. In the Beyond, they'd bathed in the magic day in and day out, but that magic had an outlet—their bodies became canvases for the power. Some had wings; some had horns or fangs.

Sensitives couldn't process magic that way. Instead, we just kept absorbing more and more magic, until we lost ourselves completely. Until we became wraiths, pale and dangerous shadows of the humans we'd once been, our lives devoted to seeking out more magic, filling that horrible need.

I'd learned eight months ago that I was a Sensitive, part of that unlucky percentage. I'd been in the store's second-floor storage room, moving a large, star-shaped sign to a better spot. (Along with walking sticks, my dad had loved big antique gas station signs. The sticks, at least, were easier to store.) I'd tripped on a knot in the old oak floor and stumbled backward, falling flat on my back. And I'd watched in slow motion as the hundred-pound sign—and one of its sharp metallic points—fell toward me.

I hadn't had time to move, to roll away, or even to throw up an arm and block the rusty spike of steel, which was aimed at the spot between my eyes. But I did have a split second to object, to curse the fact that I'd lived through war only to be impaled by a damn gas station sign that should have been rusting on a barn in the middle of nowhere.

"No, damn it!" I'd screamed out the words with every ounce of air in my lungs, with my eyes squeezed shut like a total coward.

And nothing had happened.

Lips pursed, I'd slitted one eye open to find the metal tip

hovering two inches above my face. I'd held my breath, shaking with adrenaline and sweating with fear, for a full minute before I gathered up the nerve to move.

I'd counted to five, then dodged and rolled away. The star's point hit the floor, tunneling in. There was still a two-inch-deep notch in the wood.

I hadn't wanted the star to impale me—and it hadn't. I'd used magic I hadn't known I'd had—Sensitivity I hadn't known I possessed—to stop the thing in its tracks.

I'd gotten lucky then, too: The magic monitor hadn't been triggered, and I'd kept my store . . . and my freedom.

Another boom sounded, pulling me through memory to my spot on the sidewalk. I jumped, cursed under my breath.

"I think you're good, guys!" I yelled. Not that I was close enough for them to hear me, or that they'd care. This was War Night. Excess was the entire point.

Six years before, the Second Battle of New Orleans had raged across the city. (The first NOLA battle, during the War of 1812, had been very human. At least as far as we were aware.) It had been one of the last battles of the war and one of the biggest.

Tonight we'd celebrate our survival with colors, feathers, brass bands, and plenty of booze. It would be loud, crazy, and amazing. Assuming I could manage not to get arrested before the fun started . . .

"You finally losing it, Claire?"

I glanced back and found a man, tall and leanly muscled, standing behind me. Antoine Lafayette Gunnar Landreau, one of my best friends, looked unwilted by the heat.

His dark brown, wavy hair was perfectly rakish, and his smile was adorably crooked, the usual gleam in his deep-set hazel eyes. Tonight, he wore slim dark pants and a sleeveless shirt that showed off his well-toned arms—and the intricate but temporary paintings that stained his skin.

"Hey, Gunnar." We exchanged cheek kisses. I cursed when another *boom* sounded, followed by the sparkle of gold stars in the air.

I smiled despite myself. "Damn it. Now they're just showing off."

"Good thing you're getting into the spirit," he said with a grin. "Happy War Night."

"Happy War Night, smarty-pants. Let me check your ink."

Gunnar obliged, stretching out his arms so I could get a closer view. New Orleans was a city of traditions, and War Night had its own: the long parade, the fireworks, the spiked punch we simply called "Drink" because the ingredients depended on what was available. And since the beginning, when there was nothing but mud and ash, painting the body to remember the fallen. Making a living memorial of those of us who'd survived.

The intricate scene on Gunnar's left arm showed survivors celebrating in front of the Cabildo, waving a purple flag bearing four gold fleurs-de-lis—the official postwar flag of New Orleans. The other arm showed the concrete and stone sculpture of wings near Talisheek in St. Tammany Parish, which memorialized one of the deadliest battles of the war, and the spot where thousands of Paras had entered our world.

The realism lifted goose bumps on my arms. "Seriously amazing."

"Just trying to do War Night proud. And Aunt Reenie."

"God bless her," I said of Gunnar's late and lamented aunt, who'd been a great lover of War Night, rich as Croesus, and, according to Gunnar's mother, "not quite there."

"God bless her," he agreed.

"Let's get the party started," I said. "You want something to drink?"

"Always the hostess. I don't suppose there's any tea?"

"I think there's a little bit left," I said, opening the door and gesturing him in.

Gunnar was a sucker for sweet tea, a rarity now that sugar was a luxury in New Orleans. That was another lingering effect of war. Magic was powerful stuff, and it wasn't meant to be in our world. Nothing would grow in soil scarred by magic, so war had devastated the Zone's farms. And since there were still rumors of bands of Paras in rural areas who'd escaped the Containment roundup and preyed on humans, there weren't many businesses eager to ship in the goods that wouldn't grow here.

There'd been a mass exodus of folks out of the cities with major fighting—New Orleans, Baton Rouge, Mobile—about three weeks after the war started, when it began to look as though we weren't equipped to fight Paras, even on our own soil.

There were plenty of people who still asked why we stayed in the Zone, why we put up with scarcity, with the threat of wraith and Para attacks, with Containment on every corner, with Devil's Isle looming behind us.

Some folks stayed because they didn't have a better choice, because somebody had to take care of those who couldn't leave. Some stayed because they didn't have resources to leave, anywhere to go, or anyone to go to. And some stayed because they'd been through hard times before—when there'd been no electricity, no comforts, and too much grief—and the city was worth saving again. Some stayed because if we left, that would be the end of New Orleans, Little Rock, Memphis, and Nashville. Of the culture, the food, the traditions. Of the family members who existed only in our memories, who tied us to the land.

And some folks stayed because they had no choice at all. Containment coordinated the exodus. And when everyone who'd wanted to get out was out, they started controlling access to the Zone's borders, hoping to keep the Paras and fighting contained.

No, staying in the Zone wasn't easy. But for a lot of us—certainly for me—it was the only option. I'd rather make do in New Orleans than be rich anywhere else.

Photo by Dana Damewood Photography

Chloe Neill, author of the Chicagoland Vampires novels (*Midnight Marked, Dark Debt, Blood Games*), the Dark Elite novels (*Charmfall, Hexbound, Firespell*), and the Devil's Isle novels (*The Sight, The Veil*), was born and raised in the South but now makes her home in the Midwest—just close enough to Cadogan House and St. Sophia's to keep an eye on things. When not transcribing Merit's, Lily's, and Claire's adventures, she bakes, works, and scours the Internet for good recipes and great graphic design. Chloe also maintains her sanity by spending time with her boys—her favorite landscape photographer (her husband), and their dogs, Baxter and Scout. (Both she and the photographer understand the dogs are in charge.)